a thousand heartbeats

ALSO BY KIERA CASS

The Selection
The Elite
The One
The Heir
The Crown
Happily Ever After: Companion to the Selection Series
The Siren
The Betrothed
The Betrayed

a thousand heartbeats

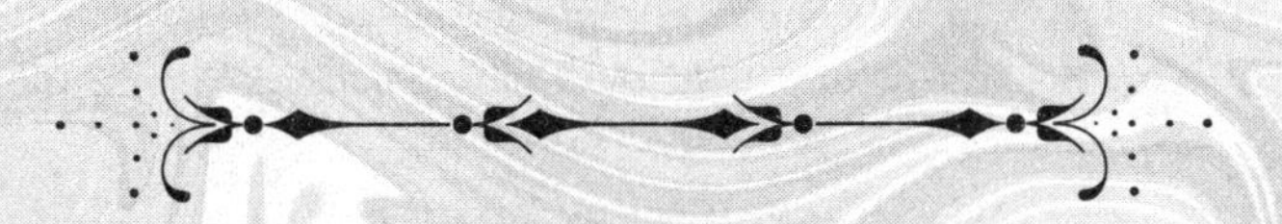

KIERA CASS

HARPER TEEN
An Imprint of HarperCollins*Publishers*

HarperTeen is an imprint of HarperCollins Publishers.

 For information address HarperCollins Children's Books, a division of HarperCollins Publishers, 195 Broadway, New York, NY 10007.
www.epicreads.com

ISBN 978-0-06-266578-2
ISBN 978-0-06-328020-5 (special edition)
ISBN 978-0-06-325991-1 (int.)

Typography by Erin Fitzsimmons
22 23 24 25 26 PC/LSCH 10 9 8 7 6 5 4 3 2 1
First Edition

To Theresa,

for all the reasons and no particular reason at all

THE ISLAND
Meckonah Castle
KIALAND
HALSGAR
KADIER
MONRIA
SIBRAL
CAPORE
SOGRE
Meckonah Castle

Vosino
Castle
STRATFEL
UNCLAIMED LAND
CADAAD
NALK
ROSHMAR
DUCAN
Vosino
Castle

Part I

At the same time that Annika was reaching to feel her sword in its hiding place beneath her bed, Lennox was wiping blood from his.

Lennox surveyed the hillside, catching his breath. Three more souls to add to the tally he'd long stopped counting. With all the lives lost at the tip of his sword, no one in the Dahrainian Army could challenge his authority. Annika, on the other hand, had drawn blood only once. And it was purely accidental. All the same, there were few who could challenge her authority, either.

The marked difference was that those who could, did.

Annika stood carefully, her legs still ever so slightly sore. She practiced her steps until she could move as gracefully as she was used to, and by the time her maid walked in, they both agreed her gait was passable. She sat at her vanity, her eyes looking at the edge of her bed reflected in the mirror. Her sword—hidden under her bed—would have to wait another day or two, but she was thrilled at the possibility of shattering one of the few rules she was still capable of breaking.

Lennox, meanwhile, sheathed his sword and strode down the quiet hillside. Kawan would be pleased with his update. Wanting to keep his situation as secure as he could, he made sure to never give him reason to be displeased. When this war was over—if it ever even started—an entire kingdom would be forced into submission, and Lennox would have his heel on the neck of it.

Annika and Lennox both focused on their upcoming day, unaware that the other existed, and blind to how they'd change the trajectory of each other's lives.

Or how they irrevocably already had.

LENNOX

I walked back to the castle, trying to decide where to stop first: my quarters or the mess hall. I looked down at my coat and boots, wiping at my cheek. The back of my hand came away with traces of dirt, sweat, and blood, and I could see splatters of all three across my shirt as well.

I'd go by the mess hall, then. Let everyone see.

I headed toward the eastern-side entrance, which was the least tended area of Vosino Castle. To be fair, the rest of it wasn't much better.

For lack of a better term, Vosino was a hand-me-down, left deserted by some forgotten kingdom and claimed as our home. Minimal effort was given to its maintenance. After all, it was only meant to be temporary.

As I walked in, I saw Kawan sitting at the head table. As usual, my mother was by his side.

No one ever joined them. Even I'd never been presented with an invitation.

The rest of the army sat as they pleased, mixing among unofficial ranks.

I drew attention the moment I entered, strolling coolly up the center aisle, my wrist resting on the hilt of my sword. Conversations dropped to whispers as people craned their necks to get a better view.

My mother noticed me first, her powder-blue eyes looking me over in a scowl. When people joined our ranks, finery and gowns were abandoned for a uniform of sorts, and most people were left with very little in the way of personal items. Mother reaped the benefits of this: she came down to eat daily in dresses once worn by someone else in the castle, the only woman in Vosino Castle afforded such a privilege.

To her right, Kawan's face was covered by the goblet he was drinking from. He slammed it on the table, wiping his wiry beard with the back of his already dirty sleeve. With a heavy sigh, he settled his eyes on me.

"What's this?" he asked, motioning to my bloodstained clothing.

"We had three attempted deserters this morning," I informed him. "You might want to send carts for the bodies before the wolves start scavenging."

"Is that all?" Kawan asked.

Is that all?

No, it wasn't all. It was the most recent act in a string of deeds done for the sake of our people, done in Kawan's name, done to prove myself. And here I was, standing silent and dressed in blood, waiting for him to finally—*finally*—acknowledge me.

I stood my ground, demanding he take note.

"I think it fairly impressive to single-handedly subdue

three young, well-trained recruits in the dark of night. To guard the secrecy of both our location and intentions and come out on the other side without a scratch. But I could be wrong."

"You often are," he grumbled. "Trista, tell your son to calm down."

My eyes flickered to my mother, but she remained silent. I knew he was baiting me; it was one of his favorite pastimes. And still, I was very close to taking a bite. I was saved by a commotion in the hallway.

"Make way! Make way!" a boy shouted, running into the room.

A shout like that meant one thing: the most recent Commission was over, and our troops had returned.

I turned around and watched as Aldrik and his lackies strolled into the mess hall, each of them pulling two cows behind them.

Kawan let out a low chuckle, and I stepped to the side as my moment was eclipsed.

Aldrik was everything Kawan was looking for. Broad shoulders and a bendable will. His messy brown hair flopped forward over his forehead as he knelt down in the same place I'd just been standing. Behind him were two other soldiers, ones he'd specifically chosen to go with him for his Commission. They were covered in red mud, and one of them was shirtless.

I crossed my arms, taking in the scene. Six cows in the mess hall.

He could have left them outside, but Aldrik clearly knew

this was by far the biggest and best conquest one of these missions had produced.

The worst? A body in a burlap bag.

"Mighty Kawan. I have brought back half a dozen cattle for the Dahrainian Army. I submit my offering before you, hoping it proves my loyalty and worthiness," Aldrik said with his head bent low.

Several people applauded, grateful for resources. As if this would be enough to feed even a fraction of us.

Kawan stood and walked over, inspecting the cows. Once he was done, he slapped Aldrik on the shoulder and turned to the crowd. "What say you? Does this offering please you?"

"Yes!" everyone shouted. Well, almost everyone.

Kawan let out a guttural laugh. "I agree. Arise, Aldrik. You have served your people well."

Applause rang out, and the crowd converged around Aldrik and his team. I used the opportunity to duck away. I could only shake my head, wondering who he'd stolen them from. I was about to mentally chastise him for being so proud of himself, but then I looked at my shirt and reminded myself exactly who I was and let it go.

It was just a job, and now my job was done, and I was going to sleep for a bit. Well, if the only woman I cared for in this castle would allow that.

I opened my door, and Thistle started yipping immediately.

I chuckled. "I know. I know." I walked over to my sloppily made bed, scruffing the fur on the back of her head.

I'd found Thistle when she was just a kit. She'd been

injured, and it seemed her pack had left her. If anyone understood that, it was me. Gray foxes were typically nocturnal—a fact I'd learned the hard way—but she always perked up when I came in.

She flopped back on the bed, showing me her stomach. I scratched her and then moved the planks from in front of the window.

"Sorry," I told her. "I just didn't want you to see me with a sword. Not like that. You can run off now if you want."

She stayed on the bed as I looked at myself in the small, broken mirror on my desk. It was worse than I'd thought. Dirt was smeared along my forehead, and blood was splattered across my cheek. I took a deep breath and dipped a towel in my basin of water, wiping away everything I'd done.

Thistle was now pacing back and forth on my bed, looking at me with what I could have sworn were concerned eyes. Gray foxes were in the canine family. She had the senses of a wolf, and I had no doubt she could smell everything on me right now. I had a feeling she knew exactly the type of person I was and just what I'd done. But she was free to come and go, and she always came back, so I hoped she didn't hold it against me.

It didn't matter, either way. I held it against me.

ANNIKA

"Here, my lady," Noemi said as she pinned the front of my dress to my stomacher. "This is the last one." She bit her lip, looking like she was debating something.

I tried to give her my most reassuring smile. "Whatever it is, just say it. Since when are there secrets between you and I?"

She nervously touched her dark curls. "It's not a secret, my lady. I'm just wondering if you're ready to see him again. To see anyone again."

Noemi chewed her lip. It was one of her many endearing habits.

I took her hand. "Founding Day is tomorrow. The people need to see their princess is well. My presence at court encourages our countrymen, and that is my primary role." I ducked my head.

If Noemi had been my real sister, she might have argued with me. As my maid, she simply replied, "Very well."

With my hair brushed and dress set, Noemi slipped me

into my sturdiest shoes, and I headed out.

Though I had lived here my entire life, I was still in awe of Meckonah Castle, with its wide-open windows, vast marble floors, and an array of galleries. But above all Meckonah's beauty, it was home.

My mother and father had forgone a church wedding in favor of exchanging their vows in the field outside.

I was born here. My first words, first steps, first everything happened for me here. I was so proud of it all, so in love with this palace and this land. There was very little I wouldn't do for it. Indeed, there was apparently nothing I wouldn't do for Kadier.

I walked slowly toward the dining hall. As I approached the door, I paused. Maybe Noemi was right—maybe it was too soon. But I'd been seen, and now it was too late.

Escalus noticed me before my father did, and he stood quickly, coming across the hall to greet me. The first real smile I'd had in weeks spread across my face as he embraced me.

"I've been aching to see you, but Noemi said you weren't up for company," he said quietly. He reached up, brushing a lock of hair from his face. Escalus and I had both been gifted our mother Evelina's ashy-brown hair and her warm brown eyes, but there was no mistaking that it was Escalus who was the echo of Theron Vedette.

"It was dull, I assure you. Nothing but me sighing about my state. Besides, I'm sure you had much more important things to tend to." I tried to sound breezy, but I sensed I was failing.

"You look different," he said, placing a comforting hand on my shoulder.

I shrugged. "I feel different."

He swallowed hard. "Is it all settled, then?"

I nodded and lowered my voice. "It's all left to Father's timing now."

"Come and eat. 'There's no sorrow cinnamon cannot fix.'"

I giggled as we walked, thinking of our mother's words. She had many cures for what ailed the soul. Sunshine, music, cinnamon . . .

But my laugh was short-lived as I came around to the other side of the table, curtsying to my father. Who was he going to be today?

"Your Majesty," I greeted him.

"Annika. Glad to see you're well again," he said pointedly. In seven words, I knew the darkness that sometimes descended on his mind was low and thick today.

Downhearted, I took my place on his left and gazed out upon the courtiers quietly eating their breakfasts. It was musical in a way, the forks and knives tinging against the china plates, making chimes among the low thrum of voices. The light fell in sheets through the arched windows, and it looked like the morning was promising us a beautiful day.

"Now that you're up and about, we need to discuss some business," my father began. "Founding Day is tomorrow, so Nickolas will be arriving tonight. I thought it would give you an excellent opportunity to propose."

"Tonight?" I'd made my peace with the decision as best I

could, but I thought I'd have more time. "How did you even know I'd return to the court today?"

"I didn't. But it needed to happen either way. He rarely comes to court without cause, and sooner is better than later. You can ask him after dinner."

Well, he'd tied all that up neatly.

"And . . . *I* have to ask?"

Father shrugged. "Protocol. You outrank him." His narrow eyes were on me; he was still angry at me for standing up to him. "And you have a . . . stouter disposition than we ever knew. So, I don't see you fainting at the idea of taking the lead."

I wanted to scream at him, to plead for my sweet father to come back to me. There was a man behind those eyes who understood me, who saw my mother in my face. And I missed him so much that I was doing everything I could to not despise *this* man.

But I was still my mother's daughter. For her sake, I kept my smile on my face, determined to preserve what was left of our family.

"No, my lord. It won't be a problem."

"Good." He turned back to his meal.

Escalus was true to his word. Cinnamon breads with icing were sitting right within arm's reach. As tempting as they were, I'd completely lost my appetite.

LENNOX

I woke several hours later with Thistle's muzzle on my leg. I looked down at her, wondering why she didn't run off to wherever it was she tended to hide most of the day. Maybe she just knew I needed her.

The berries I'd picked this morning were still in my waist-belt, and I left them in a little pile for her on the edge of the bed as I redressed myself for the rest of the day. Black pants tucked into black leather boots, white shirt under a black waistcoat. And though I had no intention of riding today, I put on my cape.

I wandered from the depths of the castle out into hazy daylight, the winds off the ocean kicking my hair up as I walked toward the fields.

I could see down the rocky path to the ocean, where people were fishing in tandem with wide nets, using the handful of tiny boats we had. Others were spread out in the fields, harvesting grains. Some fruits and nuts grew naturally in the surrounding forests and up on the mountain, and the land was farmable here if we put in the work. It was a shame that it was *so much* work.

In the distance, I heard the clanging of swords, and I walked toward the arena, intending to offer a hand in training. Once I got there, though, I could see the group was already in Inigo's capable ones, meaning I was all but useless. Hitching a foot up on the lowest plank around the arena, I settled in to survey for talent.

"That's the one," I heard someone whisper. "Killed three people this morning who tried to run. They say he's the eyes and ears of Kawan."

"If they capture someone important, he's the only one who can . . . *take care* of them," another hushed voice replied. "Not even Kawan's guards are cold enough to kill them."

"Kawan is strong, but he isn't heartless," a third chimed in.

"Do you think he can hear us?"

"If I'm the eyes and ears of Kawan, it's best to assume I can always hear," I said without glancing their way.

Then I made the mistake of looking around the arena. Every time I made eye contact with someone, they were quick to turn away.

I knew what recognition felt like. I wondered idly what it would be like to actually be known.

Then a deeper ache came to the surface, and I wondered what it would be like to be forgiven.

I kept my expression blank as I watched the fights, but my thoughts were swirling, tumbling over each other.

"Anyone impressive?"

I straightened as Kawan settled beside me.

I risked looking over at him, hoping he didn't catch the disdain in my eyes.

He didn't waste his energy on dressing to impress. He was clad in layers of old leather. His dark hair was tied back, but it was also unbrushed, and one long braid strayed over his right shoulder. It was my eyes that linked me to Mother, but the hair often tricked new recruits into thinking I was also his.

"Hard to say."

He let out a grunt. "We got two boys in this week from Sibral."

The word hung between us. Sibral was so far west they were practically neighbors to the enemy.

"That's a long trek," I commented.

"It is. They weren't looking for us, it turns out. Didn't know we existed. But they wandered to the edge of our lands, and they happily joined for lodging and warm clothes."

"Didn't know we existed," I muttered.

"Don't worry. They'll all know soon enough." He reached down, hitching up his heavy pants. "About your conquest this morning. Three against one is no small thing. But I would prefer that you stop them from running at all, rather than catching them. That would be a better use of your time. And we need the numbers."

I bit my tongue. It wasn't my fault if his little *kingdom* didn't meet people's expectations.

"What do you suggest?"

"Appropriate warning." He looked up to the sky. "I hear you're giving another lesson tonight. Make the consequences known."

I looked away, sighing. "Yes, sir."

He clapped me on the back. "Good boy. Keep an eye out here. If anyone shows promise, report to me."

With that, he strode away, people parting as he approached. It was a similar reaction to the one I received when I walked somewhere, though his was much grander. I watched him go, thinking there might be something valuable in there. If I couldn't be known or forgiven, perhaps it was enough to be feared.

ANNIKA

The scent of old books hit me the second I opened the library doors, and I felt the slightest bit of the weight I'd been carrying ease from my shoulders. I surveyed the space, taking everything in, basking in the peace the library brought me.

There was so much information in this room, so many stories. Toward the front, there were low shelves to walk through, almost like a maze, and open spaces with desks for studying. When the afternoon sun came through these windows, it was spectacular; studying in here allowed me to both read and be warmed by the sun like a cat. Bliss.

It was also a vast room, with a walkway up around a second level in the back section, and ladders in the front that made me dizzy just looking up at the highest rungs. Some of the older books were chained to the shelves; if anyone wanted to remove them from the library, they had to get permission from the king himself and then persuade Rhett—who guarded the library as if it were a living thing—to actually follow through with the command. Our collection was so extensive that neighboring kingdoms would sometimes come and borrow from us. There were even buckets of sand hidden under carved wooden benches, meant to save as much of the library as we could in the event of a fire. It was fortunate we'd never had any such incident.

As I surveyed the space, basking in the peace the library brought me, Rhett walked around a tall shelf, chuckling.

"I was wondering where you were!" he exclaimed, placing a pile of books on a nearby desk and coming over to embrace me.

Rhett was the only person in the palace who didn't bother standing on ceremony with me. Maybe it was because we'd known each other since we were children, or because he'd gotten his start as a stable hand and was used to seeing me messy and loud, but Rhett treated me like the tiara in my hair was just any other bobble.

"I've been a bit under the weather," I told him.

"Nothing too serious, I hope," he said, pulling back and flashing a wide smile.

"Not at all."

He smirked. "What are you in the mood for today?"

"Fairy tales. Ones where they get everything they ever wanted, ones with a happily ever after."

That smirk stayed plastered to his face, and he hooked his finger as if to say, *Follow me.* "Lucky for you, we got something new last week. And, because I know you so very well, my lady, I know for a fact that you haven't read . . . this one," he said, snatching a book off a high shelf, "in far too long."

He placed the well-worn novel in my hand, and I wondered if anyone else here had ever read this but me. Sometimes it felt like I was the only one in the entire palace who bothered with the library.

"This will be perfect, actually. Comforting."

"Take a new one as well," he insisted, piling it on the other. "You read abnormally fast."

"Not fast enough," I said with a smile.

He stared at me for a moment, something unfamiliar passing across his eyes. "Would you like to stay and have tea? Or, even better, I found another lock for you to try. . . ."

I sighed, wanting to stay. But tomorrow was going to be exhausting. And tonight would be even worse.

"Save the lock for next time. I'm going to be better than you one of these days."

"Will you be a superior leader? Yes. A faster reader? Of course. But quicker at picking a lock?" he said in mock outrage. "Never!"

I giggled. "One, we'll see about that. And two, I won't ever lead; I will happily live under the rule of my brother. Someday."

"All the same," he replied, his contented smile never fading.

"Thank you for the books."

"Anytime, Your Highness."

With that I was on my way. I'd been aware that my legs might bother me today, but being on my feet for so long was more painful than I'd thought it'd be. When the books slipped from my hands halfway up the stairs, I lunged a little too quickly—and I knew that something was really wrong.

I hissed at the searing sensation on the back of my left leg, and I looked around quickly, thankful I was alone.

I moved gingerly, taking longer than I cared to but unable to move any faster. Finally I reached my room, and pushed the door open.

"Your Highness!" Noemi cried as she rushed over and closed the door behind me.

I winced as I pulled up my skirts. "How bad?"

"It looks like a cut has opened up. The good news is, it's just the one. Let's get you to the bed." She put her neck under my arm, and I slowly pushed myself upright. "What in the world did you do?"

"Ate food. Went to the library. You know how reckless I can be."

Noemi chuckled as she laid me down on my stomach. "It's nice to hear you make jokes again."

I'd wondered about that, if laughter would ever come back. "Would you bring the books, please? So I have something to do?"

She ran back and fetched the books, setting them on my bedside table. I stared at the tattered cover beside the pristine one, grateful that Rhett had insisted on both. I was going to be bed-bound for the afternoon.

"His Majesty sent word that you had an important meeting tonight. He wanted me to prepare your best dress. I'd usually go with the silver, but seeing as this has opened, maybe something in a dark red would be safer?"

"That's very smart, Noemi. Thank you."

"This will sting."

"I know."

I tried not to make a sound as she did her work. The less she knew of my pain, the better. I lay there, trying to think of the words to propose to someone. Specifically, someone I had no interest in marrying.

I sighed, trying to push my disgust away. Mother and Father's marriage was arranged, and theirs was a love so grand that its end ruined my father from the inside out. When Mother went missing, he was inconsolable for months.

So I knew firsthand that a marriage of convenience needn't be a terrible thing. Besides, the palace was so large that we could probably make it through the better part of the week only seeing each other at mealtimes. I would still have my room and my library and my brother and Noemi. I'd still have the stables and all the faces I'd come to love and trust. I'd just also have a husband. That's all.

As Noemi finished her task, I picked up one of the books, getting lost in a world where the people had all their dreams come true.

LENNOX

"Don't dawdle," I commanded, leading the group of young recruits up the shallow incline, intentionally avoiding the area where I'd taken down the deserters only this morning.

The wind kicked up off the ocean, rustling the patches of grass and forcing me to yell in order to be heard. That was fine. People were used to me yelling.

"Gather here," I instructed to the dozen or so soldiers now crowding the top of the hill.

"Let's say you're out on a mission, and you get separated from the group. You get lost in that forest or you misplace your compass. What do you do?" I asked. I received a tense silence in return. "No one?"

They just stood there, arms crossed over their chests, shivering.

"Very well. If you're traveling by day, it's easy enough. The sun travels from east to west." I looked on the ground, finding what I needed almost instantly. "Take a stick, about two or three feet long, and post it upright into the ground." I shoved the stick in, making a short pole. "When the sun rises, or as soon as you can take note, place a rock at the end of the stick's shadow." I put a rock down at an imaginary shadow. "Then wait fifteen minutes or so. The sun will have moved, and so will the stick's shadow. Place a second rock at the end of the new shadow." I placed a second rock on the ground. "The imaginary line between these two rocks is the east-west line. If you head east and veer north, you will eventually run into the castle. Or the ocean. One would hope you're smart enough to tell the difference."

Nothing. Well, at least I thought I was funny.

"Traveling at night is a different game altogether. Because of that, you will need to learn to navigate via the stars."

There was a lot of weight shifting and more huddling. Why didn't anyone understand how important this was? There was a *kingdom* waiting on the other side of this. And all people cared about was the cold.

"Look up. Do you see those four stars that make a small irregular square?" More silence. "Anyone?"

"Yes," someone finally answered.

"Do all of you see it? If you don't, you need to tell me now. I can't teach you if you're already lost." Silence. "Very well. That's Ursa Major. If you trace the line of those last two stars, you should find the brightest star in the sky: Polaris. Does everyone see that?"

There were hesitant murmurs among my students.

"Polaris is almost perfectly set at true north. It doesn't move in the sky, but the other stars circle around it. If you look directly above us and focus on that spot, and then trace that to Polaris again, it will point you north. You should always be able to find the castle if you keep heading north."

I looked around to see if anyone understood. It all felt rather obvious to me, but I'd been studying the sky since before I could read—back when there were things around to be read. No one asked any questions, so I moved on.

"Another option is to pick up two sticks, then choose a bright star in the sky and line up the sticks about a meter apart just beneath your star. Then, as with the sun, you wait twenty minutes for the stars to move. If the star rises directly above your posts, you're facing east, but if it sinks behind them, you're facing west. If the star moves to the right, you're facing south, and to the left, you're facing north. Do not get those directions mixed up, or you will get hopelessly lost.

"Over the next few nights, your task is to come out here and practice, even if it's cloudy. Within the month, you should have this mastered.

"Now, look at me," I ordered, quickly gaining the attention of each soldier. "I've explained to you how to find your way in and out of here by the sky. But let me make myself clear." I took my time, making eye contact with each of them. "If you use these skills to try to run, you will come up against me. And if you do, you will regret it."

Some brave soul muttered, "Yes, sir."

"Good. Dismissed."

When the last of their shadows disappeared over the crest of the hill, I let out a breath and lay down in the grass, looking up.

Sometimes, even in my room, the castle was too loud. Echoing footsteps, asinine arguments, and unnecessary laughter. But out here . . . out here, I could think.

I started at the rustling beside me, settling only when I realized Thistle had found me.

"Ah. Out hunting? Get anything good?"

I tried to scratch her head, but she was already on the move again, so I turned my eyes back to the sky.

There was beauty there, a haunting reminder of how small we were. Father used to show me all the shapes, tell me about the characters and stories that were tied to the lines in the stars. I didn't know how much of it to take seriously, but now I liked to think that somewhere else, another father was telling his son the same stories, and that boy was thinking about the possibility in his life, and that he could be the kind of person who people turned into a legend, the kind of person people carved into the stars.

That poor boy. One day the illusion would be shattered. But I hoped he had it still, if only for a night.

ANNIKA

The moon was rising higher outside, the stars glittering around it like diamonds, though it was plain to see that they weren't all white. Some were blue or yellow, some pinkish red. The night sky was the best dressed lady at court, the stars her finest dress and the moon her perfect crown.

The room was full of music and happy people, and the dance floor was crammed with couples, old and young. And I was against a wall, looking out the window.

Cousin Nickolas was here, as promised, standing straight as a pin and looking bored. Not that he ever looked any different.

Nickolas—known as the Duke of Canisse to the general public—was tall and slender with chestnut-brown hair and guarded eyes that spoke of thoughts kept to himself. As someone who spilled too many of my thoughts, it was a trait I had once admired. He was accomplished, and proper, and a member of the only family that mattered, according to my father.

His parents had both been executed at the hand of my grandfather under suspicions of threatening the crown. His mother, Lady Leone, had royal blood in her veins through some *very* distant relative, a branch so far away on the family tree it had all but withered off. Nickolas had been spared, as he was only a baby, and once he was deemed old enough to do so, he pledged his loyalty to our family. It was possible that he might have supporters out there, but, as far as I knew, he'd never deviated from his position to support the Vedette line. That didn't stop the whispers, though, and those were enough to provoke Father to action. For a long time now, his eyes had been on the future, both Escalus's and mine.

Escalus's choices for marriage were complicated; every potential bride came with strings attached or specific benefits for the kingdom. Me? The only boy worthy of my hand was the one who could steal my position. Joining our lines meant ending any possibility of a rival to Escalus. There was no tricky math, no elaborate words. It was simple . . . to everyone but me.

I didn't have a better answer for my father than a straightforward no. But my *no* was very forcefully overruled. So I was stuck with Nickolas trailing me around the room, even when I stepped away, attempting to speak to guests. After a few minutes, he would find me and hover over my shoulder, a little too close.

"You usually dance," he commented.

"Yes. I've been unwell and am still recovering," I replied.

He made some noncommittal humming noise and stayed beside me, watching the crowd.

"You like riding, right? You'll ride out with His Majesty, His Highness, and me tomorrow, won't you?"

He always spoke like that, too. Making a statement but tagging it with a question to seem polite.

"I do like to ride. Assuming I'm feeling well, I'm sure I'll be with the party."

"Very good."

Except, if it was so good, why didn't he smile? Why didn't he *ever* smile?

I looked around the room, trying to imagine a lifetime of this. As I did in almost every situation, I asked myself what my mother would have done. But I couldn't think about what she'd do in this moment without thinking of what she'd have done in the events leading up to it. First, she'd have stood beside me. I knew that without fail. Even if it meant going against Father, even if it risked his anger, she'd have backed me. Second, if we lost, she'd have searched for the good. She would have combed over everything tirelessly looking for the bright side.

I studied Cousin Nickolas again. Yes, he was stern, cold. But maybe with that came a deep sense of responsibility. He would probably dedicate his life to upholding and preserving what was important. As his wife, I'd certainly fall under that category.

And love . . . I didn't know how deeply he was capable of feeling that emotion. I myself only had a spark of it once as a child. I smiled, thinking of that ride with Mother and the house along the road. I missed venturing out in the world. I missed her guiding hand.

I caught my father's eye, and he gave me a look as if to urge me to go ahead and get it over with. I swallowed, pulling myself taller.

"Nickolas?"

"You need some food, yes?" he guessed. "You didn't eat much at dinner."

Goodness, he was watching close. "No. Thank you. Would you join me for just a moment?"

He wore his confusion in a scowl but followed me all the same into a secluded hallway.

"How can I help you?" he asked, his eyebrows crushed together as he looked at me.

Vanish, I thought.

"I confess, I hardly know how to begin this conversation, but I hope you will be kind enough to hear me." I hated the sound of my own voice. It was distant, flat. But Nickolas didn't seem to notice. He merely gave me a curt nod, as if words would waste too much energy.

I could feel the sweat prickling at my brow. How was I supposed to lie my way into a proposal?

"Forgive me, but rank dictates I be the one to ask the question." I cleared my throat, the words needing prompting to move. "Nickolas, would you like to marry me? If not, I understand and will not be—"

"Yes."

"Yes?"

"Yes. One could only see how wise it would be."

Wise. Yes, that was the first word that sprang to a lady's head when she considered matrimony. Not words from romantic books like *wild abandon* and *fate.* "Very true. And I think it would bring our people much joy. Second only to Escalus settling down himself."

He nodded. "We shall set the example, then."

And, without any warning, he kissed me. I ought to have suspected that if his mouth had no idea how to curve itself into a smile, its ability to bend into a kiss would be awful. In one fell swoop two of my biggest life experiences—my proposal and my first kiss—were taken care of. And both were acutely disappointing.

"Let's go back in," he said, offering me his hand. "His Majesty will want to know."

I sighed. "Indeed, he will."

I placed my hand in his and marched back into the ballroom. Father was watching, and he asked the question with his eyes. I answered with mine.

Could he see that my heart was caving in? Could he see what he'd wrought? I didn't know which was worse: the thought that he couldn't, or the thought that he could and didn't care.

No. I refused to believe that. He was still in there. I knew it.

Escalus came over quickly and swooped in. "Forgive me, Cousin Nick, but—"

"Nickolas," he corrected him. "Never Nick." He made a face like a single syllable of a name was too far beneath him.

Escalus covered his amused smile quickly. "Of course. Nickolas, please allow me to cut in. It's been too long since I've danced with my sister."

Nickolas frowned. "We have news to—"

"It can surely wait for one song. Come, Annika." Escalus pulled me away swiftly. Once we were out of earshot, he spoke quickly. "You look like you're about to cry. Try to rein it in, if only for a few more minutes."

"I'll be fine," I said. "Just distract me."

We started swaying, and I thought I was smiling . . . I couldn't be sure anymore. I felt a strange emptiness, worse possibly even than losing Mother.

"Did I ever tell you about the time I tried to run away?" Escalus asked.

I scowled. "That never happened."

"It did," he insisted. "I was ten, and I'd just found out that one day I would be king. Isn't it funny? You'd have thought I'd figured it out long before then. Why didn't anyone else have people who told them how their days were planned? Why couldn't I befriend anyone I wanted to? Why were our parents already talking about my wedding?"

"That is funny," I admitted. "I feel like I knew you were going to be king before I could talk."

"Well, I've never claimed to be as smart as you. I didn't know until Father sat me down with a family tree and showed the places where you and I were drawn in. The ink was brighter, I remember that, too. Because the line was old, and we were new. Anyway. I was scared. I'd heard Father talk about defending borders and making treaties, and there were so many things that seemed too big for someone as small as me."

I looked up at him, my head tilted in sympathy. "No one

expected you to run the kingdom at ten years old, silly."

He smiled and looked around the room. "See, that was another thing I didn't quite understand. As soon as I knew the crown was to be mine, it felt immediate. It felt like I had to master everything. And I didn't want to do it, so I decided I was going to make a run for it.

"This must have been about six months after Rhett came, and he was still a child himself. But I trusted him so much, and he helped me put a bag together, and we planned which horse I was going to take."

"Wait," I said, shaking my head in confusion. "Are you telling me that *Rhett* tried to help you run away when you were ten?"

"Yes. No hesitation. I don't think he'd do anything of the sort now."

I giggled. "Much better head on his shoulders these days."

"Agreed. Anyway, he was helping me pack, and I was writing a letter to Mother and Father, apologizing for leaving. And as I was writing the letter, I put in there, 'Make sure to give the crown to Annika. She can do it better than I can anyway.'"

I looked away. "You did not."

"I did. I thought that you—at seven years old, mind you—could do more than I could at ten. I still think you could lead if you had to, Annika. I think people would follow you off a cliff if you commanded it."

"You're being ridiculous."

He pulled me closer, trying to get me to listen. "Annika, the reason I will be successful when I become king is because you will be here with me. I know that you will always tell me when I'm being foolish; if I've forgotten something, you will most certainly remember. And I know that tonight you feel like a part of you has died; I saw it when you came around the corner."

I looked away. Nickolas was right; I was too easy to read.

"But you need to find that strength in you and hold on to it. We still need you; *I* still need you."

He moved me cautiously around the floor, and I reflected on his words. They made me want to cry for a whole other reason. Nickolas and the chains of obligation felt like the absence of hope; Escalus and his faith in me felt like its full resurgence.

"Wait. Did you make it away from the palace at all? Did Father go after you?"

Escalus sighed. "I made the mistake of telling the cook I needed some food, since I was running away. She told Mother . . . who found me in the stables and talked me into staying."

"Of course she did."

"Of course she did," he echoed. "So, whatever you're feeling, know I'm thankful for you, and that, no matter what, I'm still here."

I looked up at my absurd, brave, wonderful big brother. "I'm here, too."

LENNOX

The mess hall was the same as it ever was. Loud, disorganized, and darker than it ought to be when the sun was up. I walked in, going to set my wrist on the hilt of my sword before I remembered I hadn't strapped it on for breakfast. Looking around at the many faces seeming to corner me in this morning, that suddenly felt like a bad idea.

When I could help it, I ate before or after the room was at its peak. If that didn't work, I tended to grab whatever I could eat with my hands and bolt. I stood on the edge of the space, resolving to take a piece of bread and go, even though I was much hungrier.

In the end, it didn't matter. A small girl walked over to me, shaking where she stood, looking up at me with doe-like eyes.

"What?" I demanded.

She opened her mouth, but nothing came out.

"Don't worry. I won't kill you for delivering a message."

She didn't seem convinced, and it took her another few breaths to speak.

"Kawan is asking for you," she said.

"He is?" I asked in disbelief.

She nodded. Then, having completed her task, she left as quickly as she could without actually breaking into a run.

Why in the world was he asking for me? Sighing, I abandoned breakfast and started toward his rooms, the ones I assumed belonged to the king when this castle had been erected.

I reminded myself of three things. First, that *he* sent for *me*, that I wasn't crawling to him. Second, to shove my pride as low as it could go for the time being. And, finally, to keep to the rules.

Never run away, never look away, never explain away. This was how I survived.

I knocked on the door, and he waited a few breaths before sending someone to let me in. It was Aldrik who greeted me, his expression smug. He pulled the door open wide, and I saw Kawan sitting at his desk. Behind him, his personal guards stood watch: Slone, Illio, Maston, and—walking over to join them—Aldrik.

One would have expected a revered spot like that to go to me, right? I was the son of the woman draped across his arm. I was the one who did the majority of his dirty work. I was the one most of the people in this castle feared the most.

But if I wanted anything out of Kawan's hands, I had to pull. And I refused to stoop so low. "You called, sir?" I asked, tagging the last word on in an effort to come across respectful. As the only descendant of the long-lost leader of our people, Kawan himself should be called king, though he claimed to be saving the title for when he actually held his kingdom. Anytime I tried to imagine Kawan with a ring of gold on his tangled hair, I couldn't help but think a change of location wasn't going to make him any more regal.

"I did." He looked up at me, and I had the distinct impression I was about to get punished. "The time has come for you to prove yourself. I'm sending you on a Commission."

I very nearly smiled. A Commission. At last!

The Commissions were Kawan's way of testing people, of discovering how deep their loyalties went. Only those we were sure wouldn't run were even considered, and everyone who returned had an air of . . . untouchability to them. I'd earned some of that at the end of my sword, but I wanted to have respect alongside the fear that people tended to attach to my name.

Each person chose their team and came up with their own mission. The only requirement was that the outcome had to benefit the people. Sometimes they brought back more food, sometimes more livestock, sometimes even more soldiers.

But, at least for me, there was a sense that with whatever was gained . . . nothing really changed.

That would end with me.

"I accept, sir. Gladly."

"As you know, you may choose to do whatever you like. However," he said, deliberately pausing. That dreaded sense of being punished rose again in my gut. "I will be selecting the soldiers you take."

"What?!"

A smile played on the edges of Kawan's lips. He was enjoying this. My eyes darted to my mother. Ever silent, she didn't even look at me.

"You need to prove yourself, but you're too foolhardy. I'm sending you with a carefully chosen group, people who will check you if you get out of line," he said.

People who will drag me down, I thought.

"First, Andre."

I squinted. "The . . . the one who barely talks?"

"Griffin."

I rolled my eyes. "He doesn't take anything seriously."

"Sherwin."

"I don't have the slightest idea who that even is."

"Blythe."

"A girl?"

"And Inigo." At this he seemed the most pleased he could possibly be. Why wouldn't he? If no one else could ruin my commission, Inigo certainly could. Inigo wore a scar down his face that I'd placed there myself. He wasn't about to take orders from me.

Behind him, Slone covered his mouth, trying to hide his laughter. After everything I'd done, after every life I'd taken, why was I still left trying to prove myself to these people?

I looked at my mother again. "Are you going to stay silent? A botched Commission took your husband, and now he's assuring mine will fail. You have no comments on the matter?"

She didn't seem bothered in the slightest, her icy hair

hanging over one shoulder and a smile in her eyes. "If you are the leader we know you to be, wrangling that group should be easy. I have faith."

Once again, she drew a line in the sand. Once again, I backed away.

"Very well. I'll show you exactly what I can do."

ANNIKA

I'd always loved the bells. Once, Mother brought me up to the tower where they were housed and had the keeper show me around. I touched the huge brass bells, and he let me try to pull the rope; I'd been too small to make them chime. But their sound, the clear cast of joy out from the palace, meant celebration. They rang when a royal child was born, when we had a great victory, and—the only reason I'd ever heard them—for holidays.

Today, they rang out for Founding Day. Anyone within sight of the palace would look to see us standing on the balcony. It was our job to wave to the crowd below—some might consider it a frivolous task, but it was one of my few chances to show the people of Kadier that I was here and that I cared for them. I met eyes with so many people, received kisses blown from the tips of their fingers, and I smiled, hoping they would never guess that I was anything but delighted with my place.

The wind lifted my hair, and I pulled it over my shoulder,

turning to Escalus. He looked so smart in his uniform, his military training pins along the left side of his chest.

I giggled as he blushed when yet another lady cheered his name. "You need to get used to it," I told him. "Marriage is the only thing that will save you from such adoration. And even then, you'll probably still have handkerchiefs dropped in your path. Although maybe that practice would stop if you didn't always swoop to pick them up."

He turned to me incredulously. "How could I do such a thing? A lady needs her handkerchief!"

I laughed again, and it rang out with the bells. On Escalus's other side, Father leaned forward, looking across to me. I could see by the sparkle in his eye that he was himself this morning, *really* himself.

"You are so like her today," he said. "With your hair over your shoulder like that, laughing so sweetly."

Those words from my father's lips made me want to cry. "Really?"

When he was like this, when the angry fog that had settled in his mind after Mama's disappearance lifted for a moment, my world changed. I felt hope. I saw the man who used to be so proud of me, so full of praise. I wondered if this person might apologize for words said, things done; I wondered if he might relent and let me out of this engagement. I was very tempted to ask . . . but I could be so wrong, and he could disappear again.

Just like her.

People made that comment almost daily, and it gave me pause sometimes.

I had my mother's upturned nose and ash-brown hair, and there was a portrait of her in the far corridor that reminded me my eyes were a gift from her, too. But I wondered if there was more than that.

I thought of how Escalus stood sometimes, his weight securely stationed on his left leg, and how Father did that all the time. Or the sounds of their coughs . . . I couldn't tell between the two unless I was looking. Did I have those things, too? Details I'd forgotten in the years since she'd been gone?

"Hello, my pet," Nickolas said as he came forward to join us on the edge of the balcony.

I wondered if Mother ever had to work this hard to smile, if we shared that trait, too. "Hello."

"Will you be going out for the ceremonial fox chase?" he asked as he waved to the crowd below.

I almost hated to pass on the chance. It was rare that Father let me go beyond the palace grounds anymore. But, even if I had been feeling up to it, I didn't care for the company.

"As I mentioned last night, I'm a bit under the weather. I'd love to ride, but it will be best to stay in for the afternoon," I said as a means of excusing myself. "But I know you're an excellent rider, so I'm sure you'll do well."

"I suppose," he replied. "Unless you want me to stay behind with you."

I worked to keep my voice steady. "No need for that. I'll just be sleeping anyway." I moved my eyes to the crowd, smiling and waving again.

"I've been thinking," he began as we continued to

acknowledge the people, "I don't want a lengthy engagement. Do you think you could arrange the wedding within a month?"

A month?

A strange feeling like . . . like a hand around my throat engulfed me.

"I . . . I'd have to ask His Majesty. I haven't exactly planned a wedding before," I said, attempting to disguise my fear with a joke.

"Understandable. But let's not waste any time."

I tried to think of an excuse to wait . . . not a one came to mind.

"As you wish," I finally said. The bells finished ringing, and we gave our final nods to the crowd, turning to go inside. Still to come was the fox chase and the dance young girls did in the square with their ribbons in the air. If I stayed on the balcony, I could see it from afar. Later we hosted a hunt where the children would search for painted stones hidden around the palace, and the day would cap off with a feast. Founding Day was truly my favorite holiday.

He smiled as we walked. "I'm pleased to see you so obliging. I did hope to discuss something else with you." He stopped me, holding both of my hands in his. It was a gesture so tender that I wondered for a moment where my fear had come from.

This was Nickolas, after all. I'd known him—from a distance—my whole life. He might not have been what I wanted, but he was nothing to run from.

"You are eighteen now. A proper lady, and a princess at

that. After the engagement is announced, I expect you to wear your hair up."

My heart plummeted. Not ten minutes ago, my father had rejoiced in my hair as it was. "I . . . My mother always wore her hair down. I prefer it."

"In private, that's fine. But you're not a child anymore, Annika. A lady ought to wear her hair up."

I swallowed hard. He was dangerously close to crossing a line. "*My mother* was an immeasurably magnificent lady."

He cocked his head, speaking in a tone so measured and calm it was amazing it could also be so irritating. "I'm not trying to start a fight, Annika. I simply think that you ought to show your maturity, your sense of propriety. I understand that not *all* older women pull their hair up, but most do. If you're on my arm, I expect you to be properly presented."

I let go of one of his hands so I could reach back to lace my fingers through the ends of my hair, which fell to the middle of my back. It was the same color as hers; it had the same loose curls. I kept it clean and styled; having it down was nothing to be ashamed of.

I was prepared to fight—it wouldn't be the first time—but now was not the time or place.

"Is that all?" I asked.

"For now. Off to change for the chase." He pulled up my hand and kissed it before walking away.

From across the hall, Father gave me a smile, a genuine one again.

I didn't want him to see me sad. Not on a good day. I needed to get away. I hid in a parlor while everyone got ready for the chase, and, once the palace was quiet again, I crept to my only hiding place.

I was confused when I walked into the library, and it took me a second to realize why: it was dim. Rhett had forgone drawing back most of the drapes, and the library was cast in gray shadows.

It was eerily quiet, but not empty. Rhett was there, near the front doors, sunk back in a velvet chair, toying with another lock. He looked up when he heard me coming but didn't break into his usual smile.

"Is this the new one?" I asked, carefully sitting across from him.

He nodded and handed it over. It was heavier than it looked. I pulled a pin out of my apparently offensive hair and went to work.

"Where did you find this? It looks so old," I commented, using the pin to investigate the inside of the keyhole.

"It was in a bucket in the kitchen. Someone must have found it sitting around, and no one knows where the key is anymore."

He sounded unenthusiastic, which wasn't like him. Rhett had learned how to pick locks and pockets in the packed towns on the outskirts of the country before he came to the palace for honest work.

My mother, as I said, was all about forgiveness.

He worked hard in the stables but showed a voracious hunger for learning. When the old mistress of the library passed, I suggested to my mother that a young man with Rhett's mind and determination would be the best candidate to entrust it to, and she happened to agree. He'd been a natural. Not just with the library, but with everything he practiced. He helped me with my sword fighting, even though it wasn't entirely approved, and he still found time to teach me how to pick both locks and pockets. For all my talk, I knew I had nothing close to his deftness or skill, but I loved it all the same.

"Is something wrong?" I asked offhandedly, my hairpin finally finding a point that might move.

"Heard a rumor."

"Rumors," I repeated. "Hmm. I can never decide if they're wicked or entertaining. I suppose it depends on the topic. Is the stuff they say downstairs as bad as it is upstairs?"

Rhett toyed with a long piece of straw. "Well . . . it was an upstairs rumor."

I paused my pin immediately. "Oh?"

He suddenly burst out with the words. "Are you really engaged to Nickolas? Why didn't you tell me?"

There was something about the inflection of his words, the way his eyes seemed to grow dark when he said them, that told me he was more than a little disappointed he'd found out from someone else. I didn't expect him to be so wounded over it.

"Yes. I am. It only happened last night. I wasn't trying to hide it from you. I don't particularly want to tell *anyone* yet."

"So it's true? You're actually marrying him?" There was an edge to his voice, some deep emotion stirring.

"Yes."

"Why?"

I lifted up my arms in exasperation. "Because I have to, obviously." I went back to poking the lock, doing a much worse job now that I was irritated.

"Oh." His voice softened. "So, you're . . . not in love with him?"

I looked at him with hollow eyes. "No, I don't love him. But because I love *Kadier*, I will marry Nickolas all the same. Even though it feels like someone's built a cage around my chest and my lungs can't fill the whole way. Maybe . . . maybe I've read too many books." I shrugged. "But I'd hoped for *passion*, for a love that took reason by the shoulders and shoved it off a cliff. I'd hoped for a sense of freedom within the confines of my life . . . but that's not going to happen for me. Nickolas is not my soul mate, nor is he my beloved. He's my intended, and that is all. I'm simply trying to find a way to make the best of it."

"Do you even like him?"

I sighed. "Rhett, even for us, I'm not sure these questions are entirely appropriate."

He took my hand, wrapping his fingers around mine as they held on to the lock. I could feel every callus he'd earned in his youth, every healed cut. "Isn't that the point? You could always talk to me, Annika. Honestly."

I looked into his brown eyes, brimming with tenderness. There weren't many people I could tell the truth to anymore. Escalus knew more about me than anyone, and Noemi came in a close second. Mother wasn't here, and Father couldn't be trusted anymore, not with anything truly important. But Rhett . . . he was right. I'd always been candid with him.

"What am I supposed to say?" I ventured. "I've been born to a specific role in this world. It comes with responsibilities. I'm trying to accept it with a certain level of grace. Am I in love? No. But plenty of marriages are loveless. Right now, I'm just aiming for respect."

"Fine, then do you respect him?"

I swallowed. Well, he cut right to the heart of it, didn't he?

"Annika, you can't do this."

I laughed, a tired, humorless sound. "I assure you, every avenue has been explored. If a prince and a princess couldn't stop it, I don't expect a librarian to manage it."

It was a low blow, one I'd never have made if I wasn't feeling so raw.

"I'm sorry," I said, almost immediately. "If you want to help, support me. Right now, I need every friend I can get. I need people who can remind me to look for the positive."

He surveyed the ground for a minute. "His posture is . . . remarkable. If you ever need to measure something, he'd be an excellent stick."

My laugh came out in a snort, which made Rhett laugh, which made me really laugh.

"See there," I said. "It's already better than it was when I walked in."

"I'm always here for you, Annika."

I looked into Rhett's eyes, those sincere brown eyes. At least I could always come to him.

And then, with no warning, he took my face in his hands and smashed his lips into mine.

I jumped up quickly, the lock falling from my lap to the carpet.

"What are you doing?!"

"You must know how I feel, Annika. And I know you feel the same."

"You know nothing!" I said, wiping at my mouth in shock. "If anyone had come in, do you know what they'd have done? And it would be ten times worse for you than for me!"

He stood and grabbed at my hands again. "Then don't give them the chance, Annika."

"What?"

"Run away with me."

My shoulders slumped, so tired. "Rhett."

"You just said you wanted a love that dismissed reason. If my loving you doesn't do that, then I don't know what does."

I shook my head, confused. Had I mistaken his affections all this time?

"I can't."

"You can," he insisted. "Think about it. You could walk into your room and pack every single jewel in your possession. And I can pick every pocket from here to the border. Once we get out of Kadier, no one would know you from anyone else. We could build a house. I could get a job. We can just *be*."

"Rhett, stop talking nonsense."

"It's not nonsense!" he swore. "Think about it. Annika, we could be free."

I momentarily considered his proposal. We could take any

of the horses we wanted, and, with the celebration, if we left now, we wouldn't be found missing until morning. And he was right that no one would recognize me. I'd been kept in the capital for the last three years, barely even stepping off the palace grounds. If I wasn't riding under the flag, people wouldn't have the faintest clue that royal blood coursed through my veins.

If I really wanted to, I could disappear.

"Rhett . . ."

"You don't have to decide right now. Think about it. Say the word, Annika, and I will take you far away from here. I will love you for my whole life."

LENNOX

I'd spent the entire day fuming. After all this time, this was how my Commission was going to go? And it wasn't as if I could refuse. Not backing down was my finest trait. By late afternoon, my anger had abated enough that I could mostly think straight, and I sent word through some of the younger recruits to find the five people Kawan had assigned me. I waited for them on the edge of the field, far away from the eyes and ears of the castle.

Inigo and Griffin arrived together, and I spotted Blythe's blond hair as she approached behind them. I'd balked when Kawan had said her name, but, to be fair, she was fast. Really fast. Griffin probably had redeeming qualities—I just didn't know what they were. And though Inigo wasn't my favorite person in the world, he certainly had a way with a sword. Or a fist, need be.

"What's this about?" Inigo asked.

I sighed. "We're still waiting for two more. I can see them."

Griffin and Inigo turned, looking past Blythe. She followed their lead, and took in the two figures dressed in dark gray and black coming up behind her. She propped herself up on a boulder and tilted her head in acknowledgment of Inigo and Griffin; I got a long stare.

"You wanted to see me?" Andre asked nervously as he approached.

"Yes. And I assume you're Sherwin?" I asked the stocky boy behind him.

"Yes. Sir. I mean, yes, sir."

I sighed, crossing my arms. "Well, congratulations. Kawan has assigned you all to my Commission."

At that Inigo straightened. "Assigned? That's not how Commissions work."

"And don't I know it," I replied. "But here we are. It seems that, if I am to truly prove myself, I should be capable of leading anyone into any situation."

Inigo paused. "Wait. You still need to prove yourself to him?"

It was the first time he'd acknowledged the long list of my accomplishments. It might have been the first time anyone had.

I held my arms out. "Apparently."

Inigo stared at the ground, his mind moving quickly. His eyes came to mine, clearly landing on the conclusion I'd come to before leaving Kawan's room.

"Yes," I said. "It's a setup."

"Why are you always so gloomy?" Griffin asked me, smiling all the while.

"No, think about it," Inigo began seriously, drawing our eyes to him. "There's usually a month or more between Commissions, but he's making you go right after Aldrik so people will compare your conquest to his. On top of that, he's not letting you build your own team or take time to plan. He doesn't want you to prove yourself worthy," he concluded, looking up at me. "He wants you to fail."

I pointed at him. "Absolutely. Sherwin, I didn't know you existed before this moment. Andre and Blythe, I know very little about your abilities, so I can't put much faith in you. Griffin, I can't take you seriously because you don't take anything seriously yourself. And, Inigo . . . I think everyone already knows that there's no love lost between us."

Inigo smirked. "Yes, I'd rather throw you off Govatar Mountain than help you."

"And I'd happily do the same. So you were assigned to me to drag this whole thing down. We were designed to fail."

There was a moment of silence, a pause at the funeral of my greatest personal ambition to date. Then Blythe spoke up.

"Well, I hate to disappoint you, but I don't fail." She said the last word with an air of disgust, and Inigo chuckled.

"She's right," he commented quickly. "Her aim with a bow and arrow is all but flawless, and, when it comes to perseverance, well . . . there aren't many who have what she does."

Blythe looked away. "Thanks."

"Sure."

"I can be serious," Griffin said in a whine, which made everyone laugh. "Really! I can."

"All you do is joke," I said tiredly. "You flirt. You play."

He shrugged. "Someone has to. Our lives are too dark as it is."

Well, that was a fair point. Fine, then. Blythe was good with a bow and fast. Griffin . . . well, forgetting his relentless joking, he did a fairly good job in hand-to-hand fighting. And Inigo? There was practically nothing he wasn't capable of if he decided to try.

I looked over at Sherwin. "What about you? What can you do?"

"Right now, I do a lot of farming. But Inigo is training me in combat."

I looked back to Inigo, not needing to ask.

"He has potential with a sword. The bow requires more finesse. And as for Andre, he's timid, but"—he looked over at him—"he can handle a sword better on a horse than on foot. It's impressive."

Huh. Kawan didn't seem to even know what he had at his disposal. If he had, he certainly wouldn't have assigned anyone with this sort of skill to me.

I looked back at Inigo. He was the only one who could really make the call.

"I have no intentions of failing," he told me. "Not because of you, but because of me."

"For what it's worth," I replied, "I did have a brilliant plan, but I'm going to let it go for the sake of something much more attainable, something where we'll risk little but the potential payoff is priceless."

"Is it better than more recruits?" Sherwin asked.

"Yes."

"Better than six cows?" Griffin posed, making the group chuckle.

To my surprise, even I smiled. "Yes."

"Then what is it?" Blythe asked.

I took a deep breath, thinking of the one thing we needed more than anything these days.

"Hope."

ANNIKA

Escalus had his own knock. It was amazing how two seconds of sound could lift my entire mood.

Noemi bounded over to the door, grinning from ear to ear. I kept my seat by the window, embroidery hoop in hand.

"What are you doing here?" I asked. "I assumed you'd be joining the stone hunt." I gave him a pointed look. Last year, he carried around half the stones in his arms and ended up with about twenty children trying to climb him and steal them back.

"Oh, that's been over for hours. Did I find the most stones again? Yes. Yes, I did. But I then noticed my sister didn't make it downstairs for dinner and thought she might need a little something. For you, miss," he said, handing a huge chunk of raisin bread to Noemi. She lit up like the sun, taking it in her hands.

"Thank you, Your Highness."

"Not at all. The least I could do. And this one is for you.

They're still warm," he added, setting my piece on the windowsill since my hands were full.

"Why were you in the kitchens? Did you miss dinner, too?"

He plopped down across from me, rolling his eyes in exasperation. "No, but I ran from Nickolas shortly after dessert. He's trying to get me to look at some design he has for a fortification. Says he's been studying the borders and thinks we could use some lookouts."

"Hmm. Is he right?"

"Who knows? Where's mine?" he asked.

"In the basket."

Escalus reached down and pulled his own needlework out of the notions basket and settled back on the stone bench beneath my window. We were given unique educations; we liked to share them.

"That's coming along quite nicely, Your Highness," Noemi said, looking over his shoulder.

He set it on his knee and looked up at her admiringly. "Why, thank you, Noemi. See, someone here appreciates my raw talent."

"Noemi has to say that," I teased. "She's not about to insult her future king."

Escalus looked at me in mock outrage. "That's not so! Tell her, Noemi."

She shook her head. "I wouldn't go around insulting you, sir, but I also wouldn't give you praise where it isn't due."

"See?" he insisted.

"Oh, hush," I muttered at him, winking up at Noemi.

He chuckled to himself, going back to the stitching of another circle in his design. It looked like he was making a succession of rings growing around one another, each one using a different stitch that he'd mastered. I tended toward flowers and rosy colors; he preferred symmetry and blues.

"Father had such a good day," he commented.

"I know. I wanted to spend more time with him, but . . . I was just on edge."

He kept his head down but looked up at me. "Anything you want to talk about?"

"Not yet. I'm trying to decide if I'm being childish."

Escalus smiled and shook his head. "How could you think your behavior about this childish? Marrying for your kingdom's sake is so . . . noble."

"Is it?" I scoffed.

"Annika, Nickolas has the strongest claim to the throne should something happen to Father or me. Being married to him keeps anyone who might have ever doubted us from having a single cause for war. And if something happens to me, your place on the throne is secure with him as your consort. It's difficult, I know, because he's so . . . so . . ."

"I know." There wasn't a word for the air that Nickolas gave off. *Boring* wasn't strong enough and neither was *stern*, but *wicked* was maybe too far. Whatever the word, it was hard to cast it in a positive light.

"Well, we can acknowledge he's . . . lacking in some ways. But he's strong in others. Clever, a good hunter and rider. He's wealthy, not that you need it."

"He has nothing I need. Nothing I want."

"Hmm."

"What?" I asked, peeking up to see my brother smiling.

"It's just that saying it that way makes me wonder if there is someone who does have something you want."

I rolled my eyes. "For goodness' sake."

"You can tell me."

For a split second I thought of Rhett and his proposal. He didn't care about my rank or the impropriety of the offer. He simply wanted me. I could admit there was something appealing in that . . . but I couldn't say that aloud.

"I wouldn't have to. If someone had stolen my heart, you'd figure it out long before I did."

He laughed. "And don't I know it! Noemi, how many times has she told you about that boy with the apple?"

"I stopped counting!" Noemi called from the side chamber.

"For a ten-year-old, it was rather romantic," I argued as Escalus chuckled. I heaved a sigh. "I was only trying to say that there were standards in my head. They've gone down significantly now. I feel like all I can hope for is kindness. And maybe affection."

"It will come," Escalus assured me, though his tone was cautious. "More than just affection came for Mother and Father."

"Do you remember a season when they weren't warm toward each other?" I asked, looking up from my stitches. "Were they just happy from the first day, or . . . ?"

"Well . . . I remember Father got sick once. Deathly sick. You were really young. And Mother insisted that she tend to him herself. I don't know if it was love or duty that motivated her, but they came out on the other side of that with a different attitude toward one another. After that, he just worshipped her."

"I can't imagine a scenario in which Nickolas would worship me."

"I've got it!" he said, putting the sewing aside. "We need to poison him!"

"Escalus!"

Behind me I heard Noemi giggling. She walked over, stopping beside me, and I reached up, wrapping an arm around her waist.

"I do believe that's illegal, Highness," Noemi teased.

"Not a lot, just a little!" he countered before turning back to me. "He'll think he's sick, and you can take care of him, and then you're all set."

I shook my head. "Terrible idea."

"Amazing idea. Come on, Noemi, what do you think?"

"I think . . . ," she began with a sigh, "that it's a pity your sister wasn't born first."

I doubled over with laughter, and Escalus's whole face scrunched up, amused. Noemi ran her hand down my back a few times before carrying on with her tasks, and Escalus and I fell into a comfortable silence for the better part of an hour. It was a relief to me that he never needed me to fill a space with words.

But he then reached his limit and rubbed at his eyes. "That's all I can take. Where's your sword?"

"Same place as always."

He reached under my bed and pulled out the sword. Ever since I accidentally cut his arm, the rule—our rule, anyway—was I practiced my sword work with cloth strapped around the blade.

I never asked where my sword came from. I assumed it was either one he'd used when he was younger and handed down to me, or that he had it made especially for his little sister in secret. Either way, I loved it.

He pulled it out and spun around, hitting the post of my bed.

"Hey!"

"I didn't hurt it. Up now. Time for a lesson."

I set my embroidery down and took a big bite of the bread he had bought me, walking over as I chewed.

"Show me your stance."

I put my feet shoulder width apart, digging the balls of my feet into the parquet floor.

"Good. Where do your hands go?"

I raised them to the right of my chin, acting as if I was holding the hilt of my sword.

"Shoulders down. Good. All right." He handed the sword off to me. "Your turn."

I took a long, slow breath and stepped, using the post of my bed as a target. Unlike Escalus, I didn't try to hit it. My goal was to come up on it with enough force that I could take a chunk out if I did, but with enough control that I could stop before it could happen.

Escalus watched patiently, correcting my form and offering encouragement. We only went a few minutes before I pushed too hard. My sword clattered to the floor as I winced in pain, grabbing my thigh.

"Annika!"

"My lady!" Noemi came running, but she was too late. Escalus had swept me up, setting me gingerly on the bed.

"I'm fine. I just have one wound that's not healing well."

Escalus's clear, trusting eyes looked deep into mine. "I never imagined it could get that bad between you two. Even at his worst, I . . ."

I could tell I was bleeding, and I tried in vain to keep the blood from spreading on my shift. "I know. But I can either spend my lifetime hating him for it or come to peace. Forgive." I sighed. "You should go. I'm in capable hands."

Escalus looked up at Noemi, who nodded, saying wordlessly that she would protect me. Goodness knows what would happen if anyone figured out a way to bribe Noemi. She knew every last secret.

"I'll see you in the morning," he said sympathetically. "Hopefully with a smile."

"Of course, I shall bring my smile."

"Good. Because I miss seeing you be you."

I looked up at him, trying to seem hopeful and thinking of our words to one another the night before. "I'm still here. Always."

LENNOX

I woke to the sound of Thistle coming in to sleep. She chirped, nuzzling her nose just by my ear.

"That is not helpful," I informed her. "I actually have work to do today. I need to be rested."

She let out a long sigh.

"Very well." I reached out, my hair falling across my eyes as I scratched her chin. "I may as well get up, anyway. I might actually be able to make a difference soon. We might finally leave." I whispered a thought I'd barely allowed myself to consider: "I might be known for something else in a few days. But! Not if I don't prepare."

I shoved myself up, running my fingers across my face, taking in my quarters. There wasn't much in the space that I could call my own anymore; a few vestiges from my years raised as a merchant's son, the years before Kawan showed up at our door. A bow with its quiver of arrows rested against the corner beside a guitar that had long since lost its strings. On my rarely used desk, a few books about navigating the stars sat in a pile next to an oblique calligraphy pen for my now questionable handwriting. On the far corner of the desk sat the telescope my father had given me, the lens chipped on the edge from a time I'd dropped it. The rest was clothes in various stages of cleanliness. I told myself that my small life was worth fighting for, that there were bigger things waiting on the other side.

The sky was still hazy out the small window, so I grabbed my cape and put it on over my clothes, picking up my sword as I headed to the arena. I saw the rest of my team coming around the side of the castle and told myself to pull it together. This was the beginning of everything.

"I've made sure everyone knows to excuse you from any other details you might have been assigned to today. It is imperative that I understand what each of you are capable of before we head out. So, this morning, you will either face off against Inigo or me."

At that they all fidgeted. Except for Blythe, who seemed to have expected something like this.

"But first, I want to explain why it's so important that you're all prepared for whatever comes." I swallowed. "We're going into Kadier. We're stealing the Kadierian crown. Actually, no, I take that back. We're going to retrieve *our* crown. And we're bringing it back here."

Inigo and Blythe exchanged a look, while Sherwin looked like he might faint. Griffin let out a wild laugh.

"I love it!" he exclaimed.

"This could be suicide," Inigo said.

I shrugged. "Staying here, hidden away on the outskirts, is a death of a different kind. I don't know about you, but I'm tired of waiting. If we can pull this off, it will give everyone in this castle what food and clothes and recruits cannot. If we succeed, Kawan will have to see that we are ready to reclaim our kingdom."

"How exactly do you plan on getting to the crown?" Blythe asked. "Getting into Dahrain alone might be impossible."

I shook my head. "Difficult, probably, but not impossible. It's happened twice."

She stood her ground, unconvinced. "Even if the old maps could guide us there and even if we can somehow get into their palace, there's no way the actual crown would be on display. It's certainly under guard. It might take days to find it."

"We're going to sneak in. There are some untouched clothes in storage. We're going to get the best of what's left and turn ourselves into subjects. We're going to set up camp somewhere in Dahrain, get into the palace, and establish our watch. Royals are lazy creatures with predictable habits. It won't take too long to find out where they'd keep their valuables. The danger comes in the guards. Who knows how many there might be? I can take around four at a time, and Inigo, you could probably handle about the same." He nodded. "So I need to see how well the rest of you respond to pressure. I need to know that we can succeed."

"It's bold," Griffin said.

"That's . . . that's not the right word," Inigo countered.

Blythe sighed. "One problem. The women's clothes don't go into storage; they go to your mother's wardrobe."

"I've already considered this. Tonight, while everyone is

eating dinner, I'll get into her room."

"Couldn't we just ask?" Sherwin offered.

"No," Inigo said. "If we've already been set up to fail, we can't ask for permission. We'll have to take everything we need and then some. If we succeed, they won't be able to say anything about it. If we don't . . ."

He looked at me, and I shook my head. "We're not going to fail. We're going to be patient and careful, and we're coming back with a crown in our hands."

Blythe kicked off the planks of the arena. "All right. Let's get to work, then."

She took the sword out of Andre's hand and made her way to the middle of the field.

"I'll go with her. You can take Sherwin," Inigo offered, then lowered his voice. "Start slow. Give him a chance to build some confidence. He's got potential, but he responds better to encouragement than shouting."

I took that in. "Thank you."

Inigo stepped back at the words, almost as if they could burn him. He swallowed, straightening himself up. "You're welcome."

He went off to Blythe, Andre and Griffin paired up to practice, and Sherwin stepped in front of me. I could see the panic in his eyes. On the one hand, it would have been foolish for him to not fear me, but on the other, it was not reassuring that fear read so easily on his face.

I followed Inigo's instructions, not pointing it out.

After about fifteen minutes, Sherwin's moves started to become surer. His lunges sharpened, and his response time shrank. The focus of his eyes shifted, and he started looking like a soldier. I pushed harder, and he responded, moving more aggressively. It was promising. But after a moment, I saw him looking over my shoulder, and I finally backed down, turning to see the fuss.

Inigo and Blythe were moving fast, swords clanking in time. They sparred smoothly, seeing one another's moves a second before they happened, so well matched it looked like a dance. I was entranced, so much so that I didn't dare blink for fear of missing something. After another well-placed hit, Inigo raised his left arm, and Blythe pulled back just as she was winding up to strike again, lowering her sword.

Behind me, Griffin and Andre were clapping, and Sherwin quickly joined in. Blythe and Inigo looked over at their adoring crowd, smiling at the acknowledgment.

"Excellent work, Blythe," I said.

She ducked her head quickly, sweeping a lock of hair behind her ear, saying nothing in return.

"That goes for you, too, Sherwin." I turned to him. "You just need to be as confident at the start as you are fifteen minutes in. Trust yourself from the off; you can do this."

He nodded. "Yes, sir."

"Griffin. You ready to suffer?" I called.

He held his arms out as if he were embracing the world, that smirk ever present on his lips. "At your service."

And the morning went on like that, trading sparring partners, offering insight. By the time lunch came, I was convinced more than ever that Kawan was a fool. One, he had so much at his disposal, and he failed to use it. And two, he'd accidentally handed it over to me.

ANNIKA

As much as I'd have preferred to stay in my room, it was Wednesday, and I knew that Father would be teaching Escalus; I hated missing a lesson.

Just as I reached the library doors, Rhett walked out, on his way to deliver some books. His smile had returned, and he looked perfectly at ease. I couldn't help but think, *That boy kissed me.*

There was something about this fact that left me stunned. He'd worked so hard for his place in the palace. The position, the comfort . . . people would fight for what he had.

And he was more than willing to throw it all away for me.

It was the kind of thing I read in my books, the kind of thing that made people fall. So why? Why wasn't I prepared to abandon everything for him? If he loved me like he said, it would be more of a waste to stay than go.

"Your Highness." Rhett greeted me with a rare bow as the wide door shut behind him. "Shall I prepare the horses?" His tone was playful, but the desire for an answer could be heard behind the joke.

"Not just yet."

"Not yet . . . but soon."

I giggled at his confidence. "You think you know me so well?"

He straightened, shifting his books to his opposite hand. "You doubt me? I know you prefer picking small locks to big ones, and you have a strange affection for cinnamon. Your favorite color, for some bizarre reason, is white, and you don't mind rain but hate the cold." He paused, shaking his head and making me smile even more.

"What else? You prefer evenings to mornings. You tend to put others before yourself. If you could spend the entirety of your day in a sunny patch of grass with a book, you would. Particularly that patch out in the far side of the garden."

I put my hand over my heart. "I do love it there. The pretty flowers and that smooth, round stone in the ground."

He nodded. "I know. I know everything about you. And I know that you both want and deserve more than that," he said, flicking his chin at the library door before carrying on his way.

Confused by his words, I went inside. Sure enough, I could see over the low rows of shelves near the front that Father and Escalus were at their usual table. But, surprisingly, Nickolas was there as well.

You deserve more than that. Well, yes, I supposed I did.

"You're late," Father said briskly. "Today's lesson is for the lot of you. You're the next generation of leaders for Kadier. How could you be late?"

I wanted to correct him, to tell him that he'd never formally invited me to these lessons in the first place, and I only came because Escalus started dragging me along. That I stayed because I loved it.

"My apologies, Your Majesty. I am most ready now," I said, taking my seat. I could tell he was not in the mood for pleasantries today.

Before him were several books. The largest one lay open, showing a map of the entire continent. There were the hard lines of the borders, the pretty strings of rivers lacing across them or sometimes defining them. To the north, across a small sea, sat a lump of land we owned simply titled "The Island." Mountain ranges, oceans, vast plains . . . all very typical. But there were two words on this map that sent literal chills up my spine.

The label that defined the space beyond the edges of Stratfel, Roshmar, and even Ducan: "Unclaimed Land."

A few years ago, a strange man had attempted to kill my father. I had long believed that man was from those lands. I also thought that if my mother was alive, she was somewhere out there. Distance-wise, it wasn't impossible to get to—a capable man could probably ride through in a day, day and a half—but there was the issue of a forest so thick and threatening I'd never heard a single account of anyone crossing it. Someone could go up by sea, but around the southeastern coast, the rocks were so jagged that when we tried sending a ship that way looking for Mama, we ended up with a single survivor returning on foot.

Father cleared his throat, and my eyes went to his. He

looked at us, his face stern. "You three are the future of our kingdom. And I wanted to give you a moment to think about where we've come from, and where you could take us."

He reached over and opened a book to a page he'd marked with a long ribbon, placing it over the open one that I'd been staring at before. In front of us lay the outline of Kadier. Except it wasn't Kadier.

A hundred and fifty years ago, Kadier was nameless. The land we kept had held six large clans—Jeonile, Cyrus, Crausia, Etesh, Obron Tine, and Straystan—united by language, divided by greed. This land was so good, so easy to work, that each clan scraped and fought for more, taking what they could. But the division turned out to be a bigger problem than we knew. With our backs to the ocean and our faces to Kialand and Monria—who both desperately tried to push us out to sea—we were all in a dangerous position. After decades of battles, losing land, losing lives, the six clans met and agreed to unify under the leadership of one. My four-times great-grandfather was voted to lead the masses. Back then, our clan had gone by Jeonile, changing it to Kadier in honor of a brave woman who'd fought valiantly, according to legend. I couldn't find her story in our history books, so I didn't know who she was. But the name served to unite all six clans, forsaking our old names and clinging to the new.

After evaluating skills, dividing men, harvesting resources, and much planning, the newly unified Kadier mounted an attack on Kialand, not only pushing them back but claiming some of their land as our own. When Monria heard what we were finally capable of, they came offering gifts of peace. The crown I wore had Monrian gold in it, passed down through all those years.

Early on, there were attempts from other clan leaders to take the throne, claims that their bloodline was longer, that they were blessed in ways we weren't. But we knew how to fight, and those who wouldn't kneel were buried. Through the years, the leaders of those clans tapered off, the relatives of some marrying into the royal line. It was all now down to Escalus and me on one side, and Nickolas on the other. With us united, there were no claims left. We would lead Kadier into unparalleled peace.

We stared at the faded lines, the pen strokes that had wedged us into enemies at one time. My father had a gift for making his point.

"Founding Day was yesterday. We announce Annika and Nickolas's engagement tomorrow. After seven generations, with your marriage, we'll have taken Kadier from six feuding clans to one fully unified kingdom. Our ancestors could only dream of such a thing," he said.

He swallowed, meeting each of our gazes before shifting the old map of Kadier back to the one of the entire continent. "And that is why you must work together. You will be an example for the rest of the country, an example of peace and unity. You will face obstacles, without a doubt. And there will be those trying to win your favor for their own gain.

"When your mother went missing," he said, pausing for a moment after uttering the words, "we thought it must have been done by a neighboring country, someone trying to break the peace we worked for. In fact, I was sure your people had been behind it, Nickolas." Father nodded to himself, voicing his theories, some I'd never heard. I didn't know if any of this was based on fact or if he spent his nights dreaming up answers. "When Jago had come for me a few months earlier . . . I knew he must have been working for someone. Another king out there wants me dead; they all want Kadier. They always have."

His eyes were wide, staring at nothing. "Jago . . . he wasn't working alone. He tried to kill me for someone's gain. I feel it in my bones. And when he failed, they took your mother to break me."

I didn't want to admit that he was scaring me, talking like that.

I remembered when the assassin came for my father, sneaking in at night and getting into his rooms. It was my mother's scream that woke my father and alerted the guards. Another few seconds, and they both might have been lost. Because Mama went missing shortly after, he assumed the two incidents were linked. If they were, we had no way of knowing. There was no ransom asked, no note left behind. There was no sign of struggle at all. Except for the fact that I knew my mother would never, ever leave my side, I'd almost think she just stepped out of the palace one night and never came back.

"But no one will break us," he went on. "We will be poised and prepared. One day, when we find a lead, we will do what we must to execute justice. Until then, we will be the finest examples of a royal family anyone has ever seen. Escalus, we must take care choosing your bride; every princess will come with strings attached, but a smart alliance will give us further stability. And Annika, you and Nickolas will go on a royal tour soon after your wedding, introducing yourself as a couple to the surrounding monarchs. As such, I expect you to do research on etiquette for Caporé, Sibral, Monria, Halsgar, and Kialand. Those five will be the bare minimum."

I nodded, knowing Rhett would point me in the right direction.

"We should invite them here, yes?" Nickolas suggested, sounding offended. "Surely they should be the ones to make the trek once we are married."

I exchanged a look with Escalus before replying on my father's behalf. "As the youngest newly established royal couple, it's proper that we make the event easier for our elders."

"If you insist," Nickolas said, sounding unsatisfied. "Is that all?"

I looked to Escalus again. What an impertinent question.

Father nodded. "For today."

Nickolas turned as if he was about to address me, but Escalus beat him to it.

"I hope this isn't rude, but if you two don't mind, I wondered if I might borrow my sister. We have some personal matters to discuss." Without waiting for a response, I took Escalus's arm and let him escort me out through the doors and off to another part of the castle. Anywhere, really.

"Are you all right?" he asked.

I nodded, though the gesture was hollow. "I just wish doing the right thing didn't feel so wrong."

We walked in silence for a moment before I remembered why we were here in the first place.

"Oh, silly me. What did you want to tell me?"

"Something incredibly important . . . My favorite color is blue."

I rolled my eyes. "Was that all?"

"I just wanted to see how your leg is. You scared me yesterday."

"I'm fine," I told him. "It hurts, but I didn't open a wound. I'm doing better than I thought."

"Oh, really? So when do you want to have another lesson?"

"Tonight!" I exclaimed. "But it needs to be in the stables this time, and not my room. I can't move in there."

"But I like practicing in your room."

"I need to be able to make noise, to hit things."

He huffed.

"Please!" I tugged on his sleeve over and over like a child.

"Ugh, and you think Nickolas's the worst? Fine. The stables it is."

"I knew you loved me."

He kissed my forehead. "Who doesn't?"

LENNOX

At the head table, my mother sat beside Kawan, leaning into him, her fingers coiled around the collar of his shirt. He was smiling, his face a little too close to hers, and speaking in a low tone. My stomach felt like it was falling down a hill, head over feet again and again.

I stood by the door, making eye contact with my team in turn. Inigo and Griffin were at the same table but sitting at opposite ends. Kinton—the boy who ran into the mess hall yelling when Aldrik returned—was curious about my Commission and had cornered Andre, asking questions, which worked well for the situation tonight. Sherwin was alone at a table, and, given that I'd had absolutely no idea who he was before yesterday, I had to believe that he ate alone often. Blythe was at a table with some girls, most of whom I knew by sight but not by name.

The plan was simple. I was going to go up to my mother's quarters to steal a dress. If, for some reason, she or Kawan got up from the table, Griffin and Inigo were going to launch into a fight. Kawan wasn't going to stop two people who were assigned to help me from injuring each other, so he'd let it drag out and would surely stay to watch. If that wasn't enough, Blythe had also secured someone to fight with her. I didn't know who had willingly agreed to let that girl attack them, but I was impressed by whoever it was.

Kawan and my mother were still eating, so I ran to the third floor, crossing only a handful of stragglers as they headed down to dinner. It was almost too perfect.

I pushed my mother's door open, finding it empty, as predicted. Every time I went to her quarters it felt like stepping into a distorted memory. Once, this space held three people. The corner where my bed had been was now home to a vanity. The decor was distinctly feminine now, all traces of my father erased.

For a second, I had to stop and take a shaky breath. How had she let him go so easily? How could she live in luxury while the rest of us worked and trained for war? How could she let Kawan treat her only son the way he did?

And after those thoughts crept in, a dozen more did. Why did I have to do Kawan's dirty work? Why was nothing ever good enough for him? Why was I assigned such a grim existence?

I hated everything. I hated this castle, I hated fate, I hated myself.

But after that moment of weakness, I resurrected the sure and steady walls I kept around my heart. It was much safer here with them in place.

Her wardrobe was in the back corner of the room, and I

moved over there, making sure to disturb nothing along the way.

It was only once I opened the doors that I realized I'd made a terrible mistake: I knew nothing about what looked fashionable on a lady. And if we were going to be there for multiple days, should I take more than one dress? Was my inability to pick out a proper dress going to be our undoing?

I swallowed hard, staring. Blythe had blond hair. Yellow looked nice with blue. Or green.

Right?

I pulled one of each color, rolling them into a ball and shoving them into the bag over my shoulder. I checked the wardrobe again, making sure nothing looked out of place, and closed the doors.

I crept into the hallway, hurrying down the rickety stairs, nearly falling after I stepped on a loose stone. In my room, Thistle was there, waiting for me. She sat proudly at the foot of my bed, a dead mouse by her feet.

She must have known I was stressed. Somehow whenever I was, Thistle would show up with food. She poked her nose down to it and looked up at me.

Sighing, I walked over and picked it up. "Thank you," I said. I pocketed the mouse because I just couldn't bear to have her think I'd reject it. I scratched at her head.

"You're a good girl. Look, don't touch this," I said, pointing to the bag. "If these get messed up, I'm in serious trouble." I shoved the whole thing under my bed, hoping nothing got ruined in the process.

"Not that it matters," I said. "Getting in trouble for this is the same as getting in it for anything else, and I know better than to care by now."

I reached up, scratching her head again. "Don't think that I care about you, either," I warned. "I don't."

She kept staring at me.

"I mean it."

She yipped at me before bounding back out the window, off to feed herself.

Sighing, I left, running back toward the mess hall. I stopped on an upper landing to throw the mouse out the window, wiping my hand on my pant leg before I entered the hall. I glanced quickly at Sherwin, who was still alone. Blythe met my eyes and quickly turned away, and Andre was now at the same table as Griffin and Inigo.

I walked up to Inigo, leaning down to whisper in his ear. "It's done . . . but is there a chance you know anything about women's clothes?"

He swallowed his food and looked up at me wide-eyed. "You're joking."

"I wish I was."

At that, he threw his head back, laughing wildly. It was a rare sound. A lone chuckle? Maybe. But extended, unguarded laughter wasn't something that happened in the castle often, if ever.

It was infectious, and I found myself smiling. I looked over my shoulder, and Blythe was staring at us, smiling, too.

It was strange. For a moment, the castle didn't feel so dark.

ANNIKA

Noemi crawled from under my skirt, her hair a bit of a mess once she was out. "Will that do?"

I took a few steps. "Yes, you brilliant girl. Thank you again."

She stood up, smiling to herself. The belt had been her idea, design, and handiwork. Made to go under my voluminous skirts, I could attach my sword beneath them without anyone being the wiser.

"Now, how long will you be away?" she asked. "And what should I say if someone comes by?"

The question gave me pause. It was unlikely that anyone would need me at this hour, but if they did . . . I was engaged now. Sneaking around the castle wasn't appropriate anymore. "I don't even know, Noemi. I hadn't thought . . . I was so looking forward to this, but now I wonder if I shouldn't go."

Noemi took my hand, pulling me back into the moment. "No, my lady. Just take me with you. If anyone asks, you were feeling melancholy and needed a walk around the grounds.

And, naturally, I went as your chaperone," she added in mock seriousness, which made me laugh.

"Are you sure you want to make yourself an accomplice to my crimes?"

"Oh, my lady, I think I already am."

I laughed, squeezing her hand. "I suppose you are, aren't you? Not a thing happens in my life that you don't know about. When are you going to have an adventure, Noemi? I need some secrets from you." We moved from the room, hand in hand, making our way to the stairs.

She smiled. "I think yours will have to be enough for the both of us," she said, dodging the question. "I hope you know that your secrets are all safe with me."

I sighed. "If I told you I was running away, would you judge me?"

She swallowed. "I desperately hope that you aren't . . . but no, I wouldn't judge. And if you are, please give me warning."

"I would . . . it was a joke," I claimed. "I need to find a better way to make light of my fears. I'm scared of being a bride."

Her face fell. "Come. Let's go and enjoy ourselves, if only for an evening."

We pulled up the hoods of our capes as we made our way down the stairs. I could hear Noemi's light steps shadowing mine, and that sound in itself was a comfort. I reached back, taking her hand again as we walked across the courtyard.

"Will you make me a promise, Noemi?"

"Anything," she vowed.

"I don't want you to stay my maid forever. I want you to marry when you're ready; I wasn't kidding about you having your own adventures. But please don't leave me anytime soon."

"Never, my lady. There is no other place in the world that could have a claim on my heart." Noemi's voice was bleeding with sincerity, and, selfishly, it settled my heart to know I wouldn't be left alone.

We entered the stables and found the boys talking with their heads together at the back. Escalus stood, leaning toward Rhett, his posture relaxed and his smile easy. Rhett, too, looked at ease as he passed a coin to Grayson, the young stable boy, paying him to run off and find another task for an hour or so.

It was Rhett who saw us first, and there was no denying the spark that came to his eye. Had it always been there? Maybe I'd mistaken his happiness at seeing me for simple charm. It was strange to think that all that light in his gaze belonged to me.

"Why, Noemi, are you finally ready to learn how to wield a sword?" Escalus asked, his smile growing brighter.

"No, Your Highness," she said sweetly. "I'm simply here as my lady's alibi."

He laughed and shook his head. "I don't think so. I think you're here for a lesson. Here. You can use mine," he said, escorting her to an open stall. "Just please don't cut me like my clumsy sister did."

Rhett came to stand beside me. I could feel him looking at me, maybe a little too closely. I took a deep breath and met his gaze.

"Marry me," he whispered, eyes pleading. "I adore you, Annika. I'd spend my life trying to make you happy." Then, as if thinking of an additional point for his argument, he said, "Escalus would support it. He hates Nickolas."

I tilted my head. "Hating Nickolas does not equate to supporting this. Hating Nickolas is far too easy to do, at any rate."

Rhett chuckled. "That's fair. I hate him myself." His smile was so easy. "When do you have to announce your engagement?"

"Tomorrow, I'm afraid. I don't have the privilege of making most of my choices."

He nodded. "Well, if you decide you want to make a big one, I'll be waiting. I'd give you anything you asked."

I stood up taller. "Then can I ask you to help me take a break from all the thinking I've been forced to do lately?"

"I am at your service."

Rhett had a mischievous look in his eye, but I knew I was safe. He wouldn't simply let me win—he never did—but he and Escalus shared one trait: they'd be broken if they did anything to hurt me.

I pulled my sword into a long stance, keeping Rhett at bay. He struck my blade, and I moved to parry, stepping to the side as I did so. He gave an approving nod as he walked in time, lining up across from me.

"Go easy on him, Annika," Escalus called from the far end of the stables. Noemi laughed shortly after in response.

"Not a chance!" I called back.

I felt myself falling into the dance of the fight, the beauty of it. I was familiar with Rhett's form and style, so I took a guess, a risk. When he lunged forward, I used his weight against him. I rammed down, pushing the corner of my cross guard into Rhett's, shoving down so the sword whipped in a circle and pulled squarely out of his hands. I watched as it flew, landing in a pile of hay and lying there useless.

In the moments of silence that followed, I felt the excitement around me bubble up until Escalus finally shouted. "Annika! You took his sword!"

I dropped mine, covering my mouth in shock. I'd never managed to disarm anyone.

"Well done, Annika!" Rhett exclaimed.

Instantly, Escalus was there, lifting me up in his arms and spinning me around. "So, it's official. When I am king, you will be the head of my guard."

"I can't believe I did that!" I gushed. The rush of accomplishment was so wildly vivid. It gave me a sense of possibility—if I could do something I was clearly not designed to do, maybe there were other things, bigger things, I could master as well.

LENNOX

I installed the lock on my door myself. It was a spike between two iron rings that kept it from opening even if someone lifted the latch. It wasn't sophisticated, and it wasn't pretty, but it was a step up from what everyone else had.

I stayed there, door locked, waiting for everyone to show up. I thought through what the next few days would look like. I'd start packing tonight.

The maps we had were old, and very few of us had been bold enough to go too far west before. But we could make it to Dahrain—or, as it had been renamed, Kadier—if we just kept our wits about us.

I didn't have much information about Kadier. I knew there was a king, and I knew he had a grand palace that should be Kawan's. I knew, based on the few maps we still had, that it was the largest country on the continent. I knew that it was his people who took everything from mine.

A knock sounded at the door, and I pulled the latch, watching Inigo, Sherwin, Andre, Griffin, and Blythe pour into my room.

"I'm sorry I laughed at you," Inigo said right away. "But you have to admit, it's funny."

I sighed. "I do. You have clothes for me?"

"Yes," Griffin said. "Everything's already packed. We thought that might be smarter than dragging it all down here."

I nodded. "Good thinking. And, Blythe," I started, scratching at my head as I went down to pull the bag from under the bed, "I hope these will work."

She reached in, pulling out dresses, holding them up against herself. "This should be fine. You look so worried," she commented, seeming amused.

I cleared my throat, standing up and tugging at my waistcoat. "I can't be expected to know about dresses."

She looked down at the material, a hand smoothing over the folds at the waist. "Don't worry. I still remember how to look like a lady."

There was a hint of longing in her voice, but I ignored it, moving back to the matter at hand. "All of you need to be ready to go in the morning. Grab the tents, obviously, and take a sword from the stockpile. Getting through that forest is a haul, so make sure you have extra food. I don't know how long this might take."

I swallowed, broaching a subject I wished I could avoid. "I know you all already understand that this mission is dangerous. If for some reason one of us is captured, don't give the enemy an opportunity to get information out of you. Better to die than betray the entire army. If you don't think you can handle that, tell me now."

Sherwin took a shaky breath but then drew himself up to his full height. And, short as he was, it was reassuring. Andre was giving a quiet but reassuring smile, and Griffin's eyes looked glassy, but he was nodding his head all the same. Inigo shrugged as if this were nothing. Blythe, arms still embracing the dress in front of her, cocked her head.

"I already told you: I don't fail."

I worked to suppress a smile. "Very well," I addressed the group. "Go sleep. I'll meet you at the stable after breakfast."

"Shoo!" Griffin said, swatting at something outside the window. "Sorry. I think an animal was trying to get in. You should board this up."

I peeked over, hoping Thistle was still hiding nearby. There was no way to explain her presence. "Thanks." I looked down. "See you all in the morning."

After they were gone, I stared at the open window, waiting for her to come back. I swallowed, thinking that, if I didn't return, Thistle might be the only one that cared.

When the wind brushed against my face, it was warm. A warmth I'd never felt in my life. And something in the air smelled sweet, like baking apples. The landscape was unfamiliar, so I started turning, looking for a landmark I recognized. There was nothing. No mountain, no violent ocean, no decaying castle. Instead, there was tall grass, moving as if it were waving every time it got swept up in the breeze. The land rolled a few times, kissing the horizon in the beauty of a setting sun. It was so startlingly different from any sunset I'd ever seen, so I reached out to touch it.

When I did, I saw that my fingers were leaving marks like ink on the sky. I was an oblique pen. So I stretched my hand up, and I engraved my name across the sky.

Lennox.

There was more to my name, but we didn't use it anymore . . . I decided I didn't need it anyway. The sky was mine now.

Satisfied, I lay back in the grass. It was so tall that it built a wall around me, and I stayed there, watching the sky grow darker.

I lay there, smiling in the dark, unable to see anything. The air was still so warm.

And then there was a hand caressing my cheek. Unlike the land, this touch felt familiar, like it had been with me all my life. But somehow not.

"There you are," I breathed.

"I am," a voice whispered back.

"Stay," I pleaded. "It's lonely."

There was no reply, only the same gentle stroke up my cheek and into my hair. It felt like I could truly rest, like I was both finally invisible and finally seen.

It was such a relief that when I woke up and realized it wasn't real, my eyes welled. I didn't cry. I couldn't cry. But I wanted to.

I sniffled, and at that, Thistle crept up, nuzzling my face.

"When did you sneak in?" I asked. "I just had the best dream."

She yipped.

"No, you weren't there. But don't worry, when I finally

get what belongs to me, I'll take you with me. I'm close. I'm so, so close."

The sky was changing colors, so the sun was going to make an appearance soon. Thistle knew that, and she moved up to my pillow, resting her head by mine, sighing heavily as she settled into sleep.

"Why do you come back?" I whispered. "Don't you know how dangerous it is to close your eyes near me? Everyone else knows."

She was warming my side, and I looked out the window, watching the stars disappear. It wasn't the same peace as the hand in my dream, willingly reaching out to comfort me . . . but it was the best I could ever hope to have, so I accepted it. Soon I'd put myself in a position where I wouldn't need comfort. Not comfort, not approval, not anything. And today was the first step.

ANNIKA

I woke up sore and thrilled.

"Noemi?" I asked groggily, rolling off my stomach. I kept forgetting I could go back to sleeping on my side.

"My lady?"

"What's the time?"

"Breakfast is just ending, but I've had a plate brought up." She gestured to the tray on the table near the unlit fireplace. "I thought you deserved some rest."

"Oh, you angel. Thank you." I stood, feeling the delicious ache in my legs and arms.

Noemi brought over my robe, and I settled into it. Slouching in the chair, I hooked one foot on the edge of the cushion, letting crumbs fall down my dress and sleeves. Even this tiny freedom made me smile. I took another bite and sighed in delight.

I sat up at the knock on the door. Noemi ran over and helped me sweep the crumbs from my face, pulling my hair neatly over one shoulder as she went. She patted at her own hair as she opened the door.

"The Duke of Canisse, Your Highness," she announced, letting Nickolas in the room.

"Oh," he said, seeing me there in my dressing robe. "I . . . I can come back."

"Not at all. Is there something you needed?"

"Yes. I've chosen this waistcoat for today," he said, gesturing to the pale blue fabric. "You would like to match, yes?"

I looked at him, wishing something in my heart would wake up. "Noemi, do I have something that would work with this?" I asked, but she was already crossing the floor to the wardrobe.

"I think we have a few that would do nicely," she said, pulling out two light blue gowns.

Before I could speak, Nickolas did.

"The one on the left," he said. "Very nice. I shall see you before the announcement?"

I forced a dutiful smile onto my face. "I'll meet you in the grand hallway by the balcony beforehand. I'm sure we're simply waving to the crowds."

He nodded. "Very well. See you then."

He went as quickly as he'd come, and it only took those few minutes for me to see the appeal of running off with a boy from the library. Rhett would let me choose my own clothes. Rhett wouldn't care how I wore my hair. Rhett would not only let me carry a sword but would also smile when I knocked his from his hand. . . .

As I stood there, it got harder to swallow. I hated this feeling, the sensation that the room was closing in. I knew it was shamefully selfish to get claustrophobic in a palace . . . but I couldn't help but think that I'd be able to breathe more freely in a cabin on the far edge of Kadier.

But almost as soon as the thought crossed my mind, I pictured my brother's face. It was so very tempting . . . but for Escalus's sake, I was positive I'd stay.

LENNOX

Thistle was on my heels. She seemed a bit on edge, awake when she ought to be asleep. She did that sometimes when a storm was coming, sensing things in the air that I could not. But, despite her uneasiness, the weather seemed strikingly calm. The sun was even shining through the wispy clouds. All the same, she refused to leave my side as I marched up the crest toward the graveyard.

By all means, we never should have gotten my father's body back. I didn't like to think of the strange green color of his skin. Or the look in Kawan's eyes that was eerily similar to joy when he saw my father in two pieces. But, as hard as it was, at least we had something to bury, an opportunity to have closure.

Not everyone was afforded such a luxury.

After my father's body was identified, it was brought here, honored as the first death of the war to reclaim our kingdom, a war that had yet to begin. Conveniently for me, he was buried beside another notable person in our history, someone who was important enough to be granted a proper burial site.

When others saw me out here, they assumed I came to speak to my father.

Assumptions are mistakes.

"I'm being sent on a Commission," I said. "I get soldiers of my own and everything. I think it will please you to know that I shouldn't have to kill anyone." I wiped under my nose. "I could be wrong about that. If someone catches me, I might have to," I said as if it were all too ordinary.

"Did your mother love you?" I asked, apropos of nothing. "I figured she must have. People with good mothers always have a look about them. I don't know if my mother ever cared about me. Not really. There was a time, back when Father was alive, I could have talked myself into believing it, but not anymore. I feel like I'm one more tool in her arsenal to keep Kawan all to herself, to be queen when he eventually sets up his new kingdom."

The wind whipped up my hair, and it stuck to my forehead. "Don't worry. When we invade, I intend to let the commoners live. You might not think it, but I can be merciful."

I sighed, walking in a circle. "I know that's hard to believe after everything I've done. You could certainly attest to how heartless I am."

I stared at the headstone. There was no name on it. That seemed fair. If we were forgotten, she could be, too.

"Anyway, I thought you'd like to hear of my new assignment. I'll come back to see you once it's done."

The wind off the coast danced around us, and I stayed there for a long time, holding close to the first soul I ever took. I wondered if there was another world, a place where people looked down. If so, was my father there and bothered that I bypassed his company for another? I couldn't explain why my chest tugged me six steps to the right of his grave. I hoped that if they were in the other world, a world where I assumed there were no questions and endless answers, that he understood.

Thistle ducked into some tall brush, giving me a clue that someone was near.

"Lennox?"

I turned to find Inigo walking up the path. "Is something wrong?"

"Sorry, there were some issues getting access to enough food."

"I'm heading to the kitchens next, so I'll sort it out." I paused. "Inigo, do you . . . do you remember anything about my father?"

Inigo's eyes were startled.

"It's not as if I've forgotten him," I said quickly. "It's just that I don't know what anyone else's impression of him was."

He nodded. "I remember he was decisive, like you. He always sounded smart; if someone had a question, he knew something about it. Maybe he didn't have the whole answer, but he never left a conversation without offering a piece of insight. And I remember once Old Theo fell into a horse trough, and your father laughed so hard he cried. I've never heard anyone laugh like him; it was booming."

I smiled. He did laugh like that, didn't he? Like thunder, deep and consuming.

"Thank you," I whispered. "We should head back."

"Absolutely, sir." Inigo shoved me with his elbow, and for the first time in a long time, I felt a sense of ease.

ANNIKA

I paced back and forth in the wide room behind the grand balcony. The bells had been ringing for ten minutes, and the news of my engagement was official. I could see a crowd gathering below the window, and I could hear cheers and applause from beyond the palace walls. The people were waiting for us.

"Everything will be fine," Escalus assured me, though I could see that he was hiding his own restlessness.

"It won't. Not for me." I couldn't get out more than three words at a time. There simply wasn't enough breath for it.

"Annika . . . you look pale."

"I feel . . . I feel . . ." I bent in half, one hand on the wall. I needed more air.

"Annika?" Father was hurrying up the hallway. "What's wrong?"

I went to my knees and rolled over onto my back. The cool marble floor felt good against the few inches of skin it touched. Down here, my lungs could open a little more. I just had to keep focusing on making them work.

"What do you think is wrong?" Escalus spat. "You did this to her. There had to be another way. This is the rest of her life you're talking about here."

"We've been over this. You are meant to marry internationally, and Annika is meant to consolidate the lines. This ensures peace," he said forcefully, oscillating between the two versions of himself that I was subject to now.

"There has to be an avenue we haven't explored," Escalus pleaded.

"It's already been announced. They're gathering outside." That was his only answer.

I started counting. Five seconds in, five seconds out. I could do this. *This is possible.*

"Escalus, help." I put my arms up, and he gently pulled me upright. Once I was on my feet, he tugged at my dress, putting the folds in the right places. I combed through my curls with my fingers, draping them over one shoulder. I peeked up to Escalus, and he nodded, telling me I looked acceptable.

"What's this all about?" Nickolas asked, suddenly appearing.

"I took a tumble," I lied.

"You? But you're always so light on your feet." He strode up to me and held out a small box. "Maybe this will ease the pain of your fall."

In the books, the men always knelt in this moment. They took their lady's hand as if clinging to it for life. I was getting a box shoved into my hands.

I opened it. Inside, nested between two blue velvet

cushions, was a ring. The greenish stone was an oval shape, surrounded by tiny diamonds. It was pretty enough, if not my taste.

"How lovely," Father commented, reminding me of what my lines were meant to be in this moment.

"Yes. Thank you." I slid the ring onto my left hand. It was slightly too big, but it would stay put.

"The stone, I'm sure you know, is native to . . ." His words trailed off as he properly took me in. "Annika, we went over this."

I stared at him, still too light-headed to guess at what he was talking about.

"Your hair," he said, his tone growing more frustrated.

I tried to make myself look a bit more dignified. "You specifically said after our engagement was announced."

"This is how our mother wore her hair," Escalus said, echoing my own words from Founding Day.

"Yes, and I understand the attachment, but I think Annika ought to pin it," Nickolas insisted. "Call her maid. Get her here immediately."

Escalus stood up straight, his voice dropping into a low and firm register I'd never heard him use before. "Sir, you forget your rank. You don't instruct me to do anything. Furthermore, Her Royal Highness's maid is a trusted servant, and we will not rip her from her work to appease your whims. And, finally, if you told Annika that this demand stood for after your engagement was announced, she's well within reason to want to show herself to her people a final time in the way she prefers."

Escalus was pushing breaths aggressively through his nose.

"I realize that you think marrying into this family was our only choice," he continued, "but I assure you, it is not. Annika has had several princes ask for her hand, and we've denied them because we hoped joining lines would bring peace. If you bring her misery, this can be undone in a heartbeat."

Nickolas looked to Father, whose fearful eyes betrayed him.

"I think not," Nickolas said finally. There was nothing menacing in his tone, simply an understanding of the facts. "But. If it will smooth over the process, I will concede on this point for today so that we can move forward. Don't want to keep the people waiting." Nickolas adjusted his cravat and reached for my hand. "Are you ready, my pet?"

He'd called me that before. I hoped he wasn't forming a new habit.

I glanced at Escalus, who still looked as though he was prepared to set the palace on fire if it meant ridding himself of Nickolas, and placed my hand on my fiancé's. "Of course."

Father said nothing. A flash of a moment as a little girl came to the forefront of my mind. I'd said I didn't want to go on a walk because Escalus had told me stories about witches and dragons, and I didn't want them to get me. Mother was holding my hand, and, for maybe the only time in my life, it wasn't enough. But my father took my parasol and held it like a sword. He vowed he'd use it like a wand against any witch, and that he'd slay any dragon. It all sounded so believable then.

I hated that he was beside me daily but still so far away. I could see that he was torn, a pang of regret visible in his eyes.

As he crossed to me, he whispered quietly. "I'm sorry, Evelina." He shook his head. "I mean . . . Annika."

And I wondered for a moment if he really did wish he could apologize to her.

"I'm fine," I lied, keeping my voice low. "Really."

Father straightened his coat, rank dictating that he and Escalus walk out first. Nickolas and I paused, giving proper space between their entrance and ours.

"The king seems . . . off," Nickolas commented, watching my father's fake smile.

"He's fine. I just don't think he cared for that scene."

Nickolas stood even taller, surprising me that he could grow any straighter than before. "I didn't cause a scene."

After a few waves to the adoring crowd below, Father and Escalus parted like a door, and Nickolas and I emerged, filling the center of the balcony. I held my hand in such a way that the sun would reflect off my new ring, telling everyone below the happy news was true.

And I smiled. For their sake, I pretended this cost me nothing.

Through his grimace of a smile, Escalus whispered to me. "I'll kill him."

I shook my head slightly. "If he died, it could invite a civil war. Don't risk everything over my hair. I'll survive."

And there was my new goal. Not flourish. Not enjoy.

Survive.

LENNOX

I carried four things in my waistbelt at all times: a small length of rope, a bar of oats and seeds pressed in honey, a folding blade for tasks my sword was too big for, and a button from my father's coat.

As I prepared for my Commission, I packed a larger bag with more food, a skin of water, bandages, a single change of clothes, and my tent. I slid my bow and arrows into a compartment attached to my saddle, but I didn't imagine I'd need to use them. I also took our outdated maps, hoping they'd at least get us close to the proper location.

The one thing I wished I could pack was a calmer mind. Was this mission too ambitious? If I could pull this off—if I could prove we should have gone back to our kingdom by now—every loss I'd suffered since coming to Vosino would be worth it.

Blythe showed up first. I hopped up on my horse, ready to go, and she did the same. "Inigo is grabbing a spare sword, and Griffin is right behind me. Had to kiss his girl goodbye."

"Griffin has a girl?" I asked in shock.

She smiled. "You know how I said I got someone to throw a fist at me if Griffin and Inigo weren't enough of a distraction last night? It was her. Rami. She was happy to do anything that might help Griffin."

My horse moved beneath me as I sat there, dumbfounded. "How long has that been going on?" I asked.

"About a month, I think. She's one of that group that came about five months ago. Remember?"

I did. We were all impressed with the scrappy group of twenty that ended up here, half of them crawling in after being lost in the Forest for four days. After getting rest and food, they swore allegiance to Kawan so fast it made me dizzy.

I nodded.

"Griffin told her what you said about not giving the enemy the chance to take anything from us, so she was in tears all night."

"He never said a word about her."

Blythe shrugged. "Not a lot of secrets around here . . . guess he just wanted one."

I sighed. This was why relationships were nothing but trouble.

Inigo appeared not a moment later, two swords in hand and a bag slung over his back.

"Hey," I whispered, "did you know Griffin had a girl?"

He sighed. "Rami. She's . . . ." He just shook his head.

Did *everyone* know about this but me?

Sherwin came out shortly after, guiding his horse. His

face was serious, and I could see he was concentrating, thinking about the task at hand. I appreciated that. He packed light and moved assuredly, and I found I was satisfied with him as a soldier.

Andre appeared next, looking eager and determined. Finally, Griffin showed up, his eyes shot with red. He kept ducking behind the mane of his horse to hide it. He was all jokes and teasing and exaggeration. It wasn't until I saw him changed that I realized how badly a place like this needed someone like him.

Someone like my father. Someone to take the edge off.

I glanced at Inigo, who seemed to read my mind.

"We could probably manage without him," he whispered.

I nodded. Kawan would make sure every single one of us saw the face of the war before it was all said and done—but he could have today.

"Griffin."

"Yes, sir." He kept his head hidden.

"You're staying. Kawan overestimated my numbers."

He shook his head, swallowing hard. "I can go. Lennox, I'm ready."

"I can see that you are. But I'm commanding you to stay. I don't need you."

I stared at him, willing him to relent. I knew he didn't want to be seen as a coward. I wouldn't. But this had nothing to do with that.

Finally, he let out a long breath. "Thanks, Lennox."

"Nothing to thank," I claimed. "In our absence, make sure this place doesn't fall apart, will you?"

He smirked. "Yes, sir."

"Move out," I ordered. I set the pace, urging my horse to move fast. I wanted a good distance between me and the castle when Kawan found out I'd left behind one of his hand-chosen soldiers. And I needed to get closer to Dahrain. It felt like I'd been trapped beneath water, and crossing that border would be taking a long breath.

The hardest part of the trek came early. There was woodland on the farthest edge of the land, thick but manageable. Beyond that were rolling plains full of tall grass and wildflowers, and I had to admit that galloping across those sometimes felt like skipping through a painting. It was a shame no one really knew about it. Blocking it from the other side was the Forest, a collection of wiry trees so dense, it was almost impossible to pass.

The upper canopy was too full for sunlight to get through, leaving the forest floor bare. The shorter trees didn't bother with leaves but shot out wide, spindly branches that clung on to everything and sliced clothes and arms. And it was all so tightly woven together that even finding an entry point was tricky. The only way to make it through was by tracing the little pieces of sky visible through the canopy. Very few could do that without getting horribly turned around. And since we only traveled this far west for Commissions or seeking poor, needy recruits, we didn't have a worn path.

Getting through the Forest took us several hours, but thankfully we were through it before nightfall. I sighed in relief when we saw daybreak through the other end.

The section of the continent we were currently inhabiting

wasn't terrible. We had access to the sea, somewhat farmable lands, and a level of seclusion that I preferred. But as we made our way along the borders of the other established countries, I found myself aching for their beauty. There were wide, rolling fields and streams that made music as they ran over rocks on their way to the ocean. Whenever we found a road that led past a village, the children would chase our horses, laughing and waving. There were structures being built in some places, the lands still being parceled off and claimed. Walls to keep in, walls to keep out.

We traveled as fast as we could, not stopping once. Aldrik had taken the cattle from northern Halsgar, so I chose to arc low for good measure, going along the southern edge by Cadaad, still sweeping along their border. By sunset, we had reached the boundaries of Monria. The tree line had thinned since this map was made, but I could tell it was the same place.

"Here," I said, checking that square of the map again, showing it to Inigo.

"Oh. Umm . . . I can't read the words," he said quietly.

I pulled it back for a second, not meaning to embarrass him. "You don't need the words. Look at the terrain. I think this forest is the one here, and that lake we passed was this one."

He took the map, staring at the shapes of the trees and rocks, looking up and surveying what was around us and thinking of what we'd seen. I saw as the understanding washed over his face. "I think you're right."

"Good." I turned to the others. "We'll camp beneath

those trees and leave at first light." I trotted over to the closest tree to dismount and tie up my horse.

Inigo started pulling out his tent. "For the record, I'm glad we're doing this. If we succeed, it could be the most important Commission anyone's ever done."

I scratched my horse behind his ears. "If we do it right, I agree. If we do it wrong . . . I don't even want to think about it."

"Then don't. We have a good unit here. If we keep our heads down, follow the lead of others in the palace, we should be able to do this."

"Let's hope so. But listen." I pulled him around the far side of my horse, speaking quietly. "If something happens to me, find a way to save the Commission. Make *something* out of it. Even if I don't live to see it, I want to get Dahrain back." It almost hurt to confess how badly I wanted it back. Wanting meant the possibility of losing, and I liked to keep a distance between that kind of pain and myself. "The team will follow you. Probably better than they follow me."

He swallowed. "I will. But nothing's going to happen to you," Inigo insisted. "You're too smart."

I looked down, grinding the toe of my boot into the dirt. "My father was smart. And he came back to Vosino in pieces. I don't think it would hurt Kawan too much to see me gone. So, if that's part of his plan, you keep going. You push until we get our kingdom back."

He gave me a quick nod and went to work settling in for the night.

I pulled my tent from my bag and started laying everything

out for my site. It was cool, but not so cold that we needed to make a fire.

I heard footsteps approaching and looked over my shoulder to find Blythe walking my way. "Do you need something?" I asked.

She looked back to make sure no one could hear her and asked, "Have you ever actually killed anyone?"

It was so ridiculous I almost laughed.

"Blythe, how long have you been at Vosino?"

"A year and a half. I came with the group from Roshmar after our crops failed."

That was the biggest boost we'd had in ages. Roshmar wasn't blocked by that awful forest, but there were mountains to contend with. A third of that crowd of people showed up with frostbite, and apparently they'd lost a dozen or so along the trek.

"So, then, you should know. Three earlier this week. Another handful of attempted deserters a few months ago. Remember the pirates who managed to circumvent the rocks and tried to invade from the sea? I thought my sword would be permanently stained red after that." I shrugged. "There are plenty more, but I'm afraid I've stopped keeping track. I have the bloodiest hands in the army."

She stared at me again for a moment. "Then why did you let Griffin stay behind? If you care so little about who lives and dies, why spare him?"

I straightened up, facing her fully. "That wasn't mercy. I didn't need him. Furthermore, it will be a delight to come back and see how Kawan feels about me disobeying him.

There's no loss to me."

Something in her eyes shifted as she watched me. "It was kind all the same, to care about two people in love."

"If you insist."

"I do." She stayed there a moment. "You know, even in places that are dark, even in the midst of war, sometimes, people find light in each other."

And suddenly I could see it there, in her eyes. She was asking questions I didn't want to answer.

I felt the icy hand of fear creeping up my spine.

"I'm going to assume the rush of the Commission has gotten the better of you, and I will forget this conversation ever happened."

She smiled, taking a step back. "We'll see."

I'd said I'd settle for being feared if I couldn't be known. I was wrong. I *preferred* being feared. Being known left you bare, and I was chilled to my bones at the thought of it happening to me.

"Blythe," I said, finding my voice. "That's not . . . it won't happen."

She shook her head, already backing away, all ease and confidence. "I already told you. I don't fail."

ANNIKA

The palace was like a different world when everyone went to sleep. Scattered candles lit in the main hallways, but past midnight the only light came from the moon. I looked out the wide window, seeing parts of constellations hidden by trees, thinking they were all just too far away.

I crept down to the hall at the farthest end of the palace, to the space where my father had moved one of the grandest portraits I'd ever seen.

I looked both ways to check that the space was truly empty, and settled on the floor in front of the larger-than-life painting of my mother. Her face was so beautiful, so peaceful. Even in stillness, she embodied kindness. The tilt of her head said you were pardoned for any offenses. Her quiet smile invited you to be near her.

People said I was like her. I wanted to be. I wanted to be serene and happy and good. Such simple words, maybe, but they could embody so much.

"I'm sorry I've been away," I whispered. "I'd tell you why, but I think it'd break your heart."

I swallowed, knowing that was true. If she had been present for the last month of our lives, she'd have been crushed. I kept thinking my tears were dry, but as I spoke, new pains found me, and I felt the tears come.

She was out there, right? Somewhere, she was alive. Maybe she was being held captive . . . or it was possible she had amnesia. That happened in the books. So it wasn't unimaginable that even after three years, she could walk back into the palace one day and hug me as she did when I was small. I had to believe that.

But sometimes believing hurt.

"I'm engaged. To Nickolas." I held up the ring, looking at her peaceful eyes and wishing that there would be some sort of reaction, something to gauge if I was crazy for refusing in the first place or if I should have held out. "Escalus keeps telling me I'm so noble. And if there is one gift I could give him, it would be an easy reign. But the way Nickolas speaks to me . . . I don't know. It feels like there's something mean just lurking under his surface." I shook my head.

"But I should tell you . . . I have a way out." I looked up at her, wishing for a reaction. "Rhett loves me," I confessed. "He wants me to run away with him. I think if you were here, you would approve. You gave him his position, so you must have seen something in him. And if anyone could provide for me, it's him. He'd sell the clothes off his back for me. I don't doubt it.

"The only problem is . . . I don't love him. Not like he

loves me. And I've told him so, but he says he'd be happy so long as I was around. And that means something to me, too. But . . . I don't think that's enough to run away for. If it was magical? I'd go. Because isn't it all supposed to be magical?" I asked.

"All the books say so. Even when things start out bad, you can feel it, Mother. You can tell that the prince sees the best in her, and she has hope for him, and once they get past the worst of it, they're making something so beautiful that *someone* has to write it down. I don't have that. Not with anyone. And maybe I never will," I said with a shrug. "I suppose there are worse things."

I wiped at my face. "I wish you were here. I wish I still had someone who loved me the way you did."

And there was the heart of all my pain. I was loved in some way or another by everyone around me. But no one loved me like her.

"I've decided something. Since it seems I must marry Nickolas, on the day of our wedding, I'm going to finally mark it in the books that you're dead." I stared into her eyes. "Because I know that this is the first royal wedding here in ages, and I know that the word will spread. And I know, without a doubt, if you were out there and you knew I was getting married, you'd come back. So, if you don't, I'll write it down, and that will be the end of it. I'll stop believing."

I sniffled, hating that I needed to make it so final. But for my sanity, I had to. The wondering was worse than knowing.

"I won't stop coming to visit, though," I promised. "I'll

talk to you like you're here, no matter what. And I'll tell you everything, even the bad things . . . just not all today.

"I love you," I whispered. "I wish you would come back." I drew in a deep breath, rubbing my temples. "I should go to sleep. We're riding out tomorrow. Father wants Nickolas and me to be seen by those in the country. Seeing as I rarely get to leave the grounds anymore, I'm taking the opportunity." I sighed. "Help me figure this out. You could smooth over an argument with a smile. . . . How did you do that? Teach me how. There has to be more of you in me than just my hair and eyes. I want your graciousness, and I want your strength. I hope it's all in there somewhere."

I stood and blew her a kiss. "I love you. I won't forget you."

I was standing on the bank of a beach with black sand. I looked down at it, curious, thinking there was no such thing as black sand. But still, here it was, caught between the toes of my bare feet. There was wind, so much wind, and it tugged at my gown, pulling it up and back, threatening to lift the hem above my head. I didn't know this place. And I was so alone.

But I wasn't frightened.

I reached up and my hair was down, floating out behind me, free.

Free.

I stood there for a long time, watching the waves, focusing on the place where the sky meets sea. After a while, on the edge of the horizon, the stars started to move. They were converging with planets, coming together in one bright point, growing so bright, it was more blinding than the sun.

I covered my eyes, looking to the side. And when I turned my head, a shadow was standing there.

He—for I was certain it was a he—stayed beside me. I waited for the brightness of all the stars to wash him from the beach. He was a *shadow,* for goodness' sake. The light should wipe him away. But he stayed, like even the thing that ought to make him run had no power, like even the thing that could destroy him wouldn't force him from me.

I studied this shape. He was a shadow, but a shadow of *what*? I took careful steps around him, looking for a break in the dark, for a source. There was nothing, only him. And he was still as I took him in.

"Who are you?"

There was no voice; I sensed he had no identity at all. And I sensed equally that he was curious about me, wanting to know my name, where I came from, and how I found the beach.

I looked back at him, staring into the place where his eyes should be.

"I am nobody, too," I said.

I could feel his sorrow for me.

He reached up and touched his shadowy fingers to my cheek. It was then that I felt how icelike he was, how cold he was at his core. I stared at him, looking for a smile, for kind eyes, for anything that said he was a friend, not an enemy.

There was nothing but ice.

And I sat bolt upright in bed, gasping for air.

"My lady?" Noemi asked, running from the fire she was setting.

"I'm fine, I'm fine," I insisted. "Nightmare. At least, I think it was a nightmare."

"Shall I fetch you anything? Some water?"

I shook my head. "No, sweet Noemi. Truly, it was just a dream."

I turned my gaze to the window. The night was fading fast, daylight breaking through the trees.

I lay back down, wiping the sweat from my forehead. I could still see the shadow. The memory sent a chill through me, which was unfortunate. There was no way I could get any more sleep now. A day alone with Nickolas approached—it seemed far less appealing in the daylight.

LENNOX

I awoke to birds chirping. It was the strangest thing. There weren't songbirds up by the coast, so I usually woke to Thistle parading across my chest. I stayed there in my tent for a while, just listening. I wondered if there were birds like these in Dahrain, if this was a sound I would grow accustomed to.

I tried to remember what I could from being a boy, from my life before the castle. I remembered a modest home, and I remembered my mother's stomach swelling with a younger sibling I never met. I remembered tracing shapes in mud, and I remembered bread that tasted sweeter than anything we had now.

I remembered working up the nerve to tell a girl she was beautiful. I remembered the delicate lilt of her voice as she took in the praise. I remembered joking around with my father, placing rocks in his shoes and watching until he unsuccessfully tried to shove his feet in them. I remembered feeling content with what I had, and sleeping well at the end of the day. I remembered a sense of peace and balance.

I didn't remember the birds.

Other sounds soon joined them. Inigo speaking to Blythe, and Sherwin breaking down his tent. It was reassuring, knowing they were all on task. After listening to the song in the air for one more peaceful moment, I got dressed and moved to dismantle my tent.

I'd kept my head down, trying to focus, so it took me a while to realize that Blythe was already in her dress. I had been right; the green did look nice with her hair, which she'd taken out from its usual braid and allowed to tumble down her back and over her shoulders. She peeked over at me through her tresses, and I cleared my throat and looked away. I didn't know how I felt being under such close observation.

Sherwin walked over, a bundle in his hands. "These are for you," he said, and I took in the parcel of clothes. I'd slept and woken in my black pants and white shirt. My black waistcoat was on but unbuttoned, and I had my riding cape waiting for me. As I looked down at the colorful cloth before me, I realized I'd gotten far too used to black and white. The crispness, the color of it all left me feeling exposed, and I couldn't bring myself to put it on.

"Pack it back up," I said. "I can change into it later if necessary."

Sherwin squinted and looked over to Inigo, who nodded. "Yes, sir."

There was too much coming that I wouldn't be able to control; I needed to hold tight to the things I could, if only for my own sanity.

Andre was already atop his horse when I was checking the last of my things, and Blythe was right behind him. I hopped up myself, pulling out the map again as Inigo rode up next to me.

"Can I see that when you're done?" he asked.

"Take it. I don't know if there's anything worth noting. If we head northwest, we should be able to get through Monria and into Kialand within a few hours, but it doesn't look like there are any significant landmarks between here and there. Or at least where we think *there* is."

Inigo studied the map for a long time, taking a while to analyze the terrain. "No, there's not much to help us this far out, is there? Very well. Any changes in the plan?"

"No. Head in, stay back. We might need to split into groups if we need to look less conspicuous. I'm not sure how difficult it will be to get onto the palace grounds. Today might be more of a scouting expedition. It just depends on what we find when we get there."

Inigo nodded, almost smiling. "If this feeling in my gut at the thought of seeing Dahrain today is what you were intending to bring back to everyone else . . . I don't see how anyone could top this one."

"If it goes well."

"No reason for it not to. We'll lie low."

I nodded, looking around me. Everyone was up and mounted, and no trace of our camp was left.

"Let's head out," I called, and the three others fell in behind Inigo and me.

For a while we went on in silence, moving quickly, but not at a full gallop.

"Hey, listen," Inigo eventually said, looking back to make sure there was some distance between us and the others. "I owe you an apology. So, you know, I'm sorry."

I glanced over at him, then looked away. This was a long-overdue conversation, and now that it was here, I didn't know if I could go through with it. "I'm the one who almost took your eye. I've been trying to find a way to apologize to you for ages now. But without actually apologizing because, as I'm sure you know, that's not my strong suit."

He smirked. "Well, you'd never have gone so hard on me if I hadn't gone so hard on you." He shook his head. "I've thought it over a lot, and I don't remember how it got in my head that I needed to keep you down. Lots of us felt that way, Lennox, and I still don't understand it.

"But it was as if . . . I had to be cold to you so the others wouldn't be like that to me." He stared off in thought. "I just feel like we should have been allies. We were, weren't we? And then we weren't. And then your dad died, and your defenses were down, and I just . . ." He swallowed hard. "I never stopped. And I don't know if I would have if you hadn't made it impossible for anyone to come up against you."

I sighed. "I certainly did that, didn't I?"

Sometimes I thought about that day, the day of my first kill. Sixteen years old, trying to get bigger and stronger in secret, and humiliated from Inigo's wrath earlier that day. When the opportunity came to change my life, I took it. I took it swiftly.

There were few people willing to push me after that, but Inigo was one of them. After a very public sword fight where

I came out victorious and he came out with a permanent scar, it was cemented. I was untouchable.

"Well, for what it's worth, I get it," I told him. "I feel like I do the same thing now, especially with the new recruits. I have to be hard on them so they get tough."

"You're not as hard on them as you think," Inigo insisted. "And what I was doing wasn't some sort of conditioning. I was trying to break you."

I turned my gaze to the horizon. "You nearly did."

"I'm sorry."

"I am, too. I didn't mean to almost kill you."

He put a hand up. "That's giving yourself a little too much credit. Horridly disfigured? Sure. But nearly dead? No. Never happened. I'm tougher than that."

Something close to a laugh came out of my mouth.

"You're not horridly disfigured," I said. "If anything, that scar somehow makes you look distinguished. I hated that I made you look *better.*"

He smiled. "It's because I'm so charming. Nothing can stop it."

In the distance, I heard Blythe chuckle. I peeked over at her, but she was looking away.

"So, it's done, then? We're good?" I asked.

"If you can let us be, then yes," he assured me.

"Good."

Inigo looked to the west, focusing on what lay ahead. As the sun was rising behind our backs, I had hope again that maybe we'd get what we needed today.

"I meant what I said last night," I began. "If something

happens to me, take over. The mission, at the castle, wherever. You're a good leader."

He sucked his teeth. "Of course I'm a good leader. But you're too stubborn to die, so no one will ever know."

ANNIKA

I stifled a yawn as Escalus trotted over.

"Are we boring you, Your Highness?" he teased.

"I didn't sleep well. Strange dreams. I think I'm just anxious about today."

He sighed heavily. "Can't say I blame you. We can stay together, the four of us, if you prefer."

"No. I hate to say it, but I don't think I can take Father's dark mood and Nickolas's sternness at the same time," I admitted. "Besides, I have a favor to ask of my fiancé. I'm hoping he'll be amenable."

"Then I'll hope for that, too. Ah, yes," he said, turning to the page who was approaching with his sword. "Thank you, young man."

"Why do you get a sword?" I muttered. "I wish I could bring mine."

"I know. Here, I promise I'll come by your room tonight. And if you behave, we can take the binding off and you can properly chop at something. So long as it isn't me again."

"For the last time, it was an accident! And you hardly even bled."

"Tell that to my favorite shirt! Not even Noemi could fix it, and she can fix anything."

"I am profoundly sorry to your shirt," I replied sarcastically, which he took as the joke it was. I loved how he took so many things in stride. He turned his horse so he was right beside me and bent over, kissing my forehead.

"My poor shirt has been long buried, but I shall update the headstone with that fine tribute."

I giggled.

Nickolas was finally affixed atop his horse and heading my way.

"Good luck," Escalus said as he went off to join Father.

"That stable boy is a disaster," Nickolas claimed.

In the distance, Grayson, the young stable hand we paid to keep our practices secret, was picking up a brush and extra blanket from the ground, looking disheartened. He never looked like that.

"One would *think* a royal stable hand could properly tack up a horse. I had to redo the entire thing myself."

Our stable hands were excellent. But leave it to Nickolas to invent standards above the needs of even a king.

"I'll make sure the head keeper speaks to him," I lied.

"Excellent idea, my pet."

I cringed at the name, but he didn't seem to notice.

"And your hair is much better today," he said, pointing to where I had it pinned up.

I reached back to touch it. I was so used to it down, even

when I rode; I liked the feel of the wind in it. I was looking forward to rejoicing with Noemi this evening when we took every last pin out.

"It feels a bit heavy like this," I admitted.

"But you look like such a lady," he commented.

I was more than a lady; I was a princess. He seemed to keep forgetting that.

"Thank you. I was hoping I could ask you something. You see—"

"Are you all set?" Father asked, coming up beside us. The anxiety in his eyes was acute. "You know, Escalus and I could join you."

"Escalus offered that as well, but don't fret, Father. It's just a quick jaunt to the countryside, waving to the fieldworkers, and riding home. Nothing to it."

He paused. "Perhaps we should stay together. . . ."

"Father, we'll be fine."

"It's just . . ."

"We'll have guards with us, and I have a personal escort," I said, gesturing to Nickolas. "One could only see how safe this will be."

He nodded. "I'm sure you're right."

But he didn't look sure. He looked nervous. And I realized then that this was the first time in the three years since Mother vanished that he was letting me out of his sight while off palace grounds.

"All will be well, Father. I will see you tonight when we toast Kadier's future," I promised.

"Until then," he said. There was so much broken between

us that he couldn't say *I love you.* Even if he had, I wasn't sure I could have said it back.

Instead, we turned our horses and trotted off in different directions.

I was so disheartened by the way I said goodbye to Father that I couldn't bring myself to speak to Nickolas for most of our ride. Instead, we traveled in silence past field after field. Seeing the royal standard one of the guards was holding, children ran to the roadside to hand me flowers, and I tucked as many of them in the back of my hair as I could. The news of our engagement had spread as quickly as we'd anticipated, and Nickolas and I were showered with well-wishes from the subjects of Kadier. At any moment, I could have turned to talk to Nickolas. I should have. But I found myself feeling unwelcome to do so.

Before I'd realized, we'd ridden much farther than I'd meant to. A short wooden bridge over a very shallow gulley marked where Kadier ended and Kialand began. The guards knew all too well that I'd hardly been outside the castle in ages, so leaving the country was unheard of. Nickolas didn't seem to know we were at the border at all, so I bypassed him and turned to the head guard. Abandoning propriety, he nodded his head forward and gave me a wink. I couldn't hide my smile at the glimpse of freedom.

"Earlier you mentioned you wanted to talk about something," Nickolas began. "The last time you said that, it ended in a proposal. So what is it, my pet?" He laughed at his own joke.

Ugh, he was going to call me that all the time now, wasn't he?

"I was wondering if we might live away from the palace when we get married. Just in the beginning," I added quickly, taking in the bewildered look on his face.

"Why would you want to live anywhere else? The palace is grand. The grounds are perfect. Your father has made your home so fine."

"Don't mistake me. I love my home." I looked into the distance wistfully. "But you and I . . . Nickolas, for all our years together, I feel I hardly know you. If we're going to have a successful marriage—a marriage that is an example for all of Kadier—then I think we should know each other better. And I don't think I can do that under the watchful eyes of every person at court. I just want us to be happy."

It would have been nice if I could explain that I wanted to form my opinions of him away from the eyes of everyone in the palace, and away from the protocol. I needed to *know* him.

He pulled the reins on his horse so that he was trotting in circles around me. "No one in the world will be as happy as us," he claimed. "I know you think I am a little . . . rigid, but you will see I'm right in the end. I am trying to take care of you. You will see, Annika, I will tend you so well."

I tried not to roll my eyes. "And I will be so thankful for that. But I'd still like to give ourselves some space away from the palace at first. I'd hoped for a year, but even a few months would do."

"A few months?" he replied, clearly still surprised by my request. "Annika, I can't imagine what would be gained. We will be together all the time as is, and if we stay at the palace, we benefit not only from the comfort of your home but also the wisdom of your father and brother. And how do you think they'll feel if we go? They'll think I'm stealing you away from them."

"Not if we explain," I pleaded.

"Annika, I have to say, I just—"

He broke off, and I turned to see what caught his eye. To his left and ahead of me, just at the breaking tree line, five figures on horses were emerging. They were average enough, if a bit of a surprise with how quietly they came upon us. There was one girl in a faded dress accompanied by a quartet of gentlemen, and they looked windswept and a little unsure . . . but that wasn't the thing that held my gaze.

The young man at the center lead of the pack was staring dead into my eyes. There was something so unnervingly familiar about his face that it sent chills all over my body. And what's more, he was blinking at me as if he were looking at a ghost, his skin growing paler with each passing second.

Shaking his head, he spoke to his companions. "New plan. Take them. The girl is mine."

In an instant, Nickolas was off, bolting in the other direction. I turned my horse as quickly as I could, following suit. The guards drew their swords and galloped alongside, keeping me protected. Nickolas was within my sights, but he was moving swiftly and with an air of determination.

I wished with all my heart I'd not cared what anyone might say and put my sword on the horse. I wished I had allowed my father to come with us. I wished I had anything to protect me now. I raced as quickly as I could through a dense patch of trees, trying to weave through them and shake off my attacker. I could hear his horse behind me, and I refused to look back and let him see just how terrified I was.

Nickolas was ahead of me to my right, and I saw that one of the riders had caught up with him. He got close enough to reach out and hit Nickolas with the hilt of his sword, and Nickolas slumped down in his saddle, leaning forward heavily on the neck of his horse.

"No!" I screamed, switching course immediately and heading in his direction.

By the time I'd gotten to Nickolas, his assailant was on the run, being pursued by one of the guards. I jumped from my horse and ran to my fiancé, searching for a breath, a heartbeat.

It was a foolish move, because as soon as I was on foot, my attacker was behind me.

I turned, watching him dismount so he could take me. I was cornered, but I had to try. I reached up, unsheathing Nickolas's sword, and took my stance.

LENNOX

I was taken aback by the way she quickly drew herself into a wide-legged stance, the sword held upright, next to her chin. It was hard to imagine this poor girl could fight—not with that hair swept up with wildflowers, those pristine clothes, and that soft look to her . . . a look I'd seen before—but at least she knew how to hold a sword properly.

I stood there, a heartbeat away from laughing at her, but the cold stare of her eyes told me that might be a mistake. Instead, I unsheathed my own sword and planted my feet, nodding my head as an invitation. In a flash, she was charging, swinging both hands down hard, like she hoped to lop off my arm. I blocked her and spun, amused.

She, however, was far from amused. She was enraged. She charged back at me, wielding her sword again with two hands. She swung with abandon but not recklessly; she almost certainly had held a sword before. Staring me down, she pulled at her stays, trying to adjust her dress, and she seemed frustrated that her skirts were in her way. But, even encumbered, she was light and fast—a decent opponent.

I didn't bother attacking, instead letting her come for me. Eventually, she would wear herself out, and I could grab her. Around us, I heard the sounds of swords clanging, catching sight of Inigo in my periphery as he dashed after one of the guards. Between the advantage of a surprise attack and our training, we had the upper hand. In the meantime, she pressed on, slashing down and across and any way she could manage. Whenever I expected her to drop her sword, tired of the apparent weight, she steeled herself and came back again. Time after time after time, hammering it down as if she were nothing but a cage of anger with the door finally let open.

She just. Kept. Going.

Eventually she stopped swinging and started stabbing, hoping to get through my blocks. I had long expected her to tire, but instead she surged at me again. As if she was only just hitting her stride, she took the sword in one hand and whipped it around with a flourish. Adjusting her grip, she charged at me, and I had to hop back on both feet to avoid being run through.

I looked down and saw that she'd torn a seam. That was close. Looking at her determined gaze, I realized I was going to have to do more than defend myself.

I spun and slashed, catching her off guard. She blocked me well enough, but now that I was trying, she was on edge. I went for her sword, not her, hitting it over and over, hoping to loosen her grip or, at the very least, frighten her into submission. After a few minutes of the onslaught, the poor girl lost her footing, slanting down on one knee.

When she slipped, she looked up at me with such disappointment, and that particular look in that particular set of eyes was so familiar it stopped me in my tracks. I knew those eyes. They had haunted me for years.

In my stupor, she jumped to her feet, raised her sword, and slashed down, clipping me and cutting across my upper chest. I growled in pain, and then, like a child retaliating after a slap, I swung, cutting her left arm. She cried out and dropped to her knees, grasping her bleeding wound.

I took my opportunity.

I lowered my sword so the tip was inches from her neck. "Drop your weapon."

She stared up at me, like she was genuinely thinking about saying no. But then she looked around. Apparently, she didn't see much point in carrying on.

She dropped her sword, and I pulled mine away.

"Stand," I ordered, and she did, though the look in her eyes said she hated to do it. I was used to fear or trembling, though I'd expected quiet dignity from her.

I wasn't prepared for thinly veiled rage.

I pulled the rope from my hip belt and started tying her hands. Shackles. That would have been smart to bring.

Once the girl was taken care of, I surveyed the rest of the group to see if my help was needed. Sherwin was on top of one guard, while Inigo had bound another. In the distance, Blythe and Andre were walking a third over to us.

"Is that everyone?" I called.

"Yes. One of the guards is dead," Andre reported.

The girl made the tiniest sound of sorrow.

"And what about him? Do we take him?" Inigo asked, pointing to the gentleman passed out on his horse.

"No. Didn't you notice?" I said, staring down at the girl. "He didn't even look back for her. He's useless."

There was more heartbreak in her eyes, and it stung in ways that didn't make sense. I reached into my bag and pulled out the gauze. I wrapped her arm hastily to keep it from bleeding everywhere.

"Thank you," she mumbled.

There was the quiet dignity.

Inigo came up beside me and spoke in a low voice. "What exactly did we just do?" he asked, his voice brimming with anger.

"They're from Dahrain," I told him.

"How do you know?"

"I know," I replied firmly. "Three guards. What do you think they'll tell us once we do a little convincing?"

He quietly considered this, then nodded his head at the girl. "And that one?"

"I have plans," I told him.

If those words scared her, she didn't let it show. The others moved to get the guards on their horses, hands bound and eyes downcast.

I lowered a hand for the girl's boot. "Up."

She gripped the saddle, ready to hoist herself up.

"Your Highness—" one of the guards called, and my heart stopped as those few words confirmed everything I feared. "We're sorry."

At that, she shoved my arm aside, looking back over my shoulder to see the three remaining guards chewing something. Within seconds, they fell to the ground, foaming at their mouths. Then they were dead.

"No," she whispered. "Not like this. Not for me."

I gripped her good arm. "Do you have whatever they took, too? If you do, hand it over immediately."

There was a single disappointed tear rolling down her cheek. She shook her head somberly, still looking at the men on the ground.

"I'll have you searched."

Her eyes never wavered. "I'd love to see what you find."

"Now what?" Inigo demanded.

My mind whirled. By the maps, we hadn't even touched Dahrain, but somehow I'd gotten their princess. This proved that an invasion was easier than we'd been led to believe. It also proved that I had the guts to go where my father had walked, and I could come out of it alive. And a princess was bound to have information we needed. If this wasn't a kind of hope, then I didn't know what was.

"She will be enough," I said, trying to assure myself just as much as the others. "If we want a shot of getting to Vosino tonight, we need to leave now. Let's go."

I got the princess on my horse and climbed up behind her. Sighing, I pulled on the reins and started us off toward home.

ANNIKA

After endless hours, we finally arrived at a castle in extreme disrepair.

Based on the path of the sun, my kidnapper had taken me east. It felt like we'd veered north as well, but I couldn't be completely sure. I looked at the shape of this side of the castle, hoping I could remember it if I needed to.

My rider dismounted and held up hands to help me down. It irritated me that he was almost gentlemanly. Compared to his peers, he held his head higher, his back straighter. I supposed that was why he was in charge.

It took me a while to realize he was probably very close to my age, but his frown made him look older, more menacing. His dark hair contrasted sharply with his shockingly blue eyes, and while his jaw was a straight line, his nose was bent, as if it had been broken in his youth. He was scowling as he pulled me into the castle and down the hall.

"Do you want me to hold her?" the lone girl from the group of captors asked, coming up beside me.

"No. She's mine," he replied simply.

"You should see to your wound, Lennox," she insisted, coming up beside us.

"I'm fine. Leave me be."

She didn't give in. "That was a long ride. You could get an infection. We need all—"

He whipped around at her, gripping me slightly tighter in his anger. "For goodness' sake, Blythe, enough!"

They stared into one another's eyes for a moment.

"You don't need to be so hard on her," another of the raiders commented.

"Not now, Inigo."

"Lennox?"

We all turned to another young man, his fingers interlaced with the girl beside him.

"Rami, why don't you go back inside? I'll be in soon."

She looked at him like she'd rather not, but she did as asked, locking eyes with me as she passed.

"I thought you'd be days, maybe weeks," he whispered.

"Plans changed. What do you think we can get in exchange for a princess?"

The new person looked at me, and his eyes widened into a joyful skepticism. "I have to see this," he said, falling into step behind the others.

I had been collecting information from the second I was placed on his horse. I had studied all the terrain I could, and I was trying to keep tracks of the turns we were taking in this ancient castle. And now I was learning about the dynamics of his group. In this moment, I needed to make a choice. I could either disrupt this boy's plans and get him into serious trouble, or I could stay silent and still. Him losing some level of credibility would add nothing for me, and if I was about to be placed in front of their leader, the odds of me escaping in that situation were slim.

For now, the best path was proud silence.

He pulled me into a room that reminded me of the master hall back home. It was darker, with hardly any windows, and lit by numerous torches. The tables and benches appeared to be as old as the castle itself. As we walked in, the people who were still up finishing their meals turned and watched us. It only took a few seconds for me to realize I was a secondary draw; they were looking at him.

They were looking at this *Lennox*.

He marched me up the center aisle, toward a man who looked to be as wide as he was tall; it was hard to tell, as he was sitting in a massive chair that I assumed had to be a throne. On his arm, a beautiful older woman was practically pouring herself onto him in a way I would have called indecent at home.

Lennox knelt before them and focused on the man. "Kawan, I've returned from my Commission, and I come to make my offering." He stood again, not seeming to want to be in a submissive position any longer than necessary.

The couple's eyes landed on me.

"What's this?" the man asked, staring at my face, looking horror-struck.

"Heir to the monster's throne."

The woman gaped at me. "She looks just like—"

"I know," Lennox replied. "Seeing as you've been saying we're going to reclaim Dahrain for years, I thought this might be the key to the castle."

Dahrain. It was only now that I realized he'd said this name before. Was he confused?

"You . . . you went to Dahrain?" the large man asked in shock.

"Yes. It was easy. Killed a few guards, took a princess. Imagine how simple it would be for us to take an entire kingdom with a little bit of knowledge." There was something accusatory to his tone. "Shall I bring you some answers?"

The man nodded wordlessly, still staring at me.

"Then we'll get straight to work." Lennox turned me around roughly—far more roughly than he had when he didn't have an audience—and dragged me out of the hall as quickly as he'd brought me in.

"Take her downstairs and put her in some proper shackles," Lennox said to the girl. Blythe? "Wait with her until I get there."

"Yes, sir," she replied bitterly, and pulled me away. "Come on."

Her hands were decidedly firmer than Lennox's, which surprised me. She didn't care that I was tripping down the stairs, and when we rounded the corner to what must have been their dungeons, she slammed me up against the wall, knocking my breath out of me and setting off a ringing in my head.

"Don't move," she warned.

I stood obediently against the wall as she pulled my new

restraints off a hook and brought them over to me.

"He shouldn't have yelled at you," I offered quietly.

"Don't talk, either."

She put my new shackles on *before* removing the rope, a move that showed she knew what she was doing. I had the feeling everyone here did.

She sighed, grabbing me by my injured arm and throwing me into a cell. There was something that might make an excuse for a bed against the wall, and a hole with a bar across it that doubled for a window.

"Might I . . . I need to . . ."

She pointed to a bucket in the corner.

"Oh. Lovely."

"Are the accommodations not up to your standards, Your Highness?"

I was left without a choice, so I squatted over the bucket, holding my dress the best I could with chained hands, and looked away from her. If I survived my time here, this would be the one detail I left out of the story.

"Can you tell me where I am, at least?" I asked the girl. "I've never been this far east. I didn't even know this land was inhabited."

For all I'd known, it was all but impossible to get here.

She scoffed. "I'm not surprised. Your people have gotten everything you wanted already, haven't you? No need to worry about us rounding up the scraps?"

I stood, making my way closer to her.

"Do these scraps not have a name, then?"

"We call it Vosino Castle," she spat. "If the land itself ever had a name, it's been forgotten."

I nodded. It seemed the words *unclaimed land* on our map were very, very wrong. "Remarkable. Have you been here long? This castle looks like it needs some tending."

"The castle was found a decade or so ago, and we've done our best to keep it up. We don't have your resources, though, do we, Your Highness?"

She kicked herself off the wall and started walking around the room. "I wonder what they're going to do with you," she said idly. "We haven't used the rack in ages."

I tried not to let her see that this line of thought was shaking me.

"But since you're royalty, maybe something with a little more finesse might be in order. What do you think?"

"Seeing as we don't torture people in Kadier—which is where I'm from, by the way, not this Dahrain place—I have no opinion. I can't imagine any form of brutality is better than another." I wished I could move my hands. I hated feeling so defenseless.

"Wouldn't it be fun if they just let you and me outside for a bit?" she mused. "We have an arena out there, and it looked like you could at least carry a sword from what I saw. Perhaps we should go toe to toe?"

"I'd hate to kill a lady," I replied politely. "Besides, with the way my captor was behaving, he seems more likely to be on my side than yours."

She crossed the room in three quick steps and slapped me hard across my cheek. A whimper escaped without my permission, and I wobbled a bit on my feet. This did nothing to help the headache that had been growing since she'd slammed me up against the wall.

"If it were up to me, I'd tie you to a rock and wait for the tide to come in."

"Fortunately for her, it's not up to you."

We both turned to the low sound of a calm and steady voice.

Lennox walked into the room looking much cleaner and, somehow, more sinister because of it. He'd washed his face and swept his long hair back. He was wearing a coat similar to the one he'd had on before, with tight sleeves and buckles that latched down one side. This one didn't have a slash across it.

"You can go, Blythe," he said.

She stood there with crossed arms for a moment, then turned on her heel and left.

He waited until she was gone to shut the door. The large key, it seemed, worked from either side. He locked us in and propped himself up against the wall with his arms crossed.

"So. You must be Annika," he said calmly.

I shook my head. "I'm impressed with how much you think you know about me. Especially considering that I never knew of your existence until today."

He looked away, wandering around the room much in the same way that Blythe girl had.

"I didn't know you existed, either. Well, I wasn't sure. I heard your name once," he said, turning to face me. He watched me closely, clearly hoping for a reaction with his next words. "It was the last thing your mother said before she died."

LENNOX

She was stunned into silence, her carefully calculated mask of pride quickly deteriorating as her eyes went glassy.

"What?"

"I confess, for the last three years, I wondered if 'Annika' was some sort of a prayer in a language I didn't know. The syllables rolled off her tongue so serenely, so hopefully, that I wondered if they were her way of pleading with some deity for mercy or saying goodbye to the world."

"My mother was *here*?" she let out in a whisper.

I nodded.

Her chest heaved, and I watched as her eyes dashed back and forth, searching for which question to ask first.

"She truly is dead?"

I studied her in silence for a moment, almost pitying the sound of a dying hope in her voice.

"Yes."

"And you were with her when she died?"

"I was."

"Was she . . ." She swallowed, trying so hard to keep herself together. "Was she in pain?"

"No," I admitted. "She went quickly, as painlessly as anyone could ask in this life."

A single tear fell down her cheek, passing a rising red welt. She didn't sob or faint; she didn't slip into a rage. I wondered if she knew how like her mother she was.

"Thank you for your honesty," she eked out, reaching up to carefully wipe at her cheek, wincing when she moved her left arm.

"You're welcome. I expect the same level of honesty in return. Sit." I motioned to the short stool near the side wall, and she obeyed, the bravado knocked out of her by the truth of her mother.

She raised her eyebrows. "What do you want to know?"

"Numbers, Princess. I need to know exactly how many people inhabit the kingdom that you've stolen, how many ships are in your navy. How many—"

"Wait," she said, holding up a hand. "Stolen? We haven't stolen anything."

"Oh, but you have. I know your history better than you do, Princess. I bet you've been told your whole life that your ancestors were chosen to lead the clans to victory against invaders, am I right?"

"Yes. Because they were. And we did."

I shook my head. "You might have held off those who tried to ruin the seven clans, but you stole your crown from my people, the Dahrainian clan. Most of the people here are their descendants, and the only reason we aren't currently sitting on the throne you hold is because your great-grandparents slaughtered half our clan and ran the other half off, stealing the role we were specifically chosen to take."

She had the audacity to smirk at me. "You are painfully mistaken. The land where Kadier now sits was once made up of *six* clans, not seven. And my ancestors held the bulk of it. You'd have nothing to illegally invade were it not for us."

I chuckled at her speech. "You've been lied to. The land where your little castle sits, where your pretty little bed is made, belongs to my people, the Dahrainians. We have been living in exile for generations, and we want it back. And you will help us," I told her. "Or you will die."

She stared at me, looking as if she were trying to decide if I was lying or not.

"It's all true," I insisted.

She scoffed. "Even if it is, I don't have what you're after. The soldiers you took probably didn't, either. My father keeps the census guarded. As to soldiers and ships . . . they *might* have had an idea. But seeing as I'm a second-born child, and a girl no less, I'm not privy to such information."

I stepped in front of her, lowering my gaze to hers, forcing her to look me in the eye. Goodness, that piercing stare was familiar. It was like seeing her mother all over again, only not.

"You know something," I said. "More than you're willing to say, at least. I think a girl who rides a horse like she's stolen it and wields a sword like she's a knight might have more information than she wants *anyone* to know she has."

She swallowed. There it was. No one else would have suspected her of holding much of anything, information or otherwise. But hidden under those messy curls and a flowing dress, I saw a heart and a mind the rest of the world had ignored. She'd locked them both up tight, and now the trick was to find the proper key.

I took a casual stroll around the cell, thinking. Sometimes, silence itself was enough to make some prisoners so uncomfortable that they spilled everything for the sake of filling the void. There was the possibility of torture, of course, but I never enjoyed that. Pain wasn't my goal; victory was.

The key to victory over her? Information of my own.

"I'll make you an offer. Tell me how many guards are in the palace, and I'll tell you the thing you want to know most."

"Which is?"

"I'll tell you exactly how your mother died."

"You were truly there?" she asked again, her eyes growing softer for a moment.

"I was."

She looked down, thinking. When her face came back up, she kept her eyes closed, wincing as she spoke.

"There are sixty-eight soldiers assigned to the palace on any given day. If there's a holiday or celebration of some kind, the number goes up, but it rarely surpasses a hundred."

I raised my eyebrows. She was so concise, so perfectly specific. If I could get her to keep talking, I'd have Dahrain in the palm of my hand.

"Well done, Princess." I walked back over to her, standing

in front of her stool again. "Your mother was my charge. I was in the room with her for maybe twenty minutes trying, as I am now, to get her to speak. She didn't share anything of consequence, not as far as our mission was concerned. So she was beheaded." He paused. "And I did it."

Her eyes darkened. "You?" she whispered.

"Yes."

"How could you do it?"

I tilted my head, stepping away. "She had to die. And I think you already know why."

Her eyes . . . they were as wild as the sea, raging underneath her regal upbringing. Her chest was rising and falling with angry breaths, and I could see her filling in the blank spaces of the full picture in her mind.

"Go ahead and take a guess," I offered. "I saw your face in the woods. You stood out to me instantly, the exact image of your mother. But you recognized me, too. Put the pieces together, Annika. Who am I?"

Her chest was rising and falling so quickly as the horror of it all came to her. "You're the son of that monster Jago."

I gave her a quick bow. "So you see, it was only fair. You beheaded my father."

"*I* did nothing," she said. "I didn't judge or condemn him, though he clearly deserved the punishment for his crime. And at least your father had a trial."

"You put his corpse on the back of a cart and left it to wander in the woods! It was by sheer luck that we got his body back, and you somehow think your actions were noble?"

"Her body . . ." Her voice broke. "Is she here? Is she buried here?"

"Yes."

She looked away, like she didn't want me to see the tears spill over. I gave her a moment to compose herself.

"If you had any self-respect," she said quietly, "you would remove these shackles from my wrists, give me a sword, and take me outside. I could match you now without question."

"No, you couldn't," I replied curtly. "You've got talent, I'll give you that, but I have far more experience. And I know that when you go to attack in blind anger, you make mistakes. I'd still win."

She shook her head. I couldn't tell if it was because she was disagreeing with me, clearing her thoughts, or just frustrated that she was crying. Maybe it was all three.

"I have more questions."

She laughed coldly. "If you think there's *any* way I would give you anything else now, you are deluded beyond measure."

"I wouldn't be so sure," I said. "I know more about your mother, and I'm willing to exchange what I know for what you do."

She crossed her arms, a difficult task with the chains around her wrists. "I will keep the memories I have, and you can explain to your leader how your own arrogance shut down your interrogation."

The spite in her voice, the immediate understanding that I'd rather crawl through fire than admit defeat to Kawan, pushed me to the point of rage. It nearly boiled over, but I refused to let her see how deeply she'd stabbed me.

I pulled my switchblade from my belt pouch. "You have a very slender neck, Your Highness." I pulled out a lock of her hair, holding it in front of her face. "It would be easier than this to remove your head." I cut the hair in a quick upward slice, so deftly she probably didn't even feel a tug on her scalp. I held it up, swinging the messy curl in front of her. "If I were you, I'd start talking."

"No."

Her voice was stone, immovable and cold.

"I made sure your mother didn't suffer, but I don't owe that to you. I'm still willing to tell you about her final moments, but only if you talk."

I swept away to the door, looking back at her before I left her alone in the cold. Her arms were still crossed as she stared at the opposite wall.

"I'll be back in an hour. Consider your choices well, Princess."

ANNIKA

Once he was gone, I allowed myself to cry.

I told myself it was better to know. I wouldn't have to wonder anymore. I had answers.

Your mother is dead, Annika. She's not coming back. Now you know.

I supposed some corner of my heart should be comforted by the knowledge that she didn't suffer, and that she was properly buried. But all I could do was miss her more.

If anyone should be in possession of my mother's final moments, it was me. Not him. I hated that he knew things I was desperate to hear and that he was viciously *aware* of how much it meant to me. It was surreal to speak so calmly to the man who killed the person you loved the most in the world. I'd expected someone more sinister, more ogre-like. He was all but a child. Like me.

She was close.

If I handed over numbers, even more false ones, maybe he would take me to her grave. Maybe I could finally say goodbye. The only problem was that I didn't want to give him anything now. I wanted to take from him. I wanted to find a way to make him suffer as no one could. Even if he'd given me a sword and a chance to fight him, I didn't know if I could inflict the pain I was imagining.

I wiped at my tears, trying to summon the ability to think clearly, if only for a moment. How could I get out of this? *Think, Annika.*

I pulled a pin from my hair and went to work on the shackles. I closed my eyes, trying my best to focus on the feel on the mechanism. I was shaky and tired and hungry, and if I'd been safe in the library next to Rhett, it would have been a different experience entirely. As it was, it took all I had to concentrate.

I imagined the smell of old books, the sound of Rhett's unguarded laugh. It brought a smile to my face; it slowed my breathing. In less than a minute, I heard the lock click and felt it fall from my left wrist.

I quietly walked over to the door. The lone torch left in its holder on the wall lit the better part of the hallway. It seemed he'd left me without any sort of guard. I supposed he didn't think me capable of escape.

The lock on the door was another beast entirely, and I'd need something much stronger than a hairpin to get through that. I peeked into the hallway again to confirm I was alone. This castle looked so old that it seemed a well-timed sneeze could knock it down. I gripped the handle with both hands and placed a foot on the wall, putting all my weight into pulling it from its place. The door wobbled a little, but there was no way of getting it to come loose.

Fine, then. I'd try the window.

This thing could hardly even count as a window. A round hole with one bar up the middle, no glass, no anything. If it rained, it would drain straight down onto this pitiful excuse for a bed. I could see the stains of where it had before. I took the bar and pulled on it with both hands, shaking it around. The bar certainly wasn't moving in or out . . . but it was moving from side to side.

I crawled up, looking at the base closer. This space had been so poorly tended to. The rock was all but crumbling sand, and it looked like I could chip away part of it at least. There was no way a grown man could get out of a space that wide . . . but if I moved it even an inch, I stood a good chance.

He said he'd give me an hour, but I couldn't count on him keeping his word. I used the opened cuff of my shackle and started chipping at the rock. By the time he came back, I could close the cuff, climb back down, and be lying on the bed with my restraints in place. He would be none the wiser.

"This is possible," I whispered to myself. "This is possible."

LENNOX

I laid the strands of Annika's hair across my desk, watching as they pulled up into a curl on their own. I was going to be forced to kill her, wasn't I? I was trying to remember a time since I'd been here that I was taught to show mercy. No such lesson came to mind.

Perhaps Annika would be a different case. The last time we'd had someone with royal blood in the castle, I was the only one who could manage to kill her. If I refused now, who'd tend to Annika?

Thistle whimpered from the window.

"Are you coming or going?" I asked.

She moved down, landing on my bed, lying with her head on her paws. I wasn't sure if foxes could feel concern, but her eyes said she was worried about me.

"Don't be," I assured her. I crossed the room, bending down to pet her head. As I did so, I looked at my hands. Was I really going to take the same hands that I used to care for Thistle, to show the maps in the stars, to build up an army . . . and put them to Annika's neck?

I took up my branch, wincing from my cut as I bent to get it, and threw my cape over my shoulders as I made my way outside.

The wind had picked up again, blowing my cape as I marched up to the cemetery. I took my small branch, still green and holding its leaves, and piled it on the others covering her mother's grave.

"Another tribute," I said, placing it down. "I met her. I met your last prayer," I told her. "She's angry. She doesn't look like she *wants* to be, but she is. I wonder where she gets that from. Not you."

I looked back at the castle. The side I could see showed the shabby windows down the back side, where the newest recruits lived. The legends said we'd once built fine structures. I'd never seen them.

I swallowed. "I'm afraid I'm going to have to kill her. I don't want to, but . . . she's too . . . observant. She already knows too much."

For the first time in a long time, tears welled in my eyes. I was so tired. Tired, and angry, and so ready for something new. But here I was, tied to this forsaken land and this dying castle and this plot of dirt that held a woman who cared for me too much in the few minutes she knew me. And I suddenly hated her for it.

"I don't understand why I come back here. You're *dead*! You couldn't save yourself, and you certainly can't save me. I'll never make sense of the kindness in your eyes, or why I feel like I'll spend the rest of my life apologizing to you. Your husband took my father! He's the reason my mother is in the arms of that pig! A life for a life."

I turned around and screamed into the night.

"Why did you have to be so gentle?" I shouted. "Why did you do that to me?"

I stared at her headstone, knowing I would forever be haunted by her. When I thought across all the people I'd killed, she was the only one I remembered. She didn't beg for mercy. She didn't spit in my face. She accepted the end, accepted me, and walked toward death like she'd been waiting for years to meet her face-to-face.

"Sometimes I feel that way, too," I confessed. "Sometimes, I think anything would be better than here. But I have a feeling, if the worlds are divided on the other side, that you and I won't be in the same place when it's my turn."

A tear fell down my cheek, the last one I would allow, and I looked at the headstone. I could still see her, and the image was more vivid now that I'd met her daughter. I'd remember them both forever.

Never run away, never look away, never explain it away. This was how I survived. So I would have to follow through now. I would have to get something out of Annika so I could present it to Kawan. I would have to be merciless. I refused to be seen as a failure. I'd backed myself into this corner, and now I was going to fight my way out.

No one stopped me as I stormed into the castle, winding my way down to the dungeons. I pulled the key from the far wall and jammed it into the lock. I could see through the bars in the door that she was huddled up on her bed with her back against the wall and her knees tucked under her chin. She looked over when she saw me, and I tried to read her eyes. There was still sadness there, but also a composed defiance that made me uneasy.

"Have you reconsidered?" I asked, shutting the door behind me.

"I'm in no mood to speak, especially not to you. Murderer."

The word hurt as much as the wound she'd made on my chest back in the woods.

"I prefer to think of myself as an enforcer. Besides, there hasn't been another infraction between our two peoples since that day. I'd call that progress."

"Says the man who kidnapped both me and my guards," she commented, rolling her eyes.

I nearly laughed, she was so painfully right.

"Listen, Your Highness, I need—"

"Stop calling me that," she said, turning to face me. "Not with that disdainful tone. My position is a product of my birth, and not one I could control. And I don't deserve your judgment for it."

"You're judging me for my birth, aren't you? My people are dregs to yours, so low we didn't deserve to keep what was ours, and now—"

She held up a delicate hand, unbothered by the cuffs still dangling from her wrists.

"Granted, my tour of your home was limited, but could you tell me, is there a library in this shack?"

I crossed my arms. "No."

"I didn't think so. Now, how exactly are you so sure you have any claim on my kingdom?"

"Our history is oral, passed down from generation to generation. Every last one of my people knows."

She shook her head, sighing. "I wasn't alive when Kadier was founded, and neither were you. You say its history is one thing, and I say it's another. I'd like to think, since I actually live there, that I know the truth. It's not disrespect; it's not judgment. Furthermore, I also know that you are the person who stole my mother from me. And I want nothing to do with you."

Her words were smooth and sharp.

"Very well, then, Annika. If you're so smart, then I'm sure that somewhere in that brain of yours, you're holding on to the information I need. And I am holding on to things I know you want. Things you probably want more than the chance to go home. If you cooperate, there's a chance I can give you both."

She cocked her head to the side. "You're not taking me home, so don't pretend that you are."

Her tone was so calm, resigned to the possibility of death, but I told her the truth all the same. "If I can, I will take you back to Dahrain myself."

"Before or after you invade?"

I clenched my fists and inhaled deeply. "It would be wise for you to, at the very least, stop being so difficult."

"It would be wise for you to stop murdering people."

I stood up and kicked the stool. It rolled across the room and left a huge wake of silence.

"I'm sorry," she whispered.

I looked back at her, surprised.

"I'm tired," she admitted, looking down at her hands and fidgeting with her fingers. "In a day, I've been taken from my home and witnessed the death of four of our best guards. I have no idea what happened to my fiancé, and I've learned more about my mother from you in five minutes than I have from anyone else in the last three years. It's overwhelming, given my gender and upbringing. I need sleep. If you let me sleep, I'll talk."

Fiancé. Huh. Maybe I should have grabbed him after all.

My plan had been to wear her out. To make her so delirious she wouldn't be able to help but talk. So far, all that was accomplishing was making her lash out and leaving me looking foolish.

"I'll be back at dawn. Be prepared. If you don't give me something, they'll want you dead."

Her eyelashes fluttered as she continued to toy with her hands. "I understand."

I went to leave, but then, because I couldn't help myself, I turned to her one last time.

"Do you have a favorite constellation?"

She looked over at me in surprise, which was fair. Then she made a face as if she was confessing this in spite of her better judgment.

"Cassiopeia."

I scoffed. "She's hanging upside down. Forever. Why her?"

She toyed with the ring on her finger—an engagement

ring, I assumed. "There are worse ways to exist," she said quietly. And then, as if she might regret even asking, she peeked over and asked, "What's yours?"

"Orion."

"That's so . . . everyone says Orion."

"Exactly. The guard of heaven. Everyone knows Orion."

She looked over at me, her face suddenly softer. "A decent role model, I suppose."

I nodded. "I suppose."

"You know, Orion was no saint," she said. "You could aim higher. Do better."

My heartbeat thundered in my ears, and I had to put up my armor, refusing to let her touch my soul. Her words tiptoed dangerously close to her mother's, and I couldn't hear them again. I swallowed. "I'll be back at dawn."

"Dawn."

I pulled the door behind me, locking it—and my tired heart—tight.

ANNIKA

I'd had a hunch that mentioning my femininity and my soft upbringing would send Lennox into confusion. Sometimes even unpredictable people are far too predictable.

I waited until I was sure he was long gone, then I pulled the pin back out of my hair. I thought of Rhett sitting closer than he knew he ought, of how much care he took with his work. I thought of him trying to make me laugh.

Click.

One cuff loose, one to go.

I switched hands. I wasn't as good with my left arm, and it was indescribably painful to use, but still.

This time, I thought of Escalus. I thought of him with his needle and thread, so thoughtful and quiet. I thought of him behaving the exact same way with a sword. I thought of how, if he were here, we would be focused on rescuing each other. It seemed that was all we ever did.

Click.

With that, the shackles were off.

I went to the foot of my bed and pressed the bar over. I'd managed to gain a little over an inch, forcing the bar to sit at a slant. It might just be enough. It wasn't going to work in this gown, though. Too bulky. I started pulling out pins and untying laces, peeling off the outer layers of the dress and throwing my riding coat aside. Once I was down to my shift and my stays, I thought I might have a chance. I looked myself over, wondering if there was anything else weighing me down.

There was.

I took my engagement ring off and left it neatly on my pile of discarded clothes.

I hoisted myself up, turning my head sideways to fit it through the opening. I stayed on my side, getting my arms and shoulders through, bracing on the other side of the wall. The cut on my arm throbbed with the effort, but I kept silent, working away. It was hard to believe the room was actually blocking that much of the wind, but it was. I wished I'd had a way to get my dress out with me, but it wasn't worth risking going back in now. I needed to put all the space I could between Lennox and me.

I pressed again. My hips were stuck. This was going to hurt, too. I pushed, shimmying a millimeter at a time.

"This is possible," I told myself again. It was painful work. I was sure my arm was spilling blood. My linen shift was getting torn by the rocks, and I could feel them digging into my hips. I felt my old wounds being pressed, and, even if they didn't open, it was a searing sensation against my skin.

But, pain or no, I was going to escape. I would not be

trapped; I would not be killed like my mother.

He'd said she was buried here. If I hunted, I might be able to find her. Lennox was right that there were things I wanted more than escape. I wanted to know everything. I wanted to know all of what she said to him, and why he seemed to remember it all too well. I wanted to know how she looked, and I wanted to go plant my tears by her headstone.

But I thought of Escalus. If nothing else, I needed to get home to warn him and Father that a war was on the horizon.

Once my thighs were through the window, my legs came out easily, and I flopped onto the ground very sloppily, aching so much that it was easier to crawl than walk.

I hoisted myself to my feet all the same. I had to move. I had until dawn at best before he realized I was gone. If I could get a horse, this would be so much easier, but I couldn't count on that. I needed to lie low and just keep moving.

My underdress was white. My stays were white. I might as well have been a torch in the night. I dug my hands into some freezing mud and raked it over my clothes and skin, trying to blend in with the shadows. The chill was already making its way into my bones.

Move, Annika. Move, and you'll be warm.

I saw no guards, no soldiers making rounds. But why would they bother? No one knew they were here. They were predators, not prey.

I stayed as low to the ground as I could, looking back over my shoulder too many times to count. Once the castle grew small, I moved faster. In the distance, I saw the thick tree line.

I laced my way through the trees, knowing there was open land on the other side. It felt like it took far too long to make it through that one patch of ground, tripping over roots and hitting a tree more than once. But, eventually, I saw the field. That treacherous forest was going to be waiting in the distance, but if Lennox could make it to Kadier, then so could I. I looked up, hunting for the north star, searching the sky for landmarks. I got my bearings, and I ran. I ran until my legs burned. I ran until my lungs might explode. I ran until my body was nothing but strained muscles and aching nerves.

And then, for my life, I kept going.

LENNOX

The hammering knock came on my door when the sky was still gray. I could see the sun was thinking about rising, and I wished, so deeply, that it would reconsider.

I'd hardly slept. While awake, all I saw was Annika's proud eyes, daring me to think I could best her, telling me I was wrong. When I closed my eyes, I saw her still, looking over at me, pronouncing *Cassiopeia* so elegantly, reminding me how the stories written in stars were once so beautiful and mysterious to me.

And now, in the seconds between knocks, I saw her headstone next to her mother's.

"Lennox! Get up, boy!"

I hopped up instantly, looking around my room for Thistle, making sure she was gone. Kawan didn't allow us to waste resources on animals, and he sounded like he was already in a bad mood. I didn't bother tucking in my shirt or throwing on a waistcoat. It was rare he wanted something this early, so I was already on edge.

"Yes, sir?" I said, opening the door. "What can I do?"

Behind him, Blythe was standing, arms crossed.

"She's gone," Kawan said.

I couldn't tell if my sigh was out of frustration or relief. "What?"

"I went to check on her," Blythe said. "There's a pile of clothes on the ground near the window. She broke out of her restraints, shifted the bar in the window, and ran for it."

I stood there in shock.

"She . . . she got out of her shackles?"

Kawan slapped me hard across the face. "She got out of the *castle*! On your watch! How could you let this happen? What kind of offering was this meant to be in the first place? How exactly does this serve the army? You've all but given us away! For as foolish as your father was, you're ten times worse."

It took all I had not to lunge at him. I was strong enough; I stood a chance. But there were bigger concerns than my pride at the moment.

I moved my jaw, refusing to reach up and touch my throbbing face. "How was I to know that wisp of a girl was capable of getting out of her shackles?"

"How were you stupid enough to not stay down there?" He stared into my eyes, his own so very dark. "Did memories of her poor mother come back to haunt you?" he guessed in a sarcastic tone.

The urge to throw a punch at him was growing in my stomach. I just wanted one. One.

"My only failure was not knowing my enemy," I told

him. "The point of my Commission was to show you just how easy it was to get into the land you've said we were going to take for ages. This girl might have taught us something very important today. Perhaps everyone in her country knows how to escape chains. This will change the way we hold their prisoners from here on out, will it not?"

Kawan stood there, irritated that I'd found the bright side in all this. And I had to give myself some silent applause for pulling that idea out of the air.

"Fix this," he commanded, pointing a cracked finger into my face. "Now."

He stormed down the hall, his footsteps thunderous.

"Don't move," I told Blythe as I shut the door. I grabbed my waistcoat from the night before and flung it on, as well as my belt with its pouch. I shoved my feet into boots and grabbed my riding cape. I had a sense we would need to mobilize immediately.

"When did you go down there?" I asked as I opened the door and headed toward the mess hall. I wanted reinforcements.

Blythe immediately followed. "It's been maybe thirty minutes."

"The shackles are in there?" I clarified.

"Yes. One of the cuffs has grit on it. It looks like she used it to hammer at the stone by the base of the bar in the window."

I shook my head. How clever. I wondered how many people here would have thought to do the same.

"She took off her outer layer of clothes to get through the

window, and that's all in a messy pile down there as well. If she's in her underclothes, I don't know how she'd survive the cold," Blythe added.

I nodded, thinking of the harsh winds that sometimes kicked off the sea, how she'd had no food or water since yesterday morning, and how she was blindly trying to find her way back home in the dark. Add the Forest to the equation, and it seemed all but impossible for her to succeed.

"Good point." I supposed that solved a problem for me. It was likely she'd have to die. Now if she died, it wouldn't be by my hand.

"After I inspected the cell, I went straight to tell Kawan. He wasn't pleased at being woken so early. Once I explained the situation, he went and got properly dressed, and we came to you."

I thought the timeline over, trying to remember when I'd left the girl last night. At best, she'd had a six-hour head start.

"Do we know if she got a horse?"

"No."

"Wait," I said, stopping just before the mess hall. "Why were you in the dungeons?"

A flicker of something passed across her eyes so quickly I could not name it. "I was looking for you. I wanted to see how the interrogations were going."

I sensed this was a lie, but I couldn't call her on it.

"There are animals out there," I thought aloud. "The terrain is treacherous. She had no supplies, hardly any clothes, and no clue where she was. In all likelihood, she's dead."

"Probably."

"But we have to search for her, or Kawan will hold it over me."

"Absolutely."

I huffed and went into the mess hall. "Inigo! Griffin!"

I didn't wait to see if they followed; I knew they would. I marched out to the side of the castle with the overhang that we used for stables. From here on out, I would be keeping count of horses.

I grabbed a waterskin for myself and tossed one to Blythe. By the time I had, Griffin and Inigo were running up behind us, wordlessly going for horses. We mounted up, and I started heading west. If she had even the slightest bit of sense, she would have headed for the tree line, so I chased.

ANNIKA

The sun was up, and I was without cover. My riding boots were not made for running, and I could feel blisters opening on my feet. My fingers were still stinging from the cold of night, and it was almost impossible to close them into fists without the pain blinding me. I hadn't seen anything that looked like civilization since I'd left the broken-down castle, so I had no way of asking for help.

Based on the sun, I was heading west, but that was all I had to go on. And as I came upon that awful forest, the sun was going to be of little help to me. It was getting harder to think clearly. I'd been riding on the rush of my escape for hours, but now all I could think of were the dead soldiers left to the elements, the fact that I hadn't come home like I'd promised. My father hadn't wanted to let me out of his sight, and, even at his worst, he must be worried. And I'd been so close to my mother and had to leave her behind. These thoughts ran through my mind over and over, though they were eventually joined by the practical things. Pain, hunger, exhaustion.

As I entered the thick forest, I told myself it didn't matter; all I needed was to get as far away from Lennox as possible. It seemed I'd been brought there to die, and Lennox was the one charged with the task—though he hadn't seemed to want the job. Not even when I made him angry. I shook my head. I would not sympathize with the man who took my mother from this earth.

Moving my head like that made me dizzy, and I had to lean against a tree. A branch scratched my arm, and I gasped, surprised I could even feel it at this point.

It was then that I heard the horses.

I looked behind me, and, in the distance, saw four riders. I could recognize Lennox instantly from his cape. I'd failed. I hadn't moved quickly enough.

The tree I'd stopped against was hollowed on one side, and all I could do now was crawl into the open space and hide. It offered no cover if anyone came in front of me, but it was all I had. There were only four of them, and they didn't know where I was. I told myself there was a chance they'd go past me.

I worked on slowing my breathing and pulled myself in tight, standing with my arms braced inside the hollowed-out trunk.

Don't move, don't move, don't move.

"Spread out."

I tensed up at the sound of his voice. He was startlingly close.

"The three of you, widen your search to the south. It's quite likely she's collapsed out here somewhere."

"Yes, sir," they replied, and I listened intently to the sound of three horses branching off.

I waited to hear him moving, too, but for a long time, there was nothing. But then I heard the sound of a horse taking a step, and another, and I knew he was still nearby, sweeping the grounds.

My heart was thundering in my ears.

After a few tense minutes, I saw him. He was atop the same horse from yesterday, a dark, fearsome thing. His eyes were sunk into the familiar scowl, and I saw his cheek had a raised red mark on it, similar to the one I could still feel on mine. He sighed, raking his gloved hands through his black hair, and stopped.

He seemed weary. Not weary with any kind of physical weakness . . . but as if he needed the kind of rest that sleep cannot give.

He suddenly looked up, like he heard something, even though I hadn't made a sound. With a hint of a question in his eyes, he tipped his head over his shoulder . . . and he saw me.

So this was it.

He slowly trotted over, his face empty of the victory I expected to see there. I didn't know what I thought might happen, but he simply stared at me for a moment. I was humiliated to realize I was in my shift and stays and little else, covered from head to toe in mud. This wasn't the dignified ending I'd hoped for.

I waited for him to pounce, but he simply looked at me. Then he reached down to the pocket attached to his belt and threw something at me. "Catch," he said quietly.

I instinctively put out my hands just before it hit the ground. I inspected the little rectangle in my palm. It looked like seeds pressed in molasses and wrapped in paper.

He pulled the skin of water off his saddle, took a massive swig, and dropped it on the ground.

"Oops."

He then reached up and pulled the cord that held his cape in place. The weight of it made it drop to the forest floor.

"Do not move," he instructed. "Once they finish their search, I will draw them back across the field behind you, keeping them south. When you can no longer hear the horses, and *only then*, go that way." He pointed in the direction I'd been heading originally. "The cape is thick enough to keep the thorns at bay. Before you get home, dispose of both it and the waterskin. The last time you saw me was when I left you in the dungeon. Is that clear?"

I'm sure I was still squinting at him as he said all this, my confusion obvious.

"The next time our paths cross, I will not be this lenient. When we come for our kingdom, Annika, you will die."

I lifted my head. "I appreciate the warning. Know I have no intention of sparing you, either, Lennox."

The corner of his lips lifted into a trace of a smile.

"Duly noted. Until then." He tipped his head at me, as if he were a gentleman.

I left his cape where it was for now, but the waterskin was close enough for me to stretch out and grab, so I did. I didn't care that his mouth had been on it, I put the thing to my lips and guzzled, desperate for something to drink. I came up from it gasping, looking out to make sure none of them had come back my way.

I looked down at the bar of food and decided to chance a bite, thrilled to find it was crunchy and sweet. I nearly sighed out loud it tasted so good. I took another bite and realized there was something familiar in it. Cinnamon.

I smiled to myself, quieting down and settling in to wait.

LENNOX

"No sign of her," Blythe admitted, her tone conveying her frustration.

"And you?" I asked Inigo and Griffin.

"Nothing," Inigo added dejectedly as Griffin simply shook his head.

"Any sign of an animal?" I asked.

"No," Inigo began, "but that doesn't mean one didn't get her. It's unlikely that she could have made it through that forest on her own."

I nodded in agreement. "That's it, then," I said. "Back to the castle. I will take responsibility. She was lost on my watch, and you all searched tirelessly. The blame is fully mine, and I will accept it."

"We can stand with you," Inigo offered. "At the very least, present a united front. Not your fault that girl is sneaky."

For the second time today, I nearly smiled.

"I appreciate the offer. Truly. But she was under my guard, so it falls to me. Let's get going. And drink carefully,"

I added. "My water fell off somewhere."

"Do you want to look for it?" Blythe asked.

I shook my head. "No. I want to get back to the castle and get this over with. Let's move."

I pushed through the forest quickly, keeping them to the south as I had promised. Once we broke through and cleared the field, I stopped at the edge of a bank of trees.

"Something's wrong with my saddle," I called. "Keep going, I'll be right there."

I hopped off, looking at the forest in the distance, squinting. After a moment, I saw a flash of black whip between the trees, heading southwest. Well, what do you know? She could take orders.

I reached up to the neighboring tree and snapped off a thin, low-lying branch. I was sure her mother would be interested in hearing all about this.

Kawan drummed his fingers across the arm of his chair. I imagined he liked to think of it as a throne, but it was really just the oldest, biggest chair in the castle. And this was no throne room, no ballroom. It was a mess hall. "So, she's gone?"

"We couldn't find a trace of her," I lied. I kept my tone calm and clear, projecting it as if I didn't care who in the room heard. "Based on the timing, we ought to have crossed paths. If she wasn't there, she's lost or dead."

He lifted the hand that had been doing all the drumming into the air. "But we have no body? Nothing to send back to their wretched king?"

"No, we do not. *I* do not. The blame is mine."

He stood, eyes narrowed, and took four steps to close the space between us. "I'm dying to know, Lennox. What exactly did you achieve from this mission?"

"We have learned that we can decimate their family," I insisted. "Surely now we can—"

Kawan pulled his hand back and slapped me across the same cheek he had this morning, only much more forcefully.

"You have exposed us! Your father at least was *alone*. As was our man who abducted their queen. *You* took a team and brought her to my castle! You have given away our position and our numbers in one spectacular moment of idiocy! It's possible that all our efforts are for naught now. Do you want to get your land back or not, son?"

I clenched my fist. In my periphery I saw my mother sit upright on her seat, knowing Kawan had gone too far.

"I am not your son," I muttered, my icy glare digging into his. "I will be your soldier. I will be the hands that get bloody so yours don't. I will be the leader of whatever mission you choose. But I will never, *ever* be your son."

He narrowed his eyes, daring me to challenge him again. "Everything here is mine. It would be wise of you to remember that."

Perhaps I should have held my tongue. But being unnecessarily humbled by Kawan twice in one day was a little too much for me.

"It's funny. You say everything is yours. When will the *work* be yours? I'm the one who keeps your army in line. I was the only one with enough guts to kill a queen. I'd love to know how you can possibly claim anything here as yours."

Never a man for words, he rounded quickly and punched me square in the nose, and I stumbled backward into Inigo's waiting arms.

"If you don't want to find yourself at the end of my sword," he snapped, "you will learn your place and stay there."

My place. For years now, my place had been filling the gaps where his cowardice would not reach.

My eyes went over to my mother. If she was sad to see her son bleeding, she hid it well.

"Get out of my sight," Kawan spat.

"Happily."

I shrugged myself out of Inigo's arms and moved from the room, head high and blood trickling down my neck. I stormed around the corner, unaware that Inigo, Blythe, and Griffin were on my heels.

"Here," Inigo said.

I turned, and he was holding out a handkerchief. Typically, I wouldn't have bothered, but it felt like a lot of blood.

"Thank you. And thanks for catching me." I held the cloth up to my nose and looked to the three of them. "You didn't have to stand behind me, and you didn't have to follow me out. He hates me, always has. If you stay too close, you will eventually feel his wrath."

"I think everyone gets a dose of it anyway," Griffin observed.

I gave a short chuckle, which hurt to do. "I'm sure I'll be given another task soon to make up for this failure. And it will be even more dangerous than this one, since he'd just as soon see me die as succeed. If you would rather not go, say so now."

"I'm in." Inigo crossed his arms, deciding right away.

"I'll speak for Andre and Sherwin. We'll all go," Griffin claimed.

I looked to Blythe.

"You already know."

For the first time in years I wasn't alone. Part of me was terrified by the idea, by the possibility of being known. But war was on the horizon now—with my missteps exposing us, it had to be—and if we were going to make it, I was going to have to depend on someone.

"Thank you," I said. And I took their cautious smiles as an informal agreement.

We had a team.

ANNIKA

As I drained the last of the water into my mouth, I thought of home. Though he was the person I wanted to see the least, my mind kept going to Nickolas.

He didn't even check over his shoulder for me.

I thought of our argument, of his refusal to give me time alone as newlyweds. I wasn't sure what to say to him once we met again. And even if I had words, could I say them? Our engagement was public now. It all made me feel a little bit helpless.

You just escaped your captors, Annika. You kept your cool. You broke out of a dungeon and walked through a forest your father thought was impenetrable. You somehow convinced the man who killed your mother to let you live. You are not helpless.

I stopped for a moment, standing still in a field. It was true. I'd just survived something even Escalus would have struggled with. I'd made it.

I flipped Lennox's cape behind my shoulders so it lifted in the breeze, and I pulled my exhausted, broken body taller. I was not helpless.

Encouraged, I moved forward, knowing that, no matter how long it took, I was going to make it home. As I marched, I saw, breaking over the horizon, something that looked like an army. It was a line of horses, maybe forty across and I couldn't see how deep. The sun was still high enough that I could make out the pale green of a Kadierian flag being held by the flag-bearer to the left of my father, whose crown glittered in the fading day. To his right was Escalus. And to Escalus's right, I could make out the prim figure of Nickolas.

"Escalus!" I screamed, running with all I had, my voice breaking in relief. "Escalus!"

"Halt," someone called, and the entire company stilled.

"Annika!" Escalus called, dismounting and charging toward me through the tall grass. Behind him, the entirety of the men they'd brought began cheering; their princess was safe.

I couldn't help myself; I started weeping. I could hardly move anymore, but it didn't matter. Escalus was coming to me, and all would be well now.

He crashed into me with tears in his eyes, holding on tightly, and I didn't even mind the pain. "Annika, what are you doing here?"

"What am I doing here? What are *you* doing here?"

He laughed. "Coming to rescue you, of course. Blindly heading east and praying we found you."

Tears streamed as I smiled and smiled. "It's all right. I rescued myself."

"Ha!" he called, lifting me into his arms and spinning me around. "I can't believe it. I was so afraid we'd lost you."

"You very nearly did. I have so much to tell you."

But before I could, Father and Nickolas approached.

My father looked into my eyes, and for one beautiful second, I thought he might say everything I'd been aching to hear. *Forgive me*, or *Marry who you'd like*, or *I love you.* But my father was still the king, and his mind went to matters of state.

"What do you need to tell us?" he asked, looking me over and realizing I was in my underclothes and mud.

"I met Jago's son," I told him. "There is an army out there, Father. You were right; Jago wasn't working alone. But it isn't a neighboring country waiting for us; it's something much worse. A war is coming, and we need to prepare for it."

"Are you sure?" Nickolas asked.

"Oh, look who's awake," I snapped. "Thank you so much for watching out for me in the forest."

"Annika," Father said, his tone a warning. "Without Nickolas we'd have had no idea what happened to you."

"I'll tell you what happened to me," I said, staring into my father's cold eyes. "I was left alone in the hands of a murderer."

Father huffed. "Then you won't go riding anymore."

I rolled my eyes. "That is not the answer."

"Perhaps not, but neither is scolding your fiancé."

"Enough. We need to get home," Escalus said, ever the voice of reason. "Annika, you'll ride with me."

Father went ahead, calling to the men of our preemptive victory. They cheered and sang, lifting their swords up and down in time with their song.

"Should we send the men ahead?" Nickolas asked. "After all, she's hardly dressed."

Escalus looked at my unfortunate fiancé and spoke on my behalf. "Dear Nickolas, do shut up."

Part II

At the same moment that Lennox rolled over uneasily on his thin mattress, the wisps of fabric around Annika's four-poster bed billowed in the early-morning breeze. The weather was turning. Lennox, used to harsh winds, wasn't too bothered, but Annika, whose window had been mistakenly left open, was starting to tremble.

The chilly air soaked into her skin, finally waking her, and she sat up for a moment, scanning her room with careful eyes. She'd never cared for the cold, but now it had a new effect on her. Any chill dragged her back to the dungeon of Vosino Castle. She was capable of more than anyone had guessed, though that didn't mean all her fears had been erased. They floated through her head as she lay back down, waiting for the sun to come and warm her.

Lennox, however, was already watching the sun creep over the horizon, the fog of ocean spray keeping it from being too bright. As he had every day since Annika's escape, he pictured her cornered in the woods, crouched and ready to strike. He thought that, even with her uncanny likeness to her mother, he hadn't been able to predict her moves, or guess what she was capable of.

He went over to his desk and pulled out the lock of ash-brown hair. Talking with her, even arguing with her, left him feeling seen in ways no one else in his life had managed. He still wasn't sure what to make of it. Her people were responsible for the loss of his father and the fracturing of his family, and one day his army would march upon their lands.

But she liked Cassiopeia. She held a sword. And her hair, he remembered, smelled of rosewater.

He didn't want to destroy her. But he would.

Meanwhile, Annika sat up in bed again, sighing. Creeping over to the window, she closed the panes quietly, securing them with the lock. She still shivered, and, though there were plenty of blankets, she crept down to the chest at the foot of her bed.

On top of childhood dresses and her mother's sketches was a jet-black cape with two long ties. She pulled it out and wrapped it around herself, using it to shield her body from the cold. Though Lennox had been her captor, he had also been unexpectedly generous. He could have killed her.

But he hadn't.

He said he would come for his kingdom, but what did that even mean? This palace was hers, had always been. She drew the cape closer. If she inhaled, she could smell something like the ocean on it.

He'd saved her. He'd clothed her. In a strange way, he'd shown more concern for her than her own fiancé had.

But he'd taken her mother. And if he marched on Kadier, she would fight him. For everything she ever loved, she'd have to end him.

Annika and Lennox both held the things they'd taken from the other, knowing the next time they met, one of them would die.

ANNIKA

After escaping from Lennox, I'd stayed in my room for an entire week. I had a large cut and a few scrapes that needed to heal—and so many things to think through away from prying eyes.

I'd been making peace with my mother's death. There was a sense of closure in knowing for certain, and, while I suspected we'd never recover her body, I was going to push for a proper funeral as soon as we were able.

The bigger issue at hand was that there was an army out there, poised to invade. The number of guards around the palace was increased. And not just here, but at the border as well. Should they come, we were as prepared as we could be.

But for me personally, the most important thing was that I'd made a decision. This time I would not relent.

I had a clear understanding of just what I meant to my people. When I returned from what seemed like certain death, I'd been gifted six horses, exotic foods, and so many flowers I'd never need to leave my room to walk in a garden again. And the letters! I read them all, each one full of praise, some of them tearstained from their joy and concern over my life.

I'd spent so much time worrying about my people, caring about them. Now I knew it was fully reciprocated.

"That's perfect, Noemi," I said, admiring myself in the mirror.

"Won't he be angry, my lady?" she asked, placing the simple crown on my head.

"That's kind of the point." I turned, sweeping long locks of hair over my shoulder. It was a simple statement, but an obvious one.

"He *was* knocked unconscious," she pointed out, though not very assertively.

I shook my head. "It wasn't that," I assured her. Every minute of my kidnapping was a crystal clear memory. The pain of the sword as Lennox cut my arm, the heartbreak when my guards sacrificed themselves rather than allow themselves to be used by their enemy, the hint of a smirk on Lennox's face when he found me in the woods. I couldn't forget it if I wanted to. And I knew that I could never respect Nickolas.

"If being knocked out was his only crime, then I'd be in the wrong. But he didn't even look back at me when they first appeared. He ran away and left me to follow. Any decent gentleman would have at least glanced over his shoulder, regardless of rank. I don't think there's any way to escape this marriage, but he has forfeited the right to control me."

She sighed, clasping her hands. "For someone who has noble blood, his behavior was a bit shocking. Your brother would never do such a thing."

I sighed. "Noble blood or not, he shouldn't have done it. And you're right, Escalus would have died before he let me be captured." I turned to stare out the window.

"Is it just his behavior that has you upset, my lady? You look sad." Noemi's hands moved up, still clasped but below her chin.

"I am, I suppose."

She bridged the space between us, whispering when she spoke. "You met the man who killed your mother. You watched your countrymen die. You were interrogated. You escaped from a dungeon, and then you ran home on foot. I know many grown men who'd have failed in your shoes; it's all right to be sad or angry or anything else you might feel."

"It's not all that," I confessed.

"What, then?"

I closed my eyes, remembering the change in his tone after his questions and threats had ended. "He asked me about my favorite constellation. The boy who captured me. And then I asked him his."

Noemi's eyes widened. "How could you even speak to him?"

I nodded. "I know, I know. And that's what bothers me. I know things about this person now—that he is a person at all. Now I know that he has been forced into a box of his own. You should have heard how he spoke about stars, the way he used his words in general. I know he has blue eyes in a shade somewhere between ice and sky." I swallowed hard. "But he killed my mother. He wants my home and my father's crown and everything I've spent my life serving."

Her eyes were sympathetic. "He cannot be allowed that."

I shook my head, staring blankly ahead. "He won't. I'm willing to marry Nickolas for the sake of my country, for the sake of my brother's future. And now, I'll fight off Lennox for the same reasons."

She shivered. "As many times as you've said it, it's hard to believe he's real and has a name."

"Oh, he very much does," I said, shrugging into my dress for the day. I couldn't tell her—or anyone—that his name had been echoing in my head since I'd heard it, sometimes in fear, sometimes in anger, and, most horrifyingly, sometimes in gratitude.

I swept into the dining room with my head high. I didn't often wear my crown, but today it felt fitting. The men in my life were already seated at the head table. Father, of course, sat center in his high-backed chair, surveying his food as if it had somehow offended him.

To his left, my beloved brother, Escalus. His eyes were shining, his smile welcoming, and his demeanor everything I should have been able to expect from my father.

To my father's right was an empty seat for me, and beside that was dear old Nickolas. All angles and lines, he looked sullen as he chomped on his food. It was mid-bite that he looked up and noticed me striding across the room with my hair flowing behind me, my eyes locked on his, daring him to object.

"Good morning, brother," I said as I rounded the table,

and then I even bent down to kiss my father's cheek. He was as surprised by the action as I was, looking at me with a perplexed scowl.

I spooned food onto my plate and settled into my place. It took several moments before my fiancé was brave enough to speak.

"It's very nice to see you up and about again," he ventured tentatively.

I smiled but didn't speak. I'd barred everyone but Escalus and the doctor from my room. If Father came by, no one said so, but Nickolas came thrice and was firmly turned away by Noemi.

"My pet, I do not wish to start an argument our first morning back together, but I do expect you to put your hair up after breakfast," he whispered, trying to make it sound like a gentle request. Unfortunately for him, not even that would work on me now.

I turned slowly, staring at him with chilly eyes, and he was smart enough to lean away.

"First of all, if you ever call me 'my pet' again, I will shove a fork down your throat. Second, I never agreed to put my hair up. You demanded it, and I felt I had to follow, but now more than ever, I want to look like my mother. You will not take that from me. And third, how fascinating that you still think you can tell me to do anything."

He balked, looking at me as if I'd just branded him with a hot poker. Which I was considering if he said anything else foolish.

Father shook his head. "Such childish behavior," he

complained. "Your mother—"

"Mother would have agreed with me," I shot back quickly and with finality. "And if you had spoken to me in such a manner on the topic in her presence, she would have been ashamed of you." This wounded him. I could see that. "And she never would have put me in a position where I was dependent upon such a person in the first place."

He looked at me, measuring my resolve.

"Don't force my hand, Annika," he warned. "It won't be pretty."

"As if the last time was?" I lowered my voice, leaning in.

I saw his jaw tense.

"I am not attempting to back out of my engagement. Our people will need stability now more than ever. But you, sir," I said, turning to Nickolas, "should not anticipate being allowed in my presence more than once or twice preceding our wedding, which will happen when I am ready to schedule it. And after we are married, expect to keep your distance. You may take my freedom, but you will not be permitted to touch my joy."

I stood, not finished with my breakfast but not willing to linger, and marched from the room. I felt the way my hand clasped the edge of my dress to sweep it behind me, and I remembered my mother doing the exact same thing. And I thought, *I am hers.*

LENNOX

After my monstrous mistake of letting Annika escape, new tasks were added to our daily routines. Though everyone had hoped she'd died out there, Kawan wasn't in the mood to take chances. To that end, patrols of the castle and the far perimeter of what we would call our grounds were mandatory at all times.

"Thank you for letting me come with you," Blythe said. Again.

"It's really no problem. Patrols should always be done in pairs."

"I know . . . I just appreciate it."

We were patrolling now, staying to the edge of the woods, surveying out as far as we could see. It was harder at night, more dangerous. I was debating spending the evening out here whether it was needed or not. Sleep was an elusive creature lately.

"Lennox?"

"Yes?"

"What are we doing out here?"

I finally moved my eyes from the horizon to her. "Patrolling?"

"No," she said. "I mean, we train, and we wait . . . But do you ever wonder if that land is even worth fighting for?"

I narrowed my eyes, hearing Annika's assertion that I'd been misled echoing in my head. My father had told me some of our history, and Kawan had filled in the gaps when he marched up to our house, saying our surname like a prayer. So much of what he and my father had discussed across our table lined up: the word *Dahrain*, the stories of the wars, the names of the other now-extinct clans. We didn't have to live on the outskirts of other people's land, he told us. We could go get our own one day.

"I just want to get our kingdom back," I said. "That's all I've ever wanted: a place that was truly mine."

She seemed to ponder this as we continued our slow ride. "Can I ask a silly question?"

"Sure."

"Why not here?"

"What?"

She gestured to the land behind us, the abandoned broken-down castle in the distance.

"Why couldn't we make this home? We're already here. We know the land, we know how to work it. We have resources . . . why not just start building real homes here?"

I stared at it, the place we were hiding. It was where I'd become the man I was, where I'd found Thistle, where I'd made the few friends I had. I had a corner of it all to myself, and I could make ends meet here if forced. It wasn't as if it contained no comfort to me at all, but still . . .

"I can't give up on Dahrain. And if I can't be there, I'm not sure I could stay here if Kawan did. I'd find another patch of unwanted land and make it my own if I absolutely couldn't go home."

"Just head off on your own and build a country?" she asked, her tone skeptical.

"Nah," I replied, smiling at her boldness. "Just a house. A real house. Not something for an army, something for a family."

Our eyes met.

"With anyone in particular?" she asked.

"Blythe."

"For instance, what about that girl?" she asked in a measured tone.

That girl.

There were hundreds of women in the castle; she could have meant anyone. But I knew she was talking about Annika.

"You were almost . . . gentle with her," she continued. "You're not like that with anyone."

"That girl is the embodiment of everything I hate in the world," I said firmly. "So if you're going to spend your time being jealous, I'd choose a better subject."

Blythe seemed mollified by that, and she turned her attention to the horizon again. Less than a minute had passed when she held an arm up. "Over there," she whispered.

I followed her gaze and saw three figures walking across the western field. Men. Wide shoulders and narrow waists.

Not running, so they were neither in danger nor desperate. Sacks across their backs, so they weren't in need. Clad in the same pale green as the guards who'd been riding with Annika.

"Kadierian soldiers?" Blythe asked quietly.

I nodded. "If they're on a mission to find us, that means there will certainly be more soon. If we lie low, they might turn back; it's possible they don't know what they're looking for."

"But if they do . . . ," she whispered, reading my thoughts.

I unsheathed my sword as Blythe loaded her bow.

I dug my heels into my horse, and we were off.

They were aware of us almost instantly, looking up with horror-struck faces. I wondered whether they would draw swords of their own, or turn and run. But neither happened. As we approached, all three dropped to their knees, and the one on the left pulled a white scrap of fabric out of his pocket, holding it high in the air.

"Mercy!" he called.

I held out a hand, though Blythe was already pulling to a halt.

"We come in peace," he assured us. "Our princess returned and told us all—"

"She lived?!" Blythe interrupted incredulously.

The man nodded. "She explained everything. Jago, Queen Evelina, the history of our peoples. King Theron wants to make peace."

"That's right," the middle one said. He was skittish, eyes darting between us, his hands near his chin like a rat.

"Peace?" Blythe asked. "How?"

The one who spoke first cleared his throat. "He proposes a meeting on neutral land. There's an island off the coast of Kadier," he began, fumbling as he tried to open a map. "Come and talk with him. He means to open trading, give gifts." He held up a parcel of papers.

I looked upon the meeting with a measure of skepticism. Could there truly be any peace between us? After everything that had happened? It was recognition at least, respect.

Still, I wasn't keen on trusting any of them.

"You're lying," I insisted. "You're lying *and* intruding. I will send you back to your king in a box."

"No, no, no!" he cried out. "It's true. Look. We have our knives for hunting. Otherwise, we're unarmed. We only came to deliver our message and point you to the Island," he assured me. "Take us in so that we can explain everything in full."

Nothing about this felt right. It was too easy.

But I wasn't in charge.

"Drop your weapons," I commanded. They each pulled out a short hunting knife and threw it to the ground. "Take off your supplies as well."

I dismounted, coming up to the man with the flag. "Arms out, all of you. We'll tell your tale to our leader. He will decide your fate."

ANNIKA

I strode into the royal library, feeling new. Rhett wasn't at the front desk, so I wove through the shelves, listening for a sign of him. It took a moment, but toward the far back of the room, I heard the shhh of books being slid into place. I peeked around a corner, and there he was.

Rhett stood, squinting at the names on the spines of the books, double-checking that everything was placed correctly. His passion for his work was so admirable. It struck me then that he'd never done anything without an urgency or a drive, without that passion.

He looked up, catching me watching him. In an uncharacteristic move, he shoved the books on an empty portion of a shelf, running to me, his eyes painted with worry. He threw his arms around me and spoke in a rush.

"Oh, Annika." In saying my name alone, I could hear the ache, the longing. He pulled back, looking me in the eyes, his hand cupping my cheek. "I can't believe you escaped. How are you feeling?"

That was the question, wasn't it? I still couldn't quite explain it all. I felt both thrilled and exhausted, proud and defeated, thankful and disappointed.

"It's hard to say," I admitted. "I'm assuming you heard about my mother."

He nodded. "And you looked the murderer in the eye?"

"I did."

"I think I would have tried to murder him myself if it had been me," he grumbled.

I laughed humorlessly. "Well, I suggested his giving me a sword again and letting me have a chance, but he refused. I wasn't in a position to negotiate for better."

"And still you escaped," Rhett said, his voice moving from anger to awe.

"Yes. And now that I'm feeling better, I have some research to do."

He perked up at that. "You came to the right place. What can I do for you?"

"I want the trial notes for when Jago was in court," I told him. "I want to read through the evidence and sentencing. After meeting his son, I feel like I need to know more about what happened."

Rhett nodded, considering this. "Very well, then. This way. Court documents are in the history section." We started walking, and I noticed him fidgeting with his fingers. "Did you happen to get my letters?"

"I did." I ducked my head, thinking of his notes. Vague as they were, I could read the longing in them.

"I didn't dare put anything in writing," he whispered,

even though we were alone, "but after hearing Nickolas made it back without you, I wanted another opportunity to offer my hand."

"Rhett . . . I . . ."

He smiled back at me. "I know you're going to reject me. But save it for a few minutes so I can pretend we stood a chance for just a moment longer."

His eyes were so sad, the color of hopes being dashed. I took his hand. "Then let me say this instead: Thank you. You saved my life, Rhett."

His forehead knit into ridges as he stared at me, confused.

"When they took me from the woods, they bound my hands with rope, but when I was left in the dungeon, they put me in proper shackles. I couldn't have gotten out of those if you hadn't taught me. You got me out of that dungeon as if you'd been right there beside me."

His eyes were so soft, so hopeful. "Really?"

"Absolutely."

After a moment of hesitation, he closed the distance between us, moving as if to kiss me.

"Rhett," I whispered, and he stopped, swallowing, his face mere inches from mine as he spoke.

"Sorry. I was . . . moved by your words."

"Rhett, you're my closest friend. And I treasure you, but I'm marrying someone else. So, if you cannot keep from kissing me, I'll be forced to maintain my distance in the future."

He looked at me, his eyes disappointed. "After everything that happened? Didn't he abandon you?"

I nodded. "I don't love him. I don't even respect him. If

I were free, I would never ever allow myself to be linked to a man like that. Marrying Nickolas, for me, will simply be signing a contract." I shrugged. "But there's nothing I can do about it. An army might be coming any minute now. And even if they don't come for years, when they arrive, I want them to come upon a united front. This is the best thing I can do for my people."

He stared at me in hushed awe. "I wish I was half as good as you. I can't think of much I'd be willing to sacrifice my whole life for."

I smiled. "Then do me the kindness of keeping this library well. I might not be able to keep up sword fighting, so it may be my only refuge in the future."

Rhett huffed, looking up to reach the book I needed. "If protecting this library is the only way I can love you, then I'll guard it with my life."

LENNOX

"Tell me again exactly what they said," Kawan ordered for the tenth time.

We were in a small room, discussing the arrival of our unexpected guests. My mother was there, along with Aldrik, Slone, Illio, and Maston.

"It's as I said before," I answered evenly. "They surrendered their weapons and delivered the message that King Theron has invited us to a summit on some island. Beyond this, I know nothing."

Kawan turned to Blythe. "There was no fight in them," she said, "not even when we locked them in their cells."

"Which have guards this time, I presume?" he asked, glowering at me.

"Naturally."

He leaned back and huffed, scratching his unkempt beard with his thick fingers. After a moment, he started howling with laughter, throwing his head back and slapping a hand on the table in front of him.

"Imagine that," he said. "Had I known it'd be that easy to get them to roll over, I'd have taken their princess ages ago."

"But that's the thing," I said. "We took their *queen* ages ago. No one came to seek us out then."

"Given how uncoordinated that move was, they must have thought it an isolated incident. Now they know people are coming for them, and this is a means to an end."

It didn't make sense to me. There had been three years for them to find out we'd been behind the attack. What's more, if we killed their queen and kidnapped their princess, why would they offer us peace? I didn't trust any of this. But I could speak of my distrust all day long, and it would change nothing in the eyes of Kawan.

"How do you want to proceed?" I asked.

"The first step is questioning," he said decisively. "Separate them. Ask them the same questions. Aim to find what's consistent in their statements. They don't eat or sleep until we have our answers." He paused for a minute. "And see if you can weed out the weakest one."

"For any specific purpose?" I asked.

"I haven't decided yet."

I nodded. "Might I suggest sending Blythe in for the first round?"

He looked at me with skeptical eyes. "Why?"

"You should have seen her riding with her bow and arrow. They weren't half as stricken by me as they were by her. And I think it might put them off to be questioned by a woman."

Kawan looked between the two of us. "Very well. I want information. Numbers, size of their army. I don't want peace,

I want all of it. I want to tear every single brick of their castle down." The last of his words came out in a low growl.

"Yes, sir." I turned to leave, and Blythe followed.

"Should I go straight into an interrogation?" she asked when we were out of earshot.

"I think you might need different strategies for each. The one carrying the flag would probably answer anything you asked. The one in the middle, though?"

She sighed. "He was so panicky. Maybe try to talk first? Have a conversation?"

I nodded. "That's a good idea. I think he may be the weak link of the three, but I could be wrong."

"I'll do my best," she assured me.

I reached up, placing a hand on her shoulder. "I know you will." Her eyes went wide, and I cleared my throat as I pulled my hand back. "I'm going to see if I can scrounge up some paper." Annika had pointed out our lack of a library, and while I was honored by my oral history, I knew there was also strength in the written word.

I marched to my room. In the back of my desk was my very small pile of carefully guarded blank sheets. I grabbed a few, along with one of my oblique pens. The ink was going to be another problem. I opened the jars and saw dried, powdery clumps at the bottom. I hoped that some water would bring the ink back to life. I tucked the paper and pen away and clutched a jar securely in my palm, then rushed back to Blythe.

I could hear her voice from the hallway in the dungeons, coaxing Skittish into speaking. I found two stools and set them side by side to make a desk. There was some stale water in a nearby bucket, and I dipped my fingers in it, letting the droplets run from my fingers into my dried ink.

I really hoped this would work.

We'd divided the men into separate branches of the dungeon, the idea being that if they wanted to communicate, they'd have to call out, and we'd hear it all. This meant that, from my location, I could hear Blythe's conversation, even though I couldn't see her.

"I know," Blythe said sweetly. "We crossed that terrain recently as well. Not all the way to Kadier I don't think, but I understand what you've been through."

"I hate that trek. And I hate this cell. We already told you we're here peacefully. Why are we locked up? Why did you separate me from my friends?"

"We need to talk to each of you, that's all. And you're down here for your own safety. We don't know how you'll be greeted upstairs, so we ask for your patience."

"Huh." He seemed satisfied with that.

"I'll do what I can to make you more comfortable, but I can't promise much. We live lean lives."

"Life in the barracks isn't much better."

I could almost see Blythe sympathetically tilting her head, a smile in her eyes as she asked her next question. "Is your king stingy with his soldiers? And after all the work you do!"

"He's been on edge in the years since his wife went missing, constant patrols. Do you know how many miles I walk in a week? Not enough for the pay, I'll tell you that."

"That's so sad," Blythe commented. "Does he keep a lot

of troops in the palace, then?"

"Yes, but the majority are positioned around the far edge of the grounds. He doesn't want unwelcome guests getting too close."

"I understand. We've been keeping an eye out for company ourselves," Blythe replied.

There was a moment of silence, and I wondered just what was happening.

"You don't have to worry about a thing," Skittish responded in a low voice. "You've got him scared."

"What do you mean?" Blythe matched his tone.

"He holds everything with a tight fist. His children, his crown, his kingdom. If he's willing to talk, you've spooked him."

There was another beat of silence. I could tell that Blythe was doing the exact same thing I was: reveling in the thought of an intimidated king.

"Thank you," she told him. "I'll be back with more information soon."

I listened as she opened and closed the lock. I poked my head around the corner, and I saw in her eyes the hope I felt in my chest. She hurried over to me, speaking in a whisper.

"Did you hear that?"

"I did," I confirmed, wearing possibly the brightest smile I had in a decade. "I was skeptical, but he sounds like he's telling the truth."

"Lennox, if it is true, there's a chance it could be . . ."

"Bloodless."

She nodded.

"We need to keep a record of everything they're saying." I dipped my pen into the ink and drew a test line at the top. It was a little thick, but it would work. I went to pass the pen to Blythe, but she blushed and dropped her head.

"I don't know how," she whispered.

I could see the admission was upsetting for her, so I said no more.

"That's all right. I know." I felt a little embarrassed. This was twice now that the issue had come up, and it was becoming awkward being the only one who could read. Then again, until recently, there hadn't been much use. "When we come into our kingdom, you will have so much free time, you'll laze your afternoons away reading," I told her. "I'll teach you when we get to Dahrain."

"Really?" she asked with a smile.

"Of course. Now, let's get this down before we forget."

ANNIKA

A letter from Nickolas was waiting in the morning.

"It looks like the duke slipped it under the door in the night," Noemi said.

I narrowed my eyes. "That seems awfully romantic, for him."

She chuckled. "A desperate man gets sentimental rather quickly. He might care more than you guessed."

"He wants to see me," I announced after skimming over the note.

"I'd imagine so. Will you give him an audience?" Noemi pulled out three dresses, laying them across the back of my couch for me to make my choice. Was it cruel that I wanted to wear something that would break his heart?

"I already told him he wouldn't see me alone until the wedding. We'll be together at breakfast, and that will be quite enough for one day." I slipped the note into its envelope and hopped up from bed. "I think the pink flowers today."

"Excellent choice. That's one of my favorites on—" She stopped abruptly.

I turned and saw that Noemi was staring out the window, her focus stolen for the moment.

"Are you all right?" I asked. As I came to the window, I saw exactly what was holding her attention.

Hundreds of soldiers were in the far field going through drills. It wasn't unheard of for them to train on palace grounds, but it wasn't common.

"What do you think that's about?" she asked.

I sighed. "If they're training here, they must be specifically meant for the palace."

"Do you think? That many?"

I shrugged. "For the rotations that the entire grounds require, and to keep them from getting tired, they might need that many. And with how on edge Father has been, it wouldn't surprise me if he also doubled the guards around both Escalus and me."

She nodded. "Then we shall make this room an oasis," she said, almost to herself. Her eyes were still on the horizon, but mine were on her. It meant the world that, in the midst of everything, her thoughts were on making every situation better for me.

After lacing up my stays and securing my dress, Noemi moved on to my hair. She pulled the front pieces back, leaving the rest down. As I toyed with a lock of it, I thought of my mother. I always would when I did my hair now. I pulled a flower from one of the vases, cutting the stem so it was short enough to tuck behind my ear.

Deeming me ready, Noemi opened the door and sent me on my way. But when I reached the dining room, I saw the head table was empty except for Escalus.

He looked perfectly at home up there on his own. His coat today was green, and he wore his hair swept back. I walked up to him and kissed his cheek.

"Where's Father?"

I sat in my assigned seat, even though it meant I was far away from him.

"He's in meetings."

I stared at Escalus. There was something off in his tone.

I lowered my voice. "Does this have anything to do with the literal army outside?"

He darted his eyes at the crowd ahead of us and then looked back at me and nodded.

He would tell me, just not now.

"Well, then, where is Nickolas?"

"Haven't you heard? He's been holed up in his room since breakfast yesterday. His butler said he refused his meals. I think . . . I think you broke his heart, Annika."

I rolled my eyes. "Please. Over the brief period we've been engaged, he's done nothing but order me around and ignore me. And if he thinks I'll forget that he left me alone in the forest, he's mistaken."

Escalus shrugged. "We all can act rashly under moments of pressure. Not that I agree with his actions," he added quickly.

I didn't reply. What could I say?

He cut his food, frowning at it. "Annika, you have probably realized that I can't stand Nickolas. His very presence is exhausting. But . . . if I had something important to say, I'd want to be heard out."

"Did you know he sent me a letter asking for just that?"

He chuckled to himself. "No, but I'm not surprised. Go to him, let him say his piece. If he still does not redeem himself, then fine. Have a distant, loveless marriage." He sighed. "But I know you. You'll regret losing so much time if it turns out there was love there all along."

Nickolas was situated in one of the castle's best rooms, just a few hallways away from Escalus. Drawing in a deep breath, I knocked on the door. A butler answered, his eyes widening when he saw me.

"Your Royal Highness," he greeted me, dropping into a bow.

"Is it her?" Nickolas called from deep within the room. I heard his footsteps as he dashed across the floor, wrenching the door wide open. "Annika." He made my name sound like a rope tossed to a drowning man.

His hair was a mess, his waistcoat was undone, and his cravat was hanging from his neck untied. I'd never seen him with so much as a string out of place. Nickolas was sharp edges, but here he was bent and unmade.

I could admit I preferred him this way.

"I mean, Your Royal Highness," he finally added, bending into a bow. "I hope this means you received my letter, that you are willing to speak to me. I owe you the greatest of apologies. Please come in and talk with me."

"Are you quite well, sir?" I asked, continuing to take him in.

"No!" he exclaimed, gripping his hair in his hands. "I've never been so unsettled in all my life!"

He made no move to walk me into his room, which was another sign of distress; Nickolas was all about ceremony and propriety. I looked up and down the empty halls before I spoke.

"Nickolas, I never saw us being happy together, and I'd come to terms with that. But after your behavior . . ." I shook my head. "I have no hopes of us even being friendly toward one another. Plenty of marriages among people of our rank turn out this way." I pushed the urge to cry down hard. It was shattering to admit this aloud.

"But I will not rescind my proposal, and I will make no demands of you. All I ask is to be left alone. In fact, I don't ask it. I command it. Good day."

I turned to leave, but he reached out, grabbing my wrist. "Annika."

He breathed my name in such desperation, it gave me pause. Taking advantage of my stunned state, he brought his other hand around, holding on to my hand and dropping to a knee.

"I'm so sorry. If I . . . If I knew how to express myself better, I would." He kept his eyes downcast, looking nervous. Nickolas was never nervous. "I'm thankful that you're still willing to marry me . . . but is there no hope for love in our marriage?"

I looked away for a moment. "Nickolas, if you have ever loved me, you have hidden it extraordinarily well."

When I turned my eyes back to him, he nodded. "Maybe *love* is too strong a word. But you're the only thing I've ever been sure of in my life."

And the way he said it gave me a glimpse into his fear. It was part of why Lennox had scared me so. I'd spent my life in service of my crown. The thought of someone taking it away left me lost. Even though it was hard at times, even though it meant doing things I didn't care for, I didn't want to lose it.

Kadier was my life.

It was that ever-pressing sense of duty, the crystal clear vision of my own fears in Nickolas's eyes, that tugged at the threads of my heart. Tugged, not yanked.

"If there is any truth in that, then prove it."

He let me go, putting his palms up to me. "Yes. Of course. I just . . . Give me time."

I turned and walked away, wondering what exactly I'd gotten myself into.

LENNOX

By morning we'd collected our prisoners' stories, and they all said the same thing. The numbers of guards in specific locations were similar. They all pinpointed the castle and training grounds on our old maps, even going so far as to update them to the best of their knowledge. And they all confirmed the same story: the Kadierian king wanted to meet us, discuss the future, and make peace.

I handed my report to Kawan, written in my unpracticed hand. At least the lines were mostly straight.

In my mind, the first logical questions from him would be along the lines of "When are we to meet?" or "Is everything consistent?" But Kawan had his own priorities.

"Who gave you this paper?" he asked.

It only took those five words for me to understand that what I'd guessed was true: he did not want us reading or writing.

"I rummaged through the storage. There wasn't much paper, and the ink was dry. I apologize if I unnecessarily used resources, but I thought a development of this magnitude might be worth recording."

He looked at me for a long time and then at the pages. His eyes moved jerkily across the rows of information all pointing to the same thing, but no light of understanding crossed his face.

Could . . . could *he* not read?

He cleared his throat. "You both have done a good job here. I can see you want to make up for the mistakes of your last mission." His voice was still dark, the words laced with bitterness, but I was too busy taking in the first kind words he'd ever spoken to me to be bothered by it.

There was only one reason he would pay me a compliment: he was hiding something. If he could read, it was at a rudimentary level. I had a decision to make, and quickly. Either I could expose him and watch as he was taken down a notch in front of his most trusted henchmen, or I could cover for him. For now.

"Thank you," I started. "As you can see, they've all given consistent answers. And they've updated our maps, giving us a clear location for their palace, the training grounds for their army, and the few protective outposts they have.

"The location for our meeting will be here," I said, pointing to a block of land labeled "The Island." It would take some work to get there, but Kawan was too stubborn to ask them to find someplace new. "Apparently the weather there is temperamental, so it's laid unused for ages. The king wants to discuss trading and a potential joint venture in building a road between our lands for easy transport of goods. They say he has a treasure of gifts to bestow as a means of making amends."

What the envoys didn't speak of was the kingdom itself; everything else was meaningless in my eyes.

"When is this exchange to take place?" he asked.

I shuffled my feet, trying to steady myself. "In a few days. The king will meet us there and do his best to . . . appease."

"Appease," he scoffed, smiling to himself. "We will decimate them. We will end them as surely as they thought they ended us."

I could see the greed washing over him.

"We'll kill him," he went on. "We'll kill their king on that island and toss his body in the sea. Once we're rid of him, marching into Dahrain will be easy." He scratched at his beard. "We'll take everyone, the entire army. In fact," he exclaimed, a smile growing across his face, "we won't let him get to the Island. We'll attack at sea, show him what we're capable of. Then they'll regret taking my crown."

This plan didn't sit well with me. We had a few boats for fishing, but no vessels that could carry the entirety of our army. Where would we obtain such a number of boats? How would a group of people trained for land battle fare on the open sea? Or, most obviously, why not avoid violence altogether? It seemed we were intimidating the king into submission; it might be possible to simply walk in once we were that close.

"Sir, are you certain that's the best course of action?"

Kawan's eyes slowly came up from the paper. He might not be able to read the words in front of him, but I could read that gaze. It was a demand for silence, for obedience.

"First, you two will question the men again. I want the size of their false king's party confirmed, and I want the exact time they expect to meet. Do not fail me," he warned. "In the meantime, we will plan our celebration."

"Celebration?" I asked. His mind, as always, was going in vastly different directions than it ought.

"Naturally. If our people are taking their home back, we shall feast."

I nodded and turned, knowing Blythe would be two steps behind me. She closed the door as I stood in the hallway, stunned.

"That . . . was not what I was expecting," she admitted quietly.

"Nor I. Why would he force us into battle?" I couldn't think of any reason for his decision that made rational sense. He was endangering us all.

"A celebration?" Inigo asked. "For what? To celebrate going into battle?"

We were outside, sitting on rocks and staring at the sea. It was windy enough that no one else wanted to be here and loud enough that our complaints would be lost to the air. I needed a breath, a moment away from anger clouding my mind. So far, I wasn't having much luck.

I nodded. "You know what absolutely kills me, though?"

"What?"

"The day after we're supposed to meet, when we'll either be settling in or traveling back home . . ."

Inigo sighed. "It's Matraleit."

"Exactly. And he hasn't said a thing about that. No feast, no celebration. If our people are what we're fighting for, he should at least remember our traditions."

Inigo stared at the distant sky. "I'm thankful for you. You keep track of things. I knew some of our history, but half of what I know came from others in the castle after we got here."

"I don't know why we don't have it written anywhere. It would have been helpful more than once." I shook my head, asking the question that I wished I'd asked before my father died. If Kawan found us—if he knew to be looking for certain families—where did he learn that from? My family knew about Matraleit, but there were other things *he* taught *us*. Other families corroborated his stories, and between all of us, we've built the most complete history we can. But he knew so much when he walked up to our steps . . . how?

"Don't worry," Inigo said, pushing the question away. "Just because Kawan isn't marking the occasion doesn't mean the girls aren't."

I rolled my eyes. "Are you making a bracelet for anyone?"

He laughed. "Nah. Don't think anyone wants one from me. And I'm not expecting any. *You*, on the other hand, need to be on the lookout."

"Don't start."

"You know it's coming. Might as well embrace it." He looked far too happy to find something to tease me about.

"I don't embrace things. Nothing."

Inigo chuckled, but now that he mentioned it, I looked

over my shoulder, scanning the distant fields. Sure enough, there were people gathering straw.

I swallowed hard. Matraleit was all about binding, entwining. It was about permanence. Somewhere in our past, people started weaving bracelets and giving them to the person they liked. The men did it sometimes, but it was really the ladies who enjoyed it the most. You'd see people wearing a collection of them, proud they could steal so many hearts. Sometimes they were given very seriously, like a precursor to marriage vows. Sometimes they were left anonymously, and the recipient had to riddle out who made it. The bracelets had become the symbol of the holiday itself.

I'd never received one. If I did this year, there was only one person it could have come from.

"Listen," Inigo began, "all jokes aside, don't let Kawan get under your skin. A time will come when we need to act with precision, with planning. You can't do that if you're distracted by anger."

I looked away, clearing my throat. "I know."

"So, it might be worth considering embracing *something*. If only to have anything else in your heart."

I stared at him. "I'll consider it if you promise never to speak to me like that again."

He laughed. "Deal."

I slapped him playfully on the shoulder and started my way back to my room. There were many other things crowding my head, but my thoughts turned to his advice. I didn't want to disappoint him . . . but I didn't think I was capable of heeding it.

ANNIKA

I was tugging the final stitch on my project tight when Escalus's special knock sounded on the door. Noemi lit up, rushing over to answer him.

He strode in, head high, a bunch of wildflowers in his hand.

"That's very thoughtful," I said, gesturing to the bouquets around my room that still continued to pour in. "But as you can see, I've nowhere to put them."

"I figured as much, which is why these are for your maid," he said, handing them over to Noemi. "She deserves something nice of her own. People forget she has the unfortunate task of tending to you."

"I beg your pardon!" I called in mock outrage, while Noemi laughed.

"Her Royal Highness is very good to me, sir. If anyone should ever ask, you can tell them I said so myself." She buried her face in the flowers, and I felt a little guilty.

"I try, but Escalus has a point. When was the last time I

thought to bring you something, just because? And when you do so much for me . . ."

"Told you," Escalus said, sitting down.

"I have no complaints, my lady. I'll just set these in my chamber." She trotted off, new life in her steps.

"You're so thoughtful, Escalus. To me, to Noemi . . . I can't think of a person who has wanted your attention and not received it."

"I do my best," he replied with a smile. "And so do you."

"Sometimes I wish there was more I could do. The kingdom is bigger than the castle, you know." I scowled at my stitches. "After what happened, I don't see Father letting me go anywhere for a while. If ever." Lennox would love to know that he'd ruined my life in more ways than one.

"Don't fall into a pit of despair just yet," he teased. "The people have been clamoring to see you. Maybe reminding Father of that could convince him to change his mind."

Noemi was walking back in, peeking over my shoulder. "That trim came out very nicely, my lady. That might be your best work yet."

A small but happy thought came to me. "Should we put these in your room, Noemi? Brighten the space?"

She beamed. "Truly?"

"And what about a terribly finished pillow?" Escalus asked, still working on his final seam. "I'm sure this would really tie it all together."

She laughed. "The both of you need to stop. I will take anything Your Highnesses see fit to give me, but I don't need to be showered with gifts."

Her hand was just by my shoulder, so I moved over and kissed it. "You're too good, Noemi."

"Probably one of the most trustworthy people I've ever met," Escalus added, growing serious. "Which is why you can stay while I say what I must to my sister."

"Do you know about these soldiers, then?" I asked.

Escalus sighed. "Annika, he might not admit it in front of you, but the way Father acted when you were taken . . . he felt like it was entirely his fault. He kept berating himself for letting you out of his sight. He was angry at Nickolas, too, but he had to save face—now that the engagement is public, he can't let people think he chose wrong. So, all of us are under watch, and the borders are under constant patrol. I . . ."

Escalus trailed off, thinking twice over his words. "The way he's acting, though . . . I feel like there's something bigger beyond this all, but I don't know for certain."

"What else could there be?" I asked, thinking through everything aloud. "If he attacks, he'll be the king who broke more than a hundred and fifty years of peace; he'd never do that. We have nowhere to run, and they have no real claim to the kingdom. Protecting us is all he has left."

As if on cue, there was a knock on the door. Noemi scurried over, greeting the guard, who said His Majesty wanted to see us urgently. Maybe it was because of Escalus's words, or perhaps because Father rarely asked to see us, but I felt a pit settle in my stomach as we stood and made our way to his rooms.

We knocked on Father's door, and Escalus and I exchanged

a glance as the seconds ticked by. The wait only added to my anxiety. Finally, a butler came to welcome us, and, as we walked in, a flood of people filed out, advisers and high-ranking soldiers.

Father was at the large desk, stacking papers and shoving them away. He looked up at us, all business.

"Ah. Just who I needed to see." He waved us over to the desk. Atop it, in the center, was a large map of Kadier. "Both of you, clear your plans for Thursday. I will need you present for a matter of state."

I squinted. "Both of us, Your Majesty?"

He nodded, pointing at a section of the map. I tilted my head to see that he was pointing to the Island. "Annika, what did you say they called themselves? Dahrainians? Whatever it was, we are meeting on the Island for a peace summit. And you will both be there."

My blood went cold. "Sir . . . how . . . why would you do that? Why would you invite them to be so close? I told you, they have an army. They have been training for years to invade. I beg you to reconsider."

"I've already sent an envoy. If they agree, they will arrive Thursday morning. So be ready to proceed to the docks."

I looked at Escalus, pleading. He cleared his throat. "Father, are you sure? These are the people who sent a man to assassinate you. They are the ones who successfully killed our mother and nearly did the same to Annika. How will we ever rest if they are within eyesight?"

I could see it, like the second a plate fell to the ground and shattered into a dozen pieces, the way his eyes shifted to that dark anger that took hold of him so fiercely. I sucked in a breath, waiting for the storm.

"Must you two contradict me at every turn?" he demanded. His tone turned mocking, "'I won't marry him!' 'I won't marry her!' 'I want this!' . . . It's enough! I am not your father right now; I am your sovereign. I am meeting the head of this so-called army on Thursday. I want my heir apparent on one side and the princess who escaped their clutches on the other. We will present a united front, and you will be silent about it!"

In my mind, I saw myself looking out my window, finding Lennox below me. His piercing blue eyes staring up at me, his cape whipped up by the wind. No wall would stop him, no sword.

An angry silence fell between us. His Majesty gestured to the door, and I obediently curtsied as my brother bowed, and we walked quickly from the room. I followed Escalus down the hallway, feeling the tension roll off him in waves.

We rounded a corner, and he threw his back against the wall, bringing his hand to his forehead.

"What do we do?" I asked. "Escalus. We can't go along with this."

He stared at the opposite wall, considering. "I think we have to."

"What? No! Escalus, this is clearly madness. What if you spoke to the ministers and had him declared unfit? You're of age; you can be regent now."

He shook his head. "If I declare him mad, it mars my reputation, and my children's as well. You know that. The first time I make a mistake, they will say I'm going the way of my father, and I will lose the throne. Besides," he added, taking a long, heavy breath, "if he's already sent an envoy, this plan is in motion. If they go to the Island, and we aren't there to greet them, it's an insult and practically an invitation for war. We'd endanger everyone."

I felt light-headed.

"What we need to do now is make a plan for you," he said.

"What? Why for me?"

"If this summit goes poorly, we need to arrange a place for you to hide until you can garner support and reclaim the land."

That was when I lost hope. Escalus, for all his composure, for all his thoughtfulness, had given himself away. If he wanted to make a plan for me to reclaim Kadier, he must have thought we were truly going to lose it.

LENNOX

A few hours later, our three prisoners had become honored guests. Kawan welcomed them to our celebratory feast with open arms, and we were to all follow suit.

Still, I kept a close watch. They didn't huddle together, as I'd expected, but walked around confidently, charming the room. It was easily done; Kawan had all but introduced them as our saviors.

I stayed closest to White Flag. Skittish and Spare were so tense in their shoulders, I could see that even with the warm welcome, they were going to be close-lipped. Skittish because he seemed to mistrust us, and Spare because he seemed above it all. White Flag, however, looked perfectly at ease. He had a cup of ale in his hand and was laughing loudly at something someone had said. I hung back, listening.

"The Island is supposedly beautiful," White Flag commented. "I've never seen it myself, so I'm glad we'll get to escort you."

"What gifts are the king giving us?" someone asked, hands gripped in excitement.

White Flag shrugged. "I would guess food, as we have an abundance. We also have a history of excellent leather-workers, so it wouldn't surprise me if he brought some saddles as well. But feel free to imagine better."

I rolled my eyes at his boasting. Of course there was an abundance—that's why they took it from us in the first place.

"Did they tell you we all saw your princess?" someone else asked. Their tones were all wonder and ease. How could they so quickly forget this was the face of the enemy?

He nodded and gave a chuckle. "Let me tell you, we were all surprised to hear of her escape. She's a kind lady, like her mother. None of us could guess she was also so formidable."

Something lodged in my throat.

"I don't know about formidable," someone said. "She might be clever, but I wouldn't call her strong. I wouldn't be worried if I crossed her path on a battlefield."

White Flag shook his head. "You'll never see such a thing. I wouldn't be surprised if her father literally locked her in a tower. Her brother, Escalus, on the other hand? He's all manners and decorum on the surface, but I don't doubt he could kill a man. Especially for her sake. If you cross him, run."

I'd learned a lot about this little royal family today in the unguarded words of this unwanted visitor.

According to our so-called guests, it was rare to find one sibling without the other in public. Annika praised her brother in all situations and seemed to love no one on earth so much as him. Escalus boasted about his sister's wisdom and goodness, as well as her strength. If I had to guess, he was the one who taught that girl to wield a sword. And by the account of the visitors, he didn't seem to be enthusiastic about his sister's engagement.

This one detail made my mind wander down paths I didn't care for. If he didn't like her fiancé, was it because the man in question was a buffoon—which was my guess—or because there was someone else he wanted her to be with? I also wondered why they bothered finding her a partner before him. Wouldn't his choice in spouse be much more important than hers?

As I sat lost in thought, a few of our musicians paraded in heralding the arrival of our leader and my mother. Whenever we had the rare celebration, they'd make this sort of entrance, as if they truly were royalty. Kawan with his fake throne, my mother with her stolen gowns—it was all a tasteless show.

Kawan walked in, smug as he surveyed the room. But as irritated as I was by the way he sauntered in, the way he so casually disregarded his own folly, everything was all drowned out by a rush of anger at my mother.

She was wearing Annika's dress.

The riding dress she'd left in the dungeon had been reworked to fit my mother's frame, but it was unmistakable. The cream-colored bodice, the floral embroidery. Mother's head was so high, her hand resting so lightly on Kawan's.

It enraged me.

As people applauded their entrance, I marched across the mess hall to take my mother's hand and, as calmly as I could, pull her from the room.

"What is the meaning of this?" she demanded.

"Take that dress off."

She looked at me as if I were mad. "You must be joking. This is the first gown I've owned that was actually made for royalty," she said with a smile. "Now, I'm going to go enjoy it."

I blocked her path. "You. Are not. A queen. Kawan hasn't bothered to marry you or give you an official position. You can parade around in as many pretty dresses as you like, but that won't change the fact that you are replaceable in his eyes."

She stared at me, the set of her lips conveying her anger. "Why are you always so cruel to your mother?"

I gave a loud humorless laugh. "Me, cruel to you? You stand back and do nothing while the man who sent your husband out to die strikes your son in public. How can you speak to me of what's cruel?"

She swallowed. "I do not approve of him being so violent with you, and I didn't appreciate that he did it in front of so many people. I'm very sorry for it."

I crossed my arms. "That is such a comfort. Especially knowing that if he chose to hit me again tonight, you'd keep your seat all over again."

She looked away, confirming what I already knew.

"Don't you understand?" I whispered. "He keeps you close to keep me close. No one else here has the stomach to kill a queen, to kidnap a princess, to slaughter those who would otherwise run once they realize he's never going to give them what he promised. If he loses me, this whole operation crumbles. I've wanted to run for so long, to find a better way, and the reason I haven't abandoned this all yet is because I'm waiting for you to wake up and remember I'm your son."

She moved her eyes to the floor, the cuff of her sleeve, to the torch on the wall. Anywhere but to me.

"Was there ever a time when you loved me? When you looked upon me as something dearer than a soldier?"

"Lennox, of course I loved you."

Past tense. It wasn't lost on me.

"But you look just like him," she admitted, drawing her hand to her mouth. "It kills me to look at you and see the shadow of the man I married and lost. We have to survive here, Lennox. For the sake of getting everything we came for, we have to survive."

I raked my hands through my hair, ready to rip it out. "I've been surviving for years, and it is the saddest excuse for an existence that I can think of. I'm ready to start my life, Mother. And I know, without a whisper of a doubt," I said, coming close to her, "that when I do, you will have no part in it."

The tears had been growing in her eyes for a while, but now one spilled over. "What do you want from me, Lennox?"

"I want to move forward. I want to go after our kingdom, the right way. For Father's sake. I want to know I have people on my side. And I want . . . I want my mother. But she died when she became Kawan's mistress," I said, my lips trembling, "and I don't think she's ever coming back."

She cast her eyes down but kept her chin up, refusing to be ashamed. I knew she wouldn't be. I was powerless. I could do nothing, and it made me want to scream in frustration.

"I'm sorry to be such a disappointment to you," she whispered.

"You're nothing to me," I corrected her. "You're a nobody parading as a royal. You're a fraud."

Her eyes steeled over. "Fine. Then consider yourself nothing more than a soldier to me."

"I already do."

She turned on her heel, marching back into the feast with her nose tipped up.

I reached into the pocket on my waistbelt for my father's button and rubbed it back and forth between my finger and thumb.

I'd physically buried my father, and now it was time to mentally do the same with my mother.

I walked out of the castle an orphan.

ANNIKA

"He did what?" Rhett asked, aghast. "What happens now?"

I shrugged. "We go. It's all in motion already. But what happens if they attempt to invade? I'm telling you, if Lennox thinks it's possible to successfully launch an invasion, then that's what he'll do. He'll forgo any sort of meeting and come straight for this palace."

I sighed, rubbing my temples. I'd had a low-grade headache from the moment Father announced his plans.

Rhett reached out and held my hand. "What can we do? How can I help?"

I watched the way his eyes filled with concern. Instinct told me it wasn't because of worry for himself.

He was worried about me.

"I have two requests. First, I need you to take the most important of our history books and pack them. If Lennox bypasses the meeting and comes here, you have to run and take the truth with you. This is *our* kingdom. And if we have to reclaim it at some point, you'll have the evidence."

He nodded. I could tell he already had a running list of the most essential books prepared. "That's easy. What else?"

"I want to practice with my sword. If something goes wrong with this meeting and that envoy expects to find a damsel in distress, I want them to regret it. I can see it in your eyes that you care about me too much to let me be left defenseless. Can you help me?"

He stood there, smiling. "Annika, I don't just care about you. I love you. I've never made a point of hiding it."

I could feel a blush creeping up my cheeks. Was he always going to leave me feeling torn? If I didn't have ties to Nickolas, if I wasn't honor and duty bound to him, would I happily let Rhett chase after me? I couldn't say. And, for my sake, it was probably better I didn't devote too much thought to it.

"I know you do."

"And I know you're not at ease with it. So easy to read," he said with a laugh. "But I'm happy to love you from afar. Here in this dusty old library. There are worse things."

I stared into his eyes, admiring him at the very least. "Can I ask you something that might be crossing a line?"

"As far as I'm concerned, there are no lines between you and me. You can ask me anything you want, always."

I felt my pulse grow erratic, a feeling similar to when I'd been marched into the main hall in Vosino Castle. I shook it away.

"How did you know? You say you love me. How did you know what love even looked like?"

He took a long, slow breath, coming closer. "You've read

every fairy tale in this library, Annika. Don't you know? Love doesn't look like anything," he told me in a whisper. "Love has a sound. It sounds like a thousand heartbeats happening at the same time. It sounds like the rush of a waterfall or the still of the world at daybreak. You can hear it at night, lulling you to sleep, and, in the middle of your darkest days, it breaks through like a laugh.

"The thing is, some of us have been taught to listen for it, so when it comes, it's all too easy to hear over the noise. For others, there are too many other sounds drowning it out. For them, it takes longer. But when it finally breaks through, it's a symphony."

He tipped my chin, so my eyes met his. "Just listen, Annika. Listen. It will come."

He gave me the lightest of kisses on my cheek, perhaps trying to make this sound burst into the moment.

It didn't.

But I believed him.

"I think it will be easier to hear once we get past an impending war," I teased to break off the tension of the moment.

He laughed. "You're probably right. As such, yes. I will practice with you. If you bested this Lennox, then you should be able to hold your own against whoever else comes this way. But let's not risk it." He thought for a moment. "If there are preparations being made, people will be in and out of the stables; we'll need to meet somewhere else."

"What about my favorite spot in the gardens? With the stone? The greenery is high, so no one will see, and it's far enough away that no one should be drawn to the sound."

He considered this. "Yes. That should work." He turned his head to take in the darkening sky. "After dinner?"

"I'll be waiting." As I left the library, something struck me: it was possible Nickolas had not been informed of my father's plans. Despite all my misgivings about him, it seemed cruel to keep him in the dark on this matter. I headed for his room.

"Your Royal Highness," Nickolas greeted me once I'd been announced, "to what do I owe the honor of your company?"

"Has Escalus come to see you?"

He shook his head.

"Then please let me in. There is something I think you should know."

Where Rhett had responded to the news with outrage, Nickolas merely displayed a cool air of concern.

"I do not approve of you going along. It clouds my course of action."

"In what way?" I asked.

He sighed. "As a subject, my instinct is to insist to His Majesty that I sail with you all. If things don't go smoothly, I want to defend him. But as a fiancé . . ." He looked up at me. "Lennox got ahold of you once. And, seeing as the last time was completely my fault, I feel compelled to prevent any possibility of it now. I'd want to stay at your side."

I watched as his eyes went back and forth across the floor, as if he were adding details to two separate columns in his head, trying to see if one outweighed the other.

"Can I make a vote?" I risked.

He looked up at me instantly. "Of course."

"Protect Escalus. My father will have swarms of guards at his side, and you might have realized I'm pretty handy with a sword if pressed."

I paused, not wanting to carry on.

I swallowed, admitting the hardest truth. "We all know where I rank here." He stared at me. "It's much more important that Escalus comes back safe and sound. If the kingdom loses me, everything can carry on, but if something happens to my brother? It will be disastrous." I took a deep breath. "You will be put to much better use protecting Escalus. He's far more valuable."

He looked down and answered in a voice so low, I almost didn't hear it. "Not to all of us."

I realized that, for him, this admission was tantamount to carving our names in marble or writing an opera in my honor.

"Nickolas?"

He couldn't quite meet my eyes yet. "I don't have a talent for flowery words. If I did, I'd have employed it long before now. But, for some of us . . . for me . . . it will be far more shattering to lose you than anyone else.

"Annika, all my life I've been told that protocol and propriety are imperative to being a member of your family. My tutors and caregivers raised me to be a person that no one in the kingdom could doubt was worthy of you; they failed to raise me to be a person you would find worthy as well.

"Maybe it's too late to get back on course. The woods . . .

I don't blame you for hating me. I thought our country was being attacked, and my instinct was to get the news to the palace. I should have gotten you to the palace. I feel so irrevocably stupid over it now. I'll never be able to apologize for that moment enough."

He rubbed his palms together nervously, and after years of thinking I knew who Nickolas was, I was stunned to learn that perhaps I knew nothing about him at all. I wondered if now, after this, I might hear something that sounded like love.

Not yet.

Still, this honesty was precious to me.

"It's not too late, Nickolas."

He looked up at me, his eyes showing he didn't quite believe me. "I would so like to start again, Annika. Without expectation. To know you, and have you know me."

I nodded. "I'd like that, too. But I can't begin to think of it until this has passed. If you care for me as you say, please stay beside my father and brother when we go to the Island. Protect them as best you can. Be a rational voice in their ears."

Nickolas nodded. "Your wish is my command."

LENNOX

It was too dark to go far, but I couldn't stay inside those castle walls. Not right now. Over the hush of waves rolling in, I could hear the few musicians among us doing their best to play an old Dahrainian folk song. My mother had hummed it over my head when she put me to bed as a child. If there were lyrics, they were long lost. But shouldn't I rejoice in this, the stubborn march forward with the little history we knew? All I could think was that we were being deceived, and this plan of Kawan's was going to do more to hurt us than help.

And my mother . . .

I stayed by the arena, where the light of the torches near the doorways and from the windows still gave me room to see where I was standing. And I looked in at the sodden ground, wishing I had someone to spar with, anything to give release to the feeling in my chest.

"It's too late," someone said, a teasing tone in his voice. I turned to see Inigo walking my way with a handful of people behind him.

"You're reading my mind," I told him, looking to see just who he was with. Blythe was there, of course, but also Andre, Sherwin, Griffin, and Rami. "What's going on?"

Inigo shrugged. "I saw you leave, and Blythe said it looked like you came outside. If you weren't watching the prisoners, I figured there had to be a good reason."

I rolled my eyes. "You might not have noticed, but they aren't exactly prisoners anymore. They're esteemed guests, marching us into trouble."

"You sure about that?" Griffin asked.

I looked to Blythe, who sighed. "If what they're saying is true, there's a chance Dahrain would be without its royals. We could march in and take the castle. We could reclaim our kingdom without much of a fight, if any at all. But, instead of invading an unarmed throne—which would be both remarkable for us and humiliating for them—Kawan wants to use this meeting as an opportunity to kill their king. It might be straightforward. . . . It might not."

"You've got a bad feeling about it, don't you?" Inigo asked me.

"Yes. Based on what, I cannot say, but I don't think, after everything that's happened, they truly want to meet with us without some sort of repercussions." I stared at the ground, feeling a little embarrassed to be acting on a feeling. Feelings got you nowhere but into trouble.

"Then what's the plan?" Inigo asked.

My head perked up.

"You have to have something in mind," Sherwin said. "Do you need all of us, or just a few?"

"Even as a distraction?" Rami offered. "I didn't get my

shot last time." She winked at Blythe, who giggled.

I blinked a few times, taking them in. "You . . . you want to know my plan?"

"Of course," Blythe replied quickly. "You do have one, right?"

I swallowed. I did. I almost always did.

"I think we should go and take the castle. When we march out, it wouldn't be too hard to get 'lost' in those woods. With all of us out there, a handful won't be missed," I said, feeling sure. "If I'm wrong and Kawan is able to kill their king, then we have a two-fold win: he's dead, and we have their kingdom in our hands in one fell swoop."

Inigo's eyes were on me. "And are we mentioning this to Kawan?"

I glanced around, noticing the winces on a few faces.

"I don't think so. He'd stop us if he knew, but he can't if he doesn't."

"Good," Inigo said. "We'll have to move fast. . . . We'll presumably be on foot."

"And we'll probably need to carry more supplies, for good measure," Andre added.

I nodded, not having thought that far ahead. The conversation broke down into speculation. How quickly we could move, how accurate the numbers that their princess had given us truly were. With very little to go on, they were completely on board.

I took a moment, allowing my eyes to rest on each of their faces as they spoke. Why should this action, this willingness to follow, surprise me? When I'd offered them an easier Commission than the one I intended, they'd rejected it. When I'd abandoned our plan to take Annika, they'd followed my orders. When even that plan fell apart completely, they stood beside me in front of Kawan.

I had friends.

Blythe turned her head, flashing me a bright smile of the sort she seemed to reserve just for me. I wished then that I could do what Inigo had said and embrace something. It would almost be an act of rebellion now, wouldn't it? Kawan made me feel like death was waiting around every corner, like caring about anything was a liability. Thriving would be a sweet kind of revenge.

And still, I couldn't will myself to do it.

But that didn't mean I couldn't rebel.

"Anyone here interested in learning to read?" I asked.

Griffin's arm shot up first. I noted the straw bracelet hanging proudly from his wrist.

"You know how?" Rami asked, her tone tinged with joy.

I nodded. "My father taught me. I can teach you all if you want."

"Step aside. Right-Hand Man coming through," Inigo said, putting an arm out and coming to stand beside me.

I couldn't help the chuckle. I took one of the blunt arrows that had been left in a pile beside the arena and wrote out the letters of his name in the dirt.

I-N-I-G-O.

He tipped his head to the side. "It looks . . . strong."

"It's a sturdy name," I observed. "A dependable name for a dependable person."

I didn't look up, but I heard Inigo clear his throat hard.

"Don't! I already warned you once."

He walked away, chuckling.

"My turn!" Blythe insisted, coming over quickly.

I wrote the letters of her name out slowly, knowing Blythe would want the opportunity to take them in.

"I like that one in the middle," she said, pointing.

"That's a *y*," I told her.

"It's all so pretty."

"Your name is pretty. My handwriting is not."

"But it is. Wait, write your name, too. I want to see it," she insisted, shoving my arm.

I laughed. "Hold on, hold on."

I started scrawling out the word just beneath hers. She smiled at it.

"I always thought your name sounded serious. It looks serious, too. What letter is that at the end?"

"It's called an *x*."

"I like that one the best," she commented in a whisper.

Her shoulder was brushing up against mine. And there it was again, the wish that I could simply embrace her. She turned her head, and I realized our faces were very close. I felt some long-dormant instinct wake up in me. I could kiss her if I wanted. I could lower my lips a few inches, and I felt sure she would welcome it. It would be so easy that refraining from it almost felt wrong.

But I held back all the same.

I cleared my throat, looking around at the small group we'd formed. Taking in their smiles, their easy conversation, their determination for more, another emotion I hadn't been all that familiar with floated to the surface: pride.

Their laughter lit the night.

"I've never been a part of anything like this," Rami whispered.

I smirked. "Welcome to the rebellion."

ANNIKA

Rhett's sword hit mine with such force it shot off sparks. My left arm was burning from the scar Lennox had left on it, and my right knee nearly buckled under the impact, but it held. I came back, turning around to strike him again.

At his insistence, we were both wearing multiple layers of leather-covered padding over our chests. I'd laughed at him, thinking it was foolish. But, as I'd requested, he hadn't held back. In the end, the padding was saving me from all the cuts, though I would certainly have a bruise or two.

As I'd hoped, I was too quick for Rhett, and I struck him between his shoulder blades.

"Ouch! Good one, Annika." He grimaced, pulling at the ties for his padding. "Escalus taught you well."

"Are we done?" I asked, disappointed.

"For tonight. It's starting to get late, and you still have to get up and be princess in the morning," he replied with a wink.

"It's more work than one would think."

"Oh, I know. Which is why I'm sending you off to bed."

I started tugging at the knots holding on to the padding while pacing around my favorite hiding place in the garden. It lacked the impressive flowers and fountains of the spaces closest to the palace, so no one ever came out this far but the groundskeepers. Rhett and I stuck to the pebble path that created a circle around the stone in the middle, using the incline as another point in the training. I didn't know what might be waiting for me.

"Did you see?" I asked. "There's a ship at the dock."

Rhett nodded. "I keep telling myself that it's safer for you to be by the king's side, with his elite guards. That's not that much of a comfort, though."

"I just feel so . . . lost. Everything could come apart in a matter of days, and I don't know what to do. I can't challenge my father, but I can't sit still." I shook my head. "So often lately, it feels like everything happening around me is wrong." I looked at Rhett's sympathetic eyes. "I'm sorry. I know I have no room to complain."

"You're carrying the worry of a kingdom on your shoulders, Annika."

"But that's the thing: it's never been mine. It's my father's, and, when he dies, it will belong to Escalus. I've been trying to support them both my whole life because, even if it will never be under my authority, I love Kadier. With all my heart, I love it. But I keep wondering if my love has been wasted. If it would matter if I wasn't here at all."

Rhett tossed his sword to the ground and took me by the

shoulders. "Annika, I *never* want to hear you say that again. You have no idea how I would crumble without you. I'm serious. I don't know what I'd do." He swallowed hard. "I know how much you love your brother, and I know how much you love Kadier, and because of that, I've resigned myself to the fact that you'll never run off with me. But that doesn't mean I won't fall apart if you're gone."

I gave him a sad smile. "It's not that I don't care for you, Rhett."

"I know that, too. I think, under different circumstances, we could have been happy. But you are a princess, and your love for Kadier will always win out. If you're willing to marry that idiot, it must be great indeed."

I laughed. "He's trying."

Rhett shrugged. "I still hate him."

I went to pick up my sword and head back to the palace, smiling. "I'm sure you're not alone in that sentiment, but I still want to give him the chance to grow."

"No amount of effort on his part could change how I feel about him," he said matter-of-factly. "Any man who comes between you and me? That man is my enemy."

And a chill that had nothing to do with the evening weather scurried down my back.

We parted ways at the stairs, with Rhett smiling over his shoulder at me as he went off to his room. I knew I should go to bed. I couldn't, though, not just yet.

Once he disappeared around the bend in the hallway, I moved down another. It was later than I'd thought, and the palace was still and silent. I loved it like this, when I could pretend it was all mine.

Moving quickly, I made my way to the distant hall that held Mother's painting. I still had my sword sheathed in my hands. I wondered what she would have made of that. I thought of the time she'd brought a slice of cake to my room from a party I was too young to attend. We sat on the floor by the fire, digging our forks in, not bothering with plates.

She didn't mind a good secret. I think she'd have liked that I could hold my own.

Just outside the hallway, I paused for a moment. . . . I could hear something.

Someone was crying.

I hid behind a large plant and looked down the length of the hall where Mother's painting was kept.

I was stunned into absolute silence as I took in the two silhouettes holding one another in the thin moonlight.

Escalus was unmistakable. But the girl in his arms—a figure I also knew far too well—was a shock.

"Noemi," Escalus whispered. "I'm not going to die. It's going to be a quick, diplomatic meeting. There and back in a day."

"Escalus, I don't trust those people," Noemi said, so casually saying his name. "Annika has woken up from nightmares trembling ever since she came back. They are not like us. They will not exercise the restraint that you would."

He pulled her closer. "There's nothing I can do about their actions. I can only control mine. I am no coward, so I will go." He cupped her face in his hand as if she were breakable and balancing on a precipice. "But I am also no fool. I will make my way back to you. No man—no army—could stop me."

She let out a ragged breath, and Escalus bent down and kissed her.

I now knew for a fact that all those fairy tales I'd read were right. In a single second, I felt the truth of every last one of them hit me in the chest. I might not have the privilege of knowing a fated and absolute love. But Escalus and Noemi did.

It was in the determined tone of his voice, the beautiful arch of her body into his, the very hush that fell when their lips met. They loved each other so well that they learned how to hide it in plain sight.

What's more, they loved each other though it was doomed. Even if Noemi hadn't been a servant here, Escalus was destined to marry another royal. A time would come when they would be forcefully and painfully separated . . . and they didn't care.

They loved each other too much to let it stop them now. I dared to guess they'd probably already attempted to stop it and failed.

Before I got caught and stole their perfect moment from them, I turned and went as quickly as I came.

My mind was swarming with thoughts, each crashing into another like heavy waves. First, I suddenly saw my brother in a new light. Of course Escalus brought gifts for Noemi when he brought them for me. It was probably the opposite: he only did things for me to cover the fact he was doing something for her. He complimented her as often as he could; he made Nickolas be sure she was present when we did things together. He wanted to be near her always.

And Noemi. I'd known she could keep a secret, but I was shocked to find how right I'd been. I suddenly realized I had no idea how many of her own she'd been hiding from me. Not that I blamed her. If this got out, she would be instantly removed from the palace. I wasn't sure what would be done about Escalus.

And then there was me. It didn't hurt so much that maybe I wasn't as dear to my brother as I'd believed, because I knew that nothing would change how he loved me. And it didn't hurt so much that Noemi didn't trust me with this secret, because I knew she would still protect me with everything she had. What hurt in ways I couldn't express was how jealous I was.

The thing I'd been hoping for my whole life was painfully out of my reach. I couldn't even have it the way they did: brief and beautiful. And I never would. I could see it all too clearly. Rhett adored me, and it was flattering, but I didn't feel an affection nearly as strong as he did. And . . . I didn't think I could ever feel for him what I wanted to feel for someone. I wanted to swoon, to pine. I wanted passion and tenderness and . . . a love that might not make sense on paper but was undeniable in person.

It was lost to me.

By the time my self-pity hit in full force, I was at my door. The tears came as I tossed my sword down and tugged at my boots. I undressed myself rather sloppily, throwing my clothes across a couch and storming off to my bed. I buried myself beneath the covers, trying to shut out the world. To shut out the echoing disappointment.

I wished and wished and wished that my mother were here.

LENNOX

I recognized the scent almost immediately, though I couldn't see a face. "You're far from home," I said.

"So are you," she replied.

Well, wasn't that the truth? "But I'm ready to go."

Wordlessly, she laced her fingers between mine. Tall grass and clusters of flowers lined my vision as far as I could see. I watched the back of her head, simply following as long locks of light brown hair guided the way.

I found it was easy to fall into step behind her. It was comfortable to hold her hand, soft from a life of ease. And it was sweet, the sound of her voice as she coaxed me, saying, "Just a little longer."

I walked until the fields turned into a hill, cresting. Soon, so soon, I would see it. I would see home, finally. But then I was startled awake by Thistle licking my face. I gasped a little, confused and disappointed.

Thistle yipped at me, fidgeting. I could tell she was on edge, probably because I was. She kept licking my fingertips, offering the little comfort she could. She'd been roaming more than usual lately, but I told myself that was a good thing. She was wild, after all.

I pulled myself up, scratching at her ears. I wished I had a way of explaining that I was going to be roaming myself, that I might not come back. "You'll be fine without me, though," I said. "Still, try to take care of yourself, and don't come wandering around the recruits left behind. They might mistake you for food.

"And if I don't come back, thank you for staying with me. For so long, you were the only one." I lowered my voice to a whisper. "Don't tell the others, but I still prefer your company the best."

I kissed her head and stood, and she quickly nuzzled up on my thin pillow. I smiled and went to prepare myself the best I could. I tucked my shirt into the most durable pants I had and buttoned my coat over it.

I packed as I typically did, throwing a single spare of everything into my bag, just in case. It was going to be a slow trip with so many people moving on foot. We would travel today, camp tonight, and be on water tomorrow, so I packed something to sleep on.

For a split second, I almost grabbed the lock of Annika's hair. For some reason, it felt like a talisman, something that might protect me. Something had protected her, that was for sure. But I told myself I didn't need protection. King Theron was likely coming alone with a small dispatch of soldiers; we were coming en masse.

All the same, I walked over, pulling it from the back of

my desk drawer. It still held its curl, and I twirled it around my finger. I almost felt pity for her. While she was hiding somewhere, I would be taking her castle—*my* castle.

I startled a little at the knock on the door and quickly tucked Annika's hair away. Thistle moved so she was hidden in the corner. I was surprised to see Blythe this early, and with a parcel in her hand.

"Good morning," she said.

"And to you. What's this?" I pointed at the parcel.

"I don't know. It was outside the door, so I picked it up." She held it out to me.

It looked like a bunch of black fabric tied up in twine. I tugged at the bow, and the whole thing came tumbling out. I held it up and recognized the shape of it instantly.

There was no note—how could there be?—but I knew what this was and who it had come from. No one but my mother could have had my father's riding cape.

I swallowed hard, pushing something I couldn't name down to the deepest parts of myself. Down with the childhood I so deeply missed, down with the greenish pale color of my dead father's hand, down with the vomit I tossed out the window after I killed Annika's mother, down with the dread I felt each time someone meant a fraction of something to me, down with the fear in every set of eyes when they realized I was the last person they'd ever see.

I wasn't going to cry. Not today.

"You should wear it," she decided. "You look much more dangerous with a cape flying out behind you. Besides, we don't know what's waiting for us out there."

I swallowed again, then swept the cape around me, settling it across my shoulders.

Unlike mine, it was dark, the black still crisp, which told me that even though he'd been gone for years, she'd been preserving this well. The ties were long and had tassels on the edges, and the lining was made of something nicer than mine had been. Just inside the neck was an emblem of some kind, stitched in black thread, so if you didn't know it was there, you'd never see it. I didn't know what it was, but I appreciated that after all this time, he still had his secrets.

Something about the way the cape set around me felt like a hug, and I tried not to think about that too long.

"It looks good," Blythe said. Those bright eyes were back again, the faint flush in her cheeks.

I shook my head quickly and changed the subject. "Was there a reason you came by so early?"

"There are two, actually," she said, looking down. I didn't notice it at first because of the parcel, but I could see the bracelet woven with long grass and blue fabric that she must have stolen or saved resting in her hands.

I couldn't not take it.

"Thank you," I whispered, appreciating at the very least that she had the courage to give it to me. "Please don't be upset . . . but I'm not ready to wear this."

Her face was kind, more so than I deserved. "I don't need you to wear it. I just needed to make it."

I met her eyes for the briefest of seconds and looked away, pulling at the collar of my newfound cape.

"Umm, what was the other reason?"

"Oh," she said, her cheeks pink. "Kawan asked for you.

They're putting the final supplies together."

I nodded. "Let's go."

I grabbed my bag and my sword, pausing to look back at Thistle. She blinked at me once, and I hoped I'd get to see her again. Leaving the bracelet on my desk, I closed the door and followed Blythe down the hallway.

We found a good number of soldiers outside, and I could see White Flag, Skittish, and Spare glancing around, their eyes betraying their trepidation. We did not look like a group of people going to receive an envoy—no, with horses mounted and swords being sharpened, this was clearly an army headed for war.

I saw Kawan waving me to him and marched over, my cape fluttering behind me. For something so sturdy, it was light. I appreciated its construction more and more with every passing second.

I didn't care if my closest friend was dying of hypothermia, this cape would never leave me.

As I moved, I caught the sight of my mother, still clinging to the edges of Kawan's presence. I swallowed, unsure what to say or do. I thought we'd severed every last thread that might bind us. But here I stood, wearing my father's cape, given over by her grace.

I stopped, holding my hands out, wordlessly asking her what she thought.

Even from here I could see the tears in her eyes. She nodded briefly, her smile pained.

Would I ever understand her? Would she ever understand me?

Perhaps this would have to be enough for us.

"Our guests are insisting we leave our swords here," Kawan stated.

"It will be seen as an act of aggression," White Flag replied adamantly. "His Majesty will not tolerate it."

"And why should we be forced to travel unarmed?" Kawan demanded.

White Flag shook his head. "We have been sincere from the second we were discovered. Why do you think we would give you poor advice?"

Kawan's eyes were menacing. "I still say we take weapons."

"I still say it's a mistake."

There was a silence long enough for me to swiftly pull out my sword and aim it directly at White Flag's throat. Spare and Skittish stepped back but were quickly surrounded and made no further move to run.

"It seems to me that someone who wants to make sure that we have no weapons knows without doubt that we will need them. Answer my question, and don't waste my time with a lie: The king won't be alone, will he?"

He scoffed at me. "He will most likely be accompanied by his son and a handful of guards."

Again, I had no way of proving it, but I felt in my gut this was a lie.

Kawan, perhaps finally sensing this as well, flung his hand lazily. "At this point, it doesn't matter. We're taking our weapons, and your king will be joining you in the grave shortly. Lennox," he added, almost as if it was obvious, "take care of them."

My stomach sank, but I didn't flinch. "Bind them," I said,

and Aldrik, Illio, and Slone stepped from behind Kawan, tying up our revered guests' hands in front of them. Once they were properly secure, I pointed toward the path that would lead us to the sea. "Walk."

Inigo strode up beside me. "Do you need help?" he whispered.

I shook my head. "I have to do this alone. Make sure the others are ready. I'm certain now."

I marched them down the rocky trail, listening as Skittish started speaking once we were out of earshot from the rest of the army. "Coleman? Coleman, say something! Tell him we speak the truth."

"They don't believe it, my friend. I can do no more," White Flag said, resigned.

Skittish rounded on White Flag. "What?" Tears were filling his eyes; he understood that his death was unavoidable.

Spare, who'd been leading the pack, turned as well, waiting for a better answer. We all were.

White Flag—Coleman—looked at me and then his companions. "Even if I did have more to say, I couldn't. My silence will be my final service to our king." He flicked his head back at me, assuming I'd report every last syllable to Kawan.

How little he knew.

"Keep walking. Down to the coast," I said.

After some angry glances exchanged between the three of them, they started their bitter walk toward death.

Once we made it to the black sand of our beach, I made them line up in the edge of the surf, facing me. The clouds were rolling in, threatening rain.

"I won't tolerate any more lies," I began. "Speak plainly and speak quickly. Your king, what is his greatest weakness?"

White Flag refused to speak, but Skittish still looked hopeful, like giving an answer might grant him a reprieve.

"His children. If you had one of them, he'd give you anything you asked."

"Shut your mouth, Victos!" Coleman ordered.

"And your prince?"

"His sister. She is his weakness, and he is hers. Again, all you need is one."

Coleman's hands were bound, but he swung the both of them around, hitting Victos, who fell to his knees.

"Do you want to die for this?" Victos asked from the sand.

Coleman looked at me, his eyes like knives. "I will happily die for vengeance, for future peace."

I turned to Spare, the one who'd said all but nothing from the moment they arrived. He looked to the ground, and I couldn't tell if he was simply being defiant or if he had accepted his fate.

"You. What's your name?"

"Palmer," he replied.

"Do you have anything to say for yourself?" I asked him.

Victos got to his feet, and Coleman looked over, anxious to hear what Palmer would say.

He stared at me for a moment. "Her Royal Highness says you claim our kingdom is yours."

"That is true. I do."

"She says you could offer no evidence."

"We may not have your fine libraries, but that doesn't take away the truth."

"Her sensibilities may be somewhat romantic, but she is reasonable. If you had proof, she would find a way to make peace. She's like her mother in that way."

I nodded. "And tougher than one might think."

Palmer looked at me strangely. "Of course she's tough. You'd never guess what she's been through."

My eyes narrowed. I knew some of her pain; I'd caused it myself. "What do you mean?"

He looked up at me. "If I die today, it would be my greatest shame to divulge her secrets. I cannot say more."

What loyalty she commanded.

"A final question, then: If you are so devoted to her, to her family, why are you telling me this?" I asked.

"In truth? You would have to kill His Majesty if you wanted to get the crown out of his hands. The same for His Royal Highness. But Her Royal Highness?" Palmer looked down, shaking his head. "I've watched her from afar for years—since before she lost her mother—and she might be one of the few people who understand that there are things in this world more valuable than titles and crowns. She will do what is right when she is able. She is your only key to the kingdom, if one exists. But I support them to the end if you're nothing but a liar. And I hope they live, whatever happens. No offense," he added.

I chuckled. "None taken. Thank you for your honesty."

Coleman took in a deep breath. "So, what? Are we to get on our knees?"

I shook my head. "No. You are to swim."

They looked over their shoulders at the angry sea.

"I am tired of unnecessarily spilling blood. You will swim.

If you sink, that shall be on your own head. If you live and somehow make it home, well—that land will be mine by the time you arrive, so I wouldn't recommend staying."

They stood there for a minute, stunned.

"Go on. I've got work to do."

Victos and Coleman started walking into the surf. I knew it wasn't entirely impossible to stay afloat for hours with your hands bound . . . it could be torturous, though.

"Palmer," I whispered. "Hands out."

He did as I commanded, and I cut through enough of the rope that if he tried, he'd be free soon enough and could help the others.

"A gift from one man who is telling the truth to another."

He nodded at me and followed the others into the water.

I stayed for a while, watching until they disappeared behind some rocks on the southeastern part of the shore.

I put my sword away and went to rejoin the group. I looked for the handful from last night, feeling confident that everything I'd suspected was true. This was not going to be the easy encounter Kawan thought it would. Their king was intending to take out Kawan at the very least, if not all of us. And their castle would be ours for the taking. I gave Inigo a knowing nod, and he returned it. That would have to be it for now.

Kawan startled me, lumbering into my path expectantly. "Well?"

I didn't even have to lie. "Their bodies are in the sea."

ANNIKA

My feet were bare, and the night was covered in mist. It was so thick, and, though I couldn't see anyone, I knew instinctively that I wasn't alone. The moon was mostly full, scattering light off the droplets of water in the air. I searched and there, nearby, the shadow stood, shimmering hazily against the dim night sky.

I walked toward him; he'd been expecting me.

"Where are we?" I asked.

"Home," he answered.

I scanned the night again. I still saw nothing beyond the mist, but I sensed that he was telling the truth. So, when he took my hand, I didn't flinch. Not when he moved his thumb across my fingers, not when he pressed his cold lips to the inside of my wrist, not when he slid a ring onto me.

"What's this?" I asked.

"It's mine now," he said. "And so are you."

I sat up with a gasp, clutching at my chest.

"My lady! Are you all right?" Noemi rushed to my side.

"Yes," I replied, though I couldn't say for sure.

"I think the stress is giving me nightmares."

"Did you have another one?"

I nodded. "Could you have something brought up for breakfast? I don't think I can face the crowds just yet."

"I can fetch it myself," Noemi offered. It was an opportunity to see Escalus, even from a distance, and I had no intention of stopping her. "And I can take this book back to the library if you like. I wasn't sure if you were finished."

I looked over to see what she was talking about. The book, bound in green leather, sat on the same round table in the corner where I'd left it.

The trial records. In the wake of everything else, I'd completely forgotten about it.

"Actually, could you bring that to me, please?"

"Certainly, my lady. I'll get you something to eat." She set the book on my bed, and I could see her hands were not nearly as steady as usual.

"And Noemi? If my brother is there, would you check on him? I know he must be nervous. And tell him he can come by anytime at all today if he needs me."

I could see her chest rising and falling, thrilled at a reason to speak to him.

"Of course, my lady." She sped from the room while I picked up the book.

I didn't know why I felt anxious about opening it. Lennox's name wouldn't be in here. Taking a breath, I flipped it open, moving past the other hearings that seemed frivolous by comparison. There was one about a divorce, another about property lines. Finally, I came upon the trial notes for Jago. There was no last name listed, but I could see in the transcript that he'd stated, "We have no last names." I remember being told he acted alone—but he'd distinctly said *we* there. Someone should have caught that. On the list of attendees were the names of those on the jury, a handful of influential lords, and my mother. It had been so long since I'd seen her name in writing, it felt like a dagger in my heart.

Jago gave no age, said he lived alone in unsettled land, and refused to give any information beyond that. No mention of a wife; no mention of a child.

That made no sense to me. They certainly existed.

I skipped down, disappointed that the notes were so short.

The man Jago is of a wide build with dark, unkempt hair and dark eyes, nearly black. He stands at the court with an air of ease, accepting the events before him. He does not look around the room but only at the lead juror, waiting for him to speak.

"Jago the Lone, you have been charged with attempted assassination of His Majesty, King Theron. How do you plead?"

"Guilty."

"And you do so under your own free will?"

"I do."

"What is the cause for your criminal action?"

"Justice. This kingdom is not yours. I am only sorry that I failed."

But did he say this heavily? Defiantly? Was he in his right mind or not?

And why did no one take his claim into account? He gave them a reason, and it was never mentioned again.

"Very well. Under your own admission, you are guilty of this crime, and so the court finds you to be. You will be hanged, drawn, and quartered, your body parts on display for the whole of the kingdom."

At this verdict, there is much noise in the room. Her Majesty the Queen speaks to His Majesty the King. His Majesty raises a hand and stands.

"As it was my life in question, I wish to have a say in the sentencing. I am not a wholly benevolent king, but I am no monster. Had this criminal succeeded, that punishment would be fitting. As I have lived, I move to adjust this sentence to beheading. But I wish none of his body to remain on our soil."

The jury deliberates quickly.

"The sentence will be carried out tomorrow morning at dawn."

Gavel sounds.

I looked at the page holding both the name of my mother and Lennox's father. This moment linked them, and so linked Lennox and me. No one could have guessed then that this moment would be the one that led to the loss of a queen, wife, and mother.

I wished I had a way of knowing that what Lennox said was true. If Jago came here determined to kill my father, he must have believed in his cause with all his heart. He left his family for it. He died for it. But there was nothing in our history about a seventh clan, especially not one with rights to the crown. *My* ancestors were placed in power, *my* ancestors held off invaders that nearly scattered us. That was what I had always known.

And now we were about to make peace with people who wanted to take everything from us.

I couldn't let Lennox try to take my family, my castle, my country. He'd kidnapped me. He'd killed my mother while his father got a trial.

But he also gave me a way out.

I shook the thought from my head. Lennox must go the way of his father, because my father was coming home. My brother was coming home.

I would do whatever it took to make that happen.

Noemi came back in quietly, the tray of food balanced in one hand.

"His Royal Highness intends to come and see you today. He seemed not himself."

"Understandably." I picked at the food, unsure how much of it I'd be able to stomach in the end. "Noemi, I need your help."

"Certainly, my lady. What can I do for you?"

"I need you to do something that might go against my father's wishes. Maybe even my brother's. And I need you to keep it a secret."

LENNOX

For the first time, I'd misjudged Kawan's interest in me. I'd felt certain he would be so consumed with thoughts on attack, with his plot for stealing more boats, with his flimsy plans for whatever might come next, to bother paying me any attention.

But instead, he'd put me in charge of getting everyone through the forest—and now I could not run. As I led the way, trying to find the best path for the horses, the carts, and the steady stream of people, I wondered if there would be another chance.

I could almost swear that Kawan knew about my plans. As the day carried on, he kept giving me tasks, having me carry messages back through the crowd, keeping me occupied. I exchanged disappointed looks with Blythe, Inigo, and the rest of my Commission team; we all understood that we had to abandon our mission. Kawan's eyes were oddly trained on me today.

The sun moved about as slowly as we did, and we stopped

for the night in a wide field that was supposedly on the edge of Stratfel.

Griffin worked on a fire, Rami smiling and handing him kindling. It was odd. When he'd been told to fall on his sword, they'd both wept so much that I let him stay behind. Tomorrow morning, it was possible we'd be facing something far more dangerous, but they both looked calm, satisfied.

I supposed it was because they were together this time.

I sat in the grass. Inigo settled near me, and Blythe and Andre were quick to follow. Shortly after, Griffin and Rami came over, too.

"I'm sorry things didn't work out," I said. "At this point, I don't know if there's a way to follow through."

Inigo shook his head. "We have the most recent experience navigating this terrain, and we've faced off against their soldiers. I think Kawan thinks we'll give him an edge but doesn't want to go out of his way to praise us. He'd have to share the victory if he did."

It was such a straightforward and obvious assessment that it irritated me that I didn't come up with it first.

"You're right," I said with a sigh.

"You keep saying that with an air of surprise," he shot back.

I smiled, shaking my head as I looked up at the gorgeous sky, shimmering like diamonds scattered on black velvet.

"You know, you were the one who taught me to navigate by the stars," Andre said. I looked over in surprise. He wasn't normally one to initiate conversation.

"Me too," Blythe added.

"Yep," Griffin added. "I bet everyone here knows how to find their way because of you."

I ducked my head. "Eh. It's not that hard to figure out. You all were probably exceptionally good students."

"Exceptionally terrified," Andre muttered.

Everyone had a good laugh at that.

"You told us once that there were pictures in the stars," Blythe said. "What does that mean?"

I wondered how to explain. "There are collections of stars—constellations—that have stories attached to them."

"Tell us one," Sherwin insisted.

I swallowed, looking at several sets of expectant eyes waiting for me to speak. "Umm." I moved my gaze upward, trying to think of somewhere to start. I supposed the best plan was to go back to the basics. "You all know Polaris, the star you navigate by."

"Yes," Inigo said.

I drew in the sky with my finger. "And you know the four stars that make a box trailing behind it form Ursa Major."

"Yes!" Blythe replied enthusiastically.

"Well, I'm sure I never told you that Ursa Major means Big Bear. So, she's a bear."

"A crooked line and a square? That's supposed to be a bear?" Andre asked skeptically.

I shrugged. "I didn't make them; I'm just relaying the story."

"Which is?" Blythe asked.

"Once upon a time, a god fell in love with a nymph. But this god was already married. So, when his wife found out about the nymph, she had her turned into a bear. And now she's stuck up there, spinning in place."

Sherwin looked at the stars in disbelief. "That's harsh."

"I don't know," Blythe said. "I think the wife was justified."

"Yes," Rami agreed. "I'd go after the nymph."

I shook my head. "I think she'd have been somewhat more justified in punishing her husband. The nymph didn't know he was married, but *he* certainly did."

"Then they both should be bears," Blythe said. "Lennox, pick some stars and make another bear."

I chuckled. "I don't think I have the authority to do that. Besides, most of them are already claimed."

"But we don't know that," Inigo said. "Blythe's right. Go on. Make another bear."

I huffed out something that was almost a laugh searching for something that I could call a bear.

"Fine. Over there," I said, pointing to the distance. "Not only is he a bear, but they don't even get to be close to each other while they're trapped in the sky."

Andre chuckled. "I approve."

The chatter of my companions lifted my spirits, but the pessimist in me told me not to enjoy this moment. Because the truth was the same as it ever was: caring about someone made losing them that much worse.

ANNIKA

Noemi and I spent the day in my room, so I didn't see Escalus until well after dinner. We both perked up at the sound of his knock, shoving the books I'd hastily borrowed and read, torn piles of fabrics, and various supplies under my bed before Noemi ran to get the door.

She bowed, averting her eyes as she always did at first. "Your Royal Highness."

"Good evening, Noemi." He did a double take. "Has my sister made you her doll? Your hair looks very pretty that way."

"Thank you, sir. I think she's using me as a distraction against her nerves over tomorrow," she commented with a smile.

If I hadn't been so focused on myself—on missing my mother, on hating my betrothed, on wishing for more when I had so much—I'd have seen this all much sooner. They were speaking to one another in glances, having entire conversations that I could only see; they could hear.

Of course they could. Love doesn't look like anything; love has a sound.

"Are you prepared?" I asked, wringing my hands together. "Because . . . I'm a mess."

He wrapped me up in his arms. "I am, too. But honestly, I prefer walking into the unknown over you missing for a day."

"Don't be dramatic," I said, my words slightly muffled by his coat.

"It was Mother all over again, Annika. I almost couldn't bear it."

I could feel him swallowing, pushing down the tears for my sake.

"And that's how I will feel if something happens to you," I said firmly. "She's gone, and Father's barely here, and if you're not with me . . ." I took a breath, unable to even say it. "You have to be careful, Escalus."

"I will," he whispered. "But this should be little more than a ceremony. There's no reason for either of us to be this worried. However," he said, swallowing, his eyes focused on the floor, "if I am wrong and something happens to me, you are to run. And if you become heir apparent, I want you to fight for Kadier. I want you to stand up like you did to Father, like you did to Nickolas, like you did to Lennox. Keep this country whole."

"That won't happen," I urged, close to crying.

"Listen," he said, pulling me back and holding on to my shoulders, "there are things you should know. I've always thought you could lead, and if—"

There was another knock at the door, and Noemi rushed over to open it.

"Oh! Your Royal Highness, the duke is here."

Nickolas stepped around the door, coming into view. His eyes held the same worry as Escalus's.

"Ah. I see we had the same thought," Nickolas began. "Escalus, I don't suppose you'd spare a moment for me to say good night to the prettiest girl in Kadier?"

Escalus seemed unsure of what to make of this changed creature before him. I wasn't entirely sure myself.

"Certainly," my brother finally said, letting me go.

"I love you," I said.

"And I love you. Almost more than anything," he teased with a wink. A day ago, I wouldn't have known what he meant.

"Noemi, I think I'd like a moment alone to say good night to the duke. Perhaps you should escort my brother to the garden? Remind him of why he needs to take care?" I watched as her eyes lit up, little fireflies of hope.

"As you wish, my lady."

Escalus dutifully held out his arm, and she took it, and they looked so happy to be touching one another in front of other people with permission.

"You're very generous with your servants," Nickolas noted after they'd left, though thankfully without an air of judgment in his tone.

I shrugged. "She has a role to play in life, and so do I. Our role does not define our value, and so I shall treat her—and anyone else I can—with kindness."

He nodded. "You've already shown me more kindness than I deserve. When we come back from this, I will endeavor to earn it."

I gulped, hating what I was about to say. "Nickolas, you might have noticed my father is not quite himself as of late."

He ducked his head. "I have."

"If my father's poor judgment comes into play tomorrow, please don't forget your promise. Please stay with Escalus."

He held out his hand, asking for mine. I gave it.

"I'd do anything to keep you, Annika."

And then he was slowly, hesitantly, coming closer. Had he done this any other time in any other way, I might have slapped him. But as we were looking into a very uncertain tomorrow, I tilted my head up, waiting for his kiss. And, as his lips touched mine, I listened carefully.

Nickolas kissed me intently, the way he should have kissed me the night of our engagement. It was only now I considered that he might not have been brave enough in that moment. And while this kiss was much more welcome, the only sound I heard was my crackling fire.

He stepped back, a small smile on his face. He whispered when he spoke.

"We did not get off to the most promising start. But there will be time to grow together once we're back. I'm . . . I'm not prepared to say the thing I know gentlemen say when they're about to do something dangerous . . ."

"I'm not prepared to hear it," I replied, my voice just as quiet.

He nodded, a gentle, understanding smile on his lips.

"Then I shall say good night."

Nickolas kissed my hand, bowed, and left me to my tangled thoughts.

With the door closed, I went back to work, pulling out my whetstone and sword. I didn't pause when I heard the creak, knowing it was Noemi. She came beside me, pulling out the dress we were trimming for her and both our belts with pouches on the side.

"Did you tell?" I asked.

"No, my lady. I won't lie; I was very tempted. But you're right, it's better to wait. By now I hope you trust that I can keep a secret."

I sighed deeply. "Oh, Noemi. I do."

LENNOX

I woke to the sound of birds again. It was such a peaceful way to begin the day, even one marked with uncertainty. As I came to, other sounds joined the birds: Blythe packing her tent, Andre pouring water over the embers, and Inigo groaning a little as he stretched.

I wiped the sleep from my eyes and started packing.

"What are you going to do?" Inigo asked.

I looked over at him, noting that Blythe's and Andre's gazes both followed as I did. "What?"

Inigo huffed. "I know you're still thinking about the plan. So, you've got a choice now. You have to either let it go and focus on whatever is coming for us today . . . or you can tell Kawan. You can ask for us to go ahead to the castle."

Sherwin, Griffin, and Rami had now finished their tasks and were following the conversation through silent glances.

"Look at our numbers. He might let a handful of us go," Inigo offered.

I considered for a moment. If my suspicions were correct,

and their king wasn't sincere in this treaty, a move on the castle could only make things better. If I was wrong, and they were truly trying to make peace with us, I couldn't name a single person in the army who wanted that, so even a failed attempt at the castle wouldn't ruin anything.

I sighed. "I'll be back."

I wove through the sea of people in various states of readiness for the day, marching up to Kawan. He glanced over at me, rolling his eyes before I even approached.

"Everyone toward the back ready?" he asked.

"Not yet. But I have a proposition for you."

Beside him Aldrik was running his whetstone over his sword, not bothering to acknowledge I was there. Maston and Illio were checking over carts, but I didn't see Slone or my mother.

"Make it quick," Kawan said, impatience painting his voice.

"With your permission, I'd like to take a small group to secure the castle in Dahrain. With the way the prisoners behaved yesterday, I believe this summit will be less peaceful than originally thought. I feel certain that their forces will be focused on the Island and that the throne will be unguarded. It gives us a second advantage in that, even if they take some of our number and even if they escape, they'll have nowhere to run. We'll be waiting."

I did my best to make sure my plan didn't sound like a contradiction to his but rather an addition.

Even so, he was unimpressed. "You are never content, are you?"

"Sir?"

"If you aren't showing off with your sword, then it's your wit. If not your wit, then the stars. And if none of that, then you feel you have to undo my plans and bend them to yours." His lips were curling into a snarl. "You are convinced that you're better than me, aren't you?"

The word never escaped my lips, but it flashed to my mind in an instant: *Yes.*

It was a mistake that I let my lips curl up into an exhausted smile, that I let my arms rise and fall in a moment of pure incredulity. In the split second after these motions, he reached out, grabbing me by the neck.

His breath smelled like something dying, and his voice was quiet as he spoke less than an inch from my face.

"Everyone else can fall in line. Why can't you? Do you intend to usurp me?" he asked.

If I can get a clean cut.

"Unfounded suspicion will not help us in this moment, sir," I answered calmly. "We're about to face our enemy."

He swung his arm so quickly, I didn't see it coming. But I felt the skin by my eye pull apart where he struck me, the heat of running blood following shortly after. I stumbled back, still on my feet but dizzy from the blow.

"If you can't be smart enough to humble yourself before me, I'll do it for you," he told me. "Whatever you think you're going to take from me, you will fail."

I stared at him. "All I want is what you promised. You vowed to lead our people to a life that should have always been ours. I'm offering to help you achieve that end." I raised the eyebrow that was bleeding. "It doesn't sound like I'm the one struggling with humility."

He swept a foot under mine, bringing me to the ground.

"You will learn your place!" he screamed, drawing the attention of those nearby. "And you will follow my lead, or you will, for once, find yourself on the receiving end of a blade."

"We both know you don't have the guts," I said, my pride acting a little faster than my head.

He pulled back, kicking me square in the ribs, and I curled in on myself like a child, the scent of wet grass swirling around me.

Kawan bent down, resting his hands on his knees as he spoke. "If you want to live long enough to see Dahrain, I suggest you shut your mouth." He turned back to his task, and I was left humiliated on the ground.

I stood slowly, but the rumors were traveling faster than I could, and I caught people passing whispers both before and after I could walk past them. When I got about halfway through, two of the younger recruits came running up.

"We had a question. We . . ." The boy, no older than thirteen, took in my face, blood down one end, dirt down the other, and lost his train of thought. I gave him a moment, but I was in no mood for stupidity.

"What is it?" I asked. Well, barked.

They both took two steps back, but the quiet one nudged the other, urging him to just get it over with.

"Well . . . we're in charge of taking the horses back. The sun is rising there," he said, pointing. "And I put a stick in the ground, and the shadow says that east is that way, too," he added. "And if we veer slightly north, we should hit the castle before nightfall. That's right, isn't it?"

He looked up at me, his hope at being right winning out over his fear. I couldn't help the tiny smile that tugged at my lips. "Long before nightfall. Good job."

The boy let out a ragged breath. "Thank you, sir."

"Use the bit of sky you can see in that forest, all right? Don't rely on a compass; it won't work."

They nodded. The quiet one clapped the other on the back, and they both ran off, ready to do their part. I watched them a moment, proud. I'd taught them something. They'd held on to it, and that would help us all in some small way today. I couldn't feel the ache in my ribs anymore.

I slowly made my way back to the group, the state of my face telling them everything they needed to know. Rami went to work, finding something to dip in water so I could clean off my wound.

"That settles that," Andre said.

Rami carefully wiped away the blood as Blythe and Inigo watched, grimacing at her every movement.

"All we can do is be alert today. And patient."

If Kawan had heard me say that, he'd have hit me again. Who was I to be giving orders? But I didn't care. If he was solely focused on saving himself, then someone else had to save my people.

ANNIKA

For the first time in my life, I was the one helping Noemi into a dress. I wasn't about to have her ride out beside me looking like a maid for fear the soldiers might think her expendable. And I couldn't bear to leave her behind. We all knew what it was like to sit and wait for news, how sometimes that was far more painful than knowing the truth. I wasn't doing that to her.

Her dress was one of mine, tailored by her skilled hand to her frame, and almost matching mine. Had my hair been darker or had she been kissed with freckles, we might have looked like sisters.

Using her perfect little invention, my sword was expertly hidden beneath my gown, but both of the small, leather hip belts she'd found were worn outside. We didn't have much in them—hardtack in case we needed something to eat, a flint if this stretched into the night, a few pieces of gold should I need to bribe my way out of something—but knowing I wasn't completely empty-handed helped me settle myself.

I braided her hair in the way I'd experimented the day before, and while the front pieces of my hair were braided back, the rest stayed down; I was going into this meeting looking both like the woman they'd murdered and the girl they'd failed to.

"Do I look acceptable?" Noemi finally asked, holding her arms out. "I feel a bit ridiculous."

I chuckled. "Well, it suits you. As does the color. When we get back, I think we should do away with your uniform altogether."

Her tentative smile disappeared. "What?"

"Would you not like that?"

"No, no, I would!" she replied quickly. "But people will assume I'm a lady-in-waiting, not a maid. It would be inappropriate."

"People throw that word around a lot, don't you think? 'Annika, it's inappropriate to sword fight. It's inappropriate to leave your hair down.' I'm starting to think I don't care for the term at all."

Noemi walked over, taking my hands in hers. "But a part of you does. You know it would be inappropriate to completely ignore your father, so you don't. You know it would be inappropriate to abandon your title, so you press on."

I frowned. "Those distinctions have much more to do with love than decorum. As such, no more uniforms when we return. I love you."

"And I love you. So much so that I am willing to follow you into madness, so we'd better get a move on."

I smiled. "Let's go."

We headed to the stables to choose horses. Grayson was attentive this morning, moving quickly as he completed his task.

"Thank you," I said, tossing one of the coins from my bag his way. "I'm counting on someone to hold this place together while we're gone."

He smiled up at me. "Anything for you, my lady."

Noemi and I mounted our horses, and I looked back over my shoulder at Grayson. I hoped I was wrong. I hoped that this was a straightforward summit, though even that left me uncomfortable. I just prayed that I had misjudged Lennox and that he'd either be there to receive this treaty himself or back in his damp castle. Anywhere, really, so long as it wasn't on our doorstep.

We reached the front gate, only to find a huge party waiting for us. Noemi and I exchanged a glance, surprised at just how many officers Father had chosen to take with us.

"Absolutely not!"

I whipped my head up to find Escalus on his horse, trotting over. "What?"

He pointed to Noemi. "You will go back inside this instant."

"Might I remind you that she works for me, not you," I scolded.

"And might I remind you that I outrank you here."

I wondered if the shock I felt was visible to everyone else. Escalus never pulled rank on me, not in private, not in public.

"Escalus, I'm bringing Noemi with me," I told him, keeping my voice low. "If my guess is right, and Lennox comes to the castle, I'd rather her be with me."

Escalus sighed heavily, looking at Noemi. Once again, they were having one of their silent conversations. I could see that her eyes were pleading. With every second, his will was fading. He was clearly desperate to keep her close, even if it might be dangerous.

"I want both of you behind me at every step, do you understand? Neither of you are allowed to cross my line of sight."

"Of course," I replied.

"As you wish, Your Highness," Noemi answered with a bow of her head.

We collectively joined the head of the group where Father was speaking with Nickolas. They both seemed in steady spirits today; I took that as a good sign. Father looked over at me, catching Noemi.

"Ah. An attendant. That's a good idea, Annika," he said. His voice sounded strained. "Now, make sure that you both stay behind me. Escalus, Nickolas, you as well. I will be leading the procession. Let's head to the ships. I want to make sure we're on time."

We marched along the wide road that led to the docks, a place I hadn't seen in years. Mother and I used to travel, used to go out into the country, travel to the neighboring kingdoms. I still remembered those trips, the warm greetings of our countrymen, the gift of an apple from a stranger, the flowers we'd pick and bring home for our rooms. It felt like someone else had done all those things now; that girl and I were so far apart.

When we got to the docks, I was confused. Looking over to Escalus, I could see that he was as well.

"Your Majesty," he asked, "why are there three ships?"

"Oh," Father replied nonchalantly. "I'm bringing gifts. Peace offerings. We'll be on the middle one, here." He started his horse up the gangplank, and my stomach sank. Two whole ships' worth of gifts? What was he giving them? Why was he doing this at all? It made no sense.

Once on board, we dismounted, and the horses were led safely belowdecks. Father was speaking to the captain of the ship, and Nickolas was at his side, taking everything in. He was so, so eager to please.

"How could you?" Escalus asked, coming up beside me. "How could you bring Noemi into this?"

"I didn't feel safe leaving her behind."

He shook his head. "I might not be able to protect you both. She could be hurt or worse."

"She won't be. I promise I'll run if I need to run, and she'll stay with me."

Escalus stared at me with hard eyes, saying nothing before storming off.

"Escalus!" I called.

He looked at me over his shoulder. "Are you still here?"

I swallowed, waiting. He nodded but did not speak.

And that was almost worse than nothing at all.

I hoped the meeting with the Dahrainians was peaceful. That was all the battling I could take for one day.

LENNOX

The kingdom of Stratfel was along the coast, and a huge part of their economy depended upon fishing. As such, their collection of fishing boats was extensive, so there were plenty to steal. Enough small boats to carry our people to an island, and enough to devastate dozens of Stratfelian families.

I stayed out of sight, playing no part in the thievery. I simply climbed aboard when directed, knowing I had no choice. I toyed with the ropes on the boat, tying the few knots I knew. Sheet bend, lark's head, sheepshank. I hoped the action would untie the knots in my stomach. It did not. We kept close to shore, unwilling to test the boats unnecessarily. At the same time, our eyes were out to sea, wondering if they were close.

"I don't even know what I'm looking for," Blythe admitted. "Just any ship on the horizon?"

"Essentially," I replied.

Inigo and Blythe had stayed by my side, as had Griffin and Rami.

"I don't see anything," Inigo stated dejectedly. "Were we given the wrong date?"

I shook my head. "No. This was designed to lure at least some of us into the open. They're out there."

Just then, we rounded a jagged edge of the coast, and right ahead of us were three massive frigates. Now that I could see just what they had at their disposal, my greatest fear was confirmed: this was a full-fledged assault.

"Get your weapons ready," I yelled to my crew. "Their ships are bigger, but that makes them slower. There's a chance they haven't noticed us yet, but they will soon. When that happens, be on guard. We don't know what defenses they have. We will need all of our number, so protect one another."

"Yes, sir!" they all responded.

Inigo was already adjusting the sails, using the wind and our size to our advantage. Blythe and Rami were side by side, lining up the unlit torches in neat, easy rows on both the starboard and port sides of the boat.

As my father's cape drifted out behind me, I wondered idly whether there was more to be said between my mother and me. And, most important, would today rob us of the opportunity to try?

Inigo's use of the winds was excellent, pushing us past many of our own ships easily. I stood on the front of our schooner, watching. It wouldn't be long before they realized we were on their tail, and I had my eyes on the backs of the ships, waiting for that moment. I glanced to my sides, making sure everyone I could see was ready.

When I turned to my right, my mother was there, holding on to the mast of a small boat three away from me, looking at me with something in her eyes that could almost be pride. After a moment she pointed up to her eyebrow, mirroring mine. I shrugged and gave her an almost smile. Let her think I fell, or that I got hit practicing. Now was not the time to trouble her. I nodded at her, and she nodded back. I turned, focusing on what lay ahead.

Maybe a minute later, a watchman caught sight of us. I could hear the frantic yelling over the waves.

"Light the torches," I called.

We were so close. So close. My heart was racing at the thought of that giant, beautiful ship sinking to the bottom of the sea. It would be the first step in taking down the entirety of their navy. The navy, then the monarchy, then the castle. Dahrain would be ours within days.

And then they turned.

With more agility than I'd have thought possible for a ship that large, they lined the port sides of their frigate against our sad little fleet, creating a massive wall.

"Scatter!" I called when no one else gave a command. "Throw!"

We were close enough that some of the torches made it to the deck. Several bounced off the sides but didn't make contact long enough for fire to catch. It was hard to tell from this distance if the ones on the deck were doing much damage.

The aft side of the ship closest to us looked like it had a growing plume of smoke, and that made me smile briefly before a bullet sailed past my shoulder.

"What was that?!" Blythe shrieked, ducking.

"They have muskets!" I yelled back. Of course they did.

Another bullet came our way, hitting the side of the boat and splintering the wood.

"Stay down!" I ordered. Ignoring my own words, I leaped up to survey the damage. Two or three of our boats had tipped in the wake of the frigate, and people were grasping for something to hold on to, begging for someone to throw them a rope. In another boat, someone was crying as blood spilled out of a hole in their arm.

Where was my mother? I scanned our fleet, finding her where I'd seen her last, a few boats away. Even from here, I could see the tears streaming down her face as she hurled curses and torches at the massive ship, years of grief spilling out.

I'd known she was formidable. This was something else, something deeper than the sheer determination she threw into surviving. It was almost animalistic.

Following her lead, I called back to Blythe and Rami. "Light the torches, and I'll throw them from here."

Rami passed me one first.

I remembered my father's face and threw.

I remembered my cold room and threw.

I remembered needless blood on my sword and threw.

I remembered every last thing I went through because of them, and I fought the only way I could.

Over all the screams and the muskets firing, the waves and clamor, I was brought to a halt by a voice calling out.

"Annika, get back!"

She was here.

White Flag—Coleman—had specifically said that she would be kept far from a war, so why—*why*—was she here?

There. I found her on the stern of the ship, searching for something. She was in white.

I stood there stunned as the wind picked up her hair, tossing it back and forth.

She dragged her gaze over the boats, finally meeting my eyes.

She stopped looking.

Had I been what she was trying to find?

I didn't know how much time passed as we stood there, watching each other, not moving. I sensed, in the deepest parts of myself, that we were both inviting unnecessary danger.

"Lennox! Lennox, take the torch!" Rami said.

I came back to my senses. "What?"

She stood up taller. "Take the tor—"

Suddenly, Rami was on her back, an ugly red pool growing around her abdomen. She'd been hit twice in quick succession, and the bullets were doing their work fast.

"Rami!" Griffin cried, coming over to cradle her. His lips were trembling. Everything was trembling.

She hardly made a sound, and I watched as her eyes moved from the clouds to the boat to each person surrounding her . . . until she found Griffin.

"You," she whispered as Griffin clutched her hand. "You made everything bright."

"Stop it," he ordered. "We can fix this once we get to

land. Just keep pressure on it."

There wasn't much point. Inigo already had pressure on the wound, and the blood was still pouring.

Rami kept her eyes on Griffin. "You made . . . everything . . . worth it."

"Please," he said. There wasn't anything else to ask. "Please."

"I love you," she told him, the hint of a smile on her face.

Griffin nodded. "How could you not?"

She really smiled at that.

"I love you. It won't stop," he vowed.

"No," she whispered. "No . . . it won't."

Rami reached up and traced a finger along Griffin's cheek. Then her hand fell to the deck, lifeless. Griffin let out a guttural cry, the sound shaking something in the deepest parts of me. Blythe, always so steady and cool, covered her mouth, crying as well. Inigo had stood up beside Blythe. He almost went to put a hand on her back, but he remembered the blood on them and stopped, watching her in concern.

I barely knew Rami, but all I could think about was how her brief life had been wasted, stolen. The fire of anger in my chest was rekindled, and I stood, looking back to the frigate.

Annika wasn't on the deck anymore. In her place was that coward from the Forest, the fiancé.

We had to change tactics.

"Pull back!" I called. "Pull back!" I turned to Inigo. "Set our course for the Island. We're going to take them on land."

He nodded and leaped into action, his bloodstained hands moving quickly.

"Hey!"

I turned to see the boat with Kawan on it beside me.

"Who are you to call orders?" he demanded.

I bypassed him for a moment, looking for my mother. She was still there, uninjured it seemed, except for the ghosts tormenting her mind.

I turned to Kawan. "It takes a skilled soldier maybe twenty seconds to reload a musket. Under war conditions, that slows out of fear. It becomes thirty seconds, a minute. And thirty seconds at the end of my sword or Inigo's, thirty seconds on the receiving end of Blythe's or Griffin's bow . . . that's enough time to take down a country. Get us to land so we can have that time."

He considered this, then nodded.

I looked behind me, watching as Griffin kissed Rami's forehead. He stroked her hair off her face, and he didn't let her go as we shifted our course for land.

It had been fascinating to watch how love chipped the jagged edges from someone, made them sharper in some ways and softer in others. It left me, for the first time, awed by the prospect. Love was complicated.

Complicated, but so unexpectedly beautiful.

ANNIKA

I didn't tell anyone what I saw. I didn't know if I'd ever be able to talk about it, not even to Escalus. There was a world of difference between worrying people were going to die and watching it happen.

We were at war.

There were no gifts on these boats, only tons of soldiers. We weren't making a treaty on the Island, just fighting where it wouldn't hurt our kingdom. We weren't even brave enough to be honest about it; we'd walked them into a corner.

"My lady?"

I startled at Noemi's touch.

"I'm so sorry, my lady," she said, coming in front of me.

I placed a hand on my heart, trying to steady it. "Just Annika today, Noemi. What's happening?"

"We're almost there. It seems we've suffered very little damage and almost no loss of life. Based on what he saw, His Majesty says we greatly outnumber them. It should be a quick and easy defeat."

I nodded. That was what we wanted, right? What I'd said I wanted? If it came down to them or me, it was going to be me. And if not me, at least Escalus. Escalus had to survive.

"Did you suspect?" I asked her. "That we were going to attack them?"

She shook her head, her eyes holding the same horror mine did.

"I'll go up now. I want to be out there, Noemi. I want to be beside Escalus."

"The king won't like it," she whispered.

"Oh well." I stood and made my way to the upper deck.

It was peaceful out here now, with men moving around, preparing muskets and ammunition. I had my sword at my waist, not bothering to hide my intentions anymore. Looking to the horizon, I saw the Island as we approached.

I could see there was an inlet perfect for disembarking ships of our size. Most of the land was forested, though the trees looked foreign to me, and I could see mountain peaks in the distance. The only thing menacing were the clouds coming from the northeast, thick and imposing. In my head, I'd painted this place as unwelcoming, but the trees were so green, the sky was so bright that, if I'd been forced to describe the Island in a word now, I'd have chosen *inviting.*

The men pulled the ship in to the old docks, and I mounted my horse.

Noemi went to mount up as well, as I'd instructed her to, but Escalus came over.

"No! Under no circumstances are you disembarking. It was one thing to have you come along when we thought it was a small envoy, but now that there's an entire army out there, you will not be leaving this ship." He took the reins of Noemi's horse in his hands, swallowed hard, and spoke. "I forbid it."

"I unforbid it," I called.

"Annika, do not push me today," Escalus warned.

I sighed. "If things get too intense, she can come back to the boat."

He was still angry at me, still enraged that I could be putting her in danger. But after a moment, the tension in his shoulders relaxed. "Fine. But nothing changes. You stay behind me, and you *will* leave if I give the order. Do you understand?"

She nodded. "Absolutely, Your Royal Highness." There was gravity in her voice, an understanding passing between them.

I knew he was worried for her safety—I was, too—but it would be better for both of them if they were in the same place, where they would know exactly what was happening. If there was one thing Lennox had given me, it was a strange sense of peace through knowing the truth. That, at least, I was grateful for, and I wouldn't rob my brother or Noemi of it. Not on a day like this.

I wondered about those left in Lennox's army. How many had survived the onslaught? Had they come ashore yet? Were they on their way to us now?

Were they too crushed by the numbers they'd lost to carry on?

I would have been.

Swallowing, I looked at Escalus, who was mounting his own horse, and Father as he did the same. Noemi, brushing her hair off her face, and even Nickolas. What would I do if I ended this day without a single one of them?

I pushed that thought away and followed them to land. Our soldiers were disembarking as well, marching in clean lines through the thick brush. My horse didn't seem nearly as confident here as he did back home, and it bothered me that even he could sense something was off.

I took breaths to steady myself as we made our way in silence under the canopy of strange trees. In the distance, the scattered forest broke into a clearing. The sky was split, sunlight shining brilliantly on one half, the gray of heavy rain clouds on the other. Father held up a hand as we neared the edge of the forest, and I pulled my horse to a halt.

"I see them, too," Escalus whispered.

"Which means they can see us," Nickolas added.

"No point in hiding, Your Majesty. If this is why we came, let's squash this quickly and go home," Escalus said.

Father took a long pause, looking first to Escalus and then to me. He shook his head, as if he only just now realized what he'd backed us all into. Sighing, he stared into the empty field, bracing himself for whatever came next. And then we marched.

My stomach dropped. We'd been roped into a battle we didn't know was coming. How was this supposed to end well?

I couldn't help myself. Once we were out in daylight, my eyes searched for Lennox. When I finally found him—his hair lifted by the breeze, his cape out behind him—he was already watching me. His sword was drawn, but those clear blue eyes were not nearly as menacing as I'd prepared myself for.

Those weren't the eyes that ordered me to surrender and bound my hands; those were the eyes that let me go when he could have dragged me back.

I didn't know how battles began. In my heart, I hoped that Father—now that he'd come to his senses about how terrible this was—would walk out to calmly speak to them, and that their leader would meet him halfway. I hoped that after they'd already suffered loss, they'd be willing to compromise in order to save lives. I hoped we could genuinely give them this island as a gesture of peace after taking so many of their people. I hoped we could all do better.

No such thing happened.

Without warning, the bulky shape of Kawan moved, doing so faster than I thought him capable. A bow came from nowhere, hidden under his layers of fur and leather, but the arrow was crisply visible against the graying sky, flying straight as it pierced my brother's chest.

"Escalus!" Noemi screamed, already jumping from her horse to help him.

Around me, our soldiers charged without waiting for orders. I watched my brother slump forward, taking shaky breaths as he stared at the arrow. "Don't pull it out," he warned Noemi. "That will make it worse."

So, just like that, he was going to die?

Escalus was going to die. We were far from home, and he

had an arrow lodged in his chest, close to his shoulders, with no means of removing it.

And suddenly, I was very much made for the battlefield.

Lennox was still standing where I saw him last. It was as if he knew. His people might advance, and my soldiers might charge, but he and I could go up against no one else.

I dug my heels into my horse, and he sprang into life. As I started galloping, I heard someone behind me scream my name. I ignored it, my eyes trained on Lennox. He watched me for a moment, making sure I was coming his way, then turned and sprinted away. Between the distance and his speed, he had quite the head start. That wouldn't save him today. He bolted into the forest behind him, moving nimbly around trees and jumping shallow streams. I unsheathed my sword, holding it high.

He killed my mother. He kidnapped me. His army might have just murdered my brother. So, it seemed only fitting that I ever so swiftly remove his head.

As I came up on him and went to swing, he ducked, sensing me on top of him. He turned and moved in a different direction while I pulled my horse to a stop to turn and chase him. He stopped behind a cluster of trees too tightly grown for me to follow on horseback. I circled around, trying to find a break, a way I could corner him. There wasn't one.

I knew what he was doing. If I wanted a chance at him, I had to dismount. I hated to lose any advantage I had, but it had to be done.

I hopped from my horse, staring into the piercing blue eyes of my enemy. He watched me for a moment before stepping into the light.

Quite suddenly, all the sound in the world disappeared. No wind in the trees, no birds, no swaying grass. The earth itself held its breath as we came to meet for the last time.

"Your Highness," he finally said with a bow. Then he charged.

I raised my sword to block him, thinking of what Rhett had taught me: I couldn't just fend him off; I needed to attack, to strike.

I rounded on him, swiping my sword dangerously close to his cheek. When he backed up, realizing how his perfect face had nearly been ruined, he looked almost impressed. That didn't slow him for long, and he came back at me, swinging down again. It seemed his plan wasn't to simply run me through; he was going to wear me out first and then go in for the kill.

Two could play that game.

I swung low, forcing him to bounce back or jump to the side. He was much bigger, so it was certainly more tiring for him to move like that than for me. More than once, our swords hit in ways that sent out sparks. Our strengths were different, but we were well matched, making the fight go longer than I wanted. I suspected he felt the same.

I was about to strike Lennox again when the hush surrounding us broke. I heard the strangest sound, almost like thunderous applause. I saw in Lennox's eyes that he heard it, too. In silent agreement, we both pulled our weapons back and turned to see what looked like a wall of gray clouds advancing as steadily as either of our armies. Wind and rain wrapped up together—overlapping as if fighting for dominance—crept ever closer as the darkness rolled in. This must have been the storm I'd seen in the distance from the ships, the darker side of the gray clouds now taking over the entirety of the sky.

At first, I was too in awe to do anything. How eerily stunning it was, how mysterious and grand. And then I saw the winds rip a tree up from its roots, and I started running.

Lennox was beside me in a flash, passing me by a few feet, then holding that same position as we ran.

I didn't dare look back. I could hear the rain and wind behind me, and that was all I needed to continue moving forward. I'd never seen a storm like this, didn't know how to protect myself. I couldn't hold on to a tree—those were being torn from the ground—and I didn't think dropping to the forest floor would help, either.

I was wrong: there was nothing welcoming about this land.

And then, in the distance, my salvation presented itself. In the side of one of those strange rocklike mountains, down an edge as sheer as a cliff, there was an opening. I didn't know how deep it went, but it was my only chance at shelter. The only problem was that Lennox was clearly heading toward the same place. He glanced over his shoulder, first looking at me, and then at the approaching wall of wind. His eyes widened, and he pushed himself to move faster.

So, I did the same. Unfortunately, my legs were not as long as his, and my dress was limiting me. It was only a few seconds later that I tripped over a root and fell, face-first, onto the ground. I cried out from the impact, feeling certain my ribs would be bruised. I pushed myself up to my knees, desperate to keep moving, when suddenly a hand wrapped around my arm.

"Come on!" Lennox shouted, pulling me from the dirt and dragging me toward the cave.

"Keep running," he insisted, dropping my arm once I was moving so we could hold our swords in one hand and pump with the other.

I did my best to keep up, trailing just a few steps behind him. Lennox paused at the opening of the cave, holding an arm out for me and pulling me in. We both turned, looking at the encompassing wall of gray.

"What is that thing?" I asked.

"A hurricane," he said, the words sounding more like a question than confirmation. "We've gotten them before, but not this strong and never this fast. It's going to come right over us. We have to get deeper in."

We turned, surveying the cave. There wasn't much depth that I could see. From the opening, the walls fanned back to form a sort of triangle, with two rounded corners. It looked like there was something scratched on the walls, but I couldn't be sure. All that really mattered was we were trapped in here, and there wasn't anywhere else to hide.

The sound of the wind was reaching a piercing level, and it was so close, I could feel the suction of it. I moved with Lennox to one of the corners, wishing we had more protection. I pulled my sword up as high as I could and drove it into the ground, uncannily, at the exact same moment Lennox did. He knelt, pulling me down, and we gripped our swords as the winds breached the cave.

The sound was nightmarish, loud and chaotic, and the winds were strong enough that they lifted me from the floor for a second or two at a time. I gripped my sword, hoping that I'd driven it in deep enough to hold. Looking down, I saw Lennox's knees come up, too, and I reached out for him, attempting to pull him back down. Once his legs were back on the ground of the cave, he gripped me, too. He wrapped a leg around me, and I did the same. We held on to our hilts and one another, just trying to stay alive. I felt when he readjusted his grip, and I felt when he pulled me in tighter. My legs were surely going to be bruised from where I kept slamming into the floor, and I had to imagine Lennox's arms were burning as much as mine were from the strain. And then, as if he could read my thoughts, he let out a groan through his teeth, as if giving a focus to the ache. I buried my face into his chest, digging fingers into his clothes, holding on until, as quickly as it had begun, the winds began to subside.

We were on the ground, holding our swords, tangled into one another, and panting as if we'd just run across the entirety of the Island.

We stayed still a few moments, unsure if the winds would pick up again. The howling was diminished, but still there. The new noise was now the rain.

We released our grips, looking out at the sheets of rain. The lip of the cave tilted down, so it wasn't coming in, but it wasn't anything I was looking forward to rushing into.

After having my eyes clenched shut for so long, I'd adjusted to the darkness and could make out Lennox's uncomfortable expression.

Clearing my throat, I dropped my arm and untangled my legs, moving quickly to stand. Lennox got to his feet first and, with some effort, jerked his sword upright, releasing it from the ground. If it was that hard for him, this was going to be embarrassing for me. I had to tug three times to get my sword out.

Lennox wasn't even paying attention. He was walking, surveying.

Then he took a deep breath, a wild smile playing on his face. "Are you ready to get back to the business of dying?"

"Absolutely," I replied, having no intention of losing my life today. He raised his sword as I pulled back mine, and we both hit stone.

I tried to readjust, but it didn't matter. The ceiling didn't offer much room, and, to be honest, it was going to be all but impossible to move in here; we were just as likely to injure ourselves as we were each other.

We both came to this unfortunate realization at the same time.

"So how does this end?" I asked, out of ideas. "If we can't properly fight, do we run for it?"

He pointed to the torrent outside. "Can you see your way through this?"

I turned and stared, straining. "I think I see a tree. Maybe."

"Exactly. If we run, we won't make it. So, you can attempt if you want, but I'm not dying like that."

"Neither am I," I replied.

"Then I'm afraid it's an uncomfortable truce for us, Your Highness."

I huffed. He was right, of course, and I hated that. All I could do for now was survive.

"You keep to that side of the cave, and I'll keep to this one," I ordered.

"Agreed," he replied, and we stepped away from each other, settling on the floor, staring across the cave into the eyes of our enemy.

LENNOX

The weather was not changing. I didn't know if it had been hours or if it simply felt like that, but either way, the waiting was torture.

I had no stars or sun to guide me. I had attempted counting seconds just to keep track of passing time, but it had only made me tired, and I couldn't risk falling asleep.

Across the cave, Annika was clutching her knees to her chest, clearly as cold as I was. That wind had chilled me to the bone as well, and the rain wasn't helping. But I at least had my riding cape, so I was better off than she was.

She picked at a hole on her dress, looking as if she was thinking about something more intently than she wanted to.

So was I.

Why had I gone back for her? Why had I clutched her to me when the winds came in the cave? Now, hours later, I tried to come up with an excuse. I knew her; she was resourceful. I couldn't leave her life in the hands of a storm. No, in the end, if she was going to die, it had to be at my hands. I couldn't trust it to anyone—or anything—else. Anyone would agree that I'd had to save her.

A shiver ran through me, and I finally stood.

"Please tell me you carry a flint."

Annika looked up from her corner of the cave. "What?"

"It's showing no signs of easing up out there, and you look colder than I am, so if you want to survive, a fire would be a good place to start. Do you have a flint?"

"Even if I did, what would we build a fire from?"

I rolled my eyes. That didn't sound promising. I bent down and picked up an overflowing fistful of debris blown in by the wind. "This?"

She surveyed the ground, seeming to see for the first time how much we had at our fingertips. Sighing, she drew herself up.

"Leave your sword in the corner. I'll do the same."

I smirked, walking my weapon back to my side. "I could kill you with my bare hands if I wanted to."

She held her hands out wide. "So could I. Not the point. Drop your sword."

I wiped my smile away before I turned around to face her. I felt confident that she was bluffing—her hands were more suited for a ballroom than a fistfight—but I appreciated that she was bold enough to lie. I cleared my throat as I grabbed another handful of wood to build a fire. She started building a pyramid out of the larger pieces while I shoved the smaller bits of leaves into the center.

"This cave looks man-made," I commented. "Or at least modified. It isn't a natural shape. And the texture of the walls . . . they're too smooth."

She nodded. "I keep looking at those marks on the wall,

trying to figure out what they mean."

"Well, if either of us could guess, I'd suppose it would be you. This island is yours, after all." I finished my work, looking around once again. "It was nice of whoever made this cave to leave it here, but would it have killed them to stock it?"

She sighed. "Let's not make jokes about killing today."

I probably should have held my tongue, but I was far too on edge. "Whyever not? Your father mocks my people and is intent on slaughtering the masses, so you ought to be comfortable with the topic."

"You really have no room to make comments about slaughtering," she replied sharply, refusing to look up at me as she reached into her belt. "Have you no shame?"

"No," I answered quickly. "It was beaten out of me years ago."

At that, I saw her eyes dart sideways, uncomfortable. Yes, I was saying far too much. The last person on the planet I wanted sympathy from was her.

Her hands paused on her belt, debating. Eventually, she caved, hands trembling from the cold as she pulled two small pieces of rock from the pouch. It took several hard hits for the sparks to fly far enough to hit the bits of straw and needles at the base of their fire. She pursed her lips, blowing gently, willing the fire to live.

In all, it took very little effort, and it bothered me that she was so regal that even the flames obeyed her.

She'd have no such luck with me.

She moved around, sitting her back against the bottom of the wall, and held her hands out, taking in the heat. So tiny.

Formidable, but tiny.

I, too, wanted to sit against the stone, but there was no way I was getting any closer to my target than necessary, so I sat with my back to the rain and looked across the growing fire at her. Her eyes were burning into mine. Such hatred there, such disgust. Even with all I'd done to keep her alive, it wasn't enough to undo the fact that I'd taken her mother.

I wondered what she saw in my eyes, if they looked as angry as hers.

She shook her head. "Why?"

"Why what?"

She swallowed. "Never mind."

I knew. Of course, I knew. "I told you when we met that I had information you wanted. I would have handed it all over then if you'd merely cooperated."

"And then you would have killed me."

I shrugged. "I could kill you now. Or later. Eventually it will happen. So, you should have taken the offer while it stood."

I saw the muscles in her face tighten. She wanted to know so badly, but I sensed she wouldn't allow herself the weakness of asking again.

"For what it's worth," I started, "I didn't know she was your mother. I didn't know she was anyone's mother. I was given a task, and I had to complete it. It was as simple as that."

"Simple." She shook her head. "You uprooted my life. There was nothing simple about it."

I stared at this selfish, foolish girl. "You hold on to our kingdom without a second thought. It's simple for you and ruinous for us. Don't act like you're innocent in this."

"I took nothing!"

"Oh, then do tell me about your plans to give it back," I snapped.

"We've been over this. On what grounds is it yours in the first place?"

"It was always ours!" My shout echoed in the tiny cave.

The following hush was bigger than the space allowed, and we sat in an uncomfortable silence for as long as I was able to contain myself.

"There weren't six clans; there were seven. For a very brief period my ancestors were chosen to lead the clans as a united front against Kialand. We were placed in a *royal* position by a majority vote among the chiefs. And someone in your family decided that wasn't good enough for them. Not only did they kill who they could, not only did they take what was ours, they erased us from your history to cover what they'd done. And now you eat off porcelain while we sit in the shadows." I scoffed, looking over her pretty little dress with its delicate embroidery. Who wore something like that into battle?

"Don't pretend your hands are clean," I told her. "In the end, one of us will fall and the other will rise."

"Well, aren't you lucky, then, that I had a flint, and you get to live one more day?"

"Aren't you lucky that I held on to you so that you could, too?"

She shook her head. "Don't speak to me unless it's absolutely necessary."

"Done."

ANNIKA

In my head, I sang the Kadierian anthem seventeen times. And then all the anthems I knew for other countries. Then every dancing song, every ballad, and even every drinking song I'd learned behind my father's back. The hours stretched on and on, and the steady rain was starting to make me sleepy.

To stay awake, I tortured myself with questions. How much time had passed since the battle? Did Escalus survive that hit? Did someone get him back to a ship? The tears filled my eyes as I asked the questions that scared me the most: Was I an only child now? Was I the heir?

"When you were a child and your parents told you to go to bed but you didn't want to, how did you fight it?" Lennox wondered aloud.

"Ah, so we're in the same predicament," I said, a tired smile gracing my face. "Good to know."

"Eventually, we'll have to sleep. This storm isn't moving." He looked over his shoulder to check again.

He was right. The storm outside was a torrent the likes of

which had never graced Kadier, with so much rain I bet the rivers were overflowing and roots were coming loose. "I've never seen anything like this. It's so . . . violent."

He scoffed. "You've never known violence in your life. Lucky you. I've dealt with little else." He turned, burning his eyes into mine.

"It certainly shows," I replied. "You hand it out as if it were candy."

"I can't help it if everyone around me has a sweet tooth."

I glared at him. "Fighting with you will work to keep me awake. Give me an argument, and I'll be up for hours."

"Hate arguments, do you?"

"Despise them!"

"Can't imagine why. You seem to excel at confrontation."

I finally looked away. "I rarely win, and then I'll spend the next several days thinking over what I could have said differently. I lose sleep over it. So there, fight me. Insult me."

"Very well. Where should I start?" He considered this. "You are nothing next to your brother. How about that?"

I flicked my eyes over to him and watched as he smiled, thinking this would get under my skin.

"I know," I admitted.

His shoulders slumped. "That's not how arguments work. You're not supposed to concede the point; you're supposed to insult me back. Tell me I'm haunted or something. If I've riddled out some of your secrets, you must have found some of mine."

"Maybe I have," I lied, looking up at him through the fire. "And I'm sure I'll find words for you later. But on this point, you're right. I'll never be Escalus. I know it, my father knows it, the kingdom knows it. If he's dead . . ." I could hardly think it, let alone speak it. "I was prepared to assist him, prepared to marry Nickolas even. But this . . ." I was saying far too much.

"Ah, yes. That pathetic stump of a man who deserted you in the Forest."

"That's the one," I admitted with a sigh.

He laughed. "And are you still marrying him after that? I didn't think someone with your level of . . . dignity would allow it."

"He's expressed deep regret over his decision," I told him with a shrug. "And I have to take him at his word."

"No, you don't," he said emphatically. "You don't *ever* have to take a man at his word. Take him at his action. If he abandoned you once, he'll do it again. A man like that is selfish through and through. If you were smart enough to get out of my grasp *twice*, don't be stupid enough to marry someone like him."

I narrowed my eyes. "I hardly think you're in any position to comment on my private life. Especially since you . . ." I shook my head, turning away. I could feel my lips trembling, but I refused to give him the satisfaction of making me cry. I turned to strike. "If I'm to take a man at his action, then it's easy to label you, isn't it? Murderer. Monster. Coward."

He made no attempt to deny the first two offenses I laid at his feet, but then, so quietly I nearly missed it, he said, "I'm no coward."

For a moment, I felt a strange sense of embarrassment, like

I'd broken an unspoken rule. I couldn't look at him.

"Tell me," he finally said, the pomp back in his voice, "what will Dear Nickolas say when he learns you've spent a night alone with me?"

I found the courage to meet Lennox's eyes, and he was smiling, amused again by my circumstances. I smirked right back.

"He won't. One of us will be dead before we leave this cave. I don't intend for it to be me."

Unflustered by my proclamation, Lennox continued to stare at me, the fire reflecting in his eyes and his face saying this was the most fun he'd had in ages, teasing me.

"Was that argument sufficient to keep you awake?" he asked.

"Yes. Thank you."

Lennox stood and stretched, gazing up at the ceiling, the carvings in the wall, the rain outside. Then, shaking his head, he walked around and slid down the wall of the cave, settling in a few feet away from me.

I looked at him warily.

"I'm just resting. Take it easy." After a long sigh, he leaned his head back. "Do you need to argue some more?"

I shook my head. "I don't think I could if I tried. I'm exhausted. And you know what else? I really don't feel like dying tonight. I'm not in the mood."

I could see he was suppressing a smile.

"Neither am I, to be honest."

"Then can we please call a proper truce? When the rain stops, you can attack me and avenge your kingdom . . .

whatever you like," I said, gesturing my hand gracefully through the air like this was all nothing. "But please let me rest."

He looked down at me with those startlingly blue eyes. I hated to admit that he was rather handsome. His windswept hair, his too-pink lips. There was something about him that grabbed my gaze and held it.

"Whatever you might think of me, I was raised a gentleman, and my word is my bond." He took off his glove and extended his hand. "You have my word that no harm shall come to you while you sleep."

His tone was different. As if it would offend him on the deepest level if I didn't believe him. I wasn't sure how much he could be trusted . . . but this promise I didn't doubt.

Cautiously, I reached my hand out, too. It was swallowed up in his. I could feel every callus he'd ever collected as it wrapped around the entirety of my hand. "And you have mine, as a princess and a lady."

LENNOX

When I woke, the first thing I noticed was the uncomfortable pain in my back. Ah, that's right. I'd slept up against a wall. A stone wall at that.

Then I noticed the rain. It had actually been soothing when I was trying to sleep, but now, alert, it was just a reminder that I was trapped. The sky had managed to get even darker, so it was night. I hadn't been here that long. And then, a whisper of an afterthought, I noticed the pressure of Annika's foot against my leg.

At some point, she'd curled up on her side, holding herself against the cold. The fire was low but not dead. Still, it wasn't offering much heat at the moment. I watched her breathe. In sleep, she had the same peaceful look across her face that her mother carried. It haunted me. She let out a tiny sigh, so blissfully lost to the world. I could admit I thought she was beautiful. Annika was beautiful in the same way a sunset was: so heartbreakingly sweet your soul could only stand taking in one glimpse a day.

But she wasn't all sweet. I could admit that, too. She was also angry and determined and sad in ways that confused me. It would take too long to understand her, and it was better for both of us if I never did.

It would only take a second.

I could snap her neck so quickly she wouldn't even feel a thing. It would be the most merciful of all my options.

But I'd given my word not to harm her while she slept. And though I hated to admit it, of all the lives I'd been forced to take over the years, hers would sting the most. I was not in the habit of knowing the people whose lives I ended.

As if she could sense I'd foolishly considered breaking my promise, she roused, looking around in confusion before remembering where she was. She sat up, pulling her hair back and wiping at her eyes.

"Are you ready to die yet?" she asked, her voice still sleepy.

I fought a smile as I shook my head. "Not particularly."

"Me either."

She stood and walked over to the mouth of the cave. The ceiling was so low that if she reached up and stood on tiptoes, she could touch it.

"It got worse. This rain," she said heavily. "It's so impossibly thick."

I stood, going to inspect for myself. If I squinted, I could see a cluster of trees nearby, but only barely. That was it. No clouds, no grass, and, most important, no one from either of our camps.

"I hope the others are all right," she breathed.

It seemed she was reading my thoughts. "I hate to tell you,

Princess, but unless they found cover, you and I could be the only ones left."

"Don't say that," she insisted. "Don't even think it. Aren't there people from your own army you're hoping are still alive?"

"Two," I said in a gut reaction. "What about you?"

She stared, looking sad. "Two. No, four." Then she sighed. "Maybe four and a half."

I'd have been lying if I didn't say I was shocked the number was so low. "Your brother is one. I know that," I told her. "I saw him take that hit, Princess. You might be down one of your picks already."

She swallowed hard. "He's stronger than you think. And I don't know your friends well enough to guess at both of yours, but I'd suppose one must be your girl."

I looked down at her and then back at the rain. "I don't have a girl."

She chuckled. "You most certainly do."

I glanced down at her as she pointed to her cheek. "I took a hit to the face for even suggesting you were kind to me. Blondie didn't like that at all."

With that she started sauntering back to the mostly dead fire, bending to feed it.

"So that's how you got that welt on your face." Blythe was more jealous of her than she'd admitted. "Is your precious fiancé included in your count?"

"For the sake of Kadier . . ." She poked at the fire, letting that sentence trail off. "He's the 'and a half.' Who's your other one?"

"Inigo," I admitted.

"The one with the scar?"

I nodded. She'd taken in a lot in that short time.

"Well, I hope your best friend isn't dead."

"Never said he was my best friend."

"If you want him to live, that's what he is. And if you want Blondie to live, she's your girl. Don't think I didn't notice you bypassed your mother."

I did, didn't I? I looked down at my cape. It wasn't quite enough to undo years of neglect. There was also Griffin and Andre and Sherwin . . . I guessed I'd done a better job at locking people out than I'd thought.

"I stand by my count."

She shook her head. "I can't enumerate the things I would do if it meant I got another hour in my mother's arms, and yet you don't even want yours. I don't understand."

"Maybe you shouldn't speak about my mother."

"What? Do you suddenly care about the woman you wished dead thirty seconds ago?"

"I didn't wish her dead!" I insisted.

"You all but did! Is that any way to talk about the person who brought you into this world? Even if you think she's awful or—"

"Do not speak about my mother!" I yelled, the sound echoing in the little cave.

For a moment, she was silent. But she didn't stay that way. "I didn't say anything worse than you did. And considering you took mine, if I hated your mother with my last breath, don't you think it'd be a fair trade?"

I stormed to my side of the cave, picking up my sword and coming at her so quickly she had no time to prepare. Even so, the same calm her mother wore in the moment of death was painted clean across her face. I hated her all the more for it.

"You would stab an unarmed woman?" She shook her head. "You are the coward I always assumed."

I hurled my sword back to my corner, putting my face in hers. "I am not a coward! You have no idea what I've done to have every drop of cowardice removed from my body, and you . . ." I stepped away slowly, laughing. I probably looked like I'd lost my mind. I felt like I had.

"I just realized something," I said, my eyes wild. "I can tell you everything. Because you're right: one of us will die. Either it will be you, and you will never have the opportunity to share my secrets . . . or it will be me, and I won't be here to care if you shame me in my death. So there, you want to know everything, Your Highness? Here you go."

I felt like all the tightly tied strings I'd been using to hold myself together had completely come undone. And now, Annika was going to get the wrath of it.

"My nose isn't this shape by accident," I said, pointing to it. "I've lost count how many times it was broken. My mother, who I have tried repeatedly to love, has been present for several of them and never intervened. I've probably broken more bones than I could count. I've been kicked in the gut, stabbed, cut, slapped across the face so many times I hardly feel it when it happens now. Like this," I said, pointing up to my eye. "That was a gift from Kawan only this morning. He's the only one who'll dare risk it now. Because people will always come for you when they think you're the weakest. But do you know how to make people stop making you feel small? Any idea?"

Annika shook her head, looking scared, and rightly so.

"Make them fear you," I said, the words dripping from my lips. "Kill off a handful of people. Kill some more. When the opportunity comes to kill someone important, don't flinch. When someone disobeys an order. When someone looks at you the wrong way. When the sun isn't shining. When it is. Kill. And then they think twice before so much as walking in your direction. That is the secret of staying alive."

"By making sure there's no one left to take you down?" she asked.

I shook my head. "By making sure people know you don't care about them, about anything. You want to know when my life turned a corner? When it got better? A lone wolf from our army who was determined to take vengeance for my father's death decided to kidnap a woman and put her in our dungeons. But," I went on, "no one wanted this woman's blood on their hands. I had been beaten down so many times by that point. So many times. So why not prove to them I wasn't the weakling they thought I was? I didn't know who she was, so what did it matter to me? They were too afraid to do what must be done, and so I did it."

Annika didn't flinch or look away. "My mother."

I nodded, speaking calmly now but still forcefully. "I took her life to save my own. I talked to her for maybe twenty minutes, trying to get anything useful out of her. I failed at that, so I took my sword and removed her head so quickly and cleanly, she felt nothing. And I was *praised* for it," I informed her, pointing to my chest with pride. "I'm still living off the prestige of that moment. So I actually owe your mother a huge debt of gratitude. She made my life a fraction easier than it was the day before. And if I had to do it a second time to save myself from the hell I was trapped in, I would. She got me out, and I'm thankful."

I walked away from her, slumping down to the floor against the wall. I looked out at the rain. I couldn't run. I wanted to, but I couldn't.

Annika had stayed on the other side of the fire, not even moving as I huffed and sulked and burned. When I finally met her eyes, silent tears were spilling out of them.

"Then I suppose I can be thankful, too."

ANNIKA

"Stop it," he said angrily. "I don't want your pity."

"You don't have my pity," I said, the tears coming quickly now. "You have my understanding."

Lennox's face was incredulous. "How could you poss—"

I held up my hand, and he fell silent. "Promise me that one of us will die."

He flipped his hands over and back, almost flippant about the idea. "It's inevitable."

"You *promise*?"

"Yes."

I nodded and watched him go wide-eyed as I lifted the hem of my dress. I'd sworn to myself that no one but the doctor, Noemi, and my husband would see these scars, but Lennox wouldn't believe me unless I showed him. He stared with transfixed eyes upon the length of my leg . . . until I reached the back of my upper thigh, and his expression turned to one of disbelief.

"What in the world are those?"

"Scars," I said matter-of-factly, walking back to the wall by the fire and sitting down.

"Who? How?"

I straightened my dress over my knees, telling myself not to cry again. Not just yet.

"My father has been . . . different since my mother went missing. Sometimes he's the firm but tender man I knew as a child; sometimes he's another creature altogether. He goes into fits of anger, driven by fear. He's kept me under lock and key for years now, planning out my life. . . ." I sighed. "I know he means well. But when my father told me I was to marry Nickolas, I didn't agree with the decision. In fact, I outright objected. It was the one time in my life I'd taken a stand on something, so I suppose he had no idea what to make of it. To his credit, he didn't get angry right away. He came to me with multiple arguments. He came to me with bribes. He came to me with promises. I refused them all.

"It's not as if I didn't know we were supposed to end up together; it's been talked about since I was a child. Marrying Nickolas is advantageous for everyone else, so I was supposed to accept it. But I couldn't. We got into an argument, and he pushed me. I fell onto a glass table, and . . ."

I swallowed hard. "He looked sorry, but he never apologized. I was left sleeping on my stomach for two weeks to heal, and I emerged from hiding to all the plans being arranged on my behalf. That very night, I was engaged."

I looked away to wipe the tears. "I know it was an accident, and I know he's made his rules because he's afraid of losing me. I remind myself of that when I think I can't forgive him. Sometimes, I'm more sad than angry. Even though he's still here, it's like they're both gone."

I finally risked looking at Lennox. I thought I saw sorrow in his eyes. "When the doctor was pulling out the glass, he told me that if I'd simply been obedient, it wouldn't have happened." I had to pause to shake my head. "I was so enraged at that doctor, I wanted to kill him in that moment. . . . Not that I would have, but I *thought* it. I wanted to hurt someone else to make my pain a little easier to bear. So, I'm afraid I can't judge you."

I wiped away the moisture above my lips and on my cheeks. "I can't tell you how I've been dreading my wedding night. How am I supposed to explain those marks? I'm a princess. I can't . . ." I shook my head. "I hope you won't mind too much, but if I get out of here alive, I intend to say you tortured me."

There was undeniable pain in his eyes, and he sounded so disappointed when he spoke. "No one will doubt you, that's for sure."

"True."

For a moment, there was nothing but the rush of rain and the crackle of fire. Then Lennox readjusted the way he was sitting, inching slightly closer than before.

"Listen. After I kill you, I'll have a lot of free time on my hands, so if you give me a list of names, I can make sure that doctor dies, too. Nickolas as well, if you like. Personally, I can't stand him."

I scoffed. "You don't know him."

"That's hardly the point."

And, out of the depths of my sorrow, I laughed. It wasn't bright or beautiful; it wasn't the guarded, ladylike giggle of a princess. It was a raw moment of hope in the midst of impossibility.

"First of all, that doctor was removed from his post, so I don't even know where he is now. Second, Nickolas is . . . a pain, but he doesn't deserve to die. And third, I don't want you to kill anyone, Lennox. I want to be able to forgive them. That's what my mother would have done."

So quietly, I wasn't sure I heard it, he said, "I know."

I wasn't ready to ask how.

"But there are worse things to do to someone than kill them, Annika. Surely you know that."

I shrugged. "But it's so final. Every hope, every ambition, every plan . . . all gone. You and I, we've had our dignity stolen . . ." I had to stop. My breathing hitched over the ache of it all. "At least for a little while. But to take our chance to hope for a better life, wouldn't that be worse?"

He took a stick and poked at the fire. "Isn't our hope already gone? Think about it. If you win this war, you keep the kingdom, and marry a man you despise while I return to the shadows. If I win, your country is gone. You have nowhere to go. And I will have to find a way to either follow Kawan or add yet another person to the long list of deaths at my hands. What hope is there really at the end of this for either of us?"

"You must be so much fun at banquets," I said, my voice dripping with irritation.

He laughed. "We don't have a lot of banquets."

"Then what's the point?" I exclaimed. "Why go through all the trouble of getting back something you think is yours if you have no idea how to celebrate?"

"One, it absolutely is ours. Two, I have my own way of commemorating things, good or bad."

I crossed my arms. "Fine. Tell me. How do you celebrate?"

He rolled his shoulders back. "If we both survive this, I'll show you someday."

"No. One of us has to die. That's the only reason you get to hear the truth, remember? So, death or nothing."

He smiled. "Fine. Death or nothing."

I sighed, frustrated. Lennox was too human for me to hate. In fact, this conversation that should have been uncomfortable, painful even, was so reassuring that I hoped the rain lasted a few more hours.

"It doesn't look like I can kill you yet. Do you have any more secrets you want to tell me?"

"Actually, I have a question."

He huffed, still smiling. "Here we go."

"Tell me about your girl."

His smile faltered. "I told you, she's not my girl."

"Even so. What's she like? Besides being really good at making people's faces feel like they might explode."

He missed my joke completely, shoulders slumping as he searched the cave, like perhaps the words he was looking for were carved into the walls along with these unreadable lines.

"Blythe is smart. And determined. And I appreciate that she cares about me. She literally might be the only person in the world who does. So, it's not that there's anything wrong with her, exactly . . . she's just . . . she's . . ."

"All flint and no kindling?"

He looked at me, wide-eyed. "Yes. Yes." He collapsed back into the wall, looking as if a great weight had been tossed off his shoulders. "I've never known how to say it."

"Happy to help. But you'll go back to her if she's still alive?"

He sighed. "I think so."

I chuckled. I kind of liked this girl. I wondered what the world would look like if she and I could be friends. That world didn't exist, though.

"What about you? Tell me about Nickolas."

I stuck my tongue out like a child, and he laughed.

"I'm convinced now that he cares for me, on some level at least," I said begrudgingly. "But I look at him, and I feel nothing." Felt nothing. Heard nothing. "He doesn't seem to realize how inconsiderate he is. And he's so serious."

"Well, I'm serious," he countered.

"It's not the same. Nickolas is like, well, if Blythe is all flint and no kindling, he's the water coming to kill whatever spark you might build."

"How does he keep up with you, then?" he asked. "You're all fire."

All fire. Hmm.

"He doesn't keep up. He's either in front of me setting up a wall to hem me in or far behind, trying to catch up. We've never quite been on the same page at the same time . . . and it devastates me."

There. I said it.

"Well, that settles it, I'm afraid," Lennox said, very officially. "I shall move him to the top of my kill list."

I glared at him. "No. No kill lists."

"But it's all I have," he replied, clearly playing with me now.

"Nonsense. You need something much more calming in your life. My brother does embroidery. Maybe that would work for you."

He started laughing. It was cautious, but still. "Embroidery? You must be joking!"

"Not at all!"

"Embroidery," he chuckled.

After that, he went quiet, and we sat side by side, watching the fire. I couldn't help but notice how close he was. And that, perhaps foolishly, I couldn't bring myself to fear him.

LENNOX

"Do you think it's tomorrow yet?" I shook my head. "You know what I mean."

Annika smiled. "I do think it's tomorrow yet. It's at least after midnight, don't you think?"

I sighed, feeling mournful. "Then it's Matraleit."

"Matraleit?"

"A holiday. For my people."

"Oh." Annika looked away, almost seeming guilty. "What does it celebrate?"

"The first wedding," I said with a sad smile. "The story goes that our people come from the first man and woman to walk the earth. They came to be in separate places and wandered alone across the land. When they found each other, there was no fear, no trepidation. They were immediately in love and married each other on the dome of a rock so perfect and round, it looked like a stone sun rising from the ground. All our people come from them."

"How do you celebrate?" she asked.

I sighed, thinking of Blythe's bracelet. "It's all about the knotting together of love and families—about making ties. So people make bracelets and leave them for the person they love. And they have to be woven," I said, turning to emphasize the point. "If it's carved from wood or just a single loop, it's bad luck. If you ever get a bracelet on Matraleit and it's not woven, you drop it right away!"

She laughed. "Got it. What else?" She pulled her knees in and rested her arms on them, looking at me with genuine curiosity.

I found myself smiling as I went on. "There are specific foods we eat. And there's a dance," I began. "A special one for couples."

"Really?"

I nodded, still smiling. "They say we used to go back to the rock—the one where they met—and couples would do the dance around the stone, remembering the first couple and looking to the future."

"That's really beautiful," she said wistfully. I watched as she looked around the cave. "Seeing as I'm likely to kill you," she started in a very cheerful voice.

I laughed outright at her jovial tone. "Go on, go on. You're going to kill me, and . . . ?"

"Perhaps you should celebrate it one last time. If I promise to never show it to anyone, will you teach me this dance?"

This wasn't how I had pictured spending our time, but I supposed there wasn't anything better to do.

"Sure." I pushed myself off the floor and brushed the dirt from my pants. Annika joined me on the other side of the fire. "We stand in front of each other and bow."

"If this is just a clever trick to get me to bow to you, I'll kill you on the spot," she warned.

"No, no," I promised with a smile. "It's real. Then you cup your right hand by your partner's ear." I moved my hand to the side of her head, and she put hers by mine. We were so close. It would be so easy to end her life, be rid of her. I just wasn't ready to do it. "Very good. Now you take three steps in a circle to your left. All right, now switch hands and go back the other way."

"Am I doing it right?" she asked, eyes on mine. There was something so trusting in them.

"Yes. Now, step apart so the bend in your wrist hits mine. Good. Now it's more walking in circles."

"I'm getting dizzy."

"That's the point. It's supposed to be about tying a knot, binding together, remember? Once you're here, you pull the other hand across so our arms are entwined. Just like that. And then I spin you around to undo it."

I walked through the steps a few times, and I was surprised she seemed so comfortable touching me. She didn't flinch at my nearness or comment on my weathered hands. She simply held on to me as I moved her around.

"Good," I instructed. "Dum da da da dum, then turn, dum da da da dum, and step."

I watched as she quickly caught on, smiling as she moved through the dance, even when I went faster and faster. No wonder she could move so nimbly with a sword.

We went on for a moment until she missed a turn and

landed squarely on my foot.

"Ow!" I cried, bending over.

"Sorry!" she replied with a laugh.

And it was all so innocent, so ridiculous in the light of our situation, that I laughed, too. I laughed in a way I hadn't in years, from my stomach and with my eyes pinched tight. I laughed because no one else would know. I laughed because, in this cave, I felt free.

When I stood up, wiping the tears from my eyes, I found Annika there, looking as if the stars had fallen.

"What's wrong?"

"Nothing . . . I thought I heard something. Never mind."

I nodded. Her face was expectant, hopeful.

"Well, except for the ending, you did an excellent job," I told her.

She blushed. "You're a good teacher." She stepped away and went back to the fire.

In the quiet, I considered so many things. Someone knew. Someone knew the depth of my pain, the heights of my ache, and the breadth of my regret. And even though so much of it was tied up in a moment that shattered Annika's world, she didn't seem to be judging me for it. At least, not any more than she already had.

I looked down at her. She was serene as she ran a finger through the dirt on the cave floor, as if she were finding a way to make art out of nothing. She didn't seem nervous that I was so close to her. And this was another frightening thing for me: to be close to someone so quietly and not feel completely ill at ease.

We settled into a comfortable silence, occasionally stoking the fire. I kept wondering what was going through her head. Eventually, she sighed, reaching down into the bag on her belt.

"I give up," she said, pulling out something that looked like a round, hard piece of bread. Very carefully, she pushed on it with her fingers until it snapped in half. She held one of the pieces out for me. "I had one back in Kadier, so let me warn you: it's terrible. Enjoy."

I chuckled, flipping the biscuit over in my hand, and took a bite. "Ugh! It's so dry," I mumbled around a bite.

She laughed. "I know. I assume they're made to last a while, but I think dirt might be more appealing." She shook her head. "I tried so hard to be prepared for anything, but I didn't know my father was planning an attack until we were at sea."

"He didn't tell you?"

Annika gestured to her soiled white gown. "No."

How little did the man trust her?

I cleared my throat. "Well, growing up as I did, you learn to be ready for everything, so I wasn't surprised by your ships at all," I lied.

Annika held my gaze. There were words in this stare, but I didn't know what they were. I tried to guess at what she was saying, tried to decode every syllable of her silence. Something about it was beyond me, past what I could understand.

"What?" I finally asked.

She shook her head.

I cleared my throat.

"Who taught you about constellations?" she asked, seeming desperate for a change of direction. She popped the last bite of the hard biscuit into her mouth and wiped her hands together quickly.

"My father. He oversaw that and what little I know of philosophy and religion. Mother focused on my handwriting and music." I shrugged. "I don't have much use for any of that anymore."

"When did you stop?"

I thought for a moment. "You promise one of us will die, right?"

"Yes!" she replied, her eyes more devilishly playful than I'd thought a princess's could be.

I chuckled. "Fine."

I turned to face her, and she moved to face me, too. Our knees were millimeters apart. "Everything stopped when Kawan found us."

A little line knit together across her forehead. "Found you?"

I took my last bite, looked at the fire, and turned back to her. "Your people have never heard of us, right?"

She shook her head. "I've always been told that there were six clans, that they were united under ours, and that we were the ones who led the war against Kialand. When we won, we gave our new country a new name to unify us all, and we have been prosperous and peaceful ever since."

"We truly have been erased," I sighed. "The Dahrainian people were scattered for generations. Kawan had been following rumors and names, trying to unify as many of our descendants as he could. I didn't know it, but my father's surname was one of few notable ones in our history. Kawan was thrilled to find us.

"Kawan was also the one who discovered Vosino Castle. It had been abandoned for ages; I still remember the smell when we moved in. We started training, planning to one day take back what was ours. My father would tell me when he put me to bed that, one day, I would rest my head where our people always had." I swallowed, looking at the ground. "As it is, I haven't even seen it."

I was quiet for a moment, feeling the gravity of that ache. Clearing my throat, I went back to my story. "After a year or so, a few people trickled in, looking for somewhere new to settle. Several bad seasons drove even more to test out the unclaimed land, only to find that it had actually been claimed by us. The hungry, uneducated . . . people no one seemed to miss. We took them in. We fed them, clothed them, taught them. Most of our army is made up of people who were cast off by their own country."

She considered this. "I like the idea of taking in people who feel like they have no home. If your final goal wasn't to move into my house, I'd admire it."

I found I couldn't reply. I changed the subject. "What about you? Who taught you about the stars?"

"Oh. I did," she admitted with a smile. "I've spent a lot of time in our library, teaching myself the things I really want to know. That's how I learned the names of the stars. And the only reason I knew how to use a flint. And that's how I started using a sword, but Escalus found out about it and took over that instruction." She looked away for a moment, seeming embarrassed. "Then I accidentally cut him one time. My father found out, and he put an end to that."

I smiled. "Except you didn't stop."

She shook her head, still smiling. "Escalus works with me a few times a week, and I keep my sword hidden under my bed, tucked on pegs I placed in the frame myself."

Every word from her was like rubbing your eyes after a long night and watching the world come into focus. "You are the most bizarre princess I've ever come across."

She laughed. "Do you have more than one in your acquaintance?"

"No," I admitted. "But I've never heard of another who denies direct orders, studies what she wants, and then, just for fun, can also pick locks."

"Ah. I have to credit Rhett for that skill."

For reasons I couldn't name, my smile vanished. "Who's Rhett?"

"He's the librarian. But I knew him back when he started as a stable hand. My mother wanted me to have a wide range of friends, which is probably why I feel like Noemi is more a sister than a servant. Anyway, Rhett taught me a lot. I feel responsible for him."

She made a face as if she'd just realized something.

"Are you two close?"

She nodded. "In a way. It's like . . . . you, you're in a position where people might not want to be near you because they've made an assumption about you. But for me, everyone wants to be close because of their assumptions. Rhett doesn't really pay attention to any of that."

That made sense. If everyone wanted to be close because of a crown, of course she would have feelings for someone who wanted her despite it.

"Do you think that water's safe?" she asked, pointing to the rain.

"Moving water should be fine to drink."

"Good." She hopped up, walking over to the edge of the cave. Then she looked over her shoulder, asking a question that had the ring of a command. "You coming?"

She really was a royal, wasn't she? "Yes, Your Highness."

She stood with her hands cupped, the force of the rain pushing them down as she tried to scoop up the water. I put my own hands out, but the rain was so very heavy it even moved mine.

"Here," I said, placing mine beneath hers. It was just enough to hold her hands steady and let them fill. She was still for a moment, looking at our hands together. Hers were all but swallowed by mine. She eventually placed her lips to the water and slurped it up in the most wonderfully unladylike manner. When she was done, she let her hands get wet again so she could wipe them down her face.

"How do I look?" she asked.

Hopeful. Messy. Even more beautiful than your mother.

"About the same."

She smirked and shrugged. When she was done, she wordlessly put her hands beneath mine, pushing them out into the rain so I could get a drink for myself. She was not that strong, but our hands together did more than they could apart. It was strange to be so casually touched, but for the first time, I found myself not bothered. In fact, it was nice.

Annika pulled our hands back inside, and I drank and felt so much better. I followed her lead and ran a wet hand down my face.

She wasn't paying attention to me anymore; she was walking back to the fire, ready to warm her hands. She took a few steps and then took three steps to her left with her hand in the air as if cupping the cheek of her partner. I watched as she idly went through the dance I taught her, moving as if this dark cave were a ballroom, a hint of a smile on her lips.

And I thought to myself there might not be anything more dangerous in this world than this girl.

ANNIKA

I told myself that the noise I'd heard had been the rain. It was something hitting the mountain, or a tree falling, or anything else really. It would have made perfect sense considering the situation we were in. But every time Lennox smiled or touched me or even looked at me a certain way, I would hear it again.

The sound of a thousand heartbeats.

In the echo of it, I heard so many other things more clearly. I heard my love for my brother, so pure and hopeful, and even my love for my father, fractured and slow, but still there. I heard my love for Noemi, piercingly sweet and sustained. And my love for Rhett. It sounded soft, not encompassing in any way. There was a tinge of obligation to it, which surprised me.

But what was louder than all of that was the painful certainty that I'd finally felt the love I'd read about in hundreds of books, the overwhelming and crushing weight of true love. And it was attached to the one person I could never have.

I swallowed. "I need to tell you something." I was playing with the hole in my dress again. "But I'm not sure you want to hear it."

He bent down, coming into my view. "At this point, I don't think either of us can keep secrets. Besides, I'm still planning to kill you, so you might as well say it while you can."

He smiled hesitantly, and I did, too. Look at those eyes. This was not the face of a killer.

"After we spoke in the dungeon, I was curious. So I went to the library and got the records of your father's trial."

"What?" He took me and turned me to face him. "There are records?"

I nodded. "It was very brief. I won't say any more if you'd rather not hear."

"No! Please, tell me. What did it say? What happened?"

I could feel myself trembling, afraid of the aftermath of this confession. "The notes suggest he was calm on trial. He didn't give an age or disclose anything about his family. I think he was trying to keep you a secret, to protect you."

Lennox looked at the ground.

"Should I stop?"

He swallowed. "No. I want to hear."

"He also said 'We have no last names' in the notes, so they called him Jago the Lone."

Lennox was toying with the hem of my dress. "That's true. We stopped using them in the name of unity. If someone comes to camp and has a name already in use, it's changed. There's only one of anyone in Vosino."

"Oh." I didn't know what to say to that. "He . . . he

pled guilty to attempting to assassinate my father. The jury wanted him to be hanged, drawn, and quartered."

Lennox's hand tightened around the edge of my dress. I could sense this was anguish; he wasn't going to hurt me.

"The notes say that my father interceded so he would have a swift beheading."

A shiver went through him at the thought.

"I'm sorry. That's . . . that's all I know."

Lennox nodded, breathing heavily for a moment. "Kawan likes to send us on Commissions to prove our loyalty to the cause. Going to the palace was my father's. I don't know why he went that far; it wasn't like him at all. I have so many questions I can't ask Kawan, and now I can't ask my father. I guess . . . I'll never know." He swallowed again and looked up at me. "Your father really changed his sentence?"

"My father pronounced it, but it looks like it came at my mother's suggestion."

His lips were trembling. "He nearly took her husband, and still . . ."

I had hoped to bring Lennox peace; it would be the only gift I could give him. Soon, the rain would stop, and we would run, and everything would collapse back into chaos. Before it was all over, I just wanted him to have this.

"I lied to you," he whispered.

"What?"

"I wouldn't do it over again. If I had another chance, I'd get her out." He looked up at me. "Your mother . . . she looked at me and said, 'You're just a child. You shouldn't have the weight of this on you for the rest of your life. Make someone else come in.' I . . . I expected her to plead for her life, but instead she pleaded for mine. She knew what was coming, and I could see she was heartbroken over it. Still, in the end, I was the one she wanted to save."

His breaths came quickly now, painful and sharp. "I didn't even know her name, and she refused to give us any information that might make it easier to hurt you. She cried and mourned, but she didn't cave. Annika, you are so much like her."

I'd heard those words thousands of times. I never believed them as much as I did right now.

"I stepped . . ." He had to stop and wipe at his tears, his face red. "I made her get on her knees, because I was about her height then. She did it without fighting. She said, 'Oh, Escalus. Oh, Annika.' Those were her last words. I thought she was praying in a language I didn't know."

And then I was crying, too. That was all I could ever know, all there was left to tell. Now I would simply cherish that she loved me to her last breath.

"I need you to know, it was fast," he said urgently. "She felt nothing, and I handled her so carefully. And I need you to know . . ." He was bawling now, falling apart. "I need you to know I'm sorry. I'm so, so sorry. I have to carry it forever, just like she said. And I deserve it . . . but even so, you have to know, even if no one else can, that I regret it every single day. I wouldn't do it again, Annika. Even if it meant living the rest of my life in a different kind of hell, I wouldn't, and I need you to know that.

"I'm so sorry." He buried his head in his hands, and I

saw all too clearly this had destroyed him. He'd made a joke before about being haunted. But he really, truly was.

And so, it was easy then—to see the best of my mother in myself, and to give Lennox the one thing he needed more than anything.

I put my hand on his cheek, expecting him to recoil. He didn't. I waited with my hand there as he wiped at tears, looking ashamed of them, though he had no need to be. He'd been forced to hold this inside, alone, for years.

"Lennox. Lennox, look at me. Please."

He took a moment, catching his breath. Finally, he came up, his brilliant blue eyes rimmed in red. I had to imagine mine looked as rough as his.

"I forgive you. Fully. Freely. I forgive you."

He sat there, looking into my eyes for a long time. Oh, I was tangled in the worst way, wasn't I?

"I lied again," he whispered, his gaze open and clear. "I'm not going to kill you. I didn't want to in the first place, no matter what your people have done to mine. No matter what happened to my father. I'm so tired of killing, Annika."

I shook my head. "Oh dear. You've done it now. No more secrets for you."

He smiled. "A fair price, I suppose. But you needn't worry. I won't tell anyone anything you've said anyway."

"Thank you," I replied, finally letting my hand drop.

He sat up a little taller, shoving his hair back. "What about you? Are you still going to kill me?"

I looked at this boy—who had somehow, against my wishes, taken full possession of my heart—and sighed. "Well, it is an awful lot of work."

He smiled, turning so he could face the fire. His arm was against mine. "I agree. Nothing but work."

"Princesses don't work. Not like that, anyway."

I listened as his breaths slowed, finally steadying. I could even feel how his shoulders were slouched in relief next to mine. It had to be a bittersweet feeling, letting all those secrets out.

I stared ahead, but I could feel his eyes on me. I wondered what he found when he looked at me.

It didn't matter. Just like Lennox, I had questions I could never ask.

LENNOX

For the first time in years, I could feel my lungs expand to their full capacity. My shoulders felt lighter. Even the colors in the cave had changed. I was a new man.

Annika pulled a piece of hair over her shoulder and toyed with the end of it, much the way I did with the lock of her hair I had hidden away in my room. I wondered if it would bother her to know I'd kept it.

"So, what would you say?" she asked suddenly. "Two in the morning? Three?"

I nodded. "I think so."

"How much longer could this possibly last?"

"Honestly, I don't know. Between the rain and that wind, the land isn't safe. If anyone else is out there, I hope they've found shelter."

"Under normal circumstances, I would say that Escalus could get through this. He's very clever. But injured as he was . . ."

I swallowed hard. "I'm sure your brother is alive. If he has half your determination, nothing so trivial as an arrow will take him."

"I hope you're right. And I hope your friends are safe."

I nodded to myself. "I hope so, too." After a moment, I added, "Should I hope Dear Nickolas is safe? Does it save you heartache if he's not?"

She sighed. "He needs to live. Our marriage strengthens the family line, consolidates the power, and keeps the monarchy going. Maybe I shouldn't tell you that," she said with a sad smile. "But it's true."

"So, you'll marry him, even though you don't love him?"

"I have to." Something in her tone was bitter.

It was then that I realized I was on the edge of wanting something I could not have. I wanted Annika.

I wanted her as my own. I wanted her to look at me, and, even with all the horrible things I'd done, find someone she wanted to be with, too. My vague disdain for Nickolas was instantly clear. He didn't want to stand next to her with his head high, deserving her. But I did.

"Can I ask you something that might be incredibly rude?" I ventured.

"I'm not sure. Seeing as we both might walk out of here alive, I'm hesitant to tell you the truth now." But she said it all with a ghost of a smile on her face.

"All the same, can I ask?"

She nodded.

"Have you ever been in love?"

She glanced up at me and then away, and I watched blissfully as her cheeks flushed. "Most of what I know of love,

I found in the pages of books. But I think there might have been once," she admitted.

I felt all my hopes crash. *Might have been once* sounded very distant.

"I was ten," she began, a bright smile growing on her face. "My mother and I were traveling. We'd gotten a little off course, and we passed by a small house in the country.

"A woman was beating a rug on a line, and her husband was coming out of the house, wiping his hands off with a cloth. And their son . . . he was sitting on the steps with a book. We came up, and my mother asked for directions, but I could not take my eyes off their son. Just before we started off, he jumped up, ran over to a basket, and produced two apples. One for me and one for my mother.

"He handed the apple to me and our fingers touched, and he said, 'You're the most beautiful girl I've ever seen.'" She giggled a little to herself, remembering.

But something loud was crashing in my ears, heartbeat upon heartbeat.

"His father said, 'Son, you cannot say such things to a stranger.' But I looked at him and said, 'Seeing as—'"

"'It's true, he may say it as much as he likes,'" I finished.

Annika stared at me, surprised, as she should be. I could scarcely believe it myself.

"Lennox . . . How . . . ?"

"You know how."

Her eyes were welling, watching me in awe. "You're the boy with the apple? I've been telling that story about you ever since."

"And you're the girl on the horse. I've been keeping you a secret ever since."

Eyes still glittering with tears, she smiled and shook her head. "So that was your father," she said sweetly. "I can't remember much of his face, but I do remember his smile. It left an impression."

"That means I met your mother, too. I don't remember anything about her from that day. I think I was too focused on you."

I had to be blushing. I hoped Annika didn't catch that.

"It was, what, just a few minutes? But I've never forgotten how you made me feel that day."

I shook my head. "I should have known you were royalty. Who else would answer that way?"

She laughed. "I know, I know. I hope I've gained a little humility over the years."

"You have," I told her. "Still unmistakably regal, though." I swallowed, confessing. "Still beautiful."

She pressed her lips together, like she didn't want to smile. It was a losing battle.

I wanted to tell her that it meant something. That if she'd only been in love once, and it was with me, then she should consider me now. I wanted to beg her.

And then the ground started shaking.

ANNIKA

"What's that?" I gasped.

Lennox took a few seconds, hands flat on the floor of the cave. "Earthquake," he said. "Get up."

I raced behind him to the mouth of the cave, yelping when I fell forward as the ground pitched beneath my feet.

Lennox caught me, bringing me upright. He looked at me with wild eyes. "If this goes on for too long, it can crack the mountain. We could get trapped in here. We have to run."

"Run where?"

He pointed. "Remember the patch of trees? We'll stand next to that first tree and hope it doesn't fall. Hold my hand, and do not let go. You hear me, Annika?"

I nodded, looking at the tree. "This is possible," I murmured.

"Run!"

He led the way, and once we made it to the tree, he placed me between himself and the trunk. I looked back at the cave, only able to find where we'd been because I could see the faint glow of our fire.

His eyes were whipping left and right, darting around the tree, looking up. The ground was still moving, and I widened my stance, gripping the tree with one arm and Lennox with the other. I kept my eyes trained on our shelter, hoping we'd be able to get back to it. We weren't going to survive out here.

"Lennox!" I pointed to the cave, watching as a river of rocks tumbled down, covering most of the entrance. I thought I could still see a glow from the fire, but I wasn't sure if it was real or if I was just hoping.

Lennox pulled me to the left, holding me tight. I felt another tremor as one of the neighboring trees fell inches away from where we were standing. I stared aghast at where it had landed, realizing I'd have broken a leg or worse had he not moved me. How many times had he saved me now? His eyes went back to watching for danger while I scanned to see if the cave was still open.

The ground shook a little more violently, and Lennox tripped, falling into me. I took the opportunity to hold him close. I needed him to know that, as much as he had me, I had him.

That one jerk of the ground seemed to be the grand finale of a very disturbing show, and the earth stopped moving under my feet.

Lennox kept me in his arms, and I kept him in mine, staying still another moment longer. I was breathless with both fear and relief. It was over, and we were both, somehow, still alive.

His eyes came down to mine, drops of water coming off his messy hair in steady streams. His chest was pressed to mine, and I could feel his heart beating wildly. He swallowed hard, then looked back over his shoulder.

"It's there," I said, pointing to the cave. "I think we can get back in."

"You can see it better. You lead," he said, and I took his hand, moving us back in the direction of the cave. The ground was covered with tree limbs to cross and rocks to dodge, and the rain had made the ground so soft. We trudged on, making our way back to safety.

The entrance was a sliver of what it had been, and we both had to turn on our sides to squeeze through. We searched for cracks in the rock, signs that our safe haven might come crashing in. I was no expert, but it looked intact to me.

I went to walk deeper, but Lennox stopped me. "Take off your wet clothes here. We don't want to soak the ground. We need somewhere dry to sleep or we'll be sick, on top of being hungry."

He went to pull off his boots, and tiny puddles dripped out of them when he did. I thought he'd go for his black stockings next, but instead his shirt came up and over his head. He was swift, laying it out as neatly as he could over a wide rock that was blocking our entrance. And I was left in horror, staring at the map of scars across his body.

"This really isn't the time to be shy," he commented when I hadn't moved. "Besides, it's not as if I haven't seen you in your stays before." His tone was meant to be playful, but I just couldn't laugh.

Huffing, he came over and started pulling at the strings holding the front of my dress together. "This is called shock," he said quietly. "It happens when you go through something frightening and your mind doesn't know what to do with it. You're all right. We'll rest, and you'll feel better."

I shook my head, unable to do much more.

"It's not that," I whispered. His hands kept moving, loosening the strings and being careful of not touching me otherwise.

"Then what?" he asked. Not annoyed, not bothered, just curious.

I pointed to his chest. He looked down.

"Oh." He pulled his hands back, his expression suddenly self-conscious. "I've grown used to them. I suppose it would be . . . jarring for someone else." He stepped back. "Finish the rest of your laces."

I obeyed, untying my dress.

"Boots off," he commanded, and I lifted each leg so he could tug them free. He placed a hand around each of my calves. "Your shift is mostly dry, and so are your stockings, so they can stay."

I shrugged out of my dress, draping it on one of the big rocks as he did.

"We need to make the fire bigger so it will last the rest of the night. And we'll have to sit close. You can have my cape. Come on," he insisted, taking me by the arm. "You're absolutely in shock right now. Sit down."

He planted me by the fire and draped his cape across me as I sat there, stunned.

If shock was what happened when too much hit your heart and your head at once, then I most certainly was there. I was in love with Lennox. I knew that now. I sat in a daze as he rushed around the cave, scraping together debris to throw on the fire. Once it looked steady, he piled more twigs and leaves to throw on it beside us and sat down, though not as close as he had been before.

"If you want me to put my shirt back on, I can. I don't want you to be uncomfortable."

"It's not that," I eked out, finding the strength to face him. "It's just . . ." I lifted a hand and pointed at the long, diagonal mark across his chest. "The biggest scar is from me."

He looked down at it. "How do you think I feel?" he asked, bringing my attention back to him. He very gently ran a finger across the scar on my left arm, the one left when he'd retaliated.

I sighed. "I'm not upset about that one. As scary as it was at the time, it reminds me I had at least one adventure in my life."

"And I don't mind mine at all," he confessed, looking down. "It's all that ties me to you."

A thousand heartbeats.

What . . . what did he mean by that?

"Well," he added shyly, "it's not the only thing I have. I, um, I kept that lock of your hair that I cut. Sometimes, when I'm low, I wrap it around my finger. Like this."

He pulled out a piece of my hair, still dripping wet, and showed how he laced it through his fingers.

Ten thousand heartbeats.

"I kept your cape," I confessed in a whisper. He looked up, astonished. "I use it like a blanket at night. It smells like the ocean, like you."

"Your hair smells like rosewater," he said softly. I watched as those eyes, blue as the clear sky, looked down at my lips, then back up, asking without a word. He leaned in closer. "Are you afraid of me?"

I shook my head and our noses brushed. "No."

"I've never kissed anyone," he whispered. "I'm a little afraid of you."

"Then it's lucky for us both that you're very brave."

His lips touched mine.

And the sound was deafening.

He reached up, putting his hand on the nape of my neck, holding me so very cautiously, and I laid a hand on his chest, no doubt touching the very scar I'd left on him. His skin was so cold, matching mine, but I felt the warmth of that kiss.

When we parted and I looked into his eyes, I saw someone new.

And, for the first time since we'd entered the cave, I felt true fear.

It was one thing for me be silently in love with him—to go home empty, with nothing but the ache of his absence. But it was another thing entirely to force him to do the same. And I was terrified of the second that moment came.

LENNOX

The earth readjusted, centering itself on a brand-new axis. Annika was at the heart of my world; apparently, she always had been.

Without hesitating, she moved, settling herself between my legs and pulling the cape across the both of us.

She curled into me, pulling her hair away so I'd stay dry, and I wrapped my arms around her. It was so easy. I understood now why anyone dared to let someone else have control over their heart. She could do whatever she wanted. She could throw my heart back into that hurricane, and I would thank her for it. I was hers. I was Annika's.

And there was nothing to be done about it.

She stayed there, keeping her head tucked just below my chin. She seemed to be listening to my heartbeats. And I realized I was absentmindedly moving my thumb up and down her arm.

"Lennox?"

"Yes?"

"I know you said you don't use your surname anymore. But do you remember what it was?"

I smiled. In one brilliant moment I found myself positively thrilled at the idea of her contemplating my surname.

"Ossacrite."

"Lennox Ossacrite. Do you have a middle name?" She looked up at me expectantly, hopefully. I hated to disappoint her.

"No. Do you?"

"Several. I'll spare you."

I chuckled, keeping my hands on her. Had I ever known such peace?

"If this . . ." She fidgeted a little, unable to look up at me. "If it's just me, you can say so," she posed. I supposed that "this" could have meant a dozen things, but I knew it only meant one. "I'm tougher than I look. I can take it."

"I already know how tough you are. And I know you're trying to offer me a path out. But I don't need it, Annika. It's not just you." I held her a little closer. "It feels like . . . fate."

"That's what scares me. In the books, fate is rarely kind." I felt her let out a long breath. "Tell me there's a way. Give me hope."

"You're the one who gets out of chains and dungeons. Maybe you should be giving the hope out here."

She laughed, looking up at me. "You're really going to make me do all the work? Fine."

And then she grabbed me by my neck and kissed me. She kissed me as if she'd done it a thousand times before, as if she knew I belonged to her and no one else. And I welcomed it. I welcomed my ruin.

I kissed her over and over, toppling over as she giggled, lacing myself in her arms. If the ground was cold, I didn't feel it. We moved as close as we could, folding ourselves up under the cape.

"What's this?" she asked, noticing the stitching on the inside of the collar. The emblem was circular with a flowering branch filling up the center. I didn't recognize the shape of the leaves, so I assumed it was merely decorative.

"I wondered that myself. This cape was my father's, and I only just received it. Maybe he dabbled in embroidery as well."

That brought a smile to her face, and I was thrilled. I found a new game to play, a competition with myself. How many times could I make Annika smile in a minute? In an hour? Could I make a record? Could I top it?

I'd happily play that game for the rest of my life.

We lay there, holding each other for a long time, not speaking. She traced a finger across the stubble on my chin, and I played with a long piece of her hair. I was starting to warm up, and I looked over her shoulder to make sure the rain wasn't letting up.

I wasn't sure what would happen when it did.

"I have another question," I told her. "Can you tell me about Dahrain? Or, Kadier. Whatever you prefer to call it. Tell me what it's like there."

Her smile was sad. "It's beautiful. Around the palace, it's mostly well-trimmed lawns with strategically planted trees to create paths. But past that, there are rolling plains, with lots of farms. In the winter, the snow comes, but I've never known a harsh one. It looks like the world has been dipped in glass. And when it gives way to spring, the hillsides are decked with color, flowers announcing the ground is reborn. There's space, plenty of it, and if I wasn't obligated to live at the palace, I might go make a home for myself in the country." She was quiet for a moment. "I don't know what your stories and legends say, but if they're good, then they're probably all true."

Tears stung at my eyes. I wanted to see it for myself. I wanted to breathe in the air.

Annika's hand was on my cheek, trying to offer what comfort she could.

"I'm so sorry," she said.

"I don't know how to fix this."

"I'm not sure there's an easy answer," I said.

"There is. There is something obvious, and we're missing it."

"Are you always this optimistic?"

She smiled up at me. "Usually."

"I like it. It's a marvelous change of pace for me."

Her tone was playful. "So you think we're doomed?"

"Obviously," I replied, trying not to smile and failing. "Let's check my record, shall we? I set out to simply fetch something from my homeland, came back with you. I tried to question you, you escaped. I went into battle, ended up cornered. I vowed to kill you, and, well, you can see how good that's going."

She laughed, and I wished I could wake up and fall asleep to that sound.

"If it's any comfort, I think you're failing in the right direction."

I nodded, brushing my hand along the edge of her chin. "You may be right."

Her eyes were growing heavy. It had been a long and impossible night. We'd started with a fight and ended it in each other's arms.

"You can rest," I told her. "You're safe."

"I know," she whispered. "I just don't want to miss anything."

I moved over, kissing the skin just by her ear, breathing my words. "But if you sleep, maybe you'll dream up all our answers. You're a very clever girl."

"I really am," she mumbled.

I chuckled, coming back to face her. She traced lines on me with her hands. Collarbone, battle scar, jawline. I held on to the piece of her hair that kept falling forward, flipping it through my fingers over and over. She fell asleep first, and I watched her, finding comfort in her slow and steady breaths.

"Are you awake?" I whispered.

Nothing.

"Good. Because I am brave, but even I have my limits." I put my lips close to her ear. "I love you. In spite of all that's happened, and regardless of what comes next. I am hopelessly yours."

And there. That was it. I now had no more secrets.

ANNIKA

I woke to the distinct feeling of gentle kisses along my shoulder. I had moved in the night and was facing the dying fire, and Lennox was holding me. I felt the warmth of him across my back, and where his arm wrapped around my waist. I was trying to think of the last time I'd slept so well. I was also trying to remember the last time I'd felt this happy.

Lennox stopped kissing me and buried his nose in my hair, just behind my ear.

"Done so soon?" I asked.

"I've finished all my research on your shoulder. I am most intrigued by this spot just behind your ear, so I'm dedicating all my attention to it now. Also, your wrists. They're next on my list."

I giggled. "While you're back there, please feel free to whisper sweet nothings into my ear."

I felt his lips move ever so slightly forward, his breath tickling my skin. "I have breakfast."

I bolted upright, turning on him, watching as he moved to lie on his back, hands cradling his head. He seemed so easy, so unguarded. And, goodness, he was handsome.

"Please tell me you have one of those oat things that you threw to me in the woods. Please!"

He hopped up and walked over to where his shirt was. I hadn't noticed him taking off his belt as well, but it was sitting there, too. He reached inside the pouch and there, wrapped in some paper and twine, were the same bars he'd given me in the woods.

I bounded over. "I've been dreaming about these things."

He smiled. "They're my favorite."

He had two and went to hand me both. "Stop. You need one, too." I bit into it, noting it wasn't quite as crunchy at the last time. Probably because of the rain. It was still positively delicious. "Is this molasses?"

"Honey."

"Honey . . . that makes sense. I was thinking about asking our cook to attempt to remake these, but I didn't even know where to start."

"I can show you," he said. "But only if you show me how to hold my stance to do that spin block you do with your sword. Or am I too tall for it?"

"No, you're not!" I insisted. "Just let me enjoy this first, and I'll show you."

He walked around with his bar sticking out of his mouth, which was hitched up into a perfect little smile. He put his hand down on his shirt, touching it in a few places. He did the same to my dress.

He started shrugging back into his shirt, taking a bite and talking around it. "Your dress is still wet on the bottom, but not much. Do you want it?"

I shook my head. "Not yet. Swords first."

He smiled. "If you insist, Your Highness."

I licked my fingers, enjoying the last of the food. Unless something fell into our laps, that was all we had left. I stuck my fingers out into the rain to rinse them, and I realized I could see more than I'd been able to last night. I could make out the entirety of the cluster of trees we'd run to when the earthquake hit. I could make out trees and rocks farther away even.

The storm wasn't done yet, but it was weakening.

I ignored it and went to find where I'd left my sword. "I'm not sure we'll be able to raise these, but I'll try for demonstration purposes."

He stood there, arms crossed, smirk across his face. "If this was your plan all along, I have to applaud you. It's worked so well."

"Ha, ha. Idiot. Go get yours, too."

He pushed off the rock, still smiling. Even the way he walked looked good.

"All right. You stand like this." I showed him. "Keep your weight on the ball of your foot and then push this way. You let the momentum pull the sword around."

I did it very slowly, because it was just too tight a space to really move.

Lennox tried, but it clearly wasn't going to be possible in the cave. "I think I understand the mechanics," he said, leaning his sword up against the rock near the opening. "I'll practice with Inigo when I get back."

As soon as he said it, he froze. It was like a spell had been broken. We both were going to have to make plans for what came next.

I put my sword against the wall as well and walked over to my dress. I pulled it on like a coat, searching the ground.

"Where's my ribbon?"

Lennox started looking with me, eventually finding it behind the boulder my dress had been sitting on. He handed it to me, looking sad. I started the lacing process, and he stood a few feet back, watching the ground in front of me.

"I'm thankful for Vosino, but I don't want to go back to Kawan," he said. "I'd almost rather be alone and build a house in some of the unclaimed land on the outskirts where I could forget all about him, and he could forget all about me."

"Would he forget about you?"

Lennox shook his head. "Not if he's alive."

I tugged the ribbon tight and tucked it into the neckline of my dress. "What if . . . what if you came back with me?"

He smiled. "Your forgiveness means more to me than I can ever say. But in Kadier, I'm a criminal. If I go there, I'll be tried. And, seeing as your mother is no longer here to dispense mercy, we both know what will happen to me."

I winced, unable to stomach the thought.

"What if we didn't give them your name? Or what if we told them you defected?"

"If I was cleaned up, it's possible Dear Nickolas wouldn't recognize me, but it'd be risky. And, even if he didn't, how could I do that? Live in your comfortable palace while the rest of my people are left in hiding? Live under your father's reign when I should be free in it?" He shook his head. "Annika, believe me when I say I want to be wherever you are more than anything. But I'm no coward. I can't leave them behind."

I looked down. "You're right. I wouldn't ask that of you."

"Besides," he said, coming closer. I felt myself relax when his arm wrapped around my waist. "I am the only one attempting to keep Kawan in check. If I don't go back, whatever comes next will be barbaric."

I leaned my forehead into his chest. He couldn't promise another attack wouldn't come; no one could. I was thankful that he would at least be able to try.

"What if . . . what if you came back with *me*?" he offered.

I looked up at him, wishing more than anything that I could. "I don't know who has lived or died. If my brother has died, I'm heir apparent. If my father has also died, I'm queen." He stared at me for a moment, not having considered this. "If I don't go back, the kingdom goes to Nickolas. Trust me, no one wants that."

He swallowed hard. "You're going to marry Nickolas, aren't you?"

I nodded. "In Kadier, he's my only choice." I looked to the ground, finding myself wildly jealous. "You have someone waiting for you, too."

"It's not the same," he insisted quietly.

The tears were close to breaking through, but then I noted something on his shirt. "Do you have a dog?"

He looked down, taking in the strands of gray fur on his shoulder. "No. I have a fox. Her name is Thistle."

"Thistle? I love that. How do you even tame a fox?"

"Well, it's not as if she's a pet," he stressed. "We're not allowed to have any; they take resources from the livestock. But I found her as a kit. Her paw was injured, and I treated her. She's very smart. I leave my window open so she can come and go as she likes." He shook his head. "Gray foxes are nocturnal. I can't tell you how many nights she's come in only to run around my room, knock things over, and then just hop out the window again."

I chuckled. "It must have been hard to leave her and not explain."

"It's hard to leave even when you can."

Wordlessly, a lifetime's worth of conversations were happening. While I kept hearing heartbeat upon heartbeat, I wondered if he could hear every fiber of my body screaming that I loved him.

I wanted to say so. I wanted him to be able to wrap himself in it like I could with his cape. But some part of me worried that if I let those words out, they would make cuts that may never heal.

I knew that he felt something . . . but I didn't want to back him into a corner with my affection. And then, as if the Island was telling me to just let go, I heard the rain come to a stop.

It changed the sound of the cave entirely. I could hear him breathing now, it was so quiet.

We stood there for a moment, a whisper apart, simply

watching each other. Finally, Lennox looked at the crack in the rock, at the picture of a world outside coming into focus.

"Am I a coward for suggesting we stay here?" he asked.

I shook my head, smiling sadly. "Not a coward, but also not a realist."

He nodded. "If we must go, is it better to part ways of our own will rather than wait for someone to discover us?"

"I think so," I replied. "I don't want a soldier finding me with you. I don't know if I'll be able to stop them."

His lip trembled like he might cry. Before he could, I moved in, kissing him. I threw my arms over his shoulders, keeping him close. If his laughter brought on a thousand heartbeats at once, this kiss was a thousand goodbyes.

I pulled back, tears stinging. I had to make myself go now or I never would. I moved away, brushing the dirt from my dress for something to do.

"Wait," he said. Lennox pulled a small knife from his waistbelt. He carefully reached up and cut part of the tie from his cape, the tassel swaying as he moved.

"What are you doing?" I protested. "That's your father's!"

He reached out wordlessly, tying it around my wrist. Not just tying, but looping the strand over itself. "I hope you still sleep with my cape sometimes, but this is much easier to carry around," he said.

I held out my hand, marveling at the dark fabric against my skin. I had stores upon stores of jewels back in my palace, but I'd never loved a bracelet more. I smiled up at him.

"My turn," I said, reaching down and pulling at the lace around the hem of my dress with my teeth. I looked up, watching him swallow hard.

"You don't have to . . ." His words were cut off as I pulled out his dirt-covered wrist. I looped my bracelet around itself as many times as the lace would allow, grateful that he let me, grateful for this beautiful tradition that he shared with me.

He let out a slow breath, staring at the lace, looking awed.

"By the way, did you have that switchblade on you the whole time?"

He looked down at the tiny object in his other hand, confused by the question. "Yes. Sorry," he added, shaking his head. "I should have given it to you to use."

"No," I said. "We laid down our swords because we couldn't swing them in here, but you could have attacked me from the start. And you didn't."

He smiled down at me and finally shrugged. "You had a hold on me from the second you left a scar on my chest. What can I say?"

"That was the moment?" I asked in shock.

He nodded.

"You're insane," I told him.

"You're perfect," he replied.

I was very close to losing my will to leave him.

"I have to go," he said, reading my mind. "If I don't soon . . ."

"I know," I told him. I held up my wrist, the tassel swinging like a charm. "Thank you."

He held up the dingy lace on his. "Thank *you*."

I walked over, picking up my sword and looking back into the depths of the cave. The footsteps from where we'd danced, the remnants of a tiny fire, the markings I couldn't understand on the wall. I wanted to remember it just like this for the rest of my life.

Lennox looked out from the thin opening, surveying the area. "If you go north, you should make it back to where you docked." I nodded, hoping that someone would be waiting for me. "Annika . . ."

"Yes?"

He took a deep breath, struggling to look me in the eye. "I have to assume another battle will come. If that happens, and if we lose, can you promise me something?"

"Of course."

"The dance I taught you. I want you to share it with others. I just want something of my people to live on if we don't. Will you promise me?"

I drew in a shaky breath. "I promise. And if this battle comes, and we lose, I beg you to let people—especially the commoners—leave peaceably. I want my people to live on, too."

"I give you my word. And . . . don't forget this," he said, pointing back to the cave. "Don't let time convince you it didn't happen."

"Or you."

Lennox looked deep into my eyes one last time and bent to kiss me. His hand was laced in my hair as he stood for a moment with his forehead against mine. After a shaky breath, he pulled away, taking one last look, and started walking south. I watched him for a moment, clutching the bracelet against my wrist with my other hand, and then I turned, too, trying not to cry.

LENNOX

I had rules. I'd ingrained them into myself until they were second nature.

Never look away. Never walk away. Never explain away.

This was how I survived.

But looking away from Annika? Walking away from Annika? That felt more like dying than living.

I paused when I was far enough away that I knew the mouth of the cave would be blocked by the roll of the hill. I could see the mountain, jagged and foreboding. If I looked close enough, I could even see the place where the rocks that had nearly blocked off the entrance had come from. It left a strange, hollow feeling in my chest. This made perfect sense, seeing as my heart was happily tangled in the hair of Annika Vedette.

I held out my hand, looking at the loops of lace. I loved it.

I loved it, but I couldn't wear it. They'd see. They'd know I was with someone, and if they figured out it was her, they'd expect her to be dead. I'd have to explain more than I was prepared to. I stopped for a moment, looking around to make sure I wasn't being followed. Beneath a tree, I slowly unwound it, though it pained me to undo anything Annika had made. It was so, so dirty from the ground of that cave. I shoved it into my belt and shook out my hand, already feeling naked without it.

There. That was it. All the proof of my entire life being changed was gone.

My best guess was that the army would head south toward where the boats we'd stolen were docked.

The few glimpses of the sun I was getting from behind the clouds were telling me I was heading in the right direction. I soldiered on, and crested the horizon just before the slant to the sea.

There they were.

The survivors—more than I could have guessed—were all here, looking for salvageable boats and scavenging wreckages for usable parts. Ever resourceful, ever determined. I found myself swelling with pride. We were still here.

"Lennox!" someone called out. Not someone. Blythe.

And to my shock, once she said my name, the entire army went up in cheers. I could see Blythe running toward me, eyes bright, smile plastered across her face.

"I knew it," she said when she approached. "I knew you'd make it through."

"Of course," I said. And then I kissed her cheek.

She was so eager, so happy to finally be kissed, that she embraced me, too, trying to make the moment last. And I?

I was hoping to do as Annika said, move on with someone who cared about me and put our time together in a jar, never to be forgotten.

It took about four seconds to realize that would never, ever happen.

I saw my mother running through the sparse crowd, tears in her eyes. For the first time in years, my mother threw herself into my arms, reaching up and touching my face.

"I never worry," she said. "You are so strong and smart, I know you'll find your way out of anything. But this time? This time I thought that storm might get the best of you."

"It tried."

Her smile was sad. "Sometimes it aches that you look so much like your father . . . but watching you walk back from the dead . . ." She shook her head, unable to say any more.

"How did you survive the rain alone?" Blythe asked.

The girl I'm destined to love helped me build a fire. She fed me and held me. She mended my long-dead heart. I owe her my life ten times over.

"I found a cave to shelter in. Where were you all?"

Blythe shook her head. "We were able to build a crude sort of covering. It was starting to fail at the end, so it's good the rain stopped when it did."

I turned to my mother. "You?"

"Hid in a thicket of trees with really tight branches with three others."

"Inigo did that, too," Blythe said.

"Inigo made it! Oh, thank goodness."

Blythe laughed. "Don't let him hear you talking like that or he'll say you've gone soft."

I shrugged. "Maybe I have. Come on. Let's find a boat."

We walked down to the coast together, but as Kawan came into view, my mother distanced herself from me. I tried not to let it sting.

"You're alive," he said as a way of greeting. His tone implied an air of disappointment.

"Yes. What's the plan?"

"We're waiting—"

"Lennox!" Inigo said, running up the coast. I held out a hand to shake and wrapped the other around his back, and he did the same to me. Smiling, he turned to Kawan. "There are more boats just around the rocks. It looks like most are seaworthy. We're in better shape than we thought."

"Good. Start mobilizing the soldiers." Kawan waved a hand at us, and we started walking.

"I heard a cheer earlier," Inigo said. "That for you?"

I nodded. "I didn't know anyone cared."

"It's a lot more than that, my friend," he said, looking back over his shoulder to make sure we were far enough away. "When Kawan came over that hill, *no one* was happy."

My face shifted. "You're joking."

"No," Blythe confirmed. "It wasn't just that they didn't care, they were angry. *I'm* angry. He nearly got us all killed. No one's pleased he made it out of his own stupid plan alive."

"Well, that's none of my business," I said. "Not yet anyway."

"Let me know when it is," Inigo said.

I looked to Blythe, who nodded.

"I will."

ANNIKA

I trudged over hills, heading north and holding Lennox's bracelet against my wrist. I had watched until he crested the hill, thankful that he hadn't looked back. I might have lost my resolve.

He'd said I was strong, but I wouldn't have made it without him. Not only did he take care of me, he listened to the hardest secrets I'd ever kept and held them without judgment. I owed him more than my life.

I looked up from my thoughts and saw a pale green flag fluttering in the distance. I raised my hands, waving them while I ran, and I called out. I suddenly realized with a flood of disappointment that I would not be able to explain away my bracelet. I quickly unwove it and shoved it down my stays. For now, I had to tuck him and my love safely away. The boy with the apple would have to be my most closely guarded secret. After a few minutes, two soldiers came running my way, meeting me halfway.

"Your Highness," one greeted me. "The duke has been most worried about you."

Nickolas was alive.

"I am well, so do not concern yourself with me." I looked back. "How long ago did the ship carrying my brother leave for Kadier?"

They exchanged a look. "We couldn't leave, Highness. The waves were too high. One of the ships sank."

I stopped in my tracks. I took a deep breath, bracing myself. "Is my brother alive?"

"Yes."

I nearly burst into tears I was so relieved. "And my father?"

"He is alive but unstable. He's . . . somewhat incoherent."

I nodded. "Take me to Escalus at once."

They moved ahead of me, clearing a path once we reached the remaining troops. I rushed up the gangplank, following them to the captain's quarters. Just outside, Nickolas was pacing.

He had his hand over his mouth, staring at the planks as he crossed them, looking as if the weight of a country was on his shoulders. I imagined he was guessing it very well might be.

"Nickolas?"

His head jerked up, eyes wide. He let out a ragged breath and rushed over to me. "You're alive! Annika!" He stepped back, looking into my eyes, his face painted in wonder. "I thought we'd lost you."

And then, doing as I knew I must, I went up on my tiptoes and kissed him. It was brief, but it was enough for the soldiers to see, and it was enough to show Nickolas where he sat in my future.

"My brother?"

"This way," he said, placing a hand on my back and leading me into the captain's quarters. He lowered his voice. "His Majesty is belowdecks. He's . . ."

"I know."

"His Highness is in charge. I tried to get him to set sail, but he refused to budge until you returned."

I shook my head, walking over. Noemi was crouched beside my brother, wiping sweat from his brow with a cloth, her touch as gentle as a whisper.

I let out a ragged breath seeing her alive and well. She covered her mouth and had to look away for a moment, composing herself.

But neither of us could bring ourselves to smile.

Escalus opened his eyes, but only just. "My prayers . . . have . . . been answered," he eked out.

"Let us get you home so that mine can be as well."

"How?" he mumbled. I knew the rest of the question: How did I survive?

There was a boy, and he held me through the rain and the cold. He told me the truth, and he brought me peace.

"I saw the edge of the hurricane coming and found a cave on the side of a mountain. It was deep enough to wait it out."

"So that's what a hurricane looks like," Noemi said. "How did you know?"

I swallowed. "I've read about them."

She nodded. It was easy to believe.

"Well, let's be thankful you're safe," Nickolas said, placing a hand on my shoulder.

"Where were you?" I asked him.

"At first, I walked, trying to get back to the ships. But I knew I wasn't going to make it, so I hunkered under a cluster of trees. I've only just dried out."

"And you think it's miraculous I'm alive?" I shook my head. "Can we leave now?" I pleaded. "Escalus needs a proper doctor."

"Yes," Escalus said. "Noemi. Nickolas." He looked wearily at the two soldiers by the door. "Jattson. Mamun." They saluted in return. "You four stand . . . witness. I am . . . making Annika regent. My father . . . must heal. Follow . . . her command."

I stood there, stunned by his words. Regent? It made me all but queen. I was in no way prepared for such a role.

"Escalus? Are you sure?" I asked.

He nodded. "I need time. I am . . . still here," he assured me. "Time."

I looked at him, knowing he was doing his best to reassure me. So I would reassure him.

"Very well. I accept." I leaned over and whispered, "I'm still here."

And somehow, that felt so much bigger than "I love you."

"Your Highness," Nickolas whispered, pulling my attention to him. "Take a deep breath. Then go to the captain and order him to set sail. I will go with you as witness to your regency. All will be well, but we must go."

I nodded. "Yes."

I moved from the room, finding the captain waiting just outside.

"Captain. I am now in command. We must sail at once,

so my brother and father might be restored. We must ensure the safety of Kadier."

His eyes widened, but he quickly saluted me. "Yes, Your Highness." He immediately went to calling orders, and men scurried up from the coast and across the decks, getting ropes and sails into place. I was impressed with their speed, but I wouldn't be at ease until Escalus was deemed safe.

"You did well," Nickolas said quietly beside me.

"Thank you. I hope I won't let them down."

He shook his head. "It's possible that no one in Kadierian history will ever be loved as much as you. You can do no wrong."

"We'll see."

When we were finally out at sea, I watched the horizon, looking for home. What I saw instead was a smattering of shapes in the distance.

"Is that them?" I asked.

"It is," Nickolas replied. "If we didn't need to get Escalus to safety, I'd say we should go ahead and chase them now while they're weak. I can't recommend that in good faith right now."

"Nor could I. Escalus and my father are the priority now. The rest . . . we'll figure out tomorrow."

"Of course." He bowed to me and started walking, calling to the captain to ask a question.

I watched the cluster of little boats in the distance. In the books, they always spoke of pain when being parted from the one you loved.

They did not do the sensation justice.

Piercing was too small a word, as was *crushing*.

I pressed my hand to my chest, and I could feel my unraveled bracelet there, the tassel tickling my skin.

I locked Lennox away in the quietest part of my heart and willed myself to be satisfied with whatever may come.

Part III

As she had for the last several days, Annika worked until well past sunset. So, it was only now, in the latest hours of the night, that she was able to review the final petition placed in her lap today: the request by the lords for her to marry almost immediately.

Annika had no idea when an army might head her way, and she had very little left in her pocket to help her people feel secure. A wedding, a promise of an ongoing line . . . this she could give them. She stood, moving away from the endless lists of things she had suddenly become responsible for, and walked to the window. She scanned the sky for Orion.

There he was, hanging above her, the guardian of the heavens. As she pulled the black cord with its tassel from her pocket and wrapped it around her wrist, it felt as if she were being guarded as well.

In a bedroom far less grand, Lennox bent, almost as if in prayer. He knelt with a scrap of lace between his hands, looking out the window above his bed, searching for Cassiopeia. When he found her, all he could think of was Annika.

But as he watched the stars, twinkling like hope in the distance, he remembered that he could never see Annika again, never go to her side. For one day, he intended to claim everything that was his. He felt a stab of pain knowing that taking back the land might mean that Annika had to die.

In their own quietness, their own isolation, each wondered what the other was doing at that very moment. In Annika's mind, Lennox was sharpening his sword. In Lennox's mind, Annika was giving commands. They smiled to themselves, wrong as they were.

For how could they have known that they were doing the exact same thing—holding on to the tiny pieces they had of one another and wishing desperately that the other was by their side?

LENNOX

The morale around the castle was, unsurprisingly, low. I'd never thought our army vast or even strong, but now I saw that we'd been on the edge of something great.

And it had been broken.

The short battle had been disastrous. We'd lost scores of people at sea.

Even I came home feeling worse for wear.

I headed to the mess hall, which had been partially converted into an infirmary. Inigo met me at the door.

"Has Kawan been here today?" I asked.

"No. Still unwilling to show his face."

I shook my head, trying to fight back my rage. The least Kawan could do was tend to the people he'd led into a disaster.

"How long have you been up?" I asked.

"All night," he replied, rubbing his eyes. "I was going to go to sleep ages ago, but Enea's fever spiked."

He looked as broken as I felt. "Did she make it?"

He nodded but sighed. "How many do you think we've lost? I can hardly keep up."

Of course he couldn't. As usual, there were no records.

"Listen. What's important is saving the lives we can. Where should I start?"

Inigo pointed to the back corner of the room. "Those are the worst cases. Brallian lost a hand, and the infection is so bad that she might not make it through the day. Some others are so weak, it seems like they've simply lost the will to go on."

Inigo raked his fingers across his face. "Most everyone else should recover."

I nodded. "Go get some sleep."

Inigo put his hand on my shoulder, his fingers gripping as if he were holding tight to his very last hope. "Please," he whispered. "Please tell me you've got a plan to get us out of this."

I swallowed, feeling helpless.

"I don't," I confessed. "Not yet. But I will. I won't let this go on forever."

I squeezed his shoulder as I made my way to the back of the room. As I approached the huddle of the worst cases, I saw Blythe. She moved quickly and efficiently, wiping someone's brow as she met their eyes. It was strange to see her that way, mournful and serious. She stood, rubbing the ache in her neck, hair spilling over her shoulder.

Blythe was beautiful and brave. She was compassionate and persistent. She was faithful, hopeful, stronger than most of the men I knew. She was, by every measure, perfect for me.

And I wished, with all my heart, that I could find it in myself to love her.

She caught me staring and gave me a brief, sad smile as I walked over to her.

"Did you just get here?" she asked.

"Yes. You're my commander today. Tell me where to go."

She took my hand. "This way."

There was a slightly different smell toward this end of the room, something that reminded me of metal combined with aging meat. I didn't flinch. I simply had to smell it; the others had to endure it.

"Griffin wants to have a memorial for Rami," Blythe said quietly. "If you can get down to the coast at sunset, I think he'd like you there."

"I thought he'd be upset with me. She died trying to help me focus."

She shook her head. "He knows who's really to blame."

"If he wants me there, then I will be."

"Now, would you go talk with Aldrik? He's not doing well, and he's been asking for you." She pointed to the far corner . . . the dangerous corner.

I stared in unbelief in the direction she'd pointed, finding his mop of curly brown hair atop his very pale face.

I moved over quietly, not wanting to wake him if he was sleeping. His breaths were as shallow as Blythe had warned me, and watching him struggle set me on edge. His eyes flickered, and his lips lifted into a crooked, half-hearted smile.

"There you are," he managed to say.

I tried to smile back, but I wasn't sure it looked genuine. "Heard you were looking for me. If you're finally challenging me to a sword fight, I'm afraid I'm busy today," I joked.

Every blink of his eye was so slow it seemed to be asking for strength his body barely had. Still, he managed to smile. "I'm occupied myself."

I nodded. "Then how would you like to spend your day?"

He forced out a few more labored breaths. "I've spent every single day of my life here trying to become you," he said.

I shook my head. "When you get well, you'll have to aim higher. You can do far better than me."

The shade of his skin was so unnatural that I had to work hard not to stare too long.

"Lennox," he said, turning serious. "I need to tell you something. Kawan . . . he needs you. No one can touch him." Then he tilted his head a little. "Except for you."

I stilled at that, unsure of what to say. "When you went on your Commission, he was on edge the whole time, wondering what you'd do to show him up. When you came back with a princess, he lost it. He knows what you're capable of."

Aldrik stopped his slow speech to cough a few times. His coloring got worse and worse with the passing seconds. "That's why he won't come see me. Not even after all I've done for him. If you were here, he'd show, if only to make sure it was true that you were gone." Aldrik weakly shook his head.

"I should have told you sooner," he gasped. "I should have told you people would have followed you. Whatever it is that leaders hold, you have it. Why do you think Kawan hates you so?" He turned his head, coughing and then making an anguished sound, as if the action was piercingly painful.

I ignored his words and focused on him. "Let's not talk about that. What can I do to help you?"

He shook his head. "I can't feel my legs anymore. And it's like glass in my lungs. Every part of my body is either numb and gone or in pain. I . . . I don't have much time."

"Don't say that. Whatever injury this is, it may heal. . . ."

Aldrik silenced me with another weary shake of his head. "I know. I'm telling you . . . I know."

I swallowed hard.

"Lennox, you already have the strength you assume you lack. You've endured, you've survived. Don't delay. Before we're all gone, do *something.*"

I was left speechless.

"Promise me."

I nodded.

He lay back, eyes on the ceiling. Having said what he needed to, a calm came over him.

"I don't have any family here. Could you stay for a moment?" he asked.

"Do you . . ." I had to look away. "Do you want me to stay until the end?"

His lips trembled. He nodded.

I reached down, placing my hand on his. He was too weak to return the gesture.

I fought the urge to put my usual walls back up, to retreat into safety. It was rare that someone needed me so wholly. So

I let myself feel it all. The fear, the peace, the attachment, the pain. I felt it all with Aldrik so he didn't have to feel it alone.

In the end, I was glad I had. An hour later, Aldrik's skin faded from pale white to light blue, the traces of warmth in his hand disappearing completely. I pulled the blanket over his head, walked from the mess hall . . . and then I cried like a child.

ANNIKA

What everyone assumed: I'd survived the Island using only my wits and resources to carry through the long night of rain.

What everyone knew: Escalus had been severely wounded on the battlefield. After speaking with me briefly on the ship, a fever got the best of him, and he'd been incapacitated for days.

What no one knew: my father had received a wound of his own on the Island. His fever had taken him over much faster, making him talk in circles once he'd been taken to the ship, and causing him to slip into a coma before we made it home.

It was one thing for a prince to be injured or sick; it was another thing entirely for the king to be debilitated. So the extent of his condition had been kept secret from the masses, all of us hoping that he'd recover, or, at least, that Escalus would wake up soon.

When Escalus had named me regent, I thought that order

might last for all of a day or two. But neither my father nor brother were waking up. What if they never did? I was honored to help—what a privilege to lead our people, if only for a moment—but I hadn't been trained for this as Escalus had.

What was I supposed to do?

There was only one person in the world I wanted to ask that question to, one person who I knew would tell me the absolute truth. And he'd hold my hand as he did it, giving me the strength to follow through, no matter how painful the course ahead might be.

But I could never ask for his help again, never ask him *anything* again. It was one more brick on my shoulders, another thing making it harder to stand upright.

I covered my nose with my handkerchief as the doctor pierced the wound, draining fluid into a bowl. Despite how much it must have burned, my father didn't stir.

"I'm sorry, Your Highness. We're not seeing any improvement," a second doctor said. "It has simply come down to His Majesty's ability to fight."

I nodded, forcing a smile. "Then we have nothing to fear. His Majesty has never backed down from a battle."

He returned my smile, bowing a little as he stepped away.

I twisted my handkerchief in my hands and walked to the side of my father's bed, leaning over, close to his ear.

"Can you hear me? It's Annika." He didn't stir. "Father, I need you to wake up. I have so many things I need to say to you, to ask you. Please come back."

Like a child, I shook his shoulder, expecting a reaction. I was ready to cry, I felt so lost.

I swallowed and stood tall, hoping to present a facade of calm to the doctors and staff. I might be unraveling inside, but no one could know.

"You've already seen my brother today?" I asked, turning to the head doctor.

"Yes, Your Highness. His condition, too, is unchanged. But he is more stable than His Majesty."

"I know you have been rotating physicians through, but I want someone stationed here at all times. The moment my father wakes, I want to be told, regardless of the hour."

"Yes, Highness. But if His Majesty does not survive, the protocol—"

"It is treason to mention the king's death, sir," I reminded him firmly. "You will say nothing more on the subject. And you will come to me when he wakes."

"Yes, Highness," he repeated seriously, sinking into a respectable bow.

It was a strange thing to feel like my every request was law. But what was truly worrying was that a time might come very soon when my words *would* be law. What would I do if something important happened and I had no idea how to address it?

"I'm off to see my brother. Thank you so much, Doctor."

I moved quickly, hoping that, somehow, if I moved fast enough, I'd catch him waking up. Turning the corner to Escalus's room, I caught Nickolas on his way out. He paused, shifting his weight to one leg, looking a little weathered from the worry.

"Any change?" I asked as I came to a stop.

"None," he replied, shaking his head. "The maid said he's murmured something a time or two, but nothing intelligible. Though if he were to speak, she'd be the one to know—she hasn't left this room for more than a few moments."

I put a hand on his shoulder, sensing that he was holding his opinions back. "Good. Noemi is faithful and trustworthy, and I think it would comfort Escalus if he woke to a familiar face."

"But who is tending to your needs? You have no proper maid these days. It's unfitting; you're practically queen."

He had no way of knowing how repulsive that word, *queen*, was at the moment. To even think the word felt like wishing for the death of what little family I had left. *Regent* I could accept. *Regent* meant they would wake up.

"You needn't worry," I said. "I have several maids coming in to help, and as you can see, I'm still all in one piece. Now, I want to go in and see my brother with my own eyes. If you could, please go to the kitchens for me and approve the menus for the week."

He gave me a quick, shallow bow. But what were such ceremonies now? "Your Highness, any job you want to pass to me, I will happily take."

He moved on his way, and I quietly opened the door to Escalus's room. As predicted, Noemi was there, just by his bed. She wasn't fast enough, and I caught the tail end of the movement as she pulled her hand away from his.

When she turned and saw it was me, she hopped to her feet to curtsy. "Your Highness."

"None of that," I said as I crossed the room and embraced

her. "Have you eaten? Slept?"

She let out a long sigh. "Yes. But . . . I want to be able to report the moment he wakes. I've been so afraid someone would force me to leave." She looked over her shoulder at him, as if he might rouse at her saying so.

"Look at me," I said. "If you tell them you are here at my command, no one can contest it. Use my name at will. Throw it around as much as you like. No one here would protect Escalus as you would."

She let out a shaky breath. "I just wish he'd open his eyes. Whatever comes after, I can bear . . . I mean, for the sake of Kadier, of course. I just hope he comes back soon."

"He will," I said, more to convince myself than her. "Escalus said he was still here. He wouldn't leave me stranded."

LENNOX

My hands were blistered from digging a grave for Aldrik. I knew it was a little shallow, but it was the best I could do on my own. Kawan sure as hell wasn't coming to bury his closest soldier, and I wasn't about to pull anyone away from work that badly needed doing. Besides, it gave me time to think.

I spent a lot of the time looking toward the graves I visited the most: my father's and Annika's mother's. I'd left the branch I'd taken from the Island for her the day we came back, but I hadn't stopped to talk. There was so much to say then that I didn't know where to start. I still didn't. So, for now, I told her nothing, asked her nothing.

I'd never felt more alone.

Rami wasn't going to get a grave. Her body had been lost when the hurricane tossed the boats over, and in some ways, it was for the best. We'd barely been able to transport the living back to Vosino. But I knew Griffin was struggling. It felt like the whole affair left us with little in the way of closure, and for him it was a hundred times worse.

When I started the descent down the rocky side of the coast that led to the sea, I found only Griffin waiting at the bottom. He was quietly assembling the wood for the memorial, looping saplings together to make a wreath. Beside it lay a small pile of kindling and what looked to be some of Rami's clothes. He'd already started a bonfire and looked focused on his task.

"I wasn't sure you'd make it," he said when he saw me, his tone surprisingly light. "I know you've been busy."

"I have, but I wanted to be here for you." I kicked at the ground a little. "I've been wanting to tell you I'm sorry. For back on the boat. I would have done something if I could have."

"There was nothing you could do." He waved his hand. "Besides, if it wasn't for you, she might never have talked to me."

I squinted, coming closer. "What?"

His smile was genuine now. "I was sitting in the mess hall, listening to a group of girls talking at the table behind me. And one particularly melodic voice was complaining, saying that the tall soldier with the black hair was too mean." He chuckled. "She said you flung a stick at someone and left him with a cut over his eye. With your reputation, she was terrified it might get worse.

"I knew immediately who she was talking about, so I jumped in and told her you were the absolute worst and that she shouldn't bother giving you a single thought more than she already had," he admitted, looking up at me. "And then she smiled, and something in me just . . ."

He was lost trying to find the words.

"Yeah. I know."

He nodded. "So, anyway, thanks for being a giant, irrational oaf. I got to be in love because of it."

I'd seen him go through the range of emotions in the short time since he'd lost Rami. Despair, rage, and even a dark kind of humor. Seeing him also almost peaceful was strange. Strange but welcome.

I turned at the sound of footsteps and saw Blythe, Inigo, Sherwin, and Andre coming toward us with a handful of others who must have been close to Rami as well. Together, we formed a semicircle around the place where Griffin was building his floating memorial.

"Thank you all for coming," he said. "I thought it might be nice if we shared some memories of Rami. We all knew her in different ways, and I'd love to hear what all of you have to say. And then we can send off her memory."

Blythe raised her hand. "Can I go first?"

Griffin nodded, and Blythe smiled.

"What I loved about Rami was how gentle she was. It seems impossible with our way of life, but Rami still had softness in spades. Seeing how she lived inspires me to do the same. Thank you for that, Rami."

"She was always so generous," one of the girls said. "Rami and I came here at the same time, and, while we were both grateful for warm meals, we were still hungry. So she took it upon herself to go wading into the water, and she caught a bunch of tiny crabs." She laughed to herself. "They were so small! Even if she'd eaten all of them, it wouldn't have filled her up. But she brought them to the room I share with five other girls, helped start a fire, and cooked them right there to share with us."

She shook her head. "To this day, that's the best meal I ever had. It was bland and it was small, but it was made with loving hands and eaten in happy company. I owe that to her."

As each story, each memory went on, I saw Rami's life through the prism of a dozen different windows. Each of these people experienced her in a different way, but the common thread of her kind heart was woven through every anecdote.

Before I'd realized it, everyone had spoken but Griffin and me, and it dawned on me that I was going to have to say something about a girl I barely even knew. When all the eyes fell on me, I panicked. And all I could say was the truth.

I cleared my throat, studying the ground. "Honestly, I hardly knew Rami at all. But what I do know is, in the middle of battle, when I got lost for a moment, she brought me back to reality. She encouraged me to fight, to keep going."

The sniffles that had started a while ago were growing thicker, some turning into sobs.

"If that was all I knew of her, it would be enough for me to mourn her. Like so many of you said, she was brave. Braver than me, that's for sure. But now, because of you all, I know so much more. And I'm sorry to not have had the chance to know her better."

I met Griffin's eyes, and they were full of tears. But something in his face spoke of gratitude. He swallowed a few times and looked out to the sea.

"Rami," he eked out, inhaling sharply, "there were so many things I wanted to say, and I'm sorry I'll never get to. But for now, let me tell you goodbye with the one thing I hope you always knew: you are my heart."

He was quiet for a moment after that. He carefully placed her uniform on the wreath, pulled a torch from the bonfire, and walked the whole thing into the ocean until he was about waist-deep. He lit the kindling and pushed it off into the surf.

Griffin slowly trudged back to land, standing with us as we watched the flames drift into the distance.

He looked at me, and the unspoken question in his eyes was the one everyone had been asking since we'd come back: *Lennox, what are you going to do about this?*

For years, all I'd wanted was my kingdom. I wanted my freedom. I didn't want to be under Kawan's thumb or at my mother's mercy. I didn't want anyone to care about me or for me to have to care about them.

But then I got a taste of what it felt like when you were brave enough to lower the drawbridge between your heart and another's. The fear came accompanied by an unmatched peace. It allowed you to find more space in your lungs for air, sight for new colors. A life without it was hardly worth living.

I'd spent my life full of hate for the Kadierians.

But now I saw how much I loved my people. And that was worth moving mountains for.

"We all agree that there has to be a better way to reclaim

our land than what we've been trained for," I started.

"Yes," Inigo said immediately.

"The problem is, I'm not entirely sure what that is. And there's the issue of Kawan. If he knew how deeply we doubted him, he'd kill us all."

I gave them time to take in those words, to really consider that they could lose the chance to see Dahrain.

"But," I started again, "if our lives are already on the line, I'd rather risk it standing up to him than pointlessly fighting the Kadierians. And if you feel the same way . . . then, when I have a plan, I will lead you."

ANNKA

For the sake of my people, I showed up at dinner with a smile on my face.

While the details of my family members' health weren't public, it was clear that some lords and ladies had guessed the situation was serious. Serious enough that I was regent, at least. My hope was to be able to stabilize things before anyone could discover the truth of what had happened. So, as I sat in my father's chair, surveying the people in front of me, I finally spoke aloud the one thing I knew must be done.

"Nickolas," I began. His head turned quickly, eyes attentive, ready to meet whatever need I voiced. "I think it's time for us to plan our wedding."

He stared at me, confused but not displeased. "Now? With . . . with everything that's happening?"

"That's exactly why we should plan. In fact, I think we should make a big fuss about it. Tell everyone I'm designing my gown and that you're having the gold for our bands brought in from Nalk. Talk about it at every opportunity. That way, when my father and brother are better, we'll have something to celebrate. And if . . ." I choked on the word. *If* could leave you breathless. "Well, whatever may come, we shall carry on the line and console our people."

He nodded. "I know none of this has happened the way you hoped. It's not exactly how I planned it, either. But I agree. Should we set a date?"

"Let's speak of the wedding as if it's very close. We can pick the date within the next few days once we have a better idea of what's happening with my family."

He nodded. "Understood. Do you still want to live away from the palace?"

My eyes flickered to the people before me, eating and laughing, not knowing how dire things were between a collapsing royal family and a potential invasion. And those in the country had less means and fewer connections to the heart of everything happening. My relationship with Nickolas would need time to grow, but it would have to wait until they were safe.

"No. I want to be here."

That brought a smile to his face. "Very well. I truly will have the gold brought in from Nalk. And you shouldn't burden yourself with the wedding arrangements; pass those along to your maid."

"She's rather occupied at the moment, but don't worry. I'll delegate."

Nickolas took a bite of food before coming back to me. "I don't mind watching over Escalus. He's very nearly my brother now. If anyone should be at his side in your stead, it's me."

I took his hand, a falsely cheerful note in my voice. "As your regent, I am commanding you to worry about this no more. I promise you that I am in good hands, and that Escalus is well tended. You will have so much work to do yourself that you'll have no time to sit at bedsides anyway."

He looked up at me, his eyes softening. He lifted my hand to his lips and kissed it. I heard a dozen different voices go "aww" as he did so. The sound solidified my resolve. I had to marry someone. If it couldn't be the man I loved, Nickolas would do.

"If you command it, then I shall happily bend to your will."

I wasn't sleeping deeply enough to dream. I wished I could. I knew now that was the only way I could see Lennox. As it was, my sleep was thin and broken, and the only thoughts I had of him were memories.

I rubbed my eyes, giving up for the time being, and moving to step into slippers. I flung my robe on and marched across the palace.

Perhaps I should have felt uncomfortable in the silence or wished for more servants and guards to line every wall. Instead, I found the isolation soothing. I laced my bracelet around my wrist as I made my way to my mother's painting and sighed as I settled down in front of her. "I've been named regent, Mama, and I've been ruling Kadier all on my own." I spread my arms out wide. "I wish you could see. I feel like

I'm finally doing something.

"Escalus has always said that marrying Nickolas was noble. And I know that's how I'll end up serving Kadier in the end . . ." I could feel the sob rising in my throat, but I shoved it back down. There was no time for tears, not now.

"I wish I could tell you everything," I confessed. "But I feel like if I pull at that thread, I might unravel like a tapestry. For everyone else's sake, I cannot fall apart."

I stared at her for a long time, enjoying the silence, enjoying her. "Do you remember when we used to go on rides together? Do you remember the boy with the apple?"

I smiled up at her. "I bet you do. You remembered everything."

She looked down upon me, her eyes ever conveying wisdom and patience. I knew she had her faults, too. I knew she wasn't perfect. But she was always searching for the best of herself, and that was all she ever offered to me. And I so badly wanted to take the best of what I had and hand it over in spades.

"Don't worry," I told her. "What is death to you and me? Your memory is still breathing. I'm keeping it alive."

LENNOX

I stood outside my mother's door, afraid to knock. There was a good chance that she'd choose Kawan over me—she'd been doing that every single day since my father died—but I needed to finally know where her true loyalties lay.

After my hundredth deep breath, I knocked. I heard her scuffling around, coming to the door. I didn't know if I just tricked myself into thinking her eyes lit up when she saw me. But I wasn't seeing things clearly anyway. It took me a moment to see that her hair wasn't done, and her dress was wrinkled.

"Lennox," she breathed.

"Could I come in for a minute?"

She nodded her head jerkily and opened the door wide. Her bed was unmade, but it was otherwise pretty tidy. It looked much like it did when I snuck in to steal a dress for Blythe, though her presence somehow made the whole place feel a little less hollow.

"Is there something in particular you wanted to talk about?" she asked.

Why did you let him beat me so many times? Why didn't we just leave? Would you forget all about him for me? Would you follow me?

Did you love me?

"Are you happy?" I finally asked.

She stared at me. "What do you mean?"

"It's just . . . before we came here, when it was just you and Father and me . . . we were happy, right?"

She looked down and smiled, her mind seeming to picture one memory after another. "Yes. We were almost too happy."

I fiddled with my fingers, picking at the corner of a nail. "So . . . are you happy now? Was that all because of him? Did we lose that when Father died?"

She looked away for a moment, her eyes welling. "Maybe. But I'm not sure that we could have done any better."

"Why?" I said, more to myself than to her.

"The truth is, people grieve at different paces. When someone moves too quickly, it hurts the others. And if someone is too slow, that hurts as well. Sometimes I wonder if you're *still* grieving. And I . . . I had to be fast."

I swallowed, not wanting to cry.

"So you kept walking and left me behind?"

"Lennox," she said so softly I almost didn't hear it. I met her eyes. "Lennox, *you* left *me*."

I opened my mouth to object, but she was right. She was unhappy, and so was I. I got my own room, and I didn't look back.

I'd left her behind. I sat there, staring at the floor as she spoke.

"I always hoped you'd come back, but you didn't. I feel like—" Her words caught in her throat, and I could tell she was going to cry a second before she did. But with the tears came truth. "I've been trying to scrounge together whatever I could from the scraps life has left me. If I couldn't have your father, Kawan is a distant second place, but at least *someone* wants me. You didn't. It was easier to feel nothing than everything. . . . At least, that's what I told myself. I didn't realize how foolish it was until I thought I'd lost you on the Island."

She looked spent, like the confession took everything from her. She was as tired of living this way as I was.

I was stunned.

"I thought . . . all this time, I just thought you couldn't stand me." I risked looking up at her, still fearing I was right.

There were tears in her eyes as she shook her head. "I meant what I said. I miss him so much, there are days when it burns to look at you, you're so like him. But hate you? Never."

For a moment, we stood there in silence. There were mountains of speeches in that one word, and it took me a moment to take it in. She realized that, looking at me with tired but patient eyes. I swallowed. She nodded. And that was it.

"I need your help," I admitted. "And you can't tell Kawan. He'll kill me if he knows."

"I know."

I stood up straighter. "You know?"

"I want our kingdom back. And I know the only way to achieve that is by backing you. People have long feared you more than him, and now they respect you more than him. It doesn't surprise me it's come to this. You are your father's son.

"You said he kept me close to keep you closer," she continued. "That's true. But I stayed close to keep you closer, too. He's been different since I ran to you on the Island, and I think any relationship Kawan and I have now is simply going through the motions. And, for the sake of appearances, I'm going to have to keep doing that.

"Until you have a plan, I must stay on his arm. Do you understand me?"

I wanted to believe everything she'd said. But how could I let a single conversation—even one that hit so deep to the heart of all my pain—erase years of neglect?

"I understand," I said, purposely not promising anything.

"Good. Be careful of what you say and who you say it to. Where are you off to now?"

"The mess hall."

She nodded. "Come to the main hall around noon. He's making plans, and I think you should know about them."

"More plans?" I asked, incredulous.

"Control your temper," she reminded me calmly. "Watch your words. Just be silent and listen."

I sighed. "Very well. I'll be there."

I went to go, mulling over everything she'd said.

"Lennox?"

I turned, noting the concern in her eyes. "Yes?"

"If something happens—if you have to scrounge up whoever you can and take a chance—go. Don't wait for me. Don't look back. Go. For the sake of whatever future we might have, please go."

The request made me think she suspected I might be forced out, or that things here might become unbearable. But then I considered that she was a mother. And mothers tended to just *know.*

I nodded. "If it comes to that, I will. And if I must go, once it settles, I will come for you. I promise."

ANNIKA

I sat in my chair, surveying the desk before me. Agreements, treaties, queries, petitions. I kept wishing Escalus was awake to see me handling these tasks; he'd be so proud.

I signed the last thing in front of me, then slumped against the high back of my chair. For once, no one was there. No lords, no doctors, no guards.

Smiling to myself, I decided it was time to take a break. I pulled up my skirts and dashed from the room, taking the back stairways to my favorite patch of the garden, far from the splashing fountains and lush blooms. The high walls of greenery shielded me from the world, the smoothed cobblestone path gave me an aimless circle to roam. It was a refreshing, for a moment, to not have to think so much.

Of course, without the chores of kingdom-running in front of me, my mind went immediately to Lennox.

Us both making it out of that cave alive might have been the only grace the universe had to spare for two people so painfully star-crossed.

I wondered if he thought of me at all. And, if he did, was it only as his enemy again? Did he think of the way it felt when we kissed? I could see the moments over and over in my head. I could feel his hands in my hair, his breath on my neck, his name in my heart.

And when those moments came, I felt like running away entirely. Maybe he and I could live somewhere else, someplace no one wanted. Maybe we could build something of our own.

But I could do no such thing. Kadier was not going to be lost. Not on my watch. I'd survived the loss of my mother. I'd survived my father shifting into the darkest version of himself. I'd agreed to marry a man I could hardly stand. All of this I'd laid at the feet of the Kadierian throne, and I was not letting anyone—not even Lennox Ossacrite—come and take it.

Still, the very thought of his name did things to my heartbeat.

Lennox's love was tangled. It was dangerous but gentle, open but complex. It was more than the books prepared me for. And I wanted it with everything I had in me.

I looked around my oasis, realizing what a strange little place it was. Typically, our gardens were much more deliberately arranged, designed almost like a maze. But this was just a path centered around a stone. So simple, so . . .

I froze.

"What are you?" I asked, squinting at the rock. Now that I studied it, the thing seemed unnaturally smooth.

A chill went through me, and I bolted, looking for the groundskeepers. I twisted through the stone lanes and grass allies, passing people as they curtsied my way.

"You there!" I called, finally coming upon a gardener. He bowed deeply in respect. "Sir, I need your help. Please fetch at least two other men and some shovels. Bring one for me as well."

There was only one place for me to start now, but I felt I'd already exhausted all my resources. If there was truth to be found, I was determined to find it.

"Annika?"

I turned to the sound of my name being called out in a tone of disbelief. Nickolas, of course, was on the other end of the word.

"Do you need something?" I asked, still moving in the direction of the library.

"What in the world happened to your gown? Have you been rolling in dirt? You look an absolute mess. I told you, you need a dedicated maid again. What will people say? It's not proper to—"

I rounded on him, holding up a finger. "Nickolas, I appreciate all that you've been doing for me, but you have *got* to stop trying to bend me into whatever version of a wife you've built in your head. Either take me as I am or find someone else." I took a few quick breaths, brushing my hair off my face. No doubt he had feelings on that as well. "I am princess here. I am *regent*. If I walk around in my stays, then it is proper, and no one can say otherwise. If you want to be of help, then help."

I watched as Nickolas blinked and took breaths, as he weighed things in his head and came to the conclusion that, for now, I was right.

"My apologies, Your Highness." He swallowed and straightened his waistcoat. "There are a number of people waiting for you, which is why I've been roaming the palace for the last hour trying to find you. After everything that's happened, I couldn't dismiss the possibility that you'd been taken again, and the thought might have put me out of my right mind."

I didn't miss that he'd turned this back on me, but if he'd truly been worried, I wasn't going to poke him more.

"I am sorry to have worried you, but there is something pressing at hand. Please go tell those waiting that I apologize for any inconvenience, and I will see them tomorrow."

I pressed on toward the library, pushing through the doors in a rush.

"Your Highness," Rhett greeted me. "So nice to see— Are you all right? What happened to your gown?"

"I was digging," I explained quickly, moving to the history section.

"Ah," he replied with a laugh. Not judgment, not reproval, but laughter. "And what did you find?"

"A half-sphere. A stone so round it looks like the sun rising from the ground," I said, a chill going down both my arms again as I remembered Lennox's words. I stopped before the vast wall of books. "Rhett, I need the oldest records of the forming of our country. I need to know *everything* about how we came to be here."

He looked like he had a dozen questions. But instead of asking a single one, he pointed toward one end of the shelves. "Start here."

LENNOX

I showed up at Kawan's door about the same time his three lead soldiers arrived. They all gave me quick nods of their heads as a means of greeting, and I followed silently behind them.

"Heard you buried Aldrik," Illio whispered.

I nodded.

He looked at the stone wall for a second before turning back to me. "Glad he wasn't completely alone."

There was a bitterness in his tone that showed me Kawan was losing support on his own faster than I could move to take it. The only thing that might save him would be a foolproof, brilliant plan. For all I knew, he had one in his pocket. So, I stayed quiet as my mother had instructed, filing in behind the others.

"Why is he here?" Kawan asked, and I knew without looking that he meant me.

I glanced up to see my mother leaning into his arm, looking so comfortable it was hard to believe she'd called that coward *a distant second* only this morning.

"He's the only one who's interacted with their princess, and he talked to those soldiers who defected as well. If anyone could offer insight, it's him," she said lazily.

"I don't need insight," Kawan retorted, a smirk slowly spreading across his face. "I have everything that I require already."

Ice raced down my spine, pinning me to the floor. I knew in that moment, in his state of complete calm, that he'd actually unlocked the gates to the kingdom.

"What do you mean?" Illio asked.

Kawan's smile was still plastered across his face as he spoke. "We received two new recruits this morning, both from Kialand."

He was delaying, stringing us out.

Finally, Slone encouraged him to continue. "I assume they brought news with them?"

Kawan nodded. "The Kadierian prince is dead."

A part of my heart shattered. Annika was out there, alone, without her brother.

"Are you sure?" Mother asked, surprised.

"Yes. And it's possible the king is dead, too," Kawan added, almost giddy.

"What?" I asked, shocked.

"It's been nearly a week since he's been seen, and rumors are spreading. That the girl was named regent, meaning she is standing in for her father and brother. That the prince is dead, but the crown is hiding it, and it seems their so-called king is not far off. So all that's between us and our kingdom . . . is a little girl."

No. No, no, no.

"I wouldn't underestimate her," I warned.

"Just because she escaped you doesn't mean she can outrun an army," he insisted, his mood growing dark. But then, just as quickly, it turned back to light. "Even so, we won't need an army. All we need to do is wait."

The soldiers in the room exchanged looks.

But as they did their thinking, I did my own. I realized then that I was holding on to the hope that I'd see her again. Not on a battlefield or in the negotiations of surrender, but . . . I'd thought I'd embrace her again, kiss her. I thought I'd rest my head in the hollow of her neck and just be still.

She flitted in and out of my head so many times a day, I had to stop counting. She clouded every other desire, even the ones I knew I had to pursue to the end. I had my path and she had hers.

I shook my head, coming back to the moment.

"Sir," I ventured, "how can you be so sure of this?"

"Because, while you were stuck in the side of a mountain, I was camped beneath a cluster of trees . . . in a forced truce."

All our eyes snapped to him. I wanted to say it was impossible, but I knew from my own experience it most certainly was not.

"With whom?" Mother asked.

"Someone who wants the royal family to disappear as much as we do. And he is going to take care of everything for us," he replied, the answer so vague it was maddening.

"Take care of it how?" I needed clarity here, perfect clarity.

Kawan's smile was dark, delighted.

"She should be dead within the next week," he replied calmly. "And once that's done, our little informant will be . . . removed. In two weeks, we'll be living in the palace."

ANNIKA

"Thank you," I said to the maid whose name I didn't know as she placed food on the table beside me.

"You're welcome, Your Majesty," she replied.

"No!" I said so loudly she jumped. Her doe eyes were wide and fearful. I pinched my lips together, upset with myself. "I'm so sorry. I didn't mean to yell. It's just that I am still 'Your Highness.' My father and brother will be back to service soon. I'm simply . . . filling in the gap."

She nodded. "Very sorry, Your Highness." She curtsied and made her way quickly from the room.

"I really am—" She was gone before I could say "sorry."

I sighed, turning back to the tomes before me. I'd scoured seven history books looking for some mention of the Dahrainian people. There was nothing.

But that stone in the garden . . . it was *exactly* like the one Lennox described to me in the cave. Perfectly round, perfectly smooth. It had been all but buried in a garden, but it was there. He'd said his people would return to it and dance there. And if that detail was real—if he knew about that without ever having set foot here—then there must be more. I felt it in my bones.

The door opened without a knock, and Nickolas walked in with a tray.

"Ah. I was attempting to make a peace offering, but I see someone already brought you food," he said, nodding to the plates left on the table.

It had been a few hours since the incident in the hallway, and I still wasn't sure what to say about any of it. Did I need to apologize? If so, what for? In the meantime, I carried on conversation, hoping it would pass.

"Yes. I don't know who told them to . . ." I trailed off, noticing that Nickolas was sulking and stabbing cheeses with his fork.

"Can I ask you something?" I began again.

He peeked up. "Of course."

"Have you ever heard that there was a seventh clan?"

He squinted at me. "That . . . that's what you want to know?"

"Yes."

He sighed. "Annika. Our country is in danger of losing the majority of its royal family; you and I are supposedly planning a wedding; an army set on destroying everything we've built is waiting out there for us—and you want a history lesson?" He stared at the far wall for a second. "I don't understand where your mind is right now."

There was something so defeated in his posture that my instinct to put him in his place faltered.

"Nickolas, I'm in a position I wasn't trained for in a time when we *know* there are enemies on the horizon. I'm worried about my brother and father; I haven't been sleeping. If I seem distracted, it's because it's a lot. It feels"—I put a hand on my heart, thinking it all over—"overwhelming and wonderful and tiring and amazing. I'm doing the best I can."

He came over to kneel before me. "Then let me help. Annika, I'm capable. Go and rest. I'll receive your requests. I can read them, sort them, and summarize them for you tonight. Breathe."

I looked away. It felt like cheating to hand any of my responsibilities over to him . . . but if it was just reading reports and giving me pertinent information, was it so bad?

"Fine. But right now, I'm going to return these books to the library."

He smiled and nodded, satisfied for the time being. With nothing else to say, I scooped up my books and made my way to the library.

"Annika?" Rhett asked as I walked in the door. "Back already?"

"Yes." I placed the books on the front table. "I was going to look through these again, but it's no use. I'm not finding anything."

He sighed. "Have you considered that the lack of what you're hunting for is the answer itself?"

I shook my head. "I think there's more."

He came closer and took me by the shoulders. "All right, then. Tell me exactly what you're looking for. If it's in this library, I'll find it."

I huffed. "I'm looking for any mention of a seventh clan—the Dahrainians? I can't find a single reference to any such thing. . . . I was just so sure I was onto something."

I rubbed at my forehead, trying to massage the stress out of it. When I looked over to Rhett, he was smiling.

"Annika. Of course you're not finding anything. You're looking in the wrong place."

"What?"

"These people—the Dahrainians, you called them?"

I nodded in reply.

"They aren't in the history books. All the stories about the missing seventh clan are in mythology." He pointed to the section of the library at the center of the room, open so everyone could see what you were looking at, where the books themselves were chained to the shelves.

Mythology.

Before I could even process what that meant, the doors burst open.

Nickolas was there, out of breath from running all the way down.

"Annika," he greeted me breathlessly. "I wouldn't disturb you if it wasn't urgent, but there's someone here I think you want to meet."

I hated to admit how my heart leaped, how every last reserve of hope in my body woke up. Was he here? Did he come back to me?

"Who?"

"A soldier His Majesty sent to the Dahrainian camp as an emissary, announcing the transfer of the Island. He was kept in the castle, questioned, and then sent to swim his way home. He's the only one of the three His Majesty sent out to come back alive."

I nodded. "Take me to him at once."

LENNOX

I discovered I could communicate with Inigo and Blythe with a single glance. When I passed them sparring with a group of soldiers outside, that was all it took to get their attention. I kept walking, moving to the outskirts of the grounds, knowing without looking back they were following me.

I stopped at a boulder, trying to gather my thoughts. I might not have been shaking outwardly, but everything inside felt like it was shivering, cold and unsteady. I turned to find them both there, waiting.

"Their prince is dead," I told them.

Blythe covered her mouth, her eyes conveying her joy. "I wish I could tell Rami. I wish she could know. . . ."

I couldn't tell her why this didn't feel like good news to me, why it felt like a part of my heart had been heavy ever since I'd heard.

"There are reports that the king is also dead," I said quickly, not wanting her to see—and worse, question—my discomfort at the news about Escalus. "If not, he's close to. Their princess has been named regent. I don't know if that means the king actually lives or if they're buying time to prepare her before announcing his death. Either way, it would seem she's alone in that palace."

Inigo's eyes were on the grass, but I could see him squinting, tracing lines in the ground as he tried to find the end of his thoughts.

"What you're saying is, we only have to get rid of her? That's easy," Blythe said. "*I* could do that."

"No!" I said quickly, before catching myself. "Apparently while we were on the Island, Kawan waited out the torrent with someone from Kadier. Whoever that person is, they're going to get rid of her."

There was a charged moment of silence. Then Blythe laughed.

"This . . . this is exactly what we were hoping for, right?" she said.

Her head was whipping back between Inigo and me, waiting for one of us to confirm her guesses.

"We can't be sure. Not yet, anyway. I need to see if we can learn more about what's happening. If she's . . ." I swallowed. "If she's even still alive, and if the person Kawan spoke to was reliable. There's no way of knowing at the moment."

I saw Blythe deflate a little. "Of course. You're right." She sighed, looking back at the old castle. It seemed even grayer than usual today. "I just saw a flicker of hope, and I got worked up. Whatever you say is best, I'll follow, Lennox. We all will."

I looked at her, touched by the sincerity in her voice. "Thank you, Blythe."

"I mean it," she insisted. "The recruits, especially the younger ones . . . they're asking about you. I feel like we have a real chance now."

My smile was weak, but I gave it to her all the same.

"Blythe," Inigo finally said, "would you please give us a moment? I need to ask Lennox about something personal."

Her face was as surprised as mine, but she nodded and went on her way.

Inigo watched until she was well out of earshot.

"What are you going to do about it?" he finally asked.

"About what?"

"What are you going to do about your girl?" he asked firmly.

I looked at Blythe's retreating figure in confusion, holding up an arm in her direction. "Nothing? She seems just—"

Inigo slapped my hand down. "Blythe is crazy for you, so she can't see the truth right in front of her. I can." He stared at me, his eyes neither accusing nor angry. "What are you going to do about your girl?"

I swallowed, feeling my pulse pick up. "I don't know what you're talking about."

"You can keep this secret from everyone else, Lennox, but not from me. If we're about to storm a country with you at the helm, and you're not going to be able to remove the last stumbling block between us and everything we've ever said we wanted, I need to know." His words could have been cold accusations, but they weren't. He said everything with patience and concern. So much so that it made it all the more frightening for me. He pointed into the distance. "If we could run there right now, would you go for the throne, or would you go for her?"

Tears stung at my eyes. "How did you even know?"

"If a blind man could regain his sight, I imagine he'd look the way you did the first time you saw her in the forest. A half-naked girl escapes our castle and goes running across the continent, and you come home without her *or* your cape. We're in the middle of our first full-on battle, and you're blatantly searching for a familiar face in a place where there shouldn't be one. When we sailed back from the Island, you checked your pocket for a piece of lace at least six times that I counted. And just now you could hardly get out a sentence about her dying without your voice breaking.

"I need to know what the plan is. Because both you and I are tired of fighting a war without victors."

I allowed myself a sharp breath, pushing down tears. "Inigo . . . what do I do?

"I took her mother's life with my own two hands, and she forgave me. She *forgave* me! She told me the darkest secrets of her life; she trusts me."

He made a face. "That girl has dark secrets?"

I sighed. "I wish I didn't know about them. It hurts me to remember."

"You say she trusts you. Does she love you?"

I let out a long breath, thinking of her fingers in my hair, her wrapping my cape around her shoulders, her kisses that she gave so freely. "If she does or she doesn't, my heart would be wasted on anyone else."

He nodded. "Lennox. I swore my allegiance to you long ago. I've been waiting for you to be ready to lead; I've known for years you could do it. So give me an order. Tell me what you want, and I'll do everything in my power to make it happen."

I looked away, unable to bear his faith in me. It filled me with indescribable hope and pride, but there would always be a measure of fear right alongside it.

"We need our home back, Inigo. And I need her to live. If she dies, I die. I can't *have* her. I understand that. But Annika has to live."

Inigo crossed his arms again, back to being a soldier. "Understood." He looked down and then back to me. "What about Blythe?"

I swallowed. "I . . . I don't . . ."

"Because if she's fair game, you really ought to say so." And without another word, he marched off, leaving me stunned at how much Inigo might have been sacrificing for my sake all along.

ANNIKA

"Oh, please don't bow," I insisted, rushing into the room. The man in front of me looked worse than our army did marching back from the Island. His clothes were ripped, and I could see red marks on his wrists where he'd been bound. His lip was split but healing, and there were bruises on the patches of skin I could see.

It wasn't until he lifted his head that I recognized him. When I'd fallen into that glass table, my father had been too stunned to offer assistance, even as the blood poured through my torn dress. A guard had swooped into action, carrying me back to my rooms. It was humiliating . . . but I was thankful someone had helped me.

He helped me.

"Your Highness. Forgive my state. I wanted to see you first."

"Have you not been tended to, sir?" I had to imagine he was in need of food and rest. He shook his head. "You must be starving," I said, turning to Nickolas in desperation.

His eyes flicked back and forth between the guard and me, clearly reluctant to miss anything. "Of course," he finally said. "I'll be back as soon as I can."

He moved quickly from the room, and the guard and I were left alone.

"Before anything, I must apologize to you," he started urgently. "We tried to stop them from bringing their entire army, but it was fruitless. They gave no hints they were planning to sabotage you until that morning. I failed to protect you. It's unforgivable." His eyes went to the floor, ashamed.

"Say no more. I didn't know His Majesty intended to use our army to corner them. The whole engagement was a disaster. Just tell me what you can."

He nodded, moving his gaze up to me. "We were instructed to tell them to meet His Majesty on the Island. It was meant to be neutral ground for peace talks. The king would offer them goods and a treaty in hopes of future cooperation. That was all I was told." He shook his head.

"We allowed ourselves to be captured. They questioned us, mostly about protections on the castle. They wanted to know about fortifications, though there was one soldier with a lot of questions about our history. Coleman told their leader just enough details to get them on the boats. When the leader—Kawan—realized he was being manipulated, he ordered us killed. That same soldier from before, Lennox, walked us down to the shore. He asked a few more questions, about the country, about you."

He swallowed hard, thinking back. Meanwhile, my ears perked up at his name.

"Our hands were bound . . . he could have just run us

through. But he told us to walk into the water instead, giving us a chance to swim home. He even cut my ropes just enough that I could break out and help the others."

He turned away, lips trembling as he gathered the strength to finish his story. "We did get our arms free, but the currents were very strong, so we couldn't get back to shore. By the time we managed to beat the pull out to sea, we were so tired. . . . We just wanted to get out of the water, so I started making my way to the first land I could see. It was too rocky. We kept getting slammed into them, and . . . I think that was when we lost Coleman. I can't be sure."

I put my hand to my mouth, so moved by his brokenness that I felt I might cry myself any moment.

"I was finally able to climb out, and hoisted Victos behind me. We both passed out from exhaustion on the edge of a forest somewhere. When I came to, he was sweating and thrashing in his sleep. I ventured out, trying to find food and water, but it was impossible. I gave him what little I could gather, but it wasn't enough, and I tried to keep him out of the sun, but I had no way to keep the fever at bay. He died while I was asleep."

He had to pause again. This torture I understood. Even with all our doctors and medicines at my disposal, I couldn't heal my brother or father, and the powerlessness was devastating.

"A few people were kind enough to let me ride on the back of their carts, but being injured slowed me more than I liked. I've been told that the campaign went ahead, and that there was a storm?"

I sighed. "There was a brief battle at sea. They attempted

to burn our boats, but with our muskets, they had to keep a distance. We both continued to the Island, and once we came across one another, someone from their side shot an arrow directly into Escalus's chest. It was pure chaos after that. But a hurricane came in, and we were all forced into hiding. My brother and father are fortunate to even be alive."

It was then that Nickolas returned, a tray of food and drink in hand. He rushed in, setting them on the table beside the guard.

"I'm sorry. I've only just realized I don't actually know your name," I said.

He wiped at his eyes. "Palmer, Your Highness."

"Please eat something." I gestured to the food, and he half-heartedly picked up a piece of bread.

"So, are you currently regent, Highness?"

"Yes," I confirmed. "Appointed by my brother before we left the Island. Since then, both he and my father have been unconscious, but I am confident they will both recover."

I watched as Nickolas's eyes danced between us, questioning if I should be saying as much as I was.

"How bad are your injuries?" I asked. "I'd like to place you in one of the guest rooms for the time being and send a doctor. And then ask an enormous favor of you."

At this he looked up. "My injuries are minimal. How can I serve Your Highness?"

"I need someone to deliver something to Lennox. A gesture between leaders."

"Then you mean, it's for that other fellow," Nickolas clarified. "Kawan, isn't it?"

I shook my head. "No. I was in their midst. Kawan may be in charge, but he is not their leader."

Palmer nodded weakly. "What I'm delivering . . . would you say it was akin to extending a hand of peace?"

I considered this. "Something like that."

"Annika, are you sure this is wise?" Nickolas interjected. "Your father and brother are on their deathbeds. These people killed your mother and I have no doubt they're biding their time to get to you. How can we keep you safe if you send signs of goodwill after such aggression?"

It was a fair question. No matter what, this was likely going to end in war.

But I was the daughter of a peacemaker.

I'd fought so hard for the right to hold my sword, fought to learn how to use it. And now I knew that laying it down was a fight all its own.

"We will act with caution, but I'd like to make efforts toward ending this with no further bloodshed. Certainly you can get behind that."

His eyes flashed between Palmer and me. "Annika, I don't know if I can agree," he said lowly.

I walked over, attempting to keep this part of the conversation private. "If you are to become consort, then you must know this with all your heart: the people are first. We are second. So I need to put their needs before mine, even at the risk of my life. And I need you to support me while I do it."

He swallowed hard, looking at the ground. "Do what you will."

"Thank you."

I stepped away, returning to Palmer.

"Take as much time as you need, and if you're not comfortable riding back into their territory, say so. I can't promise your safe return, and after what you've been through, I wouldn't begrudge you in the slightest."

"If I can eat and rest tonight, I will happily leave in the morning," he replied immediately.

"So soon?" I asked. "Are you quite sure?"

He nodded. "I'd like the opportunity to look him in the eye again."

And I wished for nothing more myself.

LENNOX

I wandered around the castle grounds for a while, mulling over Inigo's request to let Blythe go. The more I flipped through my memories, the more it made sense. Inigo had stood up for her and praised her, all while walking on the outskirts of our fledgling relationship. Even when it hurt him, Inigo did his best to support Blythe without getting between her and the one thing she seemed to care about: me.

But now I knew better. He loved her. And I couldn't drag it out anymore.

I kept walking, moving back toward the castle. It was a rare thing to find Kawan outside, and even less common to find him alone. But when the figure rose up from the tall grass in the distance, it was unmistakably him. Maybe it was because I was thinking about Inigo's selflessness, or considering how to sacrifice a little more myself, but whatever the reason, I marched over to him.

He wiped the edge of a short knife, and I understood now he had been hunting. It probably wasn't the best time to talk, but it seemed all times were bad. So I continued. Even from a distance I could tell he was rolling his eyes.

"I'm in no mood," he called, looking down again to something in the grass.

"Nor am I. Still, I think we need to speak." I stopped a few feet away, not wanting to set him up for an easy punch if his temper got the best of him. "I don't know what it is about me that offends you so, but I have done my best for you—for our people—since the day my family arrived. You may not have liked my attitude, but I've completed every task you set me."

"You have been trying to undermine me from day one," he retorted.

"No, sir," I replied truthfully. "I believed, as my father did, that you would lead us back to our kingdom, that you would take your crown and set things straight. I've made many missteps, but I still hope for that."

He huffed, waving his arms around, gesturing to nothing. "And so I shall have my kingdom. Wait a week or two for this princess to die, and we'll waltz in, kill off the landowners—the descendants of those traitors who took our place—and put everything right."

"Is there no better way?" I asked.

His icy stare was all I needed to know that he'd grown tired of my voice. "Let me make myself plain. If you say another word against me or my plans or my methods, I will rid you of your tongue. I'd love to see people follow you if you can't give an order."

"I'm not speaking against you; I'm begging you for help. We lost so many on the Island, and if we've been misinformed about the royal family in Kadier, we could be set up for another—"

Kawan pulled his knife back out and pointed it directly at my face. It was very near my eye, and I feared a single breath let out the wrong way might cost me both my voice and my sight. Still, I didn't flinch. I stood, silent and still, waiting.

"One. More. Word," he threatened.

We stayed like that for a long moment. I wondered why he didn't just go ahead and kill me. He'd had plenty of chances over the years. My mother wouldn't have had anywhere else to go. Why did he want me under his thumb and not under a tombstone?

He pulled his knife back, sheathing it before reaching down to pick up what he'd been tending to in the grass. I watched in horror as he lifted a gray animal from the ground.

No. *No.*

"By the way," he started, "we don't have pets here." He held up my little gray fox, and I had to push aside every impulse in my body to tackle him. "Thank you for my supper."

He turned again, sauntering away, knowing I wouldn't follow.

In fact, I turned in the other direction and ran. I made it to the outskirts of the western gate before I bent over and vomited.

"Oh, Thistle," I whimpered, staying doubled over. It wasn't just the thought of her dying that tore me apart. It was the thought of her filling his stomach.

I bent over and retched again.

Just when it seemed he couldn't take anything else from me, he found new ways to break my spirit. If it wasn't so evil, it'd be impressive.

But now, I counted my conscience clean when it came to Kawan.

I'd tried following him. I tried obeying him. I tried reasoning with him.

But now, when the time came, I would undo him without a second thought. How it would happen, I couldn't say. But carrying his death would hardly be a burden at all now.

ANNIKA

I walked into my brother's room to find a doctor checking his pulse. Noemi's hands held her needlework, but they were not moving, perfectly still as she watched the doctor's every movement.

He leaned over and pulled at Escalus's eyelid, looking for what, I couldn't say. He placed his hand to Escalus's forehead for a moment, straightened himself, and walked over to me.

"Your Majesty," he greeted me.

"Highness," I corrected him. Why were so many people calling me that? It almost felt as if they'd been instructed, and if I had the slightest inkling of where it was coming from, I'd put a stop to it at the source instantly.

"Oh. Yes, of course. Your brother is showing signs of improvement. His pulse is a bit stronger than yesterday, and, while his temperature is still high, it appears to be dropping."

I looked over to Escalus, still pale, still motionless.

"Is . . . is there nothing more we can do?"

The doctor nodded. "I'm afraid not. I'm off to His

Majesty's room now. From the reports, it seems not much has changed in his condition, but I will send word immediately if anything is different, one way or the other."

"Thank you."

I wanted to be grateful, but I also wanted more. More action, more answers. How was it that I held all the power in our kingdom and yet felt so helpless?

I trudged over to Noemi, peeking over her shoulder at her needlepoint. "Is that one of his shirts?"

She nodded. "I've fixed two collars, and this cuff has a hole. There are a few coats that need some of the decorative work tended to, so those are next on my list. When His Royal Highness wakes up, his wardrobe will be ready for him. All he has to do now," she said, her lip trembling ever so slightly, "is come back."

I could feel the tension rolling off her, desperation drowning out hope. I was tired. Busy all day and sleepless most nights. That was the only reason I could think of for speaking so foolishly.

"You have to have faith, Noemi. If Escalus doesn't come back for me, he's certainly coming back for you."

Her needle froze. The realization of what I'd said hit us both at the same time, and we stared at each other wide-eyed as she got to her feet.

"How . . . how long have you known?" she asked in a whisper.

I could offer nothing but the truth. "Since just before we left for the Island. It was half the reason I insisted you go; I didn't want to make you wait."

She nodded. "Well?"

"Well, what?"

I looked at her sweet, worried face, realizing she was about to break. "Do you hate me?"

I bridged the distance between us, clutching her hands. "My darling Noemi, why would I hate you?"

She sniffled, shrugging. "For keeping such a secret from you. I always felt guilty, not telling you. But Escalus insisted. I'm so sorry."

I reached up, cupping her cheek. "I forgive you. I'm sad that I had to be kept in the dark, but I understand why I had to be. I would have said the wrong thing to someone, and you'd have been dismissed. And neither of us could've lived without you."

I looked down, sighing. "Nickolas keeps telling me to take you from Escalus's side, but I know how much he'd be comforted by waking to your face. The truth is, I'm a disaster without you. And not in the way you might think; not the tending to things and helping me get dressed. Rather, just the knowledge you were there if I was confused or scared. I've missed having someone to talk to."

She tilted her head. "I've abandoned you when you needed me most. Oh, my lady. Is it so bad?"

I could feel myself getting teary now. "The work is actually very satisfying. But knowing that every mistake will bear my name is terrifying. I hate that I have no one to steer me back on the right course."

"Not even the duke?" she ventured, though her tone gave away her own distaste in the idea.

"Noemi . . . something seems a bit off with Nickolas," I whispered. "He's offered to help again and again, though the manner in which he does it is so strange. But I can't tell if it's just my tired brain playing tricks on me. He doesn't seem to understand the sacrifice in it. . . ."

She nodded. "Remember that he has no rights to your work or your power. And I know you're keen to serve, but take some time for yourself. If you don't take care of the regent, then she won't be able to care for anyone else."

It was such a stupidly obvious point that I couldn't believe I hadn't thought of it sooner.

"See, this is why I need you around. You're so much smarter than me."

She chuckled. "I'm glad you think so." Her smile quickly faded. "But I need to ask you one more thing."

"Anything."

She reached up, touching her neck, nervous. "You said you didn't hate me for keeping a secret. But . . . if Escalus and I can somehow be together, would you hate me . . ." She looked away, unable to get the words out. But as soon as she began the sentence, I realized where it would end.

"Would I hate you if you became queen?"

She pursed her lips together, nodding slightly.

I'd had a taste of leadership now. I liked it. But, when Father or Escalus—or hopefully both of them—came to, it all went back into their hands. What did it hurt to have another person step in line before me?

"Who could possibly hate Queen Noemi?"

Her lip trembled. "Really?"

"You have supported me through thick and thin. And I will happily do the same for you." We stood there for a moment, hands locked, lives entwined. "But, first things first, we have to get this boy to wake up. So you take care of him, and I'll worry about everything else."

I kissed her cheek, turning to go. "Let me know if anything changes. I'll be at my desk the rest of the day."

She looked at me as if to say, *Did I not just tell you to do the opposite?*, but then smiled as if she realized I wouldn't have listened to her anyway. If that wasn't true sisterhood, then I didn't know what was.

When I was around the corner, I allowed myself to slow. I put a hand to my heart, trying to rub away the ache. I wanted Noemi to have every happiness. I wanted her to have a life that wasn't lost in service to mine. But it did hurt that she might get to rule in ways I never would.

There.

I wasn't perfect.

And now that I'd allowed myself the thought, I shoved it away. I would never permit myself to think of it again. If she and Escalus were going to have a chance, then I couldn't waver where she was concerned. If they ever got that far, the people would have their issues with a maid being elevated, so I would set the example of support. And that meant being better than I had been, better than I was now.

LENNOX

Walking patrol used to feel like a chore. Now—out of the castle, away from death and arguments and exploitation—it felt like a sort of freedom. How many times had I attempted to imagine life in my new land, finally having everything I wanted at my fingertips? I was realizing now that if I brought all the manipulation of Vosino with me to a new palace, it would be another prison.

"What are you thinking about?" Blythe asked.

Inigo was a few steps behind her, followed by Griffin. We all had our eyes on the horizon.

"The future," I replied honestly.

She smiled, blissful. "I can't wait to see it."

I looked back to Inigo and flicked my chin at him, asking without words to give Blythe and me some space. He nodded, slowing his pace and keeping Griffin by his side.

How was I supposed to explain to Blythe that she'd done nothing wrong? How was I to convince her that cutting ties now was different from when I'd attempted to before? How could I explain that this was the only way I could really show her love?

Once we got far enough away from the others, I turned back and looked at her. Her eyes were on me almost all the time, and today was no different.

"I need to tell you something," I began seriously.

She still wore her smile, but I could tell it was a delicate thing. "All right."

"First, I wanted to thank you. You've only ever seen the best in me. I've never understood why," I admitted. "I still don't. But that's meant more than I can say."

I could see it in her eyes, the knowledge that this was me rolling out something soft for her to fall on when I broke her heart. "There's a lot of good to you, Lennox," she said quietly.

I shrugged. "Maybe. More important, I want you to know that I see the good in you, too. For the longest time, all I saw was a soldier, but . . . you're much more than that."

She swallowed. "Don't drag it out," she breathed, looking away. "Just say it."

I was so, so tired of hurting other people. "Blythe . . . you and I . . ."

She shook her head. "Listen. If you're going to be a leader, then you can't just think about how you'll start things; you have to think about how you're going to end them, too. And you have to end them well." Her eyes came up to mine, cold for the first time since we started getting to know one another.

"This is the last time I finish something for you," she said, turning away.

The lingering chill was so uncomfortable, I nearly took the whole thing back. I might have made an attempt if something much bigger hadn't happened.

"Lennox?" Griffin called quietly.

"Yes?" I answered, matching his tone. Instantly, Blythe went into a crouch, and I lowered myself, too, on the lookout.

"On your left," she whispered.

I slowly turned my head, finding a masked rider on a horse with a white flag raised in the air. In the meantime, Griffin and Inigo had joined us, watching the lone rider come in.

"That's no accident," Inigo said. "He's looking for us."

"Then he can find us." I stepped out from the tree line, into the middle of the plain, while the others stayed put. He saw me almost instantly and slowed his trot even further. Once he was close enough, he called down from where he sat.

"Lennox."

I hoped my face didn't give away my surprise at his knowing my name. "Yes."

"I have a gift for you, an offering of peace. Directly from Her Royal Highness Princess Annika Vedette."

Her full title rolled out like poetry.

Whatever she'd sent me, I'd be thankful. But there was no way he could offer a better gift than what he'd just given me: the knowledge that Annika was alive.

I held out my hand. "Then deliver your package and be gone."

Something in his eyes said he was smiling behind his mask. And I felt like I'd seen those eyes before.

"I am not to hand it over until you confirm something."

I huffed. "And what is that?"

"She said I could not give you this unless you could articulate exactly what the 'sweet nothings' are."

I stood there, smiling to myself that she could manage to flirt with me across countries.

"I have breakfast," I told him quietly.

He chuckled and dismounted. He walked with a slight limp to his gait and untied a small canvas bag from around his belt, holding it out to me.

I watched his eyes for a moment, shaking my head when I recognized him.

"Palmer. So you did make it home alive. Bold of you to come back."

"I do as my princess asks," he replied.

I took the bag and looked away. "I assume she's well."

I couldn't outright ask how she was faring in the wake of losing her brother, but I needed to know *something.*

"She's as well as can be expected. She's trying to run a country, plan a wedding, and tend to her brother and father as often as possible. . . . I'm sure she's exhausted, but she'll never admit it."

Each word of the sentence was like a punch to the gut in different ways.

First, she truly was leading. I knew full well she was capable, but it pleased me nonetheless.

Second, her brother was not dead. He might be sick—close to death, even—but he was alive. As was their king.

And third . . . a wedding. I knew she was obligated to

marry Dear Nickolas, but that was supposed to be something distant. What if she was already married by the next time our paths crossed? How might that feel?

"No," I replied. "She doesn't seem the type to accept defeat."

I pulled at the strings holding the pouch together and found inside a glass jar with a perfectly fitted lid. It looked like the type of thing a lady might keep her perfume or face powder in, something delicate and made for a vanity, not a long trip. It was hard to make out exactly what was inside with the way the beveled glass distorted it, but I opened it and found a tiny slip of paper. On it was written one word.

Dahrain.

I looked beneath it and saw rich, dark soil.

She'd sent me a piece of my home.

I couldn't help the sob that came out, though it was embarrassing to do it in front of the enemy and my fellow soldiers. I held it up to my nose and breathed deep. Oh, it smelled so good, like plants, trees . . . hopes. All of it could grow in earth like this.

I could feel Palmer's eyes on me as I stared at this jar full of dirt.

"Sir, I have to know, do you intend to harm my princess?"

"What?" I asked, wiping my eyes with the back of my hand as quickly as I could.

"I need to know if you intend to kill her. If there's even a flicker of a chance, then I'll destroy you now. I failed her once before; it won't happen again."

I chuckled humorlessly. "And for some reason I thought you might be on my side."

He surveyed the horizon, and I could see the moment he spotted the others waiting behind the trees. He didn't seem surprised to find them there. "In a way, I am. If there was a possibility of solving this dispute peacefully, then I'd support you. But if you plan to hurt my princess, my prince, or my king . . . then you are my enemy."

"I cannot condone any more death. I would never hurt her myself nor wish her harm at anyone else's hand. Which is why I'm telling you this: someone in the castle is after Her Highness's life."

His eyes widened. "Who?"

"Someone who was on the Island. That's all I know. Kawan thinks your king and prince are dead; I'm going to let him keep believing that. But he's convinced the only thing between us and the crown is your princess."

His eyes darted to the grass, moving back and forth as if searching for possible names. "Nearly the entire army was there on that island," he said slowly. "Any one of them could have been cornered by Kawan."

"I don't know your court dynamics. Is there anyone in the palace who might hold a grudge against the princess?"

Palmer's eyes gave away his disbelief. "I don't know of a living soul in our kingdom who doesn't worship her. She's all goodness."

"So, in a situation where it seems like there's nobody . . . it could be anybody?" I asked.

Horror-struck, Palmer nodded.

"You need to get back immediately," I urged. "You have to keep her safe. After everything, she'll trust you above any other guard, right? She'll keep you near her?"

"We'll have to see. But I think we should both be honest." He looked at me, forcing me to hold his gaze. "At this point, could anyone keep her safer than you?"

I swallowed hard. "No. But it's also possible no one could bring her more danger than me, either."

"Regardless. You should come with me."

I looked over to the tree line, to Blythe and the others waiting expectantly. What would happen to them if I left now? After all their waiting, after putting their hopes in me, how could I just abandon them?

"I can't."

Even though I couldn't see his full expression, I could feel the wide expanse of his disappointment.

"Then let's both pray she lives." He turned and mounted his horse. "Do you have anything to send to Her Highness? A token? A word?"

A token. What of mine couldn't Annika have if she asked? She had my cape; she had a bracelet made from my tie; she had every last corner of my heart. If I could have given her something grand I would have, but I held nothing.

She held everything.

I reached into my waistbelt, pulling out the bars of oats she liked so much. "Give her these, and please tell her to keep practicing her steps."

He shook his head. "More codes. Very well. Stay safe."

"You too."

And he turned to go, looking at me over his shoulder one last time before he moved into a gallop.

"You're letting him go?" Blythe called incredulously,

running out to me with the others trailing close behind.

I nodded. "He delivered his message, and I needed him to bring one in return."

She watched him leave. "Who had a message? Aren't the king and prince dead?"

Once again, I found a way to answer without lying. "Their princess sent word."

"Oh," she said, looking displeased. "And?"

I sighed, clutching the glass jar of dirt wrapped tight in its cloth close to me. "I think . . . I think she wants peace."

Blythe scoffed. "Soon enough she won't be alive to offer peace. We can take the land. What a fool," she added, crossing her arms and watching as Palmer disappeared in the brush.

"Are you all right?" Inigo asked.

I stared into the distance but nodded in reply. "I just have a lot on my mind."

But there wasn't a lot. It was only one person. And I couldn't believe I'd just passed up an opportunity to be by her side.

ANNIKA

I'd fallen asleep with my face pressed against pages, my thoughts swirling around worries about how Lennox might receive my gift. Would it come across as if I had something he did not, instead of a glimpse of the thing he'd always wanted to see? I shook my head, trying to regain my bearings. I felt so disoriented.

When I sat up properly, there was a painful ache in my back from hunching over. I looked around blearily to see what had woken me and found Rhett's adoring smile shining down on me.

"Good afternoon, Your Highness. I'm sorry to wake you, but there's a soldier here who says he was sent on a mission for you." His tone turned the statement into a question, as if he didn't believe him.

"Oh goodness," I said, sitting up and brushing my hair back with my fingers. "Please tell me I don't have ink on my face."

He chuckled. "You look like a woman who has been hard

at work for her people. You've never been more lovely."

"Thank you, Rhett." I shook my head. "You have been such a faithful friend."

He lowered his eyes, seeming pleased, but there was also pain in them when his gaze returned to me. "Annika, I hope you know that I have always, *always* been on your side."

I nodded. "I do."

"If I crossed a line that day when I asked you to run away with me . . . well, you'll probably never understand what it feels like to fall in love with someone completely out of your reach. . . ."

I swallowed.

"But the feeling drives you to say and do the most desperately embarrassing things. I understand that you're going to marry the duke; I know that, even in my wildest of daydreams, you and I were unlikely to be together. But I hope you will never hold my heart against me. I will love you, and I will serve you, and I will be utterly devoted to you until the day I die."

The sincerity of Rhett's words was a comfort. I couldn't be what he wanted me to, but he was more of a friend than I deserved.

"How could I ever hold such kindness against you?" I replied with a smile. He returned it and then went to stand in a more respectable posture.

"He's waiting in the foyer. Shall I bring him to you?"

I looked at the mess of books I'd pulled out, all of them still chained to the shelves. "No, no. Take me to him."

I followed Rhett to the front of the library, finding Palmer leaning against a desk. He straightened up when he saw me and moved into a deep bow. I could see that, despite what he'd said, he was still in pain.

"I'm sorry to disturb your work, Your Highness, but I thought you'd like to know . . ." His eyes darted to Rhett, hesitant to share his news in front of others.

"You may proceed. Rhett is a friend."

His unsure eyes looked over Rhett again, but hesitant to disobey my orders, he proceeded. "Their leader believes the king and your brother are dead. And we have reason to believe you could be in danger from someone inside the palace."

Rhett stood up taller. "Who?"

"We don't know. For now, you need to be kept under constant watch. Might I ask to be made your personal guard? I'd like to pull a few guards I think we could trust to be in rotation, but I must be by your side."

"Of course," I replied.

Palmer turned to Rhett. "Keep Her Highness safe until I return."

"I won't let her out of my sight," Rhett vowed.

Palmer nodded. He turned to go but quickly stopped himself. "Ah," he said, coming back to me, a small smile on his face. "He said the code without hesitation. He was moved by your token, and he sends this in return." Palmer reached in his bag and pulled out a small rectangle wrapped in paper and twine. I could smell the cinnamon as soon as it hit the open air, and I felt my heart begin to race at the thrill of touching something Lennox's hands had been on. "He also said to practice your steps."

I smiled to myself. All I could think was that he'd fed me again.

"Thank you. That was a dangerous trek, and I know you've been pushed to your physical limits for me. I won't forget this."

Palmer bowed, heading off to his work.

Rhett watched as I pulled the parcel to my chest, looking at me with growing levels of confusion. I cleared my throat and wiped away my smile before walking to the seat I'd been in only moments ago.

I sat back down, moving on to the next book in the row, hoping I was getting closer.

Rhett reached down and picked up the bar, inhaling deeply through the paper. "Their leader sent you food?"

"Something like that."

"You can't possibly eat this," he said in outrage. "That guard just said someone's trying to kill you."

"He said someone *here* was trying to kill me." As the words came out, I realized there wasn't much comfort in that. I changed the subject. "I'm sure this is safe. But it doesn't matter, I'm not hungry anyway. I'm hunting for an answer."

Rhett stayed beside me, his mood souring quickly. All his words about devotion and love seemed very distant now as he studied me and the gift on the table. I ignored him, carefully looking through yet another book chained up to the shelves.

So far, the mythology was appearing to be about as helpful as the history. Actually, no, even less. Half the books were written in a dead language I couldn't read, and I had to put them back on the shelf. Still, all I could do was keep trying. For better or worse, I needed the truth.

Rhett finally interrupted my thoughts. "What exactly are you looking for about the seventh clan?"

"I'm not even sure. I'll know when I find it."

"Huh" was all he said.

He started pacing, and I wished he'd stay still because it made me anxious. But I kept reading all the same.

I shelved one book and picked up another, thankful I could at least understand this one. I felt a flutter in my chest when, a few pages in, the word *Matraleit* jumped from the text. I scanned it quickly, reading the tale of the first man and woman marrying on a dome-like rock.

It was here. The same story, only fuller.

Breathless, I kept reading. There were other stories, holidays. It was so rich, so full. I couldn't find the word *Dahrain*, but that made sense to me if this was a book documenting themselves. Why would they need to call out their own name?

Toward the end of the book, I found something that sent a wave of ice through my body. It took me a moment to fully understand why.

It was a family tree of sorts. At the upper corner of the page, clear as day, was a symbol. I recognized it immediately; it was embroidered into the collar of the cape Lennox was wearing in the cave.

I'd run my fingers over it so many times, studying it. This was the same thing in ink.

And underneath it was a word: *Au Sucrit*.

If Lennox's people had been scattered, if their entire history was oral, then it wouldn't take much for *Au Sucrit* to become *Ossacrite*.

But the lineage on the page broke off, seemingly lost to history around the same year Kadier was founded. This seemed far too convenient, the dragging of one in and another out at that exact moment.

In fact, if I toyed with the words *Kadier* and *Dahrain* in my head, they almost overlapped: *Kah-Dier-Rain*. Like, if someone wanted to, they could blur their existence over one another. Like someone could make up a person we were supposedly paying homage to with our new title but never appeared anywhere but on that one page of history. Like an easy lie.

The symbol, the name, and the timing were too much to be coincidence.

Here, chained to the halls of my library, was the answer.

But it was even deeper than that, deeper than Lennox could possibly know or guess. If he'd had even an inkling of the truth, he'd have flaunted it the first time we met, bragged incessantly.

Because next to each male name on the *Au Sucrit* tree, a single word appeared in sharp, unflinching ink.

Chief.

I'd really met my match, hadn't I?

"Your Highness?"

Rhett and I both turned to find a guard waiting. "Yes?"

"I'm Officer Kirk. I was sent by Officer Palmer. If you need to tend to something else, you may leave the library now. I'll follow wherever you go."

I could feel Rhett's eyes on me, trying to read my face. Too bad for him, I didn't even know what I was feeling. This was a lot to process, so it was good I'd been offered a way out.

"Thank you. I think we should head down for lunch. Be seen." My voice sounded mechanical, even to me, but it was all I could do.

I reached down and put the bar of oats in the pocket of my dress, and I wondered if the sinking feeling in my gut—the desire to hold that book so tight to my chest that no one else might ever read it—meant that I didn't deserve to have anything from Lennox at all.

LENNOX

"I'm afraid," I whispered.

Once again, Annika's mother was silent.

"She's in danger. I keep telling myself not to worry." I shook my head, almost laughing. "I have a scar across my chest that says she's up for any fight. But with me . . . with me at least she knew to be on guard. What is she supposed to do when the enemy could be someone with the face of a friend?"

I was brought to a standstill for a moment. I kept thinking about someone raising a hand to her. If anyone so much as plucked a hair from her head, I'd call that justification for whatever I might do to them.

"I don't know what to do. These people—my people—are suddenly championing me. And I think I can *do* this. I think I can bring us home . . . I might even be able to do it peacefully. But I don't know how to make sure she stays safe. And if something happens to her . . ."

And then I pictured it. I could see it in my head as clearly as if I'd done it myself. Annika on the ground, pale and still. Annika with bruises on her wrists and blood across her neck. Annika without her laughter and her wit and her constant affection. So really, not Annika at all. Just all the bones we leave behind.

It was such a sharp pain that I was brought to my knees. With that image in my mind, I could barely breathe. I shook my head and dug my fingers into the dirt, trying to remind myself of what was real. I was at Vosino. I was at Queen Evelina's grave. It wasn't real. It hadn't happened.

Yet.

Palmer was right. No one could keep Annika safe like I could. In her own way, she protected me, too. When we were together, it was as if we were encased in unbreakable glass, untouchable. Hadn't the Island tried to destroy us? Hadn't we survived all of it together in that cave?

No one—*no one*—could have made such a bitter situation into something sweet.

"You would be so proud of her," I whispered. "She's grown into someone so beautiful, probably even more beautiful than you remember her. And when she smiles, everything around her loses its color and edge. She's compassionate, determined, intelligent, and possibly even more forgiving than you." I smiled to myself.

"Do you know what she told me? She told me about the only boy she's ever loved. She passed him once, riding out with you. The boy told her how beautiful she was, and she said that he could say that as much as he wanted. Did she ever tell you how she felt about him?

"Would it break your heart to know that was me?"

As I sat there on my knees, I felt a knot unraveling in my stomach. It was close to the way I felt when Annika held me in her arms in the cave. A shower of warmth and calm hemming me in from all sides. I felt . . . free.

"Or maybe it wouldn't break your heart," I considered, thinking of what I knew about this woman. "Maybe it would give you some sense of relief that the boy you smiled at on the road that day found his path again. Because you were never angry at me. You never wished me ill or cursed me. You forgave me. *She* forgave me."

I looked down, swallowing. "She might also love me. But here's what she doesn't know," I confessed with a smile. "Even if she did, she couldn't love me half so much as I love her. I'm willing to rip the world in two for her."

And as I said it aloud, I knew it was true. I wanted to hate myself for it, for the fact that I was willing to give up everything, a lifetime of struggle and work, to chase something I knew I couldn't have. When I ran away from everything I had here, when I threw myself at Annika, there was no doubt in my mind that I would wind up dead.

But better me than her.

"I'll keep her safe," I vowed. "I can't bring you back. But I can keep her alive. I'll never be able to apologize to you enough. But I will be able to love her enough. It might be the last thing I do . . . but I will. I love her. Goodbye."

I took to my feet and turned my gaze from her grave to my father's. "Everyone says you were the best of men. So I, too, will be an honorable man. I'm sorry that I've failed at that so far. I hope you can forgive me. And I hope you know that I am so proud to be your son."

I bowed my head, honoring his memory for the last time.

My thoughts went immediately to planning, but I had no time to think. I heard a twig snap. There was no chance it was Thistle, so I whipped my head back to see who'd found me.

Blythe's accusing eyes dug into me. Her lips were trembling as she stood there, both heartbreak and rage painted across her face.

"How long have you been there?" I asked.

"Long enough," she replied bitterly. "So this is why I'm not enough for you? Because your eyes are set on *her*?"

"You were never not enough, Blythe. You are still more than—"

She cut me off, coming closer. "Do you know how long I've thought of you?" She swallowed hard, looking away for a moment. "Almost from the day I came to Vosino. I saw you work so hard, and do so much. I saw you quietly sacrifice for others, though you would never admit to doing such a thing. But you were distant, always on the side, and I wasn't brave enough. And then . . . we finally had a reason to talk when you got your Commission. I thought that was the beginning of everything. Are you telling me that's how I lost you?"

I sighed, feeling worse by the second, but knowing the truth was the only way through. "Blythe, there was nothing to lose. Until recently, I didn't even know I was capable of feeling anything that wasn't . . . fury."

Her expression moved from hurt to betrayed. "You said

she was the embodiment of everything you hate."

"She was . . . and then she wasn't."

"I've never left your side!" she raged. "I always believed in you and supported you. I saw the worst of you and didn't flinch. And now, when we are on the edge of getting *everything* you worked for, you're abandoning it for a girl who will destroy your life?"

I shook my head, steadying my tone. "That's the thing, Blythe. If I stay, Kawan will keep me as his dog. And if I kill him and try to lead our people, I will have to fight my whole life to hold on to that power. I can't. That part of me is dead, and I want to live. Even if it's short, even if it's painful. I want to live freely."

She stared at me, still angry, still unbelieving.

"You're a traitor, Lennox. Worse than a thief, worse than a coward. You're a traitor to your people." She went to leave, disgusted. "Because I have—" She shook her head. "Because I *had* such a great respect for you, I'll give you a head start. You get six hours. And then Kawan will know. Your mother, Inigo, everyone. They'll know you threw us off for nothing. And when we come"—she looked me dead in the eye—"you will be counted as our enemy. And allow me to remind you one last time: I. Don't. Fail."

She walked past me, leaving me chilled to the bone. In an instant, Blythe showed me she was as formidable as I'd always believed. And because I knew how capable she was, I ran back to my quarters, unable to waste even a second.

I surveyed everything I owned. What was worth taking? I took the oblique pens and threw them in my bag, as well as my father's cape. I strapped my sword to my waist, and I grabbed my empty waterskin, wishing I had time to fill it. My waistbelt was full and strapped to my side. I pulled my piece of lace out, wrapping it around my wrist; no point in hiding it now. Beyond that, everything else would just have to be a memory.

I couldn't risk being seen in the hallway; who knew who I might run into? So I slung the bag over my shoulder and escaped the same way Annika had: through the window.

ANNIKA

Officer Mamun was reliable but obnoxious to have over my shoulder. He didn't know how to stand still, so he frequently sniffled or scuffed his feet on the ground. I reminded myself that, while he was not the most dignified member of the guard, he had been specifically chosen by Palmer for some reason or another. As such, I had to believe he had skills others did not.

Though I hardly needed a guard—as if any intruder would have a chance at getting past Nickolas.

While I sat at the table, reviewing documents, my fiancé circled like a vulture, his eyes darting every which way. At least his footsteps were steady, rhythmic, and therefore almost easy to ignore. But even if I'd had complete silence, it'd be a lie to say my thoughts weren't miles away.

I had a sinking sensation in my stomach, worried that something was going wrong in worse ways than it already was. I couldn't stop thinking of everything I'd seen in that book.

The rock.

The symbol.

The surname.

It all added up. And the fact that someone felt compelled to hide this history made it that much more convincing. I felt so painfully torn, both my duty and my desire at war in my chest. How would it feel to hand over the kingdom? How would it feel to hand over that book to Lennox?

I wanted to see his face when he found out.

Scratch that.

I wanted to see his face.

I wanted to stare into those staggeringly blue eyes. I wanted to feel his lips by my ear. I wanted to get my fingers trapped in the hair along the back of his head. I wanted all of him. So badly it almost ached.

"What are you smiling about?"

"What?" I looked up to find Nickolas's inquisitive eyes on me.

"You're smiling."

"Oh. Um." I said, looking away to cover my burning cheeks. "I was . . . thinking about my mother," I lied, praying that she wouldn't mind me using her as an excuse. "You might find this silly, but I sometimes talk to one of her portraits. There's a large one in the far wing. Even in her absence, she's been like a guide to me."

He smiled back, endeared by my words. "How could I call that silly? It doesn't surprise me at all that you'd want to speak to her, in any form." He looked to the floor, crossing his arms. "Shall I have the portrait brought to the hallway here? Just temporarily, if you'd prefer. It might make everyone feel more at ease to have a sense of her presence here."

I tilted my head. "Nickolas, that's so thoughtful. Yes. Would you, please?"

He walked over, a grin still on his face, and kissed my forehead. "Haven't I been begging you for tasks? I'll take care of it as soon as I can." He came to my ear and lowered his voice. "I'd like to wait for Palmer to come back, though. This boy's fidgeting does not inspire confidence."

For once we seemed to have the same thought.

But it didn't matter what I thought of Mamun. Because the second the door flew open, he proved his worth. He sprang into action, sword unsheathed, blade balanced on the man's throat before I could blink.

But that man was only a doctor who fell backward instantly, covering his head and shouting. "Wait! Wait! I have news for Her Royal Highness!"

I jumped from my seat. "Oh, Doctor! I'm so sorry." I rushed over and offered him my hand.

"Your Highness," he said breathlessly, looking up at me. "Your brother is awake."

I ran past him, holding my skirts up to move faster. I could hear Nickolas over one shoulder and Mamun over the other. We dashed down the hallways, turning toward my brother's room and finding his door wide open.

I had to blink back sudden tears to see, but Escalus was there, propped up on pillows, looking pale and weak but very much awake.

"Ah!" I yelled, coming into the room and collapsing on

my knees by his bed, reaching up to hold one of his hands. I cried for several minutes, and everyone had the good sense not to stop me.

When I could finally breathe again, I sat there, gazing up at my precious brother. He smiled down at me. "I'm still here."

He'd heard me. Through all my dreams and prayers and worries, he heard my question, and he answered.

"I was so afraid," I confessed. "I wasn't ready for you to leave me."

His weak grin grew the tiniest bit more playful. "It'd take more than that."

Leave it to Escalus to make jokes at a time like this.

"Have they told you about Father?" I asked quietly.

He nodded. "Which is why I need to have a talk with you. Please clear the room."

"Of course."

The doctors standing by certainly heard, as did Nickolas and Noemi, but no one took a step toward the door.

"His Royal Highness asked you to clear the room," I said, looking at one of the head doctors to lead the way.

Ever the quick thinker, Noemi sprang into action. "Come, gentlemen. If you just wait in the hallway, I'll fetch you all some tea."

She held out her arms, guiding them patiently from the room, and I turned my attention back to Escalus.

"Are you in pain? Is there anything I can do?"

That tired smile was still on his face as he shook his head and squeezed my hand. I didn't realize I was still holding it.

"Annika. The doctors told me about Father's condition. I think we need to brace ourselves. I'm hoping he'll hold on to enough of his stubbornness to pull through, but we might be orphans very soon."

That word. *Orphan.* I supposed it was a title we only assigned to children, but even if you were forty or fifty or older still, did it ever not hurt to be without your parents?

He let out a heavy breath.

"We have so little time with the people we love; we shouldn't waste it. That brings me to the heart of what I need to tell you."

I turned to face him better, wanting him to know he had my full attention.

"I'm marrying Noemi," he said plainly. As the words escaped his lips, a smile crept onto them—a real one—and he looked so peaceful and satisfied to finally say the words aloud. "I don't care if Father doesn't approve, or the lords, or even you. I've only ever loved her, and I won't spend my life with anyone else by my side. I don't care if the entire kingdom falls down around us. I'm marrying Noemi as soon as I have the strength to stand."

There was something beautifully defiant in his eyes. And I found myself envious of him again. What did it feel like to no longer care?

I still cared.

I cared about the monarchy dissolving into nothing. I worried that our kingdom was about to be upended, and we'd have nowhere to go. I worried that we might all die in the process. And I worried the only way I'd ever see Lennox again might be at the tip of his sword.

Escalus had set himself free of all this, and, in the process, had tossed all the chains at me. I couldn't deny they were heavy, but I also couldn't deny I'd happily carry them for his sake.

I pulled my hand from his, fidgeting with my fingers. "You fell in love with a commoner. I've read enough books to know that this is the stuff of fairy tales."

"You're not upset?"

I smirked. "She asked the same question."

"Wait . . . *Noemi* asked you the same question?"

I nodded. "Yes. I caught you two in the far corridor just before we all left for the Island. I've been doing my best to keep her by your side." I smiled up at him. "So, no, I'm not mad at you, and I don't hate you. I'm sad, maybe. Disappointed that you didn't tell me."

He tilted his head. "And what? You have no secrets from me?"

"One," I stated honestly, though my tone was playful. "And it happens to be the same as yours: I, too, love someone I can't have."

"First, I don't love someone I can't have," he countered, still quick-witted despite being bedridden and weak. "I *will* be with Noemi. By whatever means, I will marry her. Second, I hope you don't really think you're in love with Rhett," he said. "He doesn't love you, either. He's . . . infatuated—and a bit too much, if you ask me—because you're the only girl he's ever spoken to. And you're also very charming. But he doesn't know himself well enough to love, so don't be taken in by that."

I sighed. I supposed it wasn't a shock that he could see how Rhett felt about me. Escalus was much more observant than I was. Besides, there was no way I could tell him I was actually in love with Lennox . . . so maybe I couldn't blame him too much for keeping his own secrets.

"Very well." I stood, keeping my eyes downcast so he might not read them. "Now that you're awake, shall I have them reinstate the regency powers to you?"

"No," he said. "I'm far too tired, and the doctors said you've been handling things well."

I looked up. "They did?"

Escalus nodded. "Bravo, Annika. I knew you had it in you."

I smiled to myself, pleased to have been praised. I stood. "Hopefully Father will be up and better soon, and we can put this all behind us." I curtsied. "By the way, have Noemi do some errands now so that people don't get suspicious too soon. She hasn't left your side since we got back."

He smiled. "I will. Thank you for commanding her to stay."

I shrugged. "It was the least I could do. And thank you."

"For what?" he asked, looking up with sleepy confusion in his eyes.

"For still being here."

He nodded, and in that simple motion I could see exhaustion taking over again.

"I'll come back later. Sleep."

I waited for him to respond, but it seemed like he was already fading into sleep. I backed away quietly, relieved beyond words that my brother would recover, even if it was slow.

In the hallway, the doctors were pacing, aching to get back to tending Escalus. I nodded to Noemi, and she sighed, understanding that all was as well as it could be.

I walked past them, feeling so many things. I was happy to have a few more moments as regent, tired from so much worry . . . and I was jealous. Escalus and Noemi were so very in love.

And I . . .

"Is everything all right?" Nickolas asked as I approached the corner.

I whispered back, "I have no idea."

And then, without warning, he gently wrapped his arms around me.

It was a shock, to be sure. Nickolas had always been order, protocol, straight lines. My rank dictated everything, and while he might have pushed against the line I'd drawn between us more frequently than I cared for, he'd never completely crossed it.

Except for now.

And it was the nicest possible way to do it, so I said nothing and let him hold me.

LENNOX

I rode without stopping. When the sun set, and I lost the light, I navigated by the stars, moving east and slightly south. I would find water when I got to Kadier. I would find rest when I got to Annika. Everything beyond that was superfluous.

I moved with little more in my head than the worry that someone might be following me by now. I figured I had at least a day. Kawan wouldn't be able to get that many people moving by night, not as battle worn and low as they were. It was Blythe I feared now; she might be driven to vengeance, and, if she was, it was possible I'd lost Inigo to her already.

I crossed the field where the army had camped as a group the night before we stole all the boats from Stratfel. I crossed the place where I'd first met Annika and fought with her. And I slowed my horse to a trot when I saw the glittering palace in the distance.

This was it. I was in Kadier. I was in *Dahrain.*

After all these years, after all the struggle, all I'd ever had to do was keep riding.

I paused for a moment, looking around, wondering if I would notice something, some piece of a long-lost past that had been embedded into my very bones. There was nothing.

The air was different, less briny than at Vosino. There was almost a sweetness to it. And the trees were blossoming with flowers I didn't know. The houses I passed were tidy if small. And while it was all very beautiful, none of it was familiar.

The only thing that told me I was home was this warm feeling in my gut, something that said I was exactly where I was meant to be.

While that sensation was a comfort, I still didn't know how to get into the palace. I got off my horse, walking him through the streets until I saw the palace gates. They were stone and sturdy, and the front gate was covered in gold. It was wide open, but there were guards on either side of it, so I doubted I could simply walk in. I stood there and sighed, trying to think of a plan. Of course, I could always try to break in. I could get over that wall if I found a portion without guards on either side. Or if I wandered around the back, there might be a weak section, something that wasn't well tended.

But neither of these helped with the true problem: I didn't know how to find Annika once I was in.

"Are you lost?"

I started as I looked down, finding a boy of maybe twelve or so standing right beside me. His eyes were wide, trusting, and he fidgeted as he adjusted a heavy bag thrown over his shoulder. He was too young to know what it meant to have enemies. I pitied that my peers might ruin that soon.

"In a sense," I replied. "I have a friend in the palace, but I don't have an invitation, so I don't know how to get in."

"Oh. What's his name? I work in the stables," he told me. "Maybe I know him, too."

I was about to tell this curious boy that I wasn't looking for a *him* at all . . . when an idea came to me.

"Actually, his name is Palmer. Officer Palmer." I did a quick mental inventory of what I had on me and reached into my waistbelt, pulling out my switchblade. "This is the only thing I have that would be of any value to you. It's yours if you can bring Palmer out to me. Can you do that?"

He squinted. "He's the one who was missing, right? He came back all beat up?"

I nodded. "Yes. Heard he had quite the adventure. Do you think you could bring him to me?"

The boy looked around and then pointed. "Wait under that tree over there."

In a flash, he took off, running through the gates without notice from the guards. I pulled my horse over to the tree and waited, gazing at the apples growing in the branches above me. So this was what it was like here? Trees and food grew without anyone really tending it? I shook my head. I reached up and gave an apple to my horse, and I stuffed another in my bag for later.

After a few minutes, I started getting restless. What if he couldn't find Palmer? Should I still try to break in? How long should I wait before trying?

An older man and his wife walked by. She had a cane, and

he was holding her other hand. They walked slowly, coming from who knows where and in no hurry to reach their destination. They looked as if they felt safe here, content. Whatever the faults of the Kadierians, I had to admit the common people were well tended.

Once they passed the gate, I was stunned to see Palmer walking out. When his eyes met mine, he smiled.

"I'm so glad you changed your mind," he said by way of greeting. "I fear the monarchy is sinking beneath my feet, and we need all the help we can get."

"I'm here for Annika. That is all."

He nodded. "That will be enough."

"I hope so. I need to warn you now that my departure might have sped up an inevitable invasion."

Palmer nodded. "Well, as you say, it's inevitable. At least now we have both foreknowledge and you." He took my horse by the reins and pulled him through the gates of the palace. I kept my eyes down and my mouth shut. I had no idea who had been on the Island, and I wondered if anyone besides Annika would recognize me. Dear Nickolas might if our paths crossed.

Palmer walked me around the side of the palace, and I could see we were heading straight to the stables. Annika had mentioned something about training out there, and I smiled at how little space she'd had to make herself so competent with a sword.

"Told'ya I could get him."

I turned and found the boy already back to his work, cleaning a stall.

"So you did. And, as promised, your reward." I handed over my switchblade, a little sad to part with it. "Use it well."

"Grayson, please tend this horse," Palmer requested. "If anyone asks, I received a guest from my hometown. That is all."

Grayson smiled and gave a tiny salute. "Yes, sir."

Palmer chuckled as he led me out toward the castle. "He's a good one. Her Royal Highness actually helped the last stable hand get a place in library ages ago. Rhett. Changed his life. I daresay she'll try the same for Grayson at some point."

Ah. Rhett. That was another name I knew. Palmer, Rhett, Dear Nickolas, and Escalus. These were the men in Annika's life. I had to say, I didn't care for half of them.

"Where is Annika now?" I couldn't hold back from asking. "Under guard, I assume?"

Palmer nodded. "I've come to trust you. So, don't fail me, Lennox. Everything is falling apart right now. If it sinks, I'm trusting you to keep her afloat."

"Easy," I said. "I'd do that at the risk of my life. And yours. And anyone else's, come to think of it."

He stared into my eyes, looking, I think, for a lie. He found none.

"Keep your head down. Follow me."

I traced Palmer's steps down the back hallways and staircases of the palace. Every once in a while, I allowed myself the briefest glimpse at a piece of art or furniture, but otherwise, I obeyed. He stopped at a corner, holding out an arm, and I waited.

"Let's go." He moved quickly, opened a door, and pulled

me inside as fast as he could. "You're to wait here. No one besides Her Highness or myself would be so bold as to open the door without knocking. If you hear someone else coming, hide."

"Understood."

Palmer went from the room as fast as he came, and I turned around to see exactly where I was.

Oh.

Her fingerprints were all over this room. In the half-finished needlework by the window, in the books piled by the bed, in the five dresses slung over the back of a couch, in the colors and textures and scents of everything.

I judged from the clothes scattered about that no one had been tending to her, and, while the room wasn't that cold, I chose to make her a fire all the same. Once the kindling was lit, I stepped back, walking around. I supposed some part of me should be jealous of the fine way she'd been raised. But it was easier to take heart in the fact that the girl I'd loved since I was a boy grew up in comfort. I walked over to the foot of her bed, dropping my bag there and reaching up to touch the gauzy fabric that hung down along the posters.

My hands were too dirty for this place.

"I will be outside this door until dawn."

I turned, hearing Palmer's voice outside the door. "By then, you will have to give me instructions on what your plans are."

"Plans for what?"

My heart started dancing at the sound of Annika's voice. I reached quickly into my bag.

"You'll see," Palmer replied.

He allowed the door to open just wide enough for her to walk in, making sure that no one might accidentally see me. Annika's adorably confused face looked at her hands, at the fire . . . and then at me.

She froze where she was, speechless, and even from across the room, I could see the tears in her eyes.

I tossed the apple across the room, and she caught it easily.

"Will you ever stop surprising me?" she asked.

"I hope not."

"I have so much to tell you," she whispered.

I shook my head. "Unless it's to tell me that you love me a thousand times, it can wait."

And she dropped the apple, running across the room and crashing into me, throwing us both back onto the bed.

ANNIKA

"How in the world did you get in here?" I asked as Lennox brushed his hair back lazily, a smile on his face.

"I ran away. I may have hastened any attack plans by coming here on my own, but I couldn't help it." He turned to look at me, his face inches from mine. "I can't *be* anywhere without you."

"Then don't," I breathed.

He reached over, laced his hand deep into my hair, and pulled me into a kiss.

It was as if not a single second had passed between us huddling in a dark cave and us holding each other on the satin blankets across my bed. There were no secrets, no worries, no apologies left unsaid. There was nothing other than the complete and perfect sense of being known.

I shifted so that I was half on top of him, my hair falling down around his face. And after a moment, he stopped kissing me just so he could reach up and brush his calloused fingers along my cheekbone, my hairline, my chin. He touched me like he thought I might break, like this moment might end too soon.

"I can't believe you're truly here. I've wished it a hundred times."

He swallowed. "As have I." There was something sad in his eyes, but it lingered only a moment before his smile returned. "I hear you are regent."

I propped myself up on my elbow. "The rumors are true."

He chuckled. "I must say leadership looks good on you; you're glowing." He wrapped a lock of my hair around his finger. It seemed to me that this must be a favorite of his. "My Annika, practically queen. Shall I stand and bow?"

He was flirting, toying with me. I knew that. But it brought me quickly back to the truth.

I was going to have to tell him what I'd learned, wasn't I? Because as deeply as I loved my kingdom, and as much as I was willing to sacrifice for my family, I couldn't hold on to something when I now knew it didn't belong to me.

I just . . . I needed tonight.

I shook my head. "Even if it was proper for you to do so, do you think I'd let you out of my arms now?"

He smiled at that, looking so incredibly at ease. He must have been scared, though. He'd left everything he knew, he was in an unfriendly land, and he could be caught at any moment. As if reading my thoughts, his tone grew serious.

"I'm sure by now Palmer has told you what's happening."

"Only that I'm in danger, and that it seems someone in the palace is in league with Kawan."

He nodded. "I am determined to find out who's at the bottom of this."

I ran my fingers across his face again. He was so, so beautiful. "Come here." I stood up, walking him over to the basin in the corner. I poured water over his tired hands, washing them with my own. I got the cloth beside it wet and reached up to wipe away all traces of his long night of riding through the woods. I could feel his eyes on me as I attempted to focus on my task. It was something I could get used to, being this close to him. Hours, days, lifetimes. It would never be enough.

"We're in another tricky situation," I told him.

"What's that?"

I couldn't meet his eyes, but I was sure he caught my smile. "As regent, I don't think I can let you leave my sight—seeing as you're a threat to the safety of my kingdom and all."

He pressed his lips together in thought. "Quite right. I'm very dangerous. It's probably best that you personally keep me under close observation."

"It's my duty, really. Can't get out of it."

"So dedicated. I admire that."

I stepped back, finally looking up at him. Those eyes really were dangerous. Lennox unhooked his cape and threw it along with his coat over the back of a chair. He walked around, blowing out candles as I climbed into bed, unable to tear my eyes away. He seemed quite at home here in my room, and I would be perfectly content to never see him leave it.

I crawled onto the bed, feeling safer than I had since

leaving the cave. I heard Lennox adding wood to the fire, stoking it, and moving the grate to guard it. And my heavy eyelids stirred as he settled in behind me. I felt his heartbeat against my back, the security of his arm around my waist. His nose settled into the nape of my neck, taking in long, deep breaths.

"Lennox?" I whispered.

"Yes?"

"Promise me you'll be here when I wake up. Don't disappear."

He kissed me just behind my ear. "I met you when we were children. I found you when you ran away. I held you through a hurricane. Nothing can separate me from you."

He sounded so certain that I believed him. And I finally, truly slept.

LENNOX

I finally, truly slept. With Annika a heartbeat away, it was easy. She'd rolled over in the night, and I was now staring at the most angelic face in history, her cheek on my arm. She was warm and, most important, alive, and this gave me rest I hadn't had since we'd fallen asleep together in the cave.

To be fair, she also had the most wonderful bed, and I fully intended to keep it when I . . .

When I what? Was I really going to attempt to take her kingdom now?

She let out a long breath in her sleep. She'd done this in the cave; I remembered it. I liked how her hair managed to twist up above her head, little ringlets of hazy gold. Looking at Annika made me think I'd wasted all my talent on a sword. I should have picked up a paintbrush instead. I should have known how to take this face and put it on canvas for the world. They had no idea what they were missing.

A little frown appeared between her eyebrows and she curled in closer, her knees wrapping up into my stomach, her head coming down to my chest, her hands crossed between us. How could someone so small have such a presence?

She inhaled deeply, and I knew she was waking up. I smiled, so happy I already knew this about her, and I wondered how many more of her little habits I could learn over a lifetime.

"You're here," she said groggily.

"I told you I would be. I've done many terrible things, Annika, but I've never lied to you."

She looked up, her sweet, sleepy face pleased. "True."

"I don't know when you need to start your day, but I certainly wasn't going to wake you."

She pushed herself up, hair messy, dress wrinkled. "It never really stops, so it never really starts."

"Oh," I said, wrapping an arm around her waist. "Then you can stay."

I gave a gentle tug, and she came back down with a giggle. If she'd been even the tiniest bit louder, we might not have heard the commotion by the door.

"Sir, I'm sorry. Her Highness isn't awake yet." Palmer's voice was clear as a bell, and Annika and I both bolted upright.

"I will see my bride this moment," someone replied. And seeing as I was already in her arms, I could only assume it was Dear Nickolas standing outside.

"Under the bed," Annika whispered urgently.

I hopped off the bed and rolled beneath it. I couldn't see much due to the copious ruffles hanging down, but I hoped that it would also keep anyone from seeing me. It wasn't the slightest bit dusty under here. Even her corners were perfectly tidy. And when I looked up, I saw two pegs strategically built into her frame, and upon it, her sword. I smiled, feeling almost giddy. Annika was hiding all her secrets in the same place now.

I saw Annika's dress hit the floor in a heap and caught the hem of her robe being scooped up.

"Ah!" she said suddenly, and a second later my bag, coat, and cape were hurled at my face. I clutched them, dragging them and myself deeper beneath the frame. A second later, my sword was slid across the ground, and I grabbed it, too, removing the very end from the sheath, so I'd be ready if the need arose.

"Please, sir. Her Highness has been pushing herself far too hard in the last few days especially. You of all people ought to be looking out for her welfare," Palmer insisted.

I liked that man more and more by the minute.

"How dare you? Do you have any idea—"

"You may let him in, Officer Palmer," Annika called, effectively ending the argument.

I heard the door open and the sound of shoes. "Forgive me, Your Highness. I didn't mean to wake you," Palmer said.

"Not at all," she replied. The cool tone in her voice was strange, so different from the girl I knew. But it wasn't completely unfamiliar; I'd heard her speak that way when I marched her into Vosino.

"When you're finished giving the duke an audience, I have a parcel for you. I was instructed to give it to you privately."

"Thank you. I will tend to it shortly."

A single pair of feet moved from the room. I straightened my head and closed my eyes, taking silent, calming breaths. If I was somehow found out, I had to be ready to strike.

Dear Nickolas huffed. "There's an apple on your floor."

I could sense Annika's anger in her silence. After a painfully long time, she breathed out a long sigh.

"I appreciate your care, Nickolas, but I prefer not to be awakened by shouts outside my door."

"The shouts were that insolent guard's doing," he replied calmly. "I had no such intentions until he refused me."

I heard her bare feet walking over to the basin. "Officer Palmer is trying to keep me safe; we can't be too cross with him."

"But safe from what?" he asked. "He has given me no insight as to what we're supposed to be looking out for. How can I protect you if I don't know? Why are there so many secrets around you these days? Unknown threats. Strange parcels. Is there anything else I don't know about?"

She let out a bubble of a laugh, which she tried to quickly cover with a cough. I bit my lips, trying not to laugh myself.

Ah, Nickolas, you're an idiot.

"I hate to disappoint you," she began, "but there will always be things you can't know. It's simply the nature of my life."

Bravo, my girl.

There was another charged silence.

"Then shall I keep what I know from you? Is that how a husband and wife behave?" Nickolas asked, his tone still measured.

Then shall I murder you? Talk like that one more time . . .

"I will ask you to please check your misguided anger. This sounds very close to a threat, and I will remind you that you are my subject. Whatever issues you take with the nature of my work, my position deserves some level of respect."

"I . . . why do you keep picking fights with me, Annika?"

I rolled my eyes at the accusation. He was the one instigating here.

"I came to tell you something urgent," he went on. "You scold me for showing up, keep me at arm's length, and then belittle me? What man could tolerate such treatment?"

First, you're twisting this entire situation. Second, I'd be on my knee before Annika Vedette every morning given the chance.

"There isn't such a man," he insisted, answering his own pathetic question. "With everything that's going on, with how badly this monarchy has been hit, what happens if I walk away, Annika?"

Personally? I'd throw a festival. But I don't currently have the funds.

"Nickolas, you are not welcome in my chambers, either private or professional. Do not come into my presence again until you receive an invitation."

"What?!"

Yes!

"You may see yourself out," she instructed. "And as for what happens if I don't marry you? I'll marry someone else. Someone who loves me; someone who wants me."

Someone conveniently hidden under her bed.

I could hear the coldness in his voice as he answered her. "No one could ever want you more than I do."

I heard her sigh as he walked away, the door closing behind him.

I poked my head out from under the bed. "He's incredibly manipulative."

"Is he?" she asked, still looking at the door. "Sometimes I wonder if I let my emotions get the better of me. We were both pushed into this, after all."

"No. You were perfect." She still wasn't looking at me. "Do you want me to kill him?"

"No," she sighed, crossing her arms.

I huffed. "Well, can I kill him anyway?"

"No!" she insisted, finally turning to look at me.

I smiled, showing I *mostly* meant no harm, and the tension around her melted. My Annika was back.

"You're in a rather playful mood today," she commented.

"I spent the night in the arms of the woman I love. What's there to be unhappy about?"

She was beaming at that, shaking her head. There was another knock at the door, and I quickly dashed back under the bed.

"Come in."

"Just me," Palmer announced, and I popped my head back out in relief. "Your Highness, I'm so sorry. I tried to be loud, to give you time. I have this for Lennox," he said, tossing a parcel on the ground by the bed. "I took a guess at what your plan might be, Highness. If I'm wrong, I can return these."

I crawled out and opened the package. Inside were clothes that looked identical to what Palmer was wearing.

"You guessed well. Of course, it's up to Lennox."

She understood I'd have reservations, but I knew there was no better way to stay by her side. Only Annika, Palmer, and Nickolas knew my face for certain. The first two were allies, and the third had just been banished, so I'd be as anonymous as I could hope to be. Besides, by now, Blythe had certainly wound up Kawan, and we were all in danger. I had to be by Annika's side no matter what.

"What do you say?" Palmer asked. "Will you wear it?"

I looked up at him from the ground. "Happily."

ANNIKA

Why did having Lennox behind me make me feel so powerful? I could tell I was standing straighter, walking stronger. I almost wanted someone to cross me today just to find out what would happen. I peeked over my shoulder, swooning a little over how good that boy looked in a uniform.

I was also possibly a little too giddy that I was walking around in broad daylight with him by my side. It was something so unimaginable that I'd never even dreamed about it. But here it was. Real. Happening. To me.

I rounded the corner to my brother's room and found him upright again, which was encouraging, with even more color in his face. Soon, he'd be his old self.

"And what do you have here?" he asked when he saw me, noting the basket in my hand.

I held it up proudly. "Needlework. I thought you might be bored to tears with nothing to do in bed, so I brought this along."

I held out a loop with fabric already drawn tight across it, as well as a handful of his favorite colors of thread.

"Noemi. Would you do me the kindness of threading a needle for me?" he asked. "This hand's not quite up to the task yet."

"Of course, Your Highness." She reached across the bed, and our eyes met. She seemed happier today, calmer. I wondered if it was from days of being so publicly beside the person she loved, because I could feel it doing wonders for me.

"We have much to talk about," Escalus said, watching Noemi's hands work.

"Indeed," I replied.

"First off, have you . . ."

I looked to Escalus and followed his eyes up to Lennox, who was still standing right behind me.

"Would you please give us some privacy, Officer?" Escalus asked.

"I was given direct instructions from Officer Palmer to stay beside Her Highness," Lennox replied confidently.

"Don't worry," Escalus said with a smile. "Weak as I am, I'd protect her faster than you would."

Lennox looked at my brother—really looked at him—and nodded. "Then I see we have the same goals." He dipped his head into a bow and backed up several steps, standing against the nearby wall.

"I like that one," Escalus whispered. "Doesn't bother much with formalities."

"I think he's new," I said. "What was your first question?" I finished threading my own needle and went to work.

"Have you heard anything about Father this morning?"

I shook my head. "No, but I intend to go to him next. I came straight to check on you after I woke up."

"That explains your hair," Escalus teased.

I reached up and touched it. "What's wrong with my hair? I brushed it!"

Noemi giggled. "Leave her be. You look lovely, Your Highness. Your poor brother knows nothing about ladies' hair."

"Nonsense," he protested. "I rather like yours today."

She smiled at that, looking away. "Here."

Escalus picked up the loop and went to work . . . very slowly.

"Have you picked a date for your wedding?" he asked suddenly.

I swallowed. I didn't like talking about wedding details with Lennox so close.

"Not exactly. I'm not even . . ." I shook my head. "The only thing we were waiting for was you and Father. I wasn't sure if things would go well, and we'd celebrate, or if they might not, and things would be delayed. Everyone involved knows that it could shift at any time."

Escalus nodded. "Then can I ask you for a favor?"

I scoffed. "You're heir aapparent, Escalus. I'm more in a position to ask a favor of you."

"All the same. Can I ask?"

I set my needlework down. "Ask away."

"Would you scrap that plan completely so I could get married first?"

I squinted at him for a moment, taking it in.

"I told you I wanted to get married as soon as I had the strength to stand, and I meant it."

Because I was so attuned to him, I was very aware of the small gasp that escaped Lennox's mouth.

"It sounds to me like you're trying to do this before Father wakes up so he can't undo it."

Escalus stared at me. Then he turned to Noemi. "She's too smart."

"Always has been," she commented.

"I don't know," he replied. "There was that time she nearly hacked my arm off."

"It was a scratch!" I protested. "And an accident!"

He laughed a little, which brought on a cough, and Noemi and I tensed up instantly. I watched as he clutched his upper chest. He took a few breaths, looking down.

"I'm fine," he insisted.

But the way sweat beaded along his temple told me he wasn't as well as he insisted. Stronger than yesterday perhaps, but nowhere close to well.

"Here's the thing, Annika. If I wait and something happens to Father, the lords will sweep in and do to me what they did to you. Noemi and I will be forced apart . . ." He swallowed. "I always admired how willing you were to sacrifice so much for Kadier. Genuinely, I'm in awe. But maybe I'm too selfish, because I won't. I won't marry some stranger for Kadier, or for Father, or even for you."

All I could think was, *For all we know, neither of us will have to marry for the sake of Kadier. Kadier might not even be here in a few weeks . . . a few days, perhaps.*

But there was still a part of me that hoped.

"I understand completely." I set my sewing down. "Noemi, you've been my sister in my heart half my life. You might as well be on paper, too." I smiled at her, hoping she knew I meant it.

Noemi and Escalus exchanged a happy glance, looking away again quickly.

"But, Escalus, who says you have to stand? Who says you need a grand reception? Give me until tomorrow, and I will see you're wed."

They stared at me. "How . . . ?"

"All we need is a willing priest, and even if I have to bring one in from Cadaad, I'll do it. So, rest today, because tomorrow you're getting married."

Escalus was still a little too pale for my liking, so the tears in his eyes looked more sorrowful than sweet. But he reached over to touch my hand, putting all of his strength into his grip.

"Thank you," he whispered.

"I'll leave you. I have much to arrange." A wedding to plan, another to delay, a country to lead . . . it was more than a day's worth of work.

"Understood," Escalus said.

I rose, handing my hoop to Noemi. "I didn't even get started, and I'm sure you could use something to pass the time as well."

"Thank you."

I curtsied to my brother and turned on my heel. I didn't

need to look back to know Lennox was right behind me. I knew his footsteps, recognized his breaths. He followed as I made my way down the hall, stopping in front of a door with two guards on either side. They bowed to me, and one reached and turned the handle.

I walked inside my father's room, and my footsteps echoed. The mood in here was different, somber.

I looked behind me, but Lennox's eyes were on my father. He swallowed, horrified by what he saw. I couldn't blame him.

I nodded to the doctors and walked across the room, perching myself on the edge of Father's bed. Everyone was kind enough to give me a wide berth as I bent over to speak quietly into his ear. "I don't know if you can hear me," I whispered, "but I think I might be running out of time to forgive you. I wanted you to know that I don't hold anything against you. I understand now what love can do to you. And I understand what grief can do. Because grief is simply love with no one to receive it.

"You see that boy behind me? I love him. I love him so much I'd do dangerous things for him. And if I lose him . . . the things I would do might be far more dangerous still.

"So I'm not upset that you pulled us in too tight. I'm not upset that you tried to direct every step of my life. I know that, in your own way, you were trying to protect what you had left. You have my forgiveness for everything that has happened between us."

I took a breath, knowing what was coming.

"And I trust I will have your forgiveness for whatever I do next."

LENNOX

While I was all too happy to eavesdrop at her brother's bedside, doing so at her father's felt inappropriate. I kept my distance, allowing her to say whatever she needed to. I didn't have the heart to tell her that, after all the deaths I had witnessed since the Island, I could recognize the truth from a mile away.

That man was not going to wake up.

But I had no intention of stealing her hope. Instead, I set my mind for the millionth time to the identity of Kawan's informant. There had been so many people on that island, and any one of them could have been with Kawan.

I hated to say it, but all my thoughts pointed me to Nickolas. His tone with her came across as condescending, and he was absolutely manipulating their conversations, so any argument seemed like her doing, not his. Maybe it wasn't enough to go on, but where else could I look? If Nickolas was on the Island, and if he disclosed his relationship with Annika to Kawan, then there was no one with better proximity. . . .

But there was also the tiny issue of me hating him, and

that *might* be seen as a bias where he was concerned.

I watched as Annika bent over and kissed her father's forehead, not flinching at the greenish hue in his skin. I stared at him, noting his frighteningly shallow breaths.

This was the man who ordered the death of my father, who sent his decapitated corpse off into the wilderness with no care for where it ended up.

But this was also the person who made Annika. He raised a daughter both bold and gentle, both unwavering and forgiving. I found myself, at the end of it all, unable to hate him the way I thought I should.

And so, though he couldn't see it, I bowed to him.

Annika rose and turned. I could see her eyes were brimming with tears. I followed her from the room, and I was beside her by the time I'd realized she wasn't moving. "He's not going to make it, is he?"

I sighed. "For now, you just have to wait and see. And you have to keep leading; it's what he'd want you to do."

Annika looked up at me, staring into my eyes. There were so many layers to her sadness; it seemed to run deeper than her father's potential death, deeper than the weight of a kingdom on her back. When she looked at me like that, something in my gut wanted to scoop her up and run. I wanted to get us both out of here, off to somewhere I could live out a quiet life with her.

If we could survive in the cave, we'd thrive in the countryside.

Finally, she nodded. "Follow me."

I walked two footsteps behind her as she wound her

way through the palace. We passed one grand hallway after another, some opening to vast rooms dripping with gold. Paintings, lush furniture, and statues were everywhere. Servants moved quickly to and fro, as guards stood watch along the edges of every space, and, moving through it all, were the nobles with their powdered hair and silken coats.

I might have felt disdain for these people except that all of them seemed to adore Annika. Deep curtsies were given by every single lady, and so many inquired upon her health. I had to wonder if they had any clue what was happening to their king at this very moment because no mention was made of it.

Part of me wondered, *How do they love her so?*

But a much larger part wondered, *How could they not?*

As we walked on, the din of conversation and movement died down. We finally stopped outside two tall doors, and Annika turned to me and gestured to the room behind her. "This is our library. It's been my hiding place most of my life."

I smiled, thinking of my princess and all her secret places.

"Can I show you something?"

I nodded, following as she pulled the doors wide open. Whatever I'd been expecting, this far surpassed it. The shelves went so high, some had rolling ladders attached, and the sheer number of books before me was staggering. I could still write, and I could still read . . . but it had been far too long since I'd been allowed the pleasure of being lost between pages.

"Back again? Don't you have a kingdom to run?"

I turned, looking for the voice that was greeting Annika too casually for my tastes, to find a boy with bright curls and a smile to match waiting by a large desk.

"The kingdom can wait a few minutes. I need to look at something. You see I have my guard, so I'll be fine on my own."

"Are you sure?" he asked, seeming offended by how quickly she brushed him off. "Based on what Officer Palmer said, it sounds the more people around you, the better."

Annika smiled, a serene and diplomatic expression she must have practiced thousands of times. "He's quite capable. I'm in a bit of a rush. As you said, there's a kingdom to tend to. I'll just be a moment."

She didn't wait for acknowledgment, but headed on to what she was looking for. I didn't bother looking at the boy as I passed, refusing to play whatever game he was trying to start.

We arrived at a shelf with dozens of books chained to it, and Annika pulled one out and turned quickly through the pages.

"Who was that?"

"Rhett," she replied.

"He's almost as bad as Nickolas."

She smiled—genuinely this time—and turned to me, speaking in a very inviting whisper. "We can't be too cross with Rhett. Thanks to his teaching, I once escaped the clutches of a very dangerous man."

"Is that so?"

She nodded. "And I'm very grateful. Had I not escaped

that day, I wouldn't be able to give that very dangerous man the extraordinary gift I'm about to give him right now."

I cocked my head at her, skeptical. "Which is?"

She handed the open book to me. "A glimpse at his family tree."

I looked down, gaping at the wide page before me, trying to understand what I was seeing. At the top of the page was the symbol that had been sewn into my father's cloak, that I now recognized was a crest. And beneath it was a surname eerily close to mine.

Before I knew what was happening, I was blinking back tears. "Annika . . . Annika, what is this?"

"This is a mythology book," she said, her tone apologetic. She reached out, touching the brass chain, pinning it to the shelves. "You know, I've seen chained libraries before. At a monastery in Nalk, and in the palace at Kialand as well. They keep the most valuable books like this, so no one takes them. But I've started to wonder if these books were kept right here in the open so the librarian would know exactly who was reading them, all the while making it impossible for anyone to remove them, to show them to someone else."

I could hardly take in what she was saying, still reeling from the crest, from the name.

She sighed, continuing. "It's curious that, out of everything we have here, someone in this castle once decided that the *mythology* books were the ones that needed to be chained. The only thing is, everything in this book looks like cleverly hidden facts to me. Names, dates, crests. But this one here," she said, pointing to the top of the page, "is the most striking one of all."

"I'll say. That's certainly my name," I breathed.

"No, Lennox. Look here."

She pointed her delicate finger to a single word beside my abandoned surname.

Chief.

Suddenly the edges of the room were blurry, and it was very difficult to swallow.

"It makes sense that Kawan was thrilled to find your father," she said quietly. "It also makes sense why he prefers to keep any of you from finding out more about your history. He might be the only one there who knows who you truly are. It's also most likely the reasoning behind him keeping you so close. If anyone else knew the truth and found that he'd deliberately tried to hurt you, well, that wouldn't reflect kindly on him. You are, after all, his sovereign."

The room was shifting, and I faltered, stumbling into the shelf, holding on to it for stability. I took a few long breaths. My head stopped spinning, but not my thoughts.

"Sovereign?"

She nodded. "I think your ancestors were crowned by the other six clans. I think the other chiefs laid down their titles so that yours could be king. Well," she amended, "most of them, anyway."

"But what does this mean?" I asked, still trying to reconcile the idea of royal blood in my veins with the fact that I'd been sleeping on threadbare blankets for most of my life.

"It means that if anyone had the right to come and challenge my father for his crown, it was your father. It means if anyone has the right to take my position, it's you."

I pulled my eyes away to focus on her. My vision was still blurry, but she was dry-eyed, even as she told me her kingdom should be mine.

"You left everything to come and defend me. And because of that, an army might be on the way soon. If that happens, I wanted you to know the truth. When it comes time for you to make a choice, I won't judge you for whichever one you make."

I could feel a painful lump rising in my throat. "I'm choosing—"

But before I could finish, she put her hand gently over my lips. That hand could thread a needle and wield a sword and flit through a dance and knot up my hair. And it could stop me in my tracks.

"Don't say it. Because if you tell me now that you choose me, and, in the end, you can't, that will be a pain worse than death. But if you say nothing, and you choose your crown and your kingdom, then I'll be able to live—or die—in peace. You made me no promises."

I nodded, unable to think of anything to say.

"Can we take this?" I asked. "I just want to see more. I can't believe there's an entire book."

She smiled and looked over my shoulder, waving her hand. I turned to see Rhett coming from a distance. Had he been watching us that whole time?

"Rhett, my father is likely on his deathbed, and my brother has expressed his deep desire for me to remain regent for the unforeseeable future. There is no one in this palace . . ." She stumbled over her words for a second. "There is no one in my *family* who outranks me. I want to take this book to my room for further study, so please unlock it."

His eyes darted between Annika and me. "I can't. I have to wait for the king."

"Rhett. I am regent."

He swallowed. "I . . . I can't."

I saw that she was irritated, but then an idea flashed behind her eyes so fast I almost missed it.

After a deep breath, she slowly nodded and walked over to Rhett and held out her hand to him. That charming face—the one she used when she walked in the library, the one she used when she tricked me in the dungeon—came back as she moved unusually close to him.

"Forgive me," she said quietly. "I'm exhausted. I know you're looking out for Kadier, and I truly am grateful, Rhett."

His shoulders dropped in relief. He didn't like being on her bad side. Personally, I thought he was missing out.

"Thank you, Annika. But come back and see me as often as you like."

She gave another calm tip of her head, and we were on our way.

ANNIKA

I knew I wouldn't be caught, but I moved quickly all the same. Lennox's legs were longer than mine, so he didn't seem ruffled by my pace.

"Don't let it bother you," he said. "There are other things to concentrate on. I know you did your best to get the book, and I'm thankful."

I rounded on him, smirking. "Are you still underestimating me, Lennox Au Sucrit?"

His stare was both amused and confused as I continued.

"I told you that Rhett taught me to pick locks. In fact, it's become one of my favorite hobbies. But the ones holding down those books are heavy, so it's going to take a little more than a hairpin to open them. So, I can either go scouring the palace to find the right tool . . . or I could just practice the other skill Rhett taught me . . ."

I lifted my hand to reveal a key dangling from my finger. "Which is picking pockets."

He stared at the key, dumbfounded. "How? *When?*"

I giggled. "When I took his hand. I just had to be close enough."

Lennox looked so painfully impressed. I didn't know what I was going to do when he chose the crown over me.

"You really are a spectacular woman."

I tilted my head. "Ah. You've been good at appraising me since our childhood. You're only getting better."

He let out a chuckle as I turned to take us both up to the rooms I was using to work.

"You should hold on to the key," I told him, handing it over. "If we go very late, we should be able to get in and out without him knowing the better. No one visits that library half so much as me, so he shouldn't notice the key is gone. If for some reason I can't go, perhaps you should go with Palmer. I'll feel much better if you aren't alone."

He seemed amused by my concern. "If you insist."

He trailed behind me like a shadow, quiet and steady, but I knew his thoughts had to be racing like a wildfire.

I told myself that this was only righting a wrong. And if Lennox and his army swept in and claimed the kingdom, my life would be easier, right? I wouldn't have to marry Nickolas, for starters. And there was a lot of protocol, a lot of expectations. I didn't always bear them gracefully, so maybe it would be good in some ways. . . .

But all I could think of was that the home I'd always known, the kingdom I'd always served, was not only going to be lost under my watch but at my own hands. And, most painfully, I would most certainly lose Lennox in the process.

As we moved down the hallway, I saw Nickolas emerging

from my workroom, walking at a very quick pace himself. He took one glance at me, then kept walking. He didn't even stop to either offer or demand an apology after the fiasco this morning.

"Halt!"

I stopped in my tracks, turning at Lennox's voice. Shockingly enough, Nickolas did as well.

"Are you going to acknowledge your sovereign?" he asked, glaring at Nickolas.

Nickolas scoffed, looking between Lennox and me. "How dare you even speak to me without my permission?"

"Decorum demands that you, at the very least, tip your head to your princess. Instead, you walk past her as if she were a commoner. If that's how you treat her, how do you act toward those without any rank at all?"

Lennox's question pierced me. His assessment of Nickolas's character was exactly what I hadn't been able to put into words.

If Nickolas could so easily disrespect me when I was all but queen, how would he have treated those we were charged with caring for?

He would never consider their needs. I could see it now as clearly as a sunrise. Nickolas had always been a straight line, pointed like an arrow. And his attention was always aimed toward himself.

"Officer Au Sucrit, no need to trouble this gentleman," I said, slightly dazed from figuring out something that ought to have been obvious.

But Nickolas was unfazed. "Seeing as you are without

rank, I don't need to give you an answer. And you should master a level of decorum yourself before daring to preach to me. Besides, she's the one who's forsaken me." Nickolas moved back, sneering at Lennox. "*Au Sucrit*. What kind of a name is that?"

He shook his head and walked away.

He truly was everything I'd said no to in the first place.

As Nickolas disappeared into the distance, I placed a hand on Lennox's arm. "You really didn't need to do that. He doesn't bother me."

"He bothers me," he replied. "Even if you weren't engaged to him, which makes me hate him in ways I cannot express, I wouldn't want that man anywhere near me. I really wish you'd let me kill him."

I shook my head. "You need a new hobby."

LENNOX

Annika's teasing always got the better of me, and I couldn't fight the smile as I followed her into the room. There were multiple tables with maps and books laid out; the main one that she appeared to be using was flooded with papers and multiple inkwells. She really had been busy.

"I have a question, now that you're here," she began, seeming hesitant.

"You can ask me anything you like. Always."

Taking a deep breath, she looked back down at her map. "You said before that people find you. And when they find you, you take them in. Is that right?"

I nodded. "It's an unbreakable agreement. Once you're in, you can't leave. Otherwise, the very people we're trying to fight might discover us." I rolled my eyes, and she smiled. "It doesn't surprise me that people don't know we're there, or that more don't discover us; the people we take in are the ones no one notices or misses. I'm not sure how many in our army are truly Dahrainian at this point."

She shook her head. "I can't decide if that's sad or beautiful."

"Neither can I. But we bring them in, we tell them our history until it's their own. I wouldn't know where to draw a line between someone inside the bloodline and someone outside. In the end, we share a sense of unity, a sense of pride. Maybe that's . . ."

I had to swallow, pushing down the sting of Dear Nickolas's words.

"Maybe what?" Annika asked quietly, looking up with those doe eyes that crippled every defense I possessed.

I smiled weakly. "I haven't used my surname in ages. You're the only one who knows it. It was painful, after all this time, to have him mock it," I admitted.

She turned away, moving back to her papers. "Don't listen to him. I absolutely adore the sound of it. Had I the liberty, I'd make it my own."

My eyes snapped up, staring at her. Make it her own? Did she . . . would she . . . ?

Something in my gut twisted, and I was seconds away from dropping to my knees and pleading with her to not even consider marrying that pathetic excuse for a man, no matter what came next.

"But back to my question," she started, having a much harder time looking at me now.

"Ask away."

"That first night in the dungeon, Blythe told me that the castle you live in, you didn't build it. It had been abandoned, and Kawan settled your army there."

I nodded. "That's right."

"You and all the people who need somewhere to go?"

"Yes."

She swallowed. "I know it's different because it was empty . . . but if the descendants of whoever built that castle came back and wanted it . . . would you be able to leave?"

My blood went cold. My first instinct was no. Absolutely not. Vosino was a complete disaster, but it was *our* disaster. And it wasn't much, but every last improvement made had been done at our hands. I couldn't admit aloud how reluctant I was to even consider it.

Luckily, I wasn't forced to. "Your Highness." A man with several golden bars embroidered into his uniform walked in. "I was told to see you urgently."

"Yes, thank you for coming. We need to ready the troops, General Golding. I know we were already bracing for an invasion, but I've heard on good authority that the Dahrainian Army is preparing to advance much sooner than expected."

I moved back, having already told Annika everything I knew. Once the stream of preparation began, it went on heavily for hours with no breaks. Between it all, she listened patiently to asinine requests, offered solutions to whatever problems she could solve quickly, and took petitions on behalf of multiple committees. An army was coming, and still she counted every last request as vital.

I had to admit it was all very . . . dull. I'd lived a life of training, of planning. I was always waiting for something to happen, ready for even the slightest shift beneath my feet. This looked like paperwork.

And I had to ask myself, was this all having a kingdom was?

When the sun was sinking low in the sky, Annika stretched her arms up high, bending a little as she did so. I could see the stress of it all was wearing on her.

As if on cue, Palmer walked in.

"Have I missed anything?" he asked me, keeping his voice hushed.

I discovered I own the ground you're standing on.

"No." I paused. "Well, one thing."

"What?"

"Did you know that Annika's maid, Noemi, was in a relationship with the prince?"

He gaped at me. "That's not . . . how did . . . ?"

"I was with Annika when she went to visit her brother today and he spoke about it openly. He's trying to marry before his father wakes up and forbids it. But I wonder if it's the prince's urgency or hers."

Palmer sighed, crestfallen. "Well, there's no risk of that."

I got chills, knowing that could only mean one thing, but needing Palmer to say it all the same.

Palmer looked to Annika and back to me, leaning over to whisper in my ear. "The king died. Only an hour or two ago. There's a very lengthy process to testing and making sure that a sovereign is officially deceased, not to mention the papers. If she'd been by his side, it would have been one thing, but if you aren't in the room, you have to wait."

"Is that where you've been?"

He nodded.

I swallowed. "She's been preparing for the battle. She's been bracing while he was dying."

Palmer looked down. "Maybe it was good for her to have the time. But I have to tell her now . . . and I dread it."

I turned, taking in his profile, the tense set of his jaw and the worried bent of his eyebrows. It took me ages to let Inigo in. Now, it seemed, I was ready to befriend people in hours. "Then let me. I don't mind."

I clapped Palmer on the shoulder as I passed, walking over to kneel beside Annika, noting the little knot in her forehead as she read.

"Annika?" I whispered.

"Hmm?"

"Annika, my love." At that she met my eyes. "I'm so sorry, but I have some difficult news."

She stared at me for a moment and then swallowed hard. She steeled herself, taking in a deep breath as if she already knew.

"I'm ready," she said.

I looked into her clear, trusting eyes. And I broke her heart. "I'm sorry, Annika. Your father has passed."

Her lip trembled a little, and her jaw clenched a few times.

"Does my broth—" She cut herself off, inhaling sharply, attempting to regain composure. "Does His Majesty know?"

I looked over to Palmer, who could hear us; he shrugged. "I'm not sure."

She sniffled a few times and smoothed out her dress.

"Then I must go tell him."

After another steadying breath, she rose and clasped her hands in front of her. She took a few steps and stopped, turning to whisper to me.

"Don't leave me. Not yet," she pleaded.

"I won't."

I wanted to say, "I won't *ever*." But she'd told me not to make such promises, and I wasn't about to disobey her now.

She carried on, nodding to Palmer as she passed him, looking perfectly calm. He and I fell into step behind her, braced for whatever might come.

A second later, another officer came sprinting down the hallway, slowing when he saw Annika and Palmer.

"Mamun?" Palmer asked. "What is it?"

He was breathing fast, looking back and forth between the three of us, struggling to get words out.

"Officer Mamun?" Annika tried gently. Even now she had unimaginable patience for those around her.

"Whatever it is, just say it," Palmer instructed. "There can be no secrets between this circle."

He looked at Annika, bowing deeply. "The king has died," he said.

"Yes, I've been told. I was just going to—"

"And the prince is missing," he finished.

ANNIKA

My knees went weak, but Lennox was there, arms beneath my elbows, propping me back up in an instant.

"What?" I asked weakly.

"He's gone," Mamun repeated.

I didn't believe it. There was no possible way he could be missing. Not now. I rushed past the guards, holding up my skirts. The doors to Escalus's room were open and unguarded. I dashed inside. His drawers had been rummaged through, and anything of value had clearly been taken.

I tried to push past my shock to think. Where would he be? Why would he go? What happened here?

Had Escalus been taken? Possibly.

But Noemi wasn't here, either. If he'd chosen to take his possessions of his own accord, then he probably intended to be gone for some time. And if he was gone, with easily sellable goods, and with Noemi . . .

I turned to run to my room. If he had been taken, there'd

be no clues in there. But if he'd left of his own accord, he'd find a way to tell me. I knew him. I knew what he'd do.

I threw open the doors to my room, with Lennox, Palmer, and Mamun on my heels. I scanned every surface looking for a letter. Nothing by the entryway, nothing by the fireplace . . . but there, on the pillow of my unmade bed, was a folded note. Settled upon it, the ring with the royal seal weighed it down.

I held the ring in one hand and pulled the letter open with the other, trying to slow my mind enough to read and understand.

Annika,

I'm sorry. Please, please find the strength to forgive me.

I know we had a plan, but Father's death complicates things. If he had lived long enough to acknowledge Noemi, it would have been one thing. But with him gone and me being heir apparent, you know the lords will force me to marry for advantage, especially with the near war that just happened on the Island.

And I won't do it.

I can't. Annika, I hope you one day get to know what it's like to find the person who fills the empty spaces in your heart, the person who pushes you to be all the things you wanted to be but weren't sure you could. That kind of love will make you do unimaginable things. Like this.

I am off to marry Noemi. Even as I write this, she is asking me to reconsider my plan, but I know what will happen if I stay. I pray you will forgive me for abandoning you now. In a few years, when my marriage is well established and I have an heir, I will happily return and take the burden of the crown from your shoulders. If you even want me to by that point. Honestly, what I told you the night of your engagement was true: I've always thought you'd be a better leader than me. You've thrived as regent, and I couldn't be any prouder of my talented, brave, intelligent sister. As king of Kadier, I hereby bequeath the title to you.

Long live Queen Annika of Kadier, the fairest and gentlest ruler our kingdom has ever seen.

I beg you again, for my sake and Noemi's, to find forgiveness for us. I love you, Annika. And, one day, I will come home.

Escalus

By the end of the letter, my hand was shaking so hard I could barely read his name. I was too stunned to speak. I understood all too well what it was to love someone so much that you felt driven to act in ways everyone around you would call crazy . . . but I couldn't believe he was gone.

My mother was gone.

My father was gone.

My brother was gone.

I was queen.

And all I could think was, *You said you were still here.*

I looked to Lennox, who was standing beside me, caution and fear in his eyes. I handed him the letter, still unable to speak. He read through it much faster than I did and slammed it into Officer Palmer's chest, falling to one knee.

"Long live Queen Annika!" he called so loud that anyone passing by would have also heard.

The moment he said that, Palmer and Mamun followed suit, moving down to one knee. Two guards who were just coming to the door on rounds saw the scene and knelt down as well. I felt the full and heavy weight of the crown settling on me.

It was frightening. But I also realized in an instant how much I was going to miss it when Lennox took it back.

I slid the ring with the royal seal onto my thumb, as it was the only finger it fit, and then picked up my skirts.

"Please have guards set outside my father's door; his body is not to be moved. And please keep the news of Escalus's departure quiet. I'll prepare a statement once the dust has settled." I allowed myself the briefest glimpse at Lennox, but I couldn't hold his eyes for too long.

"Officer Au Sucrit, if you'll follow me, please. Officers, now more than ever I expect you to keep an eye on the horizon. For now, I have urgent business to attend to in the library."

I walked away, holding my head high. I would be queen for less time than Escalus was king, but I would wear it well.

"Annika," Lennox said quietly. "Annika, let's go to the library tomorrow."

I didn't answer.

"Annika. You haven't eaten. You've been through a great shock. You need to rest."

I kept walking.

But then, quite suddenly, the floor tipped sideways, and I

fell into the wall. Immediately, Lennox's arms were there to hold me up again. He carefully cupped my cheek with his hand, urging me to look at him.

"Annika. Please. We don't have to do this tonight." He swallowed hard. "We don't have to do this at all."

I smiled weakly. "Aren't you happy, Lennox? A lifetime of work is paying off tonight. And so easily! Without shedding a drop of blood, you will have your crown back."

His lip trembled. "I never wanted a crown. I just wanted to live on the land where my ancestors lived. I didn't want to have to hide anymore. I could do that. I could stay here. With you. We don't have to do anything, Annika."

I reached up, running a very tired hand down his face. "You could. But you won't. Because at your heart, you aren't just a gentleman, Lennox. You're a king. And if you stayed here, enjoying this kingdom while the people you were meant to lead suffer in that castle on the edge of the world, you would grow to hate yourself. The same way I'd hate myself for staying with you once my people are forced to leave this kingdom."

His eyes locked with mine, facing the truth that we had refused to admit to ourselves.

"You and I, Lennox. We can't have both. In fact, we can't have either. Because if we ran off, we'd leave my people and yours in pure chaos. Who knows how many would die because of our cowardice? Do you think our love could survive that?" I shook my head. "One of us must lead, and one of us must go."

He was swallowing hard, his eyes darting back and forth,

finding no answers.

"I can't . . . ," he began.

"I know."

I hoisted myself up, marching on. Lennox, finding no way to refute me, followed silently. I thought about the moments in the cave before we came to an understanding with one another. Even that silence was more comfortable than this one.

I pushed the doors open, surprised to find Rhett right by the entryway. He was bent over, leaning against the desk, head hung as if heartbroken.

But then he looked up. Those eyes did not contain sorrow; they held rage.

"Where's the key?" he asked.

"You will change your tone," Lennox commanded.

Rhett stared him down with a level of contempt that sent a shiver through me.

"Where's the key?" he asked me again, his tone menacing. "You're the only one who could have taken it."

"Yes, I took the key. And I have full rights to," I said, holding up my hand with the signet ring. "I am queen."

He gaped at the ring, but before he could ask questions, I turned that hand to silence him. I reached the other hand to Lennox, who pulled the key from his coat.

"I'm sorry, Rhett. I need that book. So, stand down."

Rhett stepped away from the desk and pointed at Lennox. "I don't know who he is, or how you know him, or what he wants with those books. But he can't have them. He cannot have them, and he cannot have *you*."

"Rhett!"

"I told you, Annika. I told you long ago. You've always been mine. No one has loved you better."

He walked forward, hatred in his eyes. Only once before had he seemed dangerous to me, and that moment came back to mind with perfect clarity. He'd said, without hesitation or irony, that any man who came between him and me was his enemy. I saw now how deeply he meant that.

And I saw that there was a difference in what I was willing to do for love and what Rhett was. But then, could anything this vengeful be called love?

Just as Rhett was about to launch himself at Lennox, the sound of yelling echoed into the room.

Palmer was there, tossing a sword into Lennox's hand and, surprisingly enough, one into mine. He didn't bother sparing a glance for Rhett.

Instead, he looked between Lennox and me. "Come quickly, Your Majesty. We're under attack."

LENNOX

I unsheathed my sword, leaving Rhett to fume on his own, running behind Palmer as he started up the stairs. "Have they breached the walls?"

"Yes. Guards are on their way. We need to get people out."

"Agreed. After the battle at sea, they won't show mercy."

Palmer nodded. "I'll spread the word."

"What do I do?"

I stopped in my tracks, turning to see that Annika had kept pace with us, even in her gown and heeled shoes.

"Your job is to stay alive. Is there a good hiding place? Somewhere only you know about?" I asked.

Her eyes shifted to anger so quickly, it forced me to take a step back.

"You think I'm going to hide? Now? *My* people are about to die. *Your* people are about to die. I'm not saving my own life at the risk of any of theirs."

The way she pooled them all together, hers and mine,

gave me the courage to run into battle. And the way she was prepared to sacrifice herself in the most finite way said that her brother was more than justified in leaving her the crown.

"Then you have to stay by my side," I told her. "You can't leave me, not for a second."

She nodded, bending down to throw off her shoes. Taking the sword in her hand, she ran it through a part of her dress, making a slit up it so she could run faster.

Palmer sighed heavily. "I'm heading downstairs. You two stay on the second floor. Hopefully, no one will make it up here, but be braced for it if they do."

Without another word, he was off, calling orders. In his absence, it was easy enough to believe that nothing was happening at all. It was so quiet.

I turned to Annika. "I'm so sorry I brought this upon you."

"I'm so sorry you needed to."

I worked hard to keep the tears back. "I need you to know now that I choose you. Over the land, over the crown. I want you. I longed for Dahrain most of my life, but the only thing I've ever loved is you. If something happens, I need you to know that."

She looked at me, those eyes gliding over my features the same way they did that night in the dungeon: as if she fully intended to never see me again.

"And I choose you." She gestured around her, an exhausted but genuine smile on her face. "This is how you can know how deep my love for you went, Lennox: I've always lost everything I really love."

The anguish in her voice hit me. I knew the list of who she'd loved by heart, and was honored to find myself on it, regardless of what it cost me in the end.

I closed the distance between us, lacing my hand into her hair and pulling her lips to mine. If I had to die, at least I went to my grave the beloved of Annika Vedette.

She threw her sword to the ground so she could fling her arms around me, and I followed suit, tossing my sword aside. I gripped her to me, so satisfied by how perfectly she fit in my arms. I held her scent, her warmth, her taste all secure in my heart. Whatever came, no one would steal the memory from me.

In the distance, I heard the mayhem. We pulled apart, sparing a moment for one last look at each other. We both went for our swords, and I saw the first sight of danger in the form of a Kadierian soldier backing up the distant stairway. Putting him through his paces was Blythe, perfectly matching his steps without hesitation. I realized it was Mamun on the receiving end of her blows.

Coming up behind them were Palmer and Griffin, and Inigo was facing someone I didn't know. It seemed the entirety of everyone I knew was here in one ill-fated cluster.

"Lennox," Annika asked quietly. "Who are we fighting?"

I surveyed the scene once more. "No one if we can help it, but everyone if we must."

I caught the moment Blythe looked up from Mamun and saw me. And I watched as her eyes flicked over to Annika. The intense betrayal in her face was unmistakable. It occurred to me then that, while I was looking at a friend, she was looking at an enemy.

Mamun took a swipe, cutting Blythe's arm, but she moved as if she didn't feel a thing, marching toward me, her glare saying she was ready to make someone hurt as much as she did.

In the second it took me to get over the shock and take my stance, Annika was there, sword up, blocking Blythe in a move I could only call graceful.

"My lady, drop your sword," Annika pled.

"Move!" Blythe demanded.

Never one for speeches, Blythe was back to moving, and I found myself glued to the floor, unable to pull my eyes from the way they fought. Annika was all form, Blythe was all rage, and when they clashed, it was mesmerizing.

I turned away only when I saw Inigo beside me. Whoever he'd been fighting was motionless on the floor, and now his eyes were on me, too, asking me why I'd gone.

"You were my friend," he said.

"I am still. Perhaps more so than ever."

"You abandoned us."

"I came to save the woman I love, and, in the process, I found a way to save you, too. To save us all."

There was a split second, a moment when I saw the hope in his face, wanting to believe. But I lost the chance to explain when a Kadierian guard barreled down on Inigo.

"I need to find Kawan," I yelled.

"Why? What will he do?" Inigo called back, still swinging.

"Kill us all if he isn't stopped. I swear to you that we can end this without more bloodshed," I vowed.

"Stand down!" Annika yelled in such absolute despair that I not only obeyed but so did the majority of those surrounding.

Blythe was on the ground. A guard had drawn their sword up her back, opening a long wound, and she'd fallen. Immediately, Annika ripped off a large swath of her dress, pressing it onto Blythe's back to hold back the blood.

"No," Inigo whispered. "If anyone was going to make it, it was her."

I looked over, noting how low his shoulders were held, how loose his grip on his sword was. I'd never seen him like that; it scared me more than the attack.

Annika's fingers were at Blythe's throat. "Her heart is beating. We need to get her to the doctor." She looked up, waiting for someone to do something. In her world, that's what happened when she spoke.

And I would have thought that surely seeing the high and mighty queen of Kadier on her knees trying to save her enemy would stop the attack.

But it did not.

Griffin may have made his peace with losing Rami, but he clearly had not made his peace with who took her. In the unguarded stillness, he ran forward, sword high. The way it was positioned, it was going to take off Annika's head.

It was as if my sword moved of its own volition. I lunged forward and plunged it into Griffin's chest.

He didn't even make a sound. He merely gasped a little, falling to his knees.

I was the one crying. *I* was the one making whatever sound that was.

"Griffin," I breathed out, coming to the ground in front of him. "Griffin, I'm so sorry. I didn't . . . I . . ."

He reached up, holding on to my hand, staining it with blood. He was shaking violently. After a few labored breaths, he spoke.

"It was too hard . . . to carry on . . . without . . . her anyway."

I nodded, looking back to Annika quickly, noting the tears in her eyes before turning back to him. He'd been the light in that castle. "That's how I feel."

There was a brief flash of light in his eyes, of understanding. "Then . . . I . . . forgi—"

All the tension in his hand disappeared, and my friend was gone.

I recoiled, repulsed by myself. I didn't want anyone else to die, and his life was lost at my hands.

"Where is Kawan?" I demanded, my voice sinking deeper than I knew it could.

Inigo, Palmer, Mamun, and the nameless soldier stood silent. Annika was still bent over Blythe.

No one had an answer, and it didn't matter anyway. Another wave of soldiers came up the stairwell, deep in battle, swinging swords wildly. Now there was an added danger as we heard the occasional musket firing. We were all forced to our feet, back on edge. I carefully pulled my sword from Griffin, positioning myself in front of Annika.

"Slow them all, but spare them if you can," I ordered,

though on what authority I couldn't say. Inigo was on my right and Palmer was on my left. Mamun and the other soldier moved ahead of us, swinging with precision, hitting a thigh, an arm, a hand.

"So, what? Are we allies now?" Inigo asked.

"I have proof," I said. I saw him turn to me from the corner of my eye. "Proof of the true history of the land. Annika found it."

He looked to her, and she looked to him, tipping her head.

I had to stop speaking, trying not to focus on what I'd just done, hoping I could be careful enough not to do it again. I honed every sense in my body into the moment, keeping my movements as precise as possible. Annika was by my side, following our lead, her movements so deft it was like trying to fight a shadow.

"What are you doing?!" someone called, shock and rage in his voice. Dear Nickolas had appeared, coming from another stairwell. It didn't surprise me at all that he wormed his way around the heart of the battle.

"Saving as many as I can," she replied, her tone implying this was obvious.

"For goodness' sake," he said, daring again to contradict her.

"Move!" she yelled, pushing him aside to block another swipe of a Dahrainian sword. She barely succeeded.

"You should be hiding!" he insisted, pulling her again. And this time his foolishness went too far. He moved Annika's arm so she was defenseless, and the razor-sharp tip of the sword pierced her chest.

“Ah!” she bent, clutching the wound.

My eyes met his, and I was prepared to take at least one more life tonight. He seemed to have the sense to understand what he’d done, and he moved to carry her away.

She cried out when he lifted her, and I worried that the cut went deeper than it looked.

Gasping, she pointed at me and yelled as loud as she could, so everyone—both Kadierian and Dahrainian—would know. “He is your king! He is our king! Save the king!”

ANNIKA

This was not the worst pain I'd ever felt in my life, but that didn't mean it didn't hurt. I kept my hand pressed down hard over the wound, hoping to literally hold myself together.

The sword had managed to hit right between the boning of my stays, splitting it and me in one fell swoop. Nickolas didn't bother moving gingerly, running as fast as he could with me in his arms off to my room. Blood was trickling out, warm and wet, and the wound was stinging with every breath. I closed my eyes for a moment, trying to just stay calm.

The door had been left open, no doubt from when Officers Palmer and Mamun had heard the commotion downstairs, and Nickolas brought me in quickly, shutting the door behind us.

Then he locked it.

He stood with his arm against it for a while, catching his breath. And the first thing he chose to say to me was, "I cannot believe you."

"I did what I had to do," I told him plainly, pressing my hand over the wound. "I need something for the blood. There should be handkerchiefs in that drawer."

He shook his head. "'Save the king'? What on earth does that mean?"

"That man has a claim to the throne. That's all I can say at the moment."

"The *guard*?" he asked incredulously. I realized that I hadn't given away Lennox's real name nor his identity. And I had no intention of sharing it now.

"I know it sounds crazy. My father . . ." I raised a hand to brush back my hair, not remembering that it was covered in blood until it was too late.

"Your father is dead," he said mercilessly.

"I know."

"And soon, your brother will be, too."

Ice trickled down my back as I looked up at Nickolas, seeing something eerily familiar in his eyes.

What was it? Something stronger than determination. Something deeper than love. It was intense, consuming, and, most worryingly, frightening. It was the same look in Rhett's eyes when he charged at us in the library.

There was a name for this look: obsession.

I finally understood.

Nickolas would never have been satisfied with me. He would never have been satisfied with being called a prince. He wanted the crown and nothing less.

In an instant, his posture changed. The stiff way he

typically held himself around me melted, and he crossed the room with a lazy gait, kneeling in front of me.

He reached back, gripping me by the hair he'd always hated down. Right now, I wished it was up, too, so he'd have less to hold.

"You almost got out of my grasp once, but not this time." He smiled at me, delighted. He reached into his pocket, pulling out two golden bands. Wedding rings. "If you want to live, put this on."

I wasn't his. I never would be. But I wasn't strong enough to fight back at the moment. And I had to live long enough to get back to Lennox, to support him when the crown was turned over. So, I took the ring and slid it on my finger.

"We've been talking about the wedding so publicly, it won't be hard to convince the rest of the palace we were already secretly married. What's mine is yours; what's yours is mine," he said with a wicked grin.

"This is not going to end the way you think," I warned, feeling a little light-headed but refusing to let him see that.

"Always so difficult," he said. "Difficult and distant. That's going to change. You and I? We need each other. I need an heir to cement our lines. And you? You need to live." There was something maniacal in his eyes, but I forced myself to stay calm. I could get out of this . . . I just needed time. "Your brother, however, is standing between me and a crown, so I intend to take care of that little nuisance now. And what a perfect alibi," he said, holding his arms out.

I took a little comfort in the fact he didn't appear to know Escalus wasn't in the palace. He, at least, could be spared.

"I have been trying to get to your brother since the second we got off that boat. I knew your father wasn't long for this world, but Escalus? He's younger, more determined. But you just *had* to keep your maid by his side, didn't you?"

Nickolas rose, jerking me back by my hair one last time and leaving me on the floor. "I'm sure she'll be off hiding in the middle of this chaos, and one of these animals has probably already killed him. But just in case, I'll be off to finish the job. Stay put," he ordered. "Unless you want to end up like him, you'll learn to listen to me."

I shook my head at him, keeping my secrets and guessing at his. "Does Kawan know he's working with such a snake?"

"Kawan?" he asked.

I looked away, uninterested in the game he was playing. "You'll fail with or without him."

"I need no one. Not their leader, not you. I've been preparing for this moment alone all my life." He looked down at me, taking me by the chin. "And if you want to stay alive, keeping your mouth shut will be the first thing you learn to do."

He walked out the door, locking it behind him.

I pitied him if he thought it was really going to be that easy to keep me down. I went to my closet, using my sewing scissors to cut off my gown and stays. I folded a hand towel against the wound on my abdomen, wishing I had something better to treat it with. I shoddily laced up new stays, using the pressure to hold the towel to my stomach, shrugged into another dress, and prayed it was enough to keep me upright. I was a bloody, sloppy mess. But I had work to do.

I went to the door, peeking through the keyhole. Nickolas hadn't even been smart enough to post someone to guard me. I'd picked this lock before, so many times that I could do it in less than a minute by now. I ran back into my room, reaching under my bed. I grabbed my sword, strapping it to my waist as I headed back to the door, pulling a pin from my hair as I went.

Everything hurt. My ribs, my head, my heart. I was delirious from the day, and my hands were not as steady as I'd have liked. I used to think about Rhett in moments like this, his firm hands on mine, leading me, showing me just where to apply pressure. Now I pictured Lennox. His untidy hair first thing in the morning, his mischievous smile, his scrunched forehead when he was deep in thought.

This is possible, he told me.

"This is possible," I told myself.

I closed my eyes, focused again on the feeling of the latches. And, in a matter of seconds, I felt it give.

The hallway was empty, and I had to make a dangerous decision. How was I going to help? How was I going to save everyone?

In the end, I could only see one way. I clutched the hilt of my sword and ran.

LENNOX

"Where would he have taken her?" I asked Palmer as we ran.

"My best guess is her room. But they could be anywhere."

"Is he the informant?" Inigo asked. "Do you know?"

I appreciated that, considering everything that had happened, Inigo was immediately on board with me. He'd watched as I took Griffin's life and still had grace for me. He'd helped me move Blythe to a safe spot—her pulse had still been steady when we left—and then fell into step behind me, along with Mamun. I didn't know what Inigo's motivation was now—the kingdom, his pride, security for Blythe—but whatever it was, I was thankful to have him by my side again.

"I don't know. I hate him, and I suspect him, but I can't prove it."

Palmer led the way through the hallways that were still too new for me to know. I recognized some of the paintings as we got closer to Annika's room, and we came upon it to find the door wide open.

Dear Nickolas was in there, all right. He had taken the poker from beside the fire and was swinging it at every breakable object in the room. Palmer tilted his head, looking at the pathetic display.

"Sir, restrain yourself. We're in the middle of a battle," he said calmly.

Nickolas pointed the poker at us, his eyes wild. He looked like an entirely different man.

"Which one of you took her from this room?" he demanded. "I locked her in here for . . . safekeeping, and now she's gone!"

I scoffed, crossing my arms. "Did you forget that Her Majesty can pick locks? I certainly haven't."

He squinted at me. "Her Majesty?"

Palmer and I exchanged a look. In two words, I'd given away Escalus's disappearance.

"The prince is dead as well?" he asked, a smile creeping onto his lips. That smile . . . it was the same one on Kawan's face when my father's body was identified. It was a smile that said an obstacle had been removed, that someone else's tragedy was their victory.

I fully intended the wipe that smile from Nickolas's face permanently.

Palmer stepped in front of me. "There's no time for this. We need to find Annika."

Nickolas brandished the poker again. "You," he said, tipping his chin at me. "Why did she call you the king? What claim can a pathetic guard possibly have on this throne?"

"I wouldn't be so arrogant as to insult a guard right now," Palmer said. "There are three of us, and one of you. Plus, we have this very helpful chap who looks all too ready to rip one of your arms off," he added, pointing to Inigo.

"I'm not opposed," Inigo said calmly. I had to work very hard not to laugh.

"I'm not in the mood for games," Nickolas snarled. "Who are you?"

I sighed. "Unfortunately, I'm not in the mood for games, either," I said, pointing my sword at him and marching forward. "What exactly did Kawan give you in exchange for Annika's life?"

Nickolas backed away, the poker still in his hand. "What?"

"Whatever he promised, I can assure you it will never come."

"I have no business with your leader except to find him dead at the end of this night. The king is gone, the prince is gone, and now," he said, holding up his left hand, "through marriage, I will get the crown that should have always been mine. So, whatever she promised *you* . . . that won't be coming either."

I looked at that ring, stunned. There was no possible way.

Unless.

If Annika had been threatened with something related to her brother—who was I kidding? If he had threatened her with anything relating to another living soul—she'd have given in. She'd sacrifice herself a dozen times over.

Well, then, I'd have to release her.

I went to brandish my sword, but I paused again when Nickolas spoke.

"Why is everyone asking about Kawan?" he asked. "Annika first, and then you as well."

Inigo and I exchanged a glance. I looked over to Palmer.

"Where were you when everyone was stuck on the Island?" he asked.

Nickolas shook his head. "I do not answer to you." He turned to me. "And I will never bow to you."

He took up his poker again, swinging for my head. Mamun was in motion, and Inigo followed suit. Nickolas, it turned out, was quite the swordsman. He dodged both blades, swinging the poker with such force, he pushed them both aside. As if they'd been trained side by side, Inigo and Mamun split, surrounding Nickolas on both sides.

Dear Nickolas was left whipping his head back and forth. He shook his left hand out, and the light glinted off the golden band. It was just metal. Like a sword, like a lock. It could be broken.

I moved forward slowly. The worst parts of me wanted to take my time killing him.

But then, as if they were standing right in front of me, a dozen memories appeared before me. Griffin, seeming almost thankful to go. Annika's mother. Countless recruits with no names for me to remember them by.

And then I couldn't. I couldn't hurt him.

I brought my arm down.

It was Palmer who noticed my daze.

"Lennox?" he asked.

At that, Nickolas's head turned to me. His rage was still coming to the surface. "*You're* Lennox?" he demanded.

His temporary distraction was all Mamun needed to drive his sword into Nickolas's back. Nickolas's rage drained from his face as he fell to his knees. Inigo pulled the poker from his hands, and he was left there, dying and defenseless.

I walked over and lifted his hand, pulling the ring from it. He was too weak to stop me, so I tossed the thing into the fire.

"I don't know what you think you've accomplished, but you'll get none of it," I told him. "Not Annika, not a crown, nothing. You and Kawan are both too cowardly to win in the end."

He shook his head, his mouth growing into a maniacal smile, blood trickling from the corner. "I know nothing of Kawan. But it doesn't matter. She'll fail. She's far too weak. And, if I can't have Kadier, it will serve her right to lose it all."

"Annika? Weak?" I asked. "You're the one dying while she's saving the lives of her people and mine. She will be celebrated. And you? You will be forgotten."

His smile faded as his eyes rolled back. He slunk sideways onto the floor, and, for as much as I hated that man, his death brought me no satisfaction.

This time, it wasn't on my hands. I wanted to comfort myself in that small truth. It was difficult, though, after seeing the blank stare in Mamun's eyes.

"Have you ever killed someone in battle?" I asked him.

He nodded weakly. "On the Island. But it was . . . it was

a bit different then."

I placed a hand on his shoulder. "Do not carry this. Such losses belong to the war, not to you."

He looked up at me, his eyes more alert than they were only seconds before. "You seem a rather decent man. I see why she'd like you."

I smiled. "Then help me find her."

ANNIKA

I went to the only place that mattered: the library. Lennox had the key, but I needed that book, so, one way or another, I'd get it. When this was all over, if the incoming army overpowered the palace guards, they should have the truth about Lennox's position. And if they were defeated, I would need something to justify my decision to hand over the kingdom.

I was feeling dizzy. Too much had happened in too short a time, and I felt certain that for all my efforts, I was losing too much blood. Still. I pressed on.

Queens do not faint.

I went to the door, opening it slowly. Rhett's feelings for me had apparently run deeper than I'd thought. Maybe deeper than he thought, too. He'd made his peace with me marrying someone else; he wasn't going to stand for me *loving* someone else.

No amount of stealth was going to help me; I opened the door, and Rhett was there, almost exactly as I'd left him when the battle started.

"Have you done nothing?" I demanded. "The palace has been breached!"

"That guard. He's Lennox, isn't he?" he guessed, not bothering to acknowledge my question. "After you were kidnapped, you talked about him with an air of timidity. Not anger exactly, but concern. But then, after the Island, everything about your speech changed. There was almost a hint of longing . . ." He scoffed. "Why didn't you ever have that for me?"

"Rhett, I don't have time for this. We're in the middle of a war." I pointed past him. "If anyone is going to live, I have to get those books."

He sighed, looking me up and down. "You're going to take that pig and give him those books, aren't you?" His remaining self-control evaporated, and his scream echoed in the library. "Annika, you . . . if you hated Kadier so much, I offered you a way out! I wanted to take you away! I loved you!"

"This isn't love, Rhett!" I shouted back. "It never was. You wanted me because there was no one else. And I almost believed it was real, too, because I didn't know any better. But look at what you're doing now! You're risking the lives of so many people over this. How could you?"

He crossed his arms, thinking for a minute. It was akin to the way Nickolas had shifted in my bedroom; the Rhett in front of me felt like a stranger.

"You're right. You're the one who broke my heart. You're the one who betrayed your country, your crown. So their lives should be your responsibility, too." He walked over to his desk, picking up a satchel and looping it over one shoulder. Despite his menacing words, his demeanor was calm, and I felt relieved that he was choosing to simply leave.

But before he did so, he picked up the lamp on his desk, the fire alight, the basin full of oil.

And then he hurled it across the room, squarely hitting the shelves of our history books.

"Rhett!" I screamed in horror, surprised at how quickly the wall was picking up the flames.

"Show your people who you really are, Annika," he said, his tone low and steady. "Are you going to save our history . . . or his?"

I didn't even flinch. I ran past Rhett and started hacking at the chained shelves with my sword. It was sharp enough to get through the wood, but the chain was going to have to come with me. I could feel the wound down my ribs protesting as I moved, but I persisted. After a moment, the book and its neighbor were both free, linked by the same chain. I clutched them both, sheathing my sword, and turned, glaring at Rhett as I did so.

I pulled the books to my chest, the chain clinking together as I ran over to the history section. I couldn't set Lennox's books down—Rhett might grab them, or an ember might eat them—so I held them in one arm as I attempted to lift the seat off the nearest bench to get to the sand.

The buckets were too heavy for me to pull out with one hand, so I started scooping it out by the handful and tossing it on the flames. It wasn't enough, and I was so close to the smoke that it was getting harder to breathe.

I was going to lose this battle.

I stood back, unable to stop the tears. All the words. All the stories. All the good and bad that had built us, slowly eaten by fire. *My precious Kadier . . . I'm so sorry.*

"Why him?" Rhett demanded, suddenly beside me.

"Help me!" I pleaded, coughing from the smoke. "You've protected this library with your life; please help me save it!"

"He killed your mother! He's a *monster*!"

"Rhett, this might be all we have left by dawn! Help me keep it!"

He did nothing but yell at me. "*I* have been by your side through everything!"

I sighed, knowing it was useless. "And yet, you have disappointed me the most."

I went to leave; I couldn't bother with Rhett now. I needed to find Lennox, to see if I could still save something of this for him.

Rhett grabbed my wrist. "Are you seriously going to him? Now? Are you not going to try to save the books?"

His eyes were wild, and I was so angry that he'd throw such an accusation at me after starting the fire himself and standing by as it grew that I let the books drop, the chain linked around my arm. I pulled back and swung, aiming for his head. The books, as they always had, served me well, and Rhett dropped to the floor.

I stood over him, pulling myself together. "If Kadier is still here tomorrow, you'd better not be. I will have you imprisoned for treason."

I clutched my books to my aching chest, running for my life, for Lennox's life, for the lives I thought I stood a chance of saving.

In the hallway, I pressed on until I found four guards. "To the library!" I commanded. "Fire! Put out the fire!"

They ran past me without hesitation, and I moved on, with no idea where I was supposed to go now.

LENNOX

"Spare lives! Take captives!" Palmer yelled as we ran. Inigo and I did the same, but it didn't matter, Everywhere I looked, there were bodies. I was dreading seeing the damage with the dawn.

If we made it that long.

Mamun suggested going to the main hall. Apparently, there was still a lot of fighting there. So, I followed Palmer, hoping to find Annika at the end of these sweeping hallways.

I knew we were there when I saw the bloodstains on the floor. It was strange to see the imprint of such petite heeled shoes leaving a red trail down the hall, and I wondered if the lady who'd left them was safe. Our footsteps echoed in the spacious room. A handful of candles were still aflame, giving very little light to what appeared to be a scene of absolute destruction. Chairs had been tossed everywhere and shattered windows left leaflike piles of glass on the floor.

Annika wasn't here, either . . . but we weren't alone.

"Lennox!" Mother called from across the room. Her voice

echoed with hope. She went to move toward me, but Kawan grabbed her wrist. He was in no hurry to move. It appeared he'd found a throne.

My throne.

"You always have to do things the difficult way, don't you?" he said.

I took slow steps toward him, sensing that he, like I, was ready to cross the finish line.

"You never wait. You never listen. You never, *never* obey." He spoke with a restrained anger, letting go of my mother and using the same hand to grip the rounded edge of the throne. "But when you left and didn't show signs of returning, I thought, 'If that foolish child could get into the palace undetected on his own, then I can take it over with an army easier than I imagined.'" He raised his hands and let them drop. "And I was right."

After letting out a contented laugh while our people died around us, he continued.

"What's more, you doomed yourself! You made yourself a traitor at the finish line. Who will follow you now?" he asked.

He was enjoying this far too much.

"Did you know?" I demanded. "That day you came to our house, and you spoke to my father and convinced him to join your cause . . . did you know even then?"

His silence was the only answer I needed.

"We always thought my father came up with the idea to attack the king of his own accord. Did you send him on that mission specifically? Did you hope he would fail? That he would die?"

He twisted his neck a little, uncomfortable with the questions.

"Did you think that if you belittled me enough, you would crush me? Did you think you'd turn me into your slave? That I would never have enough backbone to take what's mine?"

"What's this about?" Mother looked between Kawan and me, waiting for an answer.

Before I could say anything, a hand gripped my hair at the scalp and a blade was at my neck. The gasp of surprise I made was nothing compared to the shouts of my mother. Palmer and Inigo turned quickly, swords at the ready.

"Drop your sword," Mamun ordered gruffly in my ear. "Or die."

Against my better judgment, I let it fall, metal clanging against the marble floor. I was left with Mamun's dirty blade pressed against my skin. All I could think was, if I'd been able to survive so much only to die like this, then what had been the point of it all?

"Shall I finish him off now?" Mamun asked.

"Not yet. I may need him still," Kawan replied. I was almost impressed that he'd chosen a lowly guard as his man on the inside—it was smart. A guard would never fight him for power, never go against him. A guard would take what he could and run to an easier life.

This also explained why Mamun was so quick to strike Nickolas down in the end. He had been dangerously close to making us believe he was innocent in this.

"As I told Nickolas, whatever he's promised you, it will

never come," I told Mamun quietly. He gave no reply.

"What of the others?" Kawan asked.

"The king died this afternoon," Mamun reported. "The prince was badly injured but woke only yesterday. Fortunately, he has fled the palace for the sake of love."

"I trusted you," Palmer said, the pain clear in his voice. "How could you do this to them?"

"You were there! You saw him push her into a table of glass," Mamun insisted. "You watched that man injure his own daughter. You saw how selfish the prince has become. You saw the king making nonsense decisions. What do we need with another generation of royals?" I could feel him shaking his head, each word more desperate than the last. "I won't serve them anymore! Not them, not the arrogant courtiers who hand their empty glasses to me like I'm a butler. No one! I want to be in a land that is free!"

"You think the man who would risk his *own people* on a doomed mission is going to give you freedom?" Palmer shouted, pointing at Kawan.

"Was not our king worse than that?" Mamun asked. And that silenced Palmer. "No. It will all be new once she's gone," he insisted. I could tell by his tone, he moved from addressing Palmer to Kawan. "The princess may be alive or dead at this point; we've no way of knowing. If she's made it this far, it's quite possible that if she came upon his lifeless body," he said, speaking of me, "she'd be very happy to join him."

"You don't know if she's alive?" Kawan asked sharply. "How can I possibly trust you if you've lost the one person whose corpse we need?"

"Oh, I'm very much alive."

Even with my hair pulled taut as it was, I wrenched my neck as far as I could, just needing a single glimpse of my Annika. She walked into the room, still barefoot, dragging her sword across the floor. Her other hand was weighed down by two books that were bound by one chain. She'd crisscrossed the chains around her wrist, and it looked painful, but she didn't seem to notice. There was a huge bloodstain seeping through the fabric where she'd been cut. On top of all that, she was covered in something—maybe dirt or ash—and looked as if she'd been through hell.

"We meet again," Annika said to Kawan by way of greeting. "I must say, for someone so determined to take over a crown, you have the manners of a dog."

"I'm not sure this is the moment to be hurling insults. I have your kingdom in my hands. Shall I order every last one of your subjects killed? All because their pathetic princess couldn't hold her tongue? Have you not been taught your place?"

She sighed, turning to look at me. She seemed unbothered by the fact that I had a sword to my throat, that her enemy was settled on her father's throne. She merely lifted her sword to point at Kawan, her voice painted with a tired irritation.

"Another one who thinks he can tell me what to do," she said.

She was right. I'd made that mistake only once.

"Get off His Majesty's throne," she commanded.

Kawan tilted his head, amused. "Your father is dead, child."

She mirrored the action, cocking her head to the side and smiling. "But the king lives. You and I both know that."

Kawan's smile disappeared instantly. "Kill him!" he shouted.

"Down!" Annika yelled.

I dropped, but not quite fast enough. She took a piece of my hair as she opened the side of Mamun's neck with her sword.

He backed away, clutching his throat, trying to stop the bleeding.

I was already on the ground, so I grabbed my sword and charged at Kawan. In the seconds it took me to cross the room, he played the last card he had in his pocket.

He pulled out a dagger, and, at first, I thought it was meant for me. Instead, he swung it around, plunging it deep into my mother's stomach.

"No!" Annika screamed, her voice not that far behind me.

My mother crumpled to the floor, but I kept my sights on Kawan, who started to unsheathe his sword. My vision turned red, and I leaped up ready to end him, once and for all. But before I could reach him, Inigo was there.

Inigo had always been a hair faster than me. Stronger, smarter, more levelheaded. I got lucky once, and he had to yield to me.

He pushed Kawan back, forcing him to stumble against the throne, blocking his escape and forcing me to stand back.

"Are you truly king?" Inigo asked me.

Annika, who was now down at my mother's side, answered for me. "Yes. Yes, he is."

"Then prove yourself just. Put him on trial. *You* came here in peace; *he* made war. Let's be better than him."

Once again, Inigo proved that he was the superior man in every way.

"I'm sure Officer Palmer would be pleased to take him to the dungeon as soon as he's able," Annika commented, keeping her tone soft as she brushed my mother's hair back from her face.

I stepped back. "Bind him," I ordered, and Inigo bowed his head, moving to throw Kawan on the ground.

"It will take more than this," Kawan muttered.

"I doubt it," I replied.

"Dowager Queen," Annika said quietly. My mother focused her eyes on Annika's. There was blood gathering in the corner of her mouth, and I knew that wasn't a good sign. I stepped away, coming to join Annika on my knees. "Do you have any commands, my lady? Anything you wish me to do?"

She smiled a little. "Is my Lennox truly king?"

Annika held up her chain-bound wrist. "Yes. I have all the proof here. And I will use what little authority I have to my name to secure his place. You needn't worry about anything, my lady."

She nodded weakly, turning to me. "You chose well. Better than your father."

Tears stung at my eyes. "Don't say such things."

She reached her hand out for mine, moving slowly, arm trembling. "I was too desperate to be brave. I'm sorry."

"I have long forgiven you. And I hope you will do the same for me."

She smiled. "Then I do have one command."

I dipped my head to her, showing her the respect she should have had ages ago. "Anything."

"Live. Live a life overflowing with joy."

My lips were trembling now. I didn't want to break down in front of her; I didn't want that to be her last sight.

"Yes, ma'am."

She gave a shaky breath and went still. And so, on the same day, Annika and I lost our last remaining parents.

I couldn't form the words to express everything I was feeling. The despair, the hope, the uncertainty. I'd gained a throne today, but I felt a hole growing in my stomach, leaving me feeling hollow.

In the end, it didn't matter if I had words or not. Finally at her limit, Annika passed out, falling heavily into my arms.

ANNIKA

As the light soaked in, forcing me to wake, I was instantly aware of a searing sensation across my torso. I went to stretch a little, and it burned even more.

I winced, putting my hand down to the ache.

"Nu-uh! That's healing. Don't touch." My eyes jerked open, unable to believe that Escalus was here. But there he was, sitting beside my bed. "Trust me when I say that recovering from a wound like that is nothing to laugh at. You need to take it easy."

I didn't even try to fight the tears.

He looked down, shaking his head. "I know. I know, and you have every right to hate me for what I did. I never should have—"

"I just need you to answer one question for me," I interrupted. He looked up at me, eyes guilty. He nodded. "Do I finally have a sister?"

His lips trembled as he nodded. He looked over, and Noemi came back from her place by the window. She was wearing a sunny-yellow dress, ruffles all up the front, bows on the ends of her sleeves. It had the earmarks of her handiwork, and I wondered if she'd worked on this dress quietly over the years, hoping one day she'd have cause to wear it.

I held my hand out for hers.

"When did you get back? How did you even know to come home?" *Home.* I shook my head at myself. I'd have to stop calling it that.

"We hadn't traveled very far in the first place. We were married in a small church a few miles away. We'd settled into an inn for the evening, but in the middle of the night, Lord Lehmann came barging into the building, shouting for everyone to arm themselves. He said an army took the castle overnight, that the entire royal family was missing, and that it was likely these intruders were coming for the land. He was in such a state, he didn't even recognize me.

"Well, I went back for Noemi and told her what he'd said. It seemed no one knew that Father had died or that I had left. The thing that scared me was that no one knew where you were, either. I didn't know if you'd died in the battle, and if that was the case, I needed to defend the throne, no matter what my plans," he said solemnly. "Noemi just wanted to find you."

He smiled up at her from his chair.

"We came up to the palace to find the gates broken and the walls crumbling. There were a shocking number of bodies, and it looked like one whole wing of the palace had gone up in flames." He shivered at the memory. "I couldn't believe this had all happened in a matter of hours."

I swallowed. He didn't even know the half of it. "What else?" I asked. "Did anyone stop you?"

He shook his head. "No. We walked in cautiously, but it seemed the fighting had already ceased by the time we got here. My only concern at that point was to find you. But a young man who was in the Dahrainian Army found me first. I pulled my sword . . . Annika, when I tell you I barely had the strength to hold it up . . ." He let out a long, tired breath. "Anyway, he asked me my name, and I told him. He said I was safe and to follow him. I had my doubts, but he took me to a hallway that wasn't completely demolished. Officer Palmer—you know him, right?"

I smiled tiredly and nodded.

"Officer Palmer was sitting on the floor with two books spread out in front of him. Beside him was that Officer Au Sucrit"—he eyed me at that, knowing everything about his identity now—"and he was studying every page like he'd found a hidden treasure."

I pushed myself up, my body hating me for it. "Lennox! Where is he?"

He watched me, astonished. "So, it's true, then?"

I swallowed. "Which part?"

"He told me many things I could barely bring myself to believe—things about our history, things about his bloodline—but the most shocking of all was his adamant insistence that he loved you more than anything in this world."

I was blinking away tears, clutching my hands together. "He said that?"

Escalus nodded.

Noemi was fighting a playful smirk. "He spoke in words sweeter than any of those books you ever read. If I wasn't already so happily married myself . . ."

Escalus looked up at her in mock anger. "Too late. You're mine now."

She giggled, looking absurdly happy.

"So, you know, then? You know that the kingdom is his."

My brother sighed heavily. "If I hadn't seen the books, I wouldn't have believed it. For my part"—he looked down, thinking over his words—"I was happy to abdicate for your sake. I don't need the position or the prestige. And I can accept abdicating in the name of righting a terrible wrong.

"The only thing that gives me pause is that I know nothing of this Lennox besides the fact that he killed our mother. And I don't want a crown that suits you so well to be taken from you. It breaks my heart to see you pushed from the throne, from the palace, and likely from the country, considering your blood. *Our* blood."

I nodded. "I've thought of all this already. I know that you don't know Lennox, but I hope you will trust me when I say that I do. He won't deny his part in taking Mother's life, but he regrets it in ways that haunt him. Do you know how many times he's spared my life?" I chuckled weakly. "Beyond that, do you know how many times he's intentionally *saved* it?

"You have nothing to fear. I . . . I'm sad to see it go, too. Escalus, the second I knew the crown was mine, I was in love with it. Not the power, exactly, but the responsibility.

I thought of all the work I'd been doing, and how it was exhausting but fulfilling. I thought of how much good I could do.

"But if the only good thing I can do with the crown is make sure it sits on the rightful head . . . then that's what I'll do."

"Must you always speak so poetically?"

Lennox's voice once again washed over me with the crashing sound of a thousand heartbeats. He'd cleaned up, and someone had given him a change of clothes. He looked like a proper gentleman now, except that he kept his hair down . . . which I liked, if I was honest.

"It only happens when I'm talking about you," I admitted.

"Ugh! And that is my cue to leave," Escalus said, picking up a cane I hadn't noticed and looping an arm through Noemi's.

She laughed. "You realize you sound the same way about me, right? Only worse."

"Of course, I do," he replied. "And I intend to do much more, but it's another thing entirely to hear it. So help me to our room." Escalus paused by Lennox's side. "Whatever you have to say, be gentle. She's only been awake for a few minutes."

Lennox nodded, and I watched with joy as Escalus and Noemi left the room arm in arm. But it was only as they left that I realized I wasn't in my room. Looking around, I had no idea where I was.

"Sorry," Lennox said. "I don't know what Escalus told you, but the majority of the palace is in shambles. We took you to one of the few untouched rooms. You're in the east corridor on the third floor, if that helps you at all."

I considered this, walking through where that would be in my mind. "Yes. It very much does."

I noted that Lennox was holding both of the books I'd salvaged from the fire. I nodded in their direction. "Ignore my brother. Tell me everything. Whatever it is you need to say, I'm strong enough to take it."

He lifted an eyebrow at me. "Are you sure?"

No, I thought. *I'm not prepared for the moment you tell me we're parting ways forever.*

But I was determined to be a queen until the very end.

"Absolutely."

LENNOX

I could see that she was bracing herself. If I broke her, she'd never admit it, taking it all with a graceful smile.

So like her mother.

"You already know the most important things: your brother and his wife are alive, and so are you and I. I'd call that a miracle in and of itself."

"As would I," she said.

"My mother died in your arms, and I don't know if anyone told you that Nickolas was killed last night by Mamun."

She sat up a little taller. "What?"

I nodded. "I can see now that Mamun was trying to hide his tracks. He didn't know how much longer he would need to keep his deal with Kawan a secret, so he took Nickolas out of the way when he started talking. Nickolas was a coward, but it seems he was innocent, in the end."

Annika shook her head. "He wasn't." She swallowed, her eyes tracing the details in the blanket covering her. "He locked me in my room and went off to kill Escalus—he didn't know Escalus had left. I picked the lock and ran."

"I'd expect nothing less from you." I nodded to myself, proud and thankful. "Bravo. Kawan is in chains, as is Mamun, and they will receive a proper trial. My friend Inigo is well, and I've found out Blythe survived the night." I smirked. "Inigo is tending to her most enthusiastically. Palmer helped set up an area to treat all the wounded, and the guards are taking care of the deceased."

She nodded. "Are you stalling? I need to know what's coming more than I need to know what's happened."

"True." I swallowed, perhaps the most frightened I'd been in my life. "I just need to ask you a question, then."

She steadied herself again, adjusting blankets and sitting up as tall as she could manage. "And what is that?"

"It is simply this: Annika Vedette, will you do me the extraordinary honor of accepting my hand?"

She stared at me, and I watched as the tears formed in her eyes. "I want to say yes more than you know . . . but if my people have to leave, you know—"

I shook my head, walking over and setting the books on her bed. "I've been poring over this book, reading names that sound familiar and coming across accounts that I swear I've heard before. But," I began, lifting the second book, "what you found here is equally as fascinating."

I flipped to a page with an old map. Here, finally, an account of all seven clans was documented. It even went so far as to give detailed maps of each clan, showing major families in each, pointing out who originally owned large sections.

"Look," she breathed happily. "There you are. We were neighbors." She drew a delicate finger over the line that marked the border between her ancestors and mine.

"Yes, we were. See how large your land was? It's not surprising your people felt betrayed when they were passed over for mine. But you know what else I found?"

She shook her head.

"This book outlines how your ancestors organized the clans to battle against the multiple invasions they were facing. I saw their military plans, their sacrifices, their work. Annika, maybe my people had something taken from us, but none of it would still be here had your ancestors not fought so valiantly. That is worth remembering. And I'm thankful for it."

"I'm glad. I'm glad we saved it. And I'm glad to hand it over to you in one perfect piece."

"Are you quite sure about this, Annika? Do you truly want to give me your kingdom?"

"No," she whispered. She looked down, lovingly touching the ring on her thumb before tugging it off and setting it in my palm. "I want to give you *your* kingdom."

I saw spots on the blanket from where her tears fell. I gave her a moment; I needed her to be able to hear me.

"You might remember that my people are not simply Dahrainians," I said gently. "They come from several countries, adopted into our protection. I have no intention of barring them from Dahrain . . . and I have no intention of barring your people, either."

She finally met my gaze.

"And I keep thinking of your mother. Down to her last breath, Annika, all she wanted was peace. Wouldn't she be so pleased to see you embracing my people as your own?"

She closed her eyes and nodded, and I dropped to my knees beside her bed.

"According to this book, you're right: I ought to be king. The crown should have passed down my line, but it wouldn't still be here if it wasn't for yours. So, for once, let's not make anyone choose. I think you and I, Annika, could be something. We could build something." I took a deep breath. "So stay with me. Marry me. Otherwise, this victory is empty. Otherwise, *I* am empty."

She turned her head, and for a moment, I feared I'd lost her.

"Annika?"

She was covering her mouth still when she turned back to me, but the crinkles beside her eyes said she was smiling.

"Sorry," she said, finally pulling her hand away and wiping at her tears. She placed her palm flat across the pages that marked our joint history, both the good and the bad. "It's just, all this time I'd been looking to fairy tales to find my happily ever afters. It seems I was studying the wrong books."

I took her hand, and she held mine back, and I felt the world settle into place.

"Lennox Au Sucrit," she began.

I didn't realize how much my name meant to me until she said it.

"I want nothing in the world but to be yours."

And that was how I, in less than a day, came to have everything.

How *we* came to have everything.

There was a knock at the door, and Palmer entered.

He looked at Annika, noting the tears in her eyes. "Are you quite well, Your Majesty?"

She smiled. "Oh, I am perfectly fine. And you, Your Majesty?" she asked, looking at me.

I was lost for a moment, unable to believe that the dream I'd always wanted had been dropped into my lap. I crossed the space between us, giving Annika the gentlest of kisses and basking in her radiant smile. "I have never been better."

Epilogue

Annika Au Sucrit watched in awe as the baby in her arms yawned. It was just a tiny movement, but it was no less extraordinary to her than a sunrise or a symphony. Lennox was just as dazzled as the child held on to the same finger that carried his wedding ring. He wouldn't admit aloud that he was terrified in equal measure, but his wife could guess.

Lennox turned his gaze to Annika, telling himself not to be surprised that she'd found something new to excel at. Had there ever been anything she couldn't do? And this new person—who seemed to have his eyes and her nose—who knew what he might accomplish one day?

They both took a moment to exist in the sweetness of becoming a family of three. They would have more time later, after the streams of visitors, but for now, they stole a few minutes for themselves.

Lennox insisted that they teach their children about her games, about how to hunt and gather the most painted rocks around the palace. Annika insisted upon teaching them his dances, about lacing together hands and spinning until they were dizzy. They both insisted on not giving their children the names of their parents but bestowing them with new ones. And they both insisted on loving the people they made to the point it annoyed them.

And they both vowed, with absolute solemnity, to tell them everything. They would talk about mistakes made on both sides and forgiveness granted by each. They would acknowledge the past, knowing that they couldn't ignore their history any more than they could constantly apologize for it. And they would trust that if, in a few generations, a lie could erase something, that, in a few more, the truth could restore it.

Annika's brother—now the duke—and his wife were the first to visit. The queen and her dearest friend—her sister—were both teary-eyed when they stared into the peaceful face of the prince. Escalus, who feared the entire process, was too relieved to see his sister healthy and alive to even notice the baby for several minutes. When Inigo and Blythe came in, Annika passed her son into Blythe's arms, watching joyfully as another thread sewed together their growing friendship. Lennox worked very hard not to cry when Inigo embraced him, knowing his closest friend was proud of him in ways he could not speak. And Palmer refused to enter the room, but stood watch by the door, tensing every time he heard the slightest cry.

There were others, too. Lords and ladies, visiting ambassadors, and a string of common people who brought gifts on behalf of their towns. And, while not everyone was entirely enthusiastic about the changes that had happened over the last year, there was no denying that the young king and queen were doing their best to repair what had been broken, to make something new from a fractured past. So the people, some with happy hearts and some with heavy, abandoned the titles Kadier and Dahrain for Avel.

It wasn't until much later that Lennox had a moment to catch his breath, holding his son in his arms as his wife fell asleep against his shoulder. They shared everything—the kingdom, the crown, their name—and now they'd made a future together. Each time something good fell into his lap, he found himself tensing, waiting for it to be ripped away. But no such thing happened. There had been challenges with each new step, but they had been manageable; they had been shared.

So, as he held everything precious to him in his arms, he promised himself to join Annika in her optimism. He would hold her hand and walk confidently into the next tomorrow.

Acknowledgments

Thank you, Dear Reader. Maybe this is the first of my books you've ever picked up, or maybe you've been walking with me for the last ten years. Either way, thank you for spending your time with people I made and in worlds I invented. The first reason I write is because the characters won't shut up, but the second reason is you. :) Thank you for everything.

A big thanks to my agent, Elana Parker, for your faith in my stories, your levelheaded honesty, and your sweet friendship across the years. Also to the rest of the team at Laura Dail Literary Agency, particularly Katie Gisondi, who works so hard to get my stories into the hands of readers across the world. I feel so fortunate to have such a wonderful team representing my books. Thank you for getting them off the ground.

Thank you to Erica Sussman at HarperTeen for answering my phone calls at random times, working so tirelessly to make my stories shine, and being such a beautiful friend. Also to Elizabeth Lynch for your lovely insight and hard work. Thank you to Erin Fitzsimmons and Alison Donalty for your beautiful design work, and also to Elena Vizerskya for the incredible cover art. Thank you to Jon Howard and Erica Ferguson for your excellent attention to detail and putting the final strokes on the manuscript. Thank you to Sabrina Abballe, Shannon Cox, and Aubrey Churchward for all of your work behind the scenes. I see y'all! A handful of people have come and gone at HarperTeen over the years, but I have never had anything less than an excellent team standing behind my books. I am so grateful for your dedication and for making my job so much fun.

A giant—like, unbelievably large—thank you to Callaway for being a spectacular husband and leader. I love you so much. Thank you for your encouragement and patience and things I can't write because I'll cry, and I'm in public right now, so yeah. Thank you to my Guyden for the nonstop jokes and superb hugs, and to my Zuzu for the incredible one-liners and your bright energy. Thank you to Theresa for all your help and for being a great friend. Sorry you had to wait, like, a million years to get your name listed here. I'm cuter than I am smart.

Thank you to Mimoo and Grumpa for being my biggest cheerleaders and for putting up with me, particularly through the years of 1996–2001. Thanks to Mimi and Papa Cass for your unending support and for loving me like your own.

Thank you to my church family at Grace Community Church for your faithful counseling and teaching. A big thank-you to the ladies in my small group—Darlene,

Summer, Cheryl, Rebecca, Patti, Bridget, Marrianne, Natalie, and anyone I might be forgetting in this moment—for your constant encouragement and love.

And, finally, I would like to thank the Lord. If you, Reader, don't happen to know, I started writing to get through a particularly difficult season of life. Writing felt like a life preserver being tossed out to me when I was drowning. I certainly couldn't have anticipated that I'd be sitting here with ten books to my credit, but I should have expected for a great and loving God to take the worst of my life and redeem it. Father, I do not deserve your goodness, and I will spend a lifetime falling short of it. Thank you for your grace.